ANGELA HUNT

the face

MIRA®

MIRA®

ISBN-13: 978-0-7783-2727-1
ISBN-10:   0-7783-2727-2

THE FACE

Copyright © 2008 by Angela Elwell Hunt.

www.MIRABooks.com

Printed in U.S.A.

Let us leave the beautiful women
to men with no imagination.
—Marcel Proust

It is the common wonder of all men,
How among so many millions of faces,
There should be none alike.
—Sir Thomas Browne

Chapter One

Sarah

The microcamera homes in on a poster of a long-necked blonde with wide eyes, a straight nose, high cheekbones, and a rounded chin—the requisite parts of a face, all of which I am lacking. The model's smile blurs as Hightower whirls around.

Though I'm sitting over six hundred miles away, when the image on my monitor settles into focus I'm seeing exactly what our officer is seeing: a shiny-wet London street. A stationery shop. A passing taxicab. Nothing to quicken the pulse…yet.

"Spock, are you reading me?" Hightower asks.

"Copy that, you're five by five," I assure him.

Hightower pans the rendezvous point from left to right. The surveillance camera, hidden in the frame of his eyeglasses, performs remarkably well, given the overcast conditions. "No sign of 'im."

I notice something odd on the monitor and lean toward the microphone at my workstation. "Hold that position, Hightower."

Dr. Mewton leans over me, her hip bumping my shoulder. She points to a small box attached to a streetlamp. "What do you make of it, Sarah?"

I click on the object and magnify the image. "Looks like a traffic cam."

"Any way to be sure it's legit?"

At his workstation, Judson lifts his head. "The address?"

"New Bond Street," I tell him. "The closest intersection is with Conduit."

The text-to-speech engine of Judson's computer repeats the address as he types in the address. "Sorry," he says, slipping headphones onto his ears. A moment later he pulls the headset free. "That traffic cam is confirmed. One of many in the Mayfair district."

Mewton moves closer. "What about that man across the street?"

I'm about to check him out when Hightower sneezes and the image on my monitor bobbles.

"Bless you," a baritone voice says in my headset.

Mewton glances at me. "Is that part of the protocol?"

I shrug as Hightower turns. A short man in a raincoat stands behind him, his face round and wet beneath a thin moustache.

"Our contact doesn't look like much of a threat," Dr. Mewton says. "He looks about as dangerous as a bookkeeper."

"Refresh my memory—" I glance over my shoulder "—but wasn't it a bookkeeper who brought down Al Capone?"

"You've been watching *The Untouchables,*" Judson says, grinning. "A Costner classic."

Dr. Mewton crosses her arms and focuses on the monitor, silently reminding us that we are in the middle of a surveillance op. I click my mouse and snap a photo of the man, then pull the image out of the frame and activate the facial recognition program. Hundreds of faces flash in the margin as the computer searches for a match.

My fingers freeze on the keyboard when the short man pulls a gun from his jacket and points it at our officer's face.

Behind me, Dr. Mewton groans as the muzzle looms large in the monitor. "What the—?"

"Excuse me—" the contact blinks rapidly beneath wire-rimmed glasses "—b-but does the bus to St. Paul's stop here?"

"You want the number eleven," Hightower replies, giving his half of the verbal recognition exchange. His hand appears in the frame and firmly pushes the weapon to the side. "And have you lost your mind? Put that away."

"I…I was nervous."

"I'm not the one you should be worried about." Hightower waits until his contact puts the gun back in his pocket, then he gestures to the right. "Would you like to get out of the rain?"

"*Cómo no,* a good idea."

Dr. Mewton and I watch in silence as Hightower walks toward the stationery shop. The scene blurs as he surveils the street in a quick glance, then his hand appears in the frame. "There." He points to a door beneath an awning.

"What's happening?" Judson calls.

"Santiago is a bit jumpy," Dr. Mewton answers. "We might have to use a cutout in the future."

"I'm sure Hightower will agree," I say. "Let's find him someone nice and calm."

The facial recognition program beeps, presenting us with a name and photograph. Our contact, known to Hightower as Santiago, is Oscar Espinosa, a Spanish national. His driver's license lists a Valencia address.

"Nice work," Dr. Mewton says, her voice dry. "The Spanish department of motor vehicles?"

I shrug. "Seemed logical."

Dr. M reads the information to Judson, who enters it into his computer. A moment later he informs us that Oscar Espinosa is a clerk in the accounting department of Saluda Industries.

Dr. Mewton exhales in a rush. "What do you know…the man *is* a bookkeeper."

"Now all we need is Eliot Ness to put those thugs away." Judson lifts his head. "Are they entering a building?"

Dr. Mewton answers for me. "Looks like a passageway."

None of us speak as Hightower opens the unmarked door and steps inside. The area beyond is dark, so we see nothing until the camera adjusts.

Beside me, Dr. Mewton shifts her weight. "Sarah?"

"I noticed that." I jot a note. "The aperture adjustment is too slow."

"Look," our bookkeeper says, more talkative now that he's off the street. "Nobody at Saluda takes me seriously, but I know what is happening in that place. I can get you names, dates, shipping manifests, whatever you want, but you must make it worth my while. I am not risking my life for nothing."

Hightower holds up a reassuring hand. "Haven't I promised we'd take care of you?"

The smaller man snorts. "I would rather take care of myself. And that is what I will do, as soon as payment is made."

"And you provide the information we need."

"*Claro,* of course."

The image on the monitor rises and falls as Hightower nods. "You'll contact me in the usual way?"

"Yes, but next time we meet in España. Give me a week or two."

"Next time, leave the gun at home."

"You do not know these people. I will carry my gun until I know my family and I have nothing to worry about."

"Fine. But pull a weapon on me again and I won't be so understanding."

Espinosa takes a deep breath and fastens the top button of his raincoat. "Will you leave first?"

"You go. I'll wait and exit through the stationery shop."

The small man bobs his head again, then opens the door and steps into a rectangle of light. Hightower turns, revealing a shadowed hallway, a glass entry to the right, and another doorway in the distance. He steps forward and focuses on a plastered wall. "Sister Luke, did you get that?"

Dr. Mewton taps the microphone near her chin. "We did. Your contact is Oscar Espinosa, a clerk in the Saluda accounting office. He ought to be able to get whatever we need for the DEA."

"His record's clean?"

"As far as we can tell."

"Good. Don't want to be wasting time with a trigger-happy janitor." The scene on the monitor tumbles and goes dark as Hightower removes his glasses. Our connection isn't broken, however, because his voice continues to buzz in my headset. "Hey, Spock."

I stiffen when he calls my code name. "Yes?"

"The Candyman working this gig with you?"

I glance at Judson, whose sightless eyes are fixed on some vacant point between my desk and the wall. "He's sitting about five feet away."

"Tell him the Yankees stink. Better yet, I'll tell him myself if I find myself at your place for a tummy tuck."

"I heard that," Judson growls into his mic. "And you'd better hope I'm not the angel on your shoulder the next time you have a hot date."

Hightower laughs. "Later, kids. It's been fun."

When he powers down his transmitter, I pull off my headset. As an employee of the CIA, I ought to be used to this sort of operation, but I always shiver in the unsettling silence of a broken connection.

Chapter Two

Renee

Like a determined taxpayer charging city hall, I grip the offensive letter and stride into the rental office. A middle-aged man sits on a stool behind a counter, a potbellied specimen of American male pride in an I'm with Stupid T-shirt, frayed blue jeans, and rubber flip-flops.

"Excuse me, are you Mr. Myers?" I point to the signature on the letter. "If so, you can stop sending these annoying eviction notices."

The man tears his gaze away from the small television in the corner and gapes at me. "I'm Todd, the assistant manager."

"Hello, Todd. I hope you can help me. I'm Renee Carey and I'm here to clean out my mother's unit. I would have come sooner, but I can't get away from my office during the week."

The man's gaze returns to the wrestling match on the TV before he grunts and reluctantly pushes himself off the stool. "Your mother's name?"

"Vivian Sims. Unit 1402."

"You got a key?"

"I thought you kept—"

"You lock it, you keep the key. But that's okay. If you've got a letter from Myers, we can get in."

Todd reaches for a pair of long-handled bolt cutters on the wall, then pushes his way through the swinging gate at the side of the counter. Without so much as a sidelong glance at my letter, he heads toward the entrance. "Come on."

"Wait." I unfold the page and point to the date. "According to this, my mother's contract expired three months ago. I think I owe you some money."

Todd halts, an uncertain look on his face. "You owe me?"

"Your company. I didn't know my mother's contract expired, and I couldn't get here until today. So I'm overdue. Or my mother is."

He gives me a lopsided smile. "Then let her pay it."

"I would, but she died eighteen months ago."

"Oh." Todd squinches his face into a question mark. "Um…our bookkeeper doesn't come in on Saturdays."

I smooth the letter on the counter and try to be patient. "It wouldn't be hard to figure out how much I owe you. We take the total amount due per year and divide by twelve, then multiply by three. I'd be happy to write you a—"

"Tell you what, lady—" Todd winks at me "—consider it on the house. So let's head out—"

"I'd rather not," I answer, returning his smile in full measure. "And I think your boss would rather I paid the extra rent, don't you?"

"But the guy who does the billing's not—"

"Have him call me on Monday." I pull a business card from my wallet and snap it to the counter. "Now let's get that unit unlocked."

I blink as we step into a bright spring day, then I follow Todd to a rectangular building that seems to be composed of little more than beige cinder blocks and tangerine garage doors. He walks at a surprisingly quick pace, probably trying to hurry back to his wrestling match, and pauses outside a roll-up door spray-painted with a stenciled 1402.

He turns to squint at me. "You sure you don't got a key?"

I shake my head. "I didn't even know Mom rented this place."

Todd swings the bolt cutters into position. "Musta signed

a two-year contract. Take what you want. Anything left behind
will be hauled to the dump by the close of business today. And
here…" He pauses to pull a card from his pocket and hands
it to me. "Call them if you find anything worth salvaging."

I glance at the crinkled card: Joseph's Coat Thrift Shop.
Quality Donations Cheerfully Accepted.

I drop the card into my purse as he applies his considerable
heft to the bolt cutters. I don't know what my mother stored
in this unit; until I began to receive eviction notices, I didn't
know this place existed behind the National Memorial Park.

With a loud snap, the bolt cutters bite through the steel
hasp. Myers knocks the dangling lock with a knuckle,
sending the broken mechanism rattling across the concrete
floor. "Here ya go," he says, bending to lift the roll-up door.

He walks away, whistling, as I stand in the opening and
stare at the shadowed remains of my mother's life. The space
beyond is not large, nor is the unit crowded. Mom must have
intended to use this place to store Christmas decorations or
seasonal clothing. After she got sick, she might have forgotten about it. Heaven knows she had more important things to
think about.

I spy a light switch on the cinder block wall and flip it. The
fluorescent lights flicker and cast a greenish glow over a
space that smells of mildew and dead rat. Two cardboard
boxes sit next to a black-spotted silk ficus that has seen better
days. A sofa rests against the opposite wall, covered by a
stained bedsheet, and a maple headboard and footboard lean
against the back of the unit. The curve of the headboard is
familiar…. No wonder, it's part of my old bed.

I rake my hand through my hair and wonder if any of this
stuff is worth a wasted Saturday and the possibility of a
broken nail. Not much here, and certainly nothing of value.
So why didn't Mom toss this junk out?

I step toward the first box and gingerly lift the lid. I expect
to find pots and pans, or other useful objects Mother's frugal

nature wouldn't allow her to throw away, but instead several manila file folders peek out at me.

I run my finger over the file tabs, reading Mother's neatly printed labels: Old Checks. Past Bank Statements. Utility Bills. Insurance Payments. Kevin.

I blink at the sight of my brother's name. Kevin has been gone more than twenty years, and the trunk containing his kindergarten art, catcher's mitt, and college diploma is moldering in my attic. So what has Mother saved here?

I pull the file from the box and flip it open. Inside I find Kevin's passport, riddled with red and green stamps, his Social Security card, and his birth certificate. His death certificate, signed by a doctor in Spain. The bulletin from the memorial service where we honored him, his wife, and their stillborn child. Two photographs of the matching urns at the columbarium. A faded *Washington Post* article reporting that a couple from Falls Church had died in Spain. And letters, many of them on official letterhead from the Crescent Chemical Company, the firm where my brother worked. All of them dated July 1986, the month Kevin died.

I walk to the sofa and toss back the sheet. Dust motes pirouette in the light, but the upholstered surface is clean. I settle into the corner of the couch and open the file on my lap. After holding my finger under my nose to resist a sneeze, I flip through the papers again, and this time a distinctive letterhead catches my eye. One letter, dated two days after my brother's death, is from a doctor working for the Central Intelligence Agency.

Why would someone from the CIA write Mom about my brother?

Chapter Three

Sarah

"Hey," Judson says. "We pulled off a flawless operation. High five."

He rolls over to me and holds up his large brown hand, which I slap only because I know he likes this little ritual. Dr. Mewton has headed off to her office, leaving us alone in the operations room.

I tuck a hank of hair behind my speech processor to hear him better. "I wouldn't call it flawless. First our contact went all squirrelly on us, then we lost the image when Hightower went into that passageway. Mewton wasn't happy about that."

"Hightower can handle himself. And it's not like we had any reason to expect an assassin to be lurking outside a stationery shop."

"Still, I don't like being in the dark. Anything can happen—" I swallow the rest of my words, remembering that Judson will spend the remainder of his life in darkness. He knows all too well that life can change in a heartbeat. He doesn't need me to tell him about the dangers of undercover work, any more than I need him to tell me about deafness.

I place my fingers on my keyboard as the bell in the tower begins to toll. Without looking out the window, I know the sun is sinking toward the watery western horizon.

"Maybe this accountant will be the contact that pays off," Judson says, rolling toward his workstation. "Maybe this time we'll give the DEA what they need to stop those murderous—"

"Hey," I interrupt, more than ready to change the subject. "How's the new voice working for you? Easier to live with than the old one?"

"Oh, yeah, much better." Judson clicks the keyboard at his station. "I've named her Esmeralda."

"Why?"

"Think about it, kid. The association will come to you." In one smooth move he turns his wheelchair to face me. "That reminds me—want to check out my Close Connection account?"

I close the uplink to the KH 12 satellite we used to surveil the streets around Hightower's location. "I don't know why you waste time with that site. It's not like you're ever going to meet one of those women."

"Hey—don't deny a crip one of his few joys in life, okay? Log on for me."

"Don't you hear the bell? It's time to go down for dinner."

"My stomach can wait. My curiosity, however, is desperate to be satisfied." He edges closer, his smile spreading. "Come on, Sarah, tinkle a little tune on those computer keys and hook me up with someone delicious."

"Do it yourself."

"In case you haven't noticed, my eyes don't work."

"Text-to-speech reads e-mail, too."

"Yeah, but text-to-speech can't peek at a picture and tell me if a lady's fine and foxy."

Mystified by the workings of the male mind, I study my friend. Despite the damage done to his body, Judson Holmes is a skilled agent, as quick with computer code as anyone I've ever met. Why would he want anything to do with women who advertise themselves online?

"Why?" The word tumbles off my tongue. "Seriously, Jud, I don't understand."

His smile shrivels. "I don't expect you do."

"What do you mean by that?"

He hesitates. "Well…you have to admit, Sarah, you're different."

"Not really."

"Yes, you are. You've spent way too much time in this place and you hang with me when you're not working. That a useless cripple should be a young woman's best friend— that ain't right."

"You're not useless and we're not talking about me." I touch his hand so he'll know I'm not kidding around. "I honestly don't get it. Why do you reach out to those women when your life is centered here now?"

"Oh, Sarah." His voice is as heavy as the brass bell tolling outside. "Smart as you are, I don't know if you can understand."

"Try me."

"Writing to those women…makes me feel like a whole man. Hearing from them makes me feel normal, not like some freak shut away from society."

I sit back, smarting from the barb in his words. I don't think he meant to hurt me, but he did.

The tower bell concludes its ringing, reminding any fisherman within hearing distance to take time for prayer. For those of us who live and work at the Convent of the Lost Lambs, though, the automated bell has more to do with flesh than spirit.

"Hear that?" I stand so abruptly that my chair rolls backward and slams into a filing cabinet. "It's dinnertime."

Chapter Four

Renee

A trembling rises from someplace beneath my ribs as I study the letters in my brother's folder. My mother has filed them in chronological order, and the first is dated the day after Kevin's death. In it, the president of the Crescent Chemical Company expresses his condolences for Kevin's untimely passing. "Following so soon after Diane's tragedy, we are in shock," the executive wrote. "If we can do anything for you, or if you have any opinion as to how we should dispose of his belongings, please let me know. Otherwise, we will donate the contents of the home to the local parish priest and have our attorney handle the estate…."

A second letter, on the same company letterhead, is from a man who identifies himself as Kevin's colleague and says he will be sorely missed. *He was good at his job and a true patriot,* John Forehand wrote. *You can be proud of the work he was doing in Valencia.*

I look away from the page as confusion clouds my thinking. Why would anyone make a point of telling a grieving mother that her son was a patriot? What had Kevin been *doing* overseas?

Ashamed to admit that I know so little about my brother's last years, I flip to the page that most interests me—the one from Dr. Glenda Mewton, Deputy Director for Special

Projects, Western European Division, Central Intelligence Agency. This letter, unlike the others, is not prefaced with paragraphs about loss and concern. Dr. Glenda Mewton comes directly to the point:

Dear Mrs. Sims:

This is to update you on the status of Sarah Jane Sims, daughter of the late officer Kevin Sims and the late Diane Sims. As you may have heard from your son, the child was born with severe facial defects as a result of Treacher-Collins syndrome. Immediately after birth the baby was transported to a field hospital, where doctors performed surgery to insert a feeding tube and a tracheotomy tube, without which the child could not have survived. The prognosis for this patient is not good, but I need you to sign the enclosed power of attorney giving me legal authority to do what is best for this child. I have also enclosed a photo so you will be able to see the severity of this case.

We have not been able to reach you by telephone, but must resolve this matter at the earliest opportunity. Please call or send a telegram to my attention at once.

I search through the letters and rattle the pages, but if Dr. Mewton enclosed a photo, my mother did not keep it.

Perhaps she couldn't bear the reminder.

I lower the letter as my heart leaps into my throat. This has to be a mistake. Kevin and Diane's baby was stillborn. I know the baby was born dead because that's what Mother told me, and my mother would sooner pluck out her eyelashes than tell a lie. At the memorial service her pastor talked about what a tragedy it was to lose father, mother, *and* child in the space of three days. The baby was supposed to have been cremated with Diane in Spain, that's why there were two urns, instead of three.

The buzzing of my cell phone breaks my concentration. I

dig through my purse and snap the phone open. Becky, my friend and the receptionist at my practice, wants to know if I need to use her pickup truck.

"No, but— You won't believe this." I lift the letter, my senses still reeling. "I think my brother worked for the CIA."

"You're kidding." I can imagine her astonished gape. "I didn't know you had a brother."

"I don't, not anymore. He died twenty years ago, in Spain."

"Twenty years—? Good grief, how old was he?"

"Thirty-two. He died when I was fifteen."

"Wow." I can almost hear her thoughts leapfrogging from one possibility to another. "Was he a spy? Oh my goodness, was he executed by a foreign government?"

"You've seen too many movies. No, Kevin lost his wife and baby, so a couple of days later he drove his car off a bridge…at least, that's what we were told. But I've just found this folder, and now nothing makes sense. If this one letter is to be believed, the little girl—my niece—was born alive and taken to some other hospital because she was in such bad shape."

Becky exhales into the phone. "What happened to her?"

I flip through the rest of the correspondence, but none of the other writers mention a child. And none of the letters give any clue as to how my mother responded to Dr. Glenda Mewton.

It has to be a mistake. Dr. Mewton must have received bad information. Maybe she wrote Mother about someone else's baby.

I hold the file by its spine and shake it, but no photograph or power of attorney form flutters out. Only Kevin's passport and his death certificate, signed by a doctor in Spain.

So maybe there was no baby.

Either that, or Mom returned the power of attorney and destroyed the picture, deepening the deception.

I lower the file to my lap. "I have no idea what happened to the little girl, but I'm thinking she must have belonged to someone else. Otherwise, someone would have followed up with us…right?"

"I don't think the CIA volunteers a lot of information," Becky says. "And they were even more closemouthed twenty years ago, weren't they?"

"I don't know." I glance out the door as a pair of young boys whiz through the alley on bicycles, their hair flying. For so long I've thought I was the last of my family… What if I've been wrong?

I could have a niece. If she survived whatever Treacher-Collins syndrome is, she'd be twenty years old now.

I know very little about birth defects and even less about the CIA, but I'm not willing to spend the rest of my life wondering if I've been sold a lie.

I'm going to learn the truth about what happened to Sarah Jane Sims.

Chapter Five

Sarah

"Sarah?"

Despite the heavy hum on the secure line, I recognize the voice immediately—it belongs to Jack Traut, deputy director of the Office for Science and Technology. Mr. Traut is Dr. Mewton's supervisor, and he's probably calling from Langley. But why is he calling at 10:00 p.m.?

I roll over, sit up, and adjust my pajama top. "Sir?"

"Catch you at a bad time?"

I ought to remind him about the five hours' difference in time zones, but instead I toss a guilty glance at the DVD playing on my computer monitor. I always feel as if I should be working when Mr. Traut calls, but for the last fifty minutes I've been watching Baby try desperately to convince Johnny Castle that she can learn to dance the merengue. I pick up the remote and press the mute button. "No, sir."

"Good. Listen, have you been briefed about the recent trouble in Slovakia?"

I bend to search through a stack of folders on my night-stand. I usually file briefings as soon as they come in, because few of them relate directly to my work. Occasionally, though, I wish I'd skimmed those pages before putting them away.

I find the Eastern European affairs folder and tug it out of the stack. "I have the briefing in front of me."

"Our people can't get a clear answer from anyone in-country, but all signs point to Hungarian hackers. Whoever attacked the Slovakian Web sites did a thorough job—every government server went down in less than twenty-four hours."

"I see that."

"Obviously, we can't have that happening on our systems. We've got some of our best people working on the defensive perimeter, but Dr. Mewton reminded me of your steganography project. Seems to me there has to be a way we can guarantee that the Slovakian situation can't happen here. Why can't we be proactive and sneak something onto the computers of whoever might be foolish enough to attack us?"

I watch Baby step into Johnny's arms as I consider the question. Steganography, the art of hiding a message inside pictures or programs, isn't a new science, but I've never considered its potential as a defensive measure. My current project is a little program I call Mona Lisa. On the surface, it's just a collection of screen savers, perfectly suitable for an office environment. But in reality, each of those pretty pictures could be used to send covert messages or secretly upload key files.

I suppose I could expand the application to include a "Trojan horse"—hidden software that could do very bad things to unsuspecting users' computers. If a hacker cracked the firewall protecting our systems, why couldn't we let him steal something that contained a secret string of deadly code? The trick would be convincing him to steal the loaded image or document…unless, of course, we loaded *all* our files with an undetectable Trojan.

"I could certainly add that dimension, sir. I think I'd enjoy the challenge."

"I'll look forward to a demonstration. Let Glenda know when you have it ready."

"I will, sir."

"Fine, fine. How's the weather out your way?"

I glance toward the window, a star-studded ebony rectangle. "Clear and pleasant. We've had a lovely summer."

"I should get out there to check up on you all more often. Keep up the good work, Sarah."

"I will. Thank you, sir."

The phone clicks and I return it to its base. Mr. Traut is right—he should come out here more often. He says we're his favorite special projects team, but you wouldn't know it if you studied his calendar. He's visited our facility only three times this year.

I study the latest briefing. According to the classified report, the Slovakian prime minister's Web site was hit on June 27. After the PM's site went down, other hacker attacks came in waves, effectively shutting down newspaper offices, television stations, schools, and banks. The assault so unnerved the Slovakian government authorities that they raised the issue at a meeting of NATO officials, equating the cyber attack with an act of war.

I lean against my pillow and push against the unruly sprig of hair that is forever falling into my left eye. Like many others in the company, Mr. Traut believes that technology has forever changed the face of war. Instead of fighting with large conventional armies, countries will either strike with small guerilla groups or wage cyber battles—and of the two types of attack, cyber war will be the more devastating. Because so many people rely on the Internet for banking, shopping, and communicating, hostile action in cyberspace could bring a country to its knees.

I watch the monitor as Baby skips across a green lawn in white sneakers and cropped pants. The story is set long before people routinely had computers in their homes and carried cell phones in their pockets. I'm sure the screenwriter wanted to portray the early sixties as a more innocent era, but I've seen this film several times, and I know that darkness lurks even at Kellerman's.

I watch a lot of movies, but I hold few illusions about life. The CIA's Convent of the Lost Lambs treats people who have been tortured and mutilated by their fellow men. Part of my job includes eavesdropping on plots and conspiracies to overthrow governments and commit murder. I know that evil lurks in every building and behind every bush outside these walls.

Perhaps that's why I enjoy films so much. In them I can enjoy a world where almost everyone has a pretty face and only the men and women who wear black have evil hearts.

If pain and sadness can shadow beautiful Baby and handsome Johnny in a lovely summer resort, I know it would haunt me, if I ever leave this place.

Not that I ever will.

Chapter Six

Renee

"So?" I lower my pen to my desk, a purposeful and relaxed gesture that should encourage Nancy to talk. "Does the BOTOX seem to be working?"

My patient, a forty-six-year-old mother in a T-shirt, shorts, and battered sneakers, crosses her legs and gives me a rueful smile. "My daughter keeps telling me that I look like I'm wearing a mask."

"Was this the sixteen-year-old?"

"Brittany, yes."

"Did you honestly expect her to say something *nice?* After all, didn't you just take her cell phone away?"

Nancy sucks at the inside of her cheeks for a moment, then snorts. "Maybe you have a point."

"And maybe your daughter wanted to put a negative spin on a noticeable improvement," I point out. "I would say you appear more rested than usual, but I want to know how you've been *feeling*. Have you noticed any improvement in your depression?"

Nancy runs a hand over her hair, which she has pulled into a tight ponytail. "Now that you mention it, maybe the injections have helped. Last week at this time I could barely summon the energy to get out of bed, but I'm here, aren't I?"

"And you're looking pretty good."

"Rested, you said."

"Rested…and a bit more relaxed than usual."

The corner of Nancy's mouth dips in a wry smile. "I still don't see how BOTOX is supposed to help me feel better. My husband thinks this treatment is a lot of hooey. He doesn't even want me coming to therapy anymore."

"When did he say that?"

"Last night. Right after he told me he'd rather eat roadkill than my pot roast."

I smooth my slacks and take a moment to evaluate my patient's statement. Nancy's Neanderthal of a husband is probably to blame for her continued depression, but she's not willing to admit that. Not yet, anyway.

"Perhaps," I edge into the topic, "your husband expressed that opinion because he noticed a change and assumed you are completely better. He'd be wrong, because depression doesn't go away overnight, but you could accept his comment as evidence that your outlook has brightened."

"But why?" Her forehead remains smooth, courtesy of the BOTOX, but a frown cuts deep parentheses into the sides of her mouth. "I don't get it."

I fold my hands. "Remember the old song about the benefits of putting on a happy face? As illogical as it may seem, the lyricist had it right. A demonstrable physiological link exists between our facial expressions and our emotions."

"We feel better because we look better?"

"Looking better is a side effect. When you wear a happy face, your emotional outlook improves because smiling promotes the release of endorphins in the brain. On the other hand, frowning causes your spirits to plummet. And when you narrow your eyes in anger, your blood pressure rises."

Nancy frowns again, and in that down-turned mouth I can read years of repressed frustration and yearning. "So what does all that have to do with cosmetic injections?"

"BOTOX isn't used only for cosmetic reasons. Because it

temporarily paralyzes certain facial muscles, doctors are finding all sorts of medical applications for it. Neurologists use it to treat migraine headaches, and we psychologists use it to paralyze the corrugator supercilii muscles in patients' foreheads—"

"To treat frowny faces?"

"To treat clinical depression." I give her a careful smile. "Have you ever heard of the partial facial paralysis known as Mobius syndrome? These patients, most of whom are born with the condition, are often unable to smile or frown. As a result, they don't experience emotions with the same intensity as normal people."

"I have days," Nancy says, "when that sort of numbness would be a blessing."

"I don't think so." I shift my gaze to the sunlit window beyond my desk. "Numbness is a blessing when we're in pain, but pain tells us when something is wrong. Discomfort motivates us to seek the help we need."

"You could always have your partner prescribe more happy pills."

"We've already tried the standard antidepressants," I remind her, "and it appears that your depression is not caused by a chemical imbalance."

I'd lay the blame for Nancy's depression at the feet of her churlish husband and her ungrateful teenage children, but the woman is blindly devoted to all three. I doubt she'd be sitting in my office if they were equally devoted to her.

"We need to try a different approach," I say, jotting a note on my legal pad. "Who knows? You might get so used to wearing a peaceful look that a smile becomes your natural expression."

If her forehead hadn't been freshly injected with BOTOX, I suspect, Nancy would lift both brows in an expression of genuine skepticism.

"So," she says, rubbing her arms, "should I keep journaling? And make another appointment?"

"Absolutely. And remember not to censor yourself. Write whatever comes to mind, and let your thoughts spill out. About your kids, your husband—everything."

"What if someone reads it?"

"Would that be a problem?"

"My husband would freak out if he knew what I was really thinking." She brings her hand to her throat, a common *I need reassurance* gesture.

"You need to be honest with yourself." I lean toward her and smile to alleviate her anxiety. "Get one of those old-fashioned diaries with a lock and key. Or journal on a computer and protect the file with a password. You don't have to share your most private thoughts with anyone, but you do have to write them down. Only when you force yourself to put feelings into words are you able to recognize them for what they are."

She sighs and reaches for her handbag on the floor. "I'll try."

"Don't try—*do*. And we'll talk about it during our next session."

Nancy nods through her tears, then thanks me and stands. "By the way," she says, settling her purse strap on her shoulder, "a few months ago you mentioned taking a long vacation. Is that coming up any time soon?"

I stand, as well. "It's not actually a vacation, but I need to check on a family matter. Before I can leave, however, I have to get a security clearance."

"Oh. Sounds mysterious."

"Trust me, my family has nothing to do with national security. But the process is taking longer than I thought it would."

She crinkles her nose. "How long does it take to check your fingerprints?"

"They check a lot more than fingerprints," I tell her, moving toward the door, "and it's already been four months since I submitted my paperwork. I've been told the process can take up to a year."

Nancy gives me the first real smile I've seen on her face in months. "So I'm okay to make an appointment for next week?"

"You're good to make appointments from now until Christmas. But don't you worry—you're going to be doing better long before the holidays."

After Nancy leaves, I close the door and lean against it. With my patients and friends, I've pretended to be calm and accepting of the process known as "getting clearance," but on most days I'm ready to scream with frustration.

Since finding that CIA connection in my mother's files, I've made inquiries and been told that I cannot have any contact with Dr. Glenda Mewton unless I have the proper security clearance. To obtain clearance, I must be in the military, hold a government job, be employed by a contractor working for the government, or apply for a position that requires a government clearance. No exceptions.

For two days I thought about giving up—allowing Sarah Jane Sims, if she exists, to live her life in the same state of idyllic ignorance I once enjoyed. But then I thought about my mother, who once spied my bleeding hangnail and drove thirty miles back to a dress shop to tell the clerk that her little girl might have bled on the zipper of a dress she had tried on. If so, she would pay for the dry cleaning.

My mother was completely committed to doing right. That's why I have to know if Sarah Sims survived…and why my mother told me she didn't.

Frustrated by my inability to move forward with the CIA, I followed a hunch and went around the U.S. government, sending a letter to the leading hospital in Valencia, the Hospital Clinico Universitario. In my barely adequate Spanish, I asked for a copy of Sarah Jane Sims's birth certificate, if such a thing exists.

I've also taken a far more significant step. In April—quietly, not wanting to alarm the other doctors in my practice—I applied for a position as a staff psychologist with the Central Intelligence Agency. I never thought I'd consider working for the CIA. But Kevin was apparently willing to sacrifice the pleasures of ordinary life to serve his country. In any case, I've come to believe that ordinary life is overrated.

In order to achieve the vaunted status of One Who Can Be Trusted with Government Secrets, I have filled out Standard Form 86, I have been fingerprinted, and I have given the government page after page of personal information, numerous references, and permission to check everything from my credit report to my college transcripts. I have been told that my medical and police records will be reviewed…and I am praying that my five speeding tickets won't be interpreted as a reckless disregard for American highway law.

I would hate to have my quest for truth crushed by my own lead foot.

Chapter Seven

Sarah

"That you, kiddo?"

As I leave the exercise room, I'm surprised to find Judson waiting in the hallway. "Who else would it be?"

"Sometimes the guards like to slip up here and work out."

"Not when Mama Mewton is prowling around."

"You've got a point there." He rolls toward me, his powerful arms propelling his chair over the tiled floor. When my fingertips brush his shoulder, he slows his pace and lowers his voice. "Did you hear the chopper last night?"

I shorten my step to match the wheelchair's progress. "I took my speech processor off so I could concentrate on a project. Is the new arrival a patient or a guest?"

"Neither. Traut came in alone. He's waiting for us in the conference room."

A shiver of anticipation ripples through my limbs as we approach the elevator. Judson doesn't seem at all nervous about this meeting with the director, but he hasn't spent the last several weeks writing a program intended to prevent national disaster.

I hope the man approves of my work.

I press the call button and cross my arms. "What time did Mr. Traut arrive?"

Judson shrugs. "I wasn't listening for the clock. It was late, though."

The elevator opens. We nod to the guard and enter, Judson wheeling to the left and spinning to face the door. A moment later we arrive on the second floor, home to our apartments, Dr. Mewton's office, operations, security, and the conference room. My hopes for a quick shower and a change of clothes are dashed when I see Dr. Mewton waiting in the hallway.

"I was about to call you on the intercom," she says, stepping forward to pluck a stray hair from my shoulder. "Holmes, you give your report first. Sarah, Mr. Traut has a copy of your program and wishes to speak to you. He'll probably want a demonstration, so grab your laptop."

I point toward my apartment, only a few feet down the hall. "Do I have time to change?"

"No."

"Breakfast?"

"There's coffee, fruit, and doughnuts on the table. Shelba will bring up anything else you want."

Of course Dr. M's thought of everything. She never misses a detail.

I wait for Judson to roll forward, then I follow, my stomach tightening with every step.

Jack Traut is devouring one of Shelba's delicious fritters when Judson and I enter the conference room. He nods at us and takes a sip of coffee as we approach the table. "Interesting program," he says, pointing to the laptop in front of him. "Mind telling me how it works?"

I glance at Judson, who rolls to his usual place at the table without comment. If he minds being overlooked by our boss's boss, he gives no sign of it.

"The concept isn't complicated," I say, sinking into my own chair. "The program works in conjunction with others that provide a layered security approach."

"Layered?"

"Like an onion." Dr. Mewton slides into her seat and

gives Mr. Traut a smile. She is, I notice as I open my laptop, wearing lipstick today. "Encryption, plus hidden directories, added to covert channels that hide data in Internet traffic."

Our boss wipes his hands on a napkin. "But if the perimeter is secure—"

"The perimeter dissolved a long time ago," Judson says. "Virtual private networks, Web mail, e-mail on smartphones, telecommuters…they all make the concept of a secure perimeter archaic. We have to be data-focused, not perimeter-focused. We have to protect the data, wherever it is, wherever it goes."

"That's why we need layers," I add. "They're the armor we wrap around our data."

Without so much as a peek in my direction, Mr. Traut looks at Dr. Mewton, then glances at Judson. "Are you two on board with this?"

Dr. Mewton doesn't answer, but Judson grins. "Just let the girl talk."

I wait—annoyed at being ignored, I'll admit—until Mr. Traut looks at me. Then I continue. "What I did was conceal mirroring code in the existing antivirus program. If—*when*—a hacker breaks through the firewall, the mirror will mash up with any malicious code that's introduced and encrypt the results. If the hacker tries to take a file, any file, the concealed code will erupt like Mt. Vesuvius once it's installed on the invading system. In other words, the hacker gets hacked…and his system gets tied up in knots."

The hint of a smile strains at Mr. Traut's mouth as he takes out his pipe and lights it. "You've tested this?"

"On several systems. I ran the first trial against a network at the Technical University of Budapest. I hacked into the TU system on a less-than-secure network and left my calling card on a proxy server I'd set up. When they came calling, our program crashed their servers in less than ten minutes."

"They're still trying to figure out what hit 'em," Judson

says, grinning in Mr. Traut's direction. "I monitored some chatter on the hacker boards—they were all buzzing."

"But they can't steal your code?"

"No, sir," I answer. "That's the beauty of it—after the mashup occurs, you'd need a supercomputer and the patience of Mother Teresa to sort it all out."

Mr. Traut finally looks at me. Then he removes his pipe and smiles at Dr. Mewton. "God may not have given that girl a face, but he certainly gave her a brain. Congratulations, Glenda, on a brilliant acquisition."

The pleasure I felt a moment ago evaporates as his words resonate on the air. The director is not looking at me, but at this moment I don't think I could bear the touch of his gaze. When I find my voice, it sounds strangled in my ear: "Thank you, sir."

Across the table, Dr. Mewton clears her throat. "I'm sure we'll be making adjustments to Sarah's program in the weeks ahead, but you can begin implementing it at Langley."

I feel like hanging my head to hide my hurt, but I doubt Mr. Traut will look at me again.

He lifts his pipe to his lips. "The assignment that brings me out today," he says, exhaling, "has the potential to eliminate all intensive interrogation techniques. I'm sure you're aware that we've come under fire for harsh interrogations in the past, but we believe this team can help us access a prisoner's knowledge without eliciting pain of any kind."

Something in his choice of words—*access knowledge?*— sounds familiar. "Are you talking about voice stress analysis?" I ask. "Or some kind of improved polygraph?"

"You're on the right track." Mr. Traut pulls a briefcase onto the table, punches in a code, and unlocks the clasps. He withdraws two copies of a spiral-bound document and slides them across the table, one to me and one to Dr. Mewton. He places a CD in Judson's hand.

"What we've acquired," he says, "is a device that records

and measures human brain waves. It's far more accurate than a polygraph or vocal scan, and far less stressful than torture."

I scan the cover of the document, which has been labeled with the project name and classification: Sensitive Compartmented Information—Special Intelligence.

I lift my chin and stare at the director's profile. "You're calling it *Gutenberg?*"

"After the man who invented the printing press. We're hoping to invent a printing method, as well…a way to publish a legible, comprehensible record of what a brain knows."

"If you've already acquired this scanner, why do you need our help?"

"Because the operating program is not infallible, nor has its potential been fully realized." Mr. Traut leans forward and speaks directly to me, and for once he doesn't deflect his gaze in reflexive discomfort. "We think you can come up with a way to render our brain scans mistake-proof. If you can fine-tune this program, our officers will never have to resort to painful interrogation."

Awareness thickens between us as I ponder the meaning of his words. If we can plumb the depths of an evil mind, perhaps we can stop terror. Dr. Mewton says evil loves darkness, and Gutenberg may be a way to shine a light into dark places. The dread of that light may be enough to stem the tide of viciousness that men exhibit to one another.

I look at Mr. Traut. "I'll do my best for you, sir."

"I'm sorry, Glenda, but it's all I can do to look at that girl." The words spill easily from Mr. Traut's lips as he stands in the elevator, not knowing that I am watching—and listening—via the security camera mounted in the corner of the car.

I swallow hard and wrap my arms around myself, shivering beneath the sweater I have pulled over my shoulders. I'm not surprised to hear this; really, I have always known he felt this way. Still…disappointment strikes like a punch to the stomach.

Angela Hunt

"Jack." Dr. Mewton's voice is low with reproof. "She has feelings, you know, and she desperately wants to please you."

Mr. Traut slips his hand into his pocket. "She's an employee. I would hope that all my employees want to do a good job."

"It's different with Sarah. *She's* different. Since you assumed your position, I think she's come to think of you as a father figure. Did you know she keeps that equivalency diploma you sent in her room? It's been hanging on her wall for over five years."

Traut shakes his head. "I didn't mean to encourage her. Not like that."

"Why shouldn't you encourage her? She's brilliant, and she'll work hard for you."

"And what else is she going to do?" He turns away from the camera to look at Dr. Mewton, but I can hear the smile in his voice.

Dr. M folds her arms and stares at the back of the guard's head. "All I'm saying is that you need to be more sensitive to her. She's a young woman, with a young woman's feelings."

The elevator stops. "I'll see you later." Dr. Mewton nods at Mr. Traut and steps out of the car.

I am about to exit the surveillance program when Mr. Traut folds his hands and looks at the guard, who has backed away from the sliding door. All I can see is the top of the guard's head, so I have no way of knowing who he is.

"You know that girl, Sarah?"

The guard nods.

"If you were trapped with her on a desert island for a year, would you?"

The guard throws up both hands and utters an expletive, then reassumes his military posture. "No way, sir."

Traut grins. "That's what I thought."

I turn off the program and head for bed. I get under the covers and leave the lamp burning.

Dr. Mewton once told me that beautiful women sleep on their backs because sleeping sideways contorts the face and causes wrinkles.

I always sleep on my side.

Chapter Eight

Renee

Christmas approaches, bringing the promise of busted budgets and the holiday blues on its wintry breath. Our office closes a full week before the holiday, and as Becky plans to host a turkey dinner for twenty-five aunts, uncles, cousins, and miscellaneous family offshoots, I decided to paint the kitchen and clean out my walk-in closet. When people ask if I have big plans for the holidays, with perfect sincerity I answer *yes.*

Since Becky and I are close, I buy her the first three seasons of *Seinfeld* on DVD. I buy a ten-pound doggie stocking for Elvis, my two-hundred-pound mastiff, and order citrus gift boxes for all my partners in the practice. I can't help wondering if this will be the last time I'll place those orders. Next year I may be a CIA shrink and bound to secrecy.

At the closing-of-the-office party, I receive tins of fruit, chocolate, and nuts from my partners, and a leather-bound copy of *Cry, the Beloved Country* from Becky. I am touched.

The day before Christmas, during a break from painting, I receive the most unsettling gift of the season: a letter from Spain containing a copy of Sarah Jane Sims's *certificado de nacimiento.* My niece's birth certificate.

A tremor of mingled fear and anticipation shoots through me as I open the narrow envelope and discover the certificate inside. Though my Spanish is rusty, I'm able to read that Sarah Jane Sims was born alive on July 3, 1986, at 6:30 a.m., to Diane and Kevin Sims. Because both her parents were U.S. citizens, Sarah had American citizenship at birth.

I pick up the envelope and shake it, afraid I've missed something, but there is no cover letter, no note of explanation. Nothing to tell me what happened to the baby.

In my den, I sink into my sofa and prop my feet on the ottoman, grateful for even this simple confirmation. I still don't know if Sarah Jane is alive today, but I do know she wasn't stillborn. My mother, the soul of integrity, lied about this girl.

Why?

The question hangs in the air, shimmering like the reflections from the dozens of glass bulbs on my Christmas tree.

Mother knew Sarah Jane Sims survived the birth. But Dr. Mewton's letter said the baby's prognosis was poor, so perhaps Mom believed the child would die. Or, having just lost Diane and Kevin, maybe she was so heartsick she couldn't bear the thought of taking responsibility for a child she would almost certainly lose as well.

I can imagine Mother looking at the baby's photo and weeping…and then signing the power of attorney and sending it off, leaving the child in what she assumed were more capable hands.

My mother was not heartless. In July, 1986, however, she was heartbroken.

I close my eyes and resign myself to the real possibility that I may never know the entire truth. My brother and his wife are gone, and so are my parents. Sarah Jane Sims may be beyond my reach as well.

When I open my eyes, I find that my thoughts have crystallized. Mom misled us about the baby, but she didn't throw Dr. Mewton's letter away. She saved it, leaving the door open for me to investigate. I can act on the facts I have in hand.

The letters in my brother's file confirm that Kevin was

working for a Spanish chemical company. He and Diane had a child who was born with severe birth defects. Dr. Glenda Mewton, employed by the CIA, took care of Sarah Jane after Kevin's and Diane's deaths.

Doesn't that girl, wherever she is, deserve to know her family?

I may not be able to get close to the mysterious Dr. Mewton without a security clearance, but I can certainly write and ask her to forward a letter to Sarah Jane Sims. If she's unable to do so, she should respond. Any polite person would.

On Christmas Eve, with the kitchen resplendent in a fresh new coat of noble gold, I climb into my flannel holiday pajamas and cuddle with Elvis on the sofa. In the glow of our twinkling Christmas tree, I pull a sheet of stationery from the coffee table drawer and write Sarah a letter. I tell her I'm her aunt, that I'm glad I've finally learned about her, and that I can't wait to meet her. I want to learn all about her, and I want to share everything I know about her father, my brother.

I sign off with a wish for a merry Christmas and a successful New Year. Then, on a whim, I adjust Elvis's flannel holly-berry necklace, hold up a digital camera, and snap a picture of the two of us. When I'm convinced we look friendly, not goofy, I head into the study to print out a copy and find an envelope.

Chapter Nine

Sarah

A frosty January wind is rattling the windowpanes by the time I get Judson strapped into the chair and ready for his first brainprinting session.

He tests the leather strap around his wrist. "Are you sure this isn't painful?"

"Completely pain-free."

"Then why are you tying me down?"

"So you won't wiggle. Now be quiet, please."

I've been working like a madwoman to prepare unique stimuli for two tests, one for Judson and one for Dr. Mewton. Judson's exam has provided me with special challenges because his blindness precludes my use of visual cues. For him, every stimulus must be either aural or tactile. Given time, I could come up with some olfactory cues, but the delivery process might be complicated.

I lift the specially designed sensing device from the table and slip it around his head. "Do you promise to sit absolutely still?"

"Do I have a choice? You're applying electricity to my brain."

"Oh. Right." I work my fingers over the device, making sure each of the more than two dozen electrodes fits snugly against his bald skull. The device, which looks like a studded shower cap, has been outfitted with electronic sensors that will measure the brain's electrical output from several different locations.

"There." I tighten the strap under his chin and check the elastic band that holds all the wires together in a thick ponytail at the back of his head. "You don't have to talk. You don't have to do anything but sit and relax. Let your brain do all the work."

"What if my brain's feeling a little nervous?"

"Tell it to trust me. I'm your friend and I won't hurt you."

"That's what they all say."

A husky note vibrates in his voice, bringing with it hints of another time when he was restrained and subjected to the whims of others. Those people, however, were not his friends, and I will not let him dwell on that episode.

After all, he doesn't let me dwell on my painful past.

I pull a set of headphones from my pocket and slip them over Judson's ears, careful not to disturb the sensors. Because the headphones will block any sound in the room, I pull the microphone from my headset closer to my mouth. "Can you hear me?"

"I'm trying to ignore you."

"That's the spirit. Just relax while I get your program ready."

I'm not sure why Judson remains tense; he knows this test is not designed to elicit panic or pain. Unlike a polygraph, the Gutenberg program doesn't attempt to indicate truth-telling or lying, nor does it measure emotion-triggered signals like heart rate, sweating, or blood pressure. The tiny sensors in the cap will record whatever electrical signals are emitted from Judson's brain approximately three hundred milliseconds after it is confronted with a stimulus of special significance—a sound, word, or feeling Judson finds familiar.

I move back to my workstation and my computer. "Almost ready."

"I still think the polygraph is perfectly adequate," Jud says, flexing his fingers. "Why is Traut making you do all this when we already have tools in place?"

"Because polygraphs have never once snagged a spy." I

open the file containing Judson's unique program and prepare to begin broadcasting. "Twice the polygraph failed to catch Aldrich Ames when he was working for the Soviets."

"Still, ninety percent reliability is pretty good."

"Tell that to the double agents who were executed when Ames exposed them. And what if you're in the ten percent of those who are falsely accused? I don't like those odds, and neither do the American courts."

"You don't have to use a polygraph in a trial. Sometimes just the threat of a lie detector test is enough to make a subject crack."

"What is it with you men and intimidation? We're supposed to be leaving all that behind, remember? Besides, if we can get this program to work reliably, the brainprint can be as conclusive as DNA when it comes to proving innocence or guilt."

Judson releases a deep chuckle. "The polygraph guys scared the spit out of me when I was training at Camp Peary. Those guys used to tell me they were *certain* I was lying. They almost convinced me—and I *knew* I was telling the truth."

"Those days are over and done, my friend. Now we let electrodes search for truths hidden in the brain."

"Have fun looking, sister. A lot of people got a lot of trash hidden in their heads."

"I don't worry about your head."

"Maybe you ought to." He lowers his voice. "By the way, Sarah…"

I stop what I'm doing when Jud's voice drops. "Hmm?"

"Did you get that satellite tasked over the coordinates I gave you yesterday?"

"Yes."

"Did you look at the photos?"

"I did."

"Did you happen to see a boy in the yard?"

I know what he's asking, and why. Jud has a son living at

those coordinates in Lubbock, Texas. A sixteen-year-old boy named Darius, who lives with his mother and stepfather.

"I didn't see a boy in any of the shots."

"Maybe you need to adjust the time. He gets out of school around three o'clock."

"I didn't see a boy, Jud. But I did see a car I'd never seen before in the driveway."

"Could you tell the model?"

"No, but it wasn't the Ford Focus or the SUV. An older sedan, maybe."

Judson smiles to himself. "The boy went and got himself a car. That makes sense, he'd be driving now."

"I hope he drives a car better than you handle your wheels. Okay, time to be quiet. I'm going to start the tape."

Judson grips the armrests of his chair and presses his lips together. For a moment he looks so vulnerable I almost laugh aloud. "I told you, Jud, it's not painful."

"Let me be the judge of that, okay?"

"Sure. Ready—three, two, one. Starting *now.*"

I click the start key and sit down, then turn off my headset so Judson won't hear any background noise bleeding through my mic. I know what he's hearing through his headphones— my voice, rattling off random words at a slow and steady pace: *Dog. Farm. Chain. Cat. Mother. Saw. Ice. Apple. Son. Ice pick. Sunshine. Light. Darkness. CST. Crash. Convertible. Basset hound.*

I chose words that pertain to things I know Judson once loved—*basset hound, farm, son, mother*—and deliberately juxtaposed them with words that are likely to remind him of stress—*ice pick, crash, chain.* I interspersed dozens of military acronyms and tradecraft terms among the cues, mingling *dead drop* and *brush pass* with such innocent words as *apple* and *tree.* Since I don't know everything about Jud's past, I might hit on an aberration—for instance, if he had a dog named Apple and associates it with an unpleasant experience—but considering how many words I've selected, those are long odds.

By the time the test is finished, Judson will probably be wild with boredom, but I'll have a printout of the unique inventory of his brain. Any word or sensation that arouses a memory or recognition in Judson's mind will emit a P300, an electrical signal that is maximal at the midline parietal area of the skull. Even stronger signals will indicate that the probing stimulus probably refers to a stored memory. The stronger the signal, the more powerful the memory.

I know Judson pretty well. And by the time this test is finished, I'll know him a lot better.

I have great hopes for the Gutenberg program. Earlier researchers have achieved a ninety-seven percent accuracy rate of determinations of "information present" or "information absent" in a subject's brain. In Missouri, a serial killer has already been sentenced to prison after a brainprinting test demonstrated that he had information in his head that matched the details of an unsolved murder. When confronted with the results of his brain scan, the man confessed to that murder and three others.

Still…brainprinting is not without challenges. Three percent of test subjects give indeterminate results, and Mr. Traut will not be happy unless our program is one hundred percent trustworthy.

Fortunately, he has given us time to work.

Chapter Ten

Renee

On the sidewalk outside the Dolley Madison Library in McLean, I break my stride long enough to admire a patch of daffodils, the first hardy harbingers of spring. The place is especially busy even for a Saturday, and I discover the reason why when I enter the common area and find a local author talking about her new book. I hug my shoulder bag close and murmur "Excuse me, excuse me" as I wend my way through the crowd, but I catch more than one scornful look as I press toward the librarian at the reference desk.

"Hi." I drop my purse and notebook on the counter, then jerk my thumb toward the author behind me. "What is it, a diet book?"

The man behind the desk smooths his tie and lifts his brows in an expression of disdain. "I believe her book is called *Getting What You Want Means Wanting What You Get.*"

"People are paying money for that?" I glance over my shoulder and shake my head. "I could have let them in on that secret in just one session."

The librarian is not amused. "May I help you?"

"Sure. I'm wondering if you have any specialized medical journals."

"Which journal would you like?"

"Well...I'm not sure. I'm looking up a condition called Treacher-Collins syndrome."

He smoothes his tie again and points to the computer carrel behind me. "May I suggest you look up the term on Google?"

"Did that weeks ago. I don't want Internet chatter, I want reliable information. Medline, for instance. Does your library have an access code?"

He blinks slowly and points me toward another computer. "Over there. If you can't access the document, get the edition number and bring it to me."

"Can't you just give me a password?"

"I cannot."

I tilt my head, surprised by the man's unhelpfulness. "All righty, then."

I move to the specified computer and hook my purse strap over the back of the chair. I glance right and left before I slide into the seat. I know I'm being paranoid, but ever since applying for a security clearance I can't shake the feeling that I'm being watched. This sensation is the reason I've come to the library instead of working at my computer in the office—hard drives have long memories, and unique Medline access codes can be tracked. Though I know my misgivings are probably silly, I don't want to find myself sitting in a darkened room while unseen inquisitors drip water on my forehead and ask why I was investigating Treacher-Collins syndrome when none of my patients have that condition.

For the past three months I've been writing letters to anyone who might help me connect with Sarah Sims. The CIA central office referred me to the Directorate for Science and Technology, where an underling suggested I write Mr. Jack Traut. That gentleman has not responded to my queries, but neither has Dr. Glenda Mewton, to whom I've been writing since Christmas.

Though I haven't received any satisfying answers or heard

anything about my security clearance, I am continuing my quest under the assumption that uncommunicativeness is standard operating procedure for the CIA.

My determination to know what happened to my niece has brought me to the library.

Over the last several weeks I've learned that Treacher-Collins Syndrome, also known as mandibulofacial dysostosis, is a hereditary condition that causes facial defects and occurs approximately once in every ten thousand births. Typical problems include eyes that slant downward, an unusually small lower jaw, an abnormally large mouth, malformed or absent ears, scalp hair extending onto the cheeks, and a cleft palate. Though the facial deformities are often severe, the condition does not affect the brain. Afflicted children usually possess normal intelligence.

I already know Sarah's condition must have been far worse than average. Why would a child with a small jaw and malformed ears need tubes to breathe and eat? Scalp hair in the wrong place, slanting eyes, even a cleft palate, would not demand immediate surgical intervention. In order to require a trach tube, Sarah would have to lack a proper nose. In order to require a feeding tube, my little niece would have had to be born without a lower jaw.

I know that standard treatment includes plastic surgery, facial reconstruction, and testing for hearing loss. Complications, many of which continue throughout childhood, include difficulty with vision, eating, speaking, and hearing.

After accessing a Medline article on the syndrome's psychological effects, I learn that while children with severe facial abnormalities may achieve a level of independent living, many withdraw from society and even become suicidal, because they do not have what most people take for granted: an expressive, functional face.

I stare into the crowd around the visiting author as the word *severe*—Dr. Mewton used that word—looms large in my consciousness. I have blithely assumed that Sarah's physical problems were resolved within a few months of her birth, but what if they weren't? What if the child faced years of painful surgeries and rehabilitation? What if she's still suffering?

If a child were born without a face…would death be a mercy?

I press my hand to my lips as my gaze roves over the people milling about in the library. A mother walks by, a toddler clinging to each hand, and older patrons automatically stop to smile at the little ones. Why? Because they're adorable. Big-eyed, shiny-haired, chubby-cheeked cherubs.

Yet in the carrel across the aisle sits a young woman in a wheelchair. One arm lies across her lap; her right hand is bent and twisted. She's tapping on the computer keyboard with clumsy fingers and concentrating so intently that apparently she hasn't noticed the slow string of drool marking her twisted mouth and chin.

No one stops to admire her. No one pauses to ask her the time or for help with the computer. Even though I suspect she's been seated at that station for longer than the allotted thirty minutes per patron, no one has approached to tell her to move on. She might as well be invisible.

My stomach twists as my imagination superimposes my beloved brother's features on that lonely face. Children can be cruel and peers can be vicious, but years of experience have taught me that indifference inflicts the deepest wound of all. Has my niece, wherever she is, come to the conclusion that her family simply doesn't care?

My throat aches with the thought.

If Sarah is dead, surely someone would tell me. After all, I've been honest about my reasons for wanting to contact Glenda Mewton. I don't give a fig about the woman and her top secret work; all I care about is finding my brother's daughter.

I can see a fork in the road ahead: one path leads to the dead end of learning that my niece died long ago, the other to a living woman. But if I find her, and finally meet her, instead of embracing me, she might spit in my face.

If I had been abandoned and left alone in a world of pain and fear, that might be my reaction.

Chapter Eleven

Renee

When my receptionist hands me the mail on a warm afternoon in May, I immediately recognize the return address on one envelope. Jack Traut, deputy director of the CIA's Directorate for Science and Technology, is writing—again—to inform me that because I lack the proper security clearance, his agency cannot answer my questions about Sarah Jane Sims or Glenda Mewton.

After skimming his note, however, I find a handwritten postscript:

> Sarah Jane Sims declines to see you. Furthermore, Ms. Sims is working on a classified project at a secure post. To divulge her location would compromise ongoing operations, expose Americans and foreign nationals to grave risk, and reveal secrets adverse to U.S. interests.

My first thought is that my niece must be some kind of Mata Hari. My second thought is that Jack Traut has just confirmed that she's alive, in contact with him, and working for the CIA…at some sort of government facility.

My vision of Sarah Sims as a blue-jeaned, wisecracking college student vanishes like a burst bubble, but no matter where she is, I refuse to believe that a twenty-one-year-old orphan wouldn't want to meet her only living relative.

I drop the letter and buzz the front desk. "Becky, do we know any lawyers who deal with the CIA?"

She laughs. "None who will admit it."

"I need one."

"Give me a minute." I heard the click of her keyboard, then she gives me a name: "Try John Lipps. He's married to Nicole, and their home number's in your address book."

I close my eyes and try to picture Nicole Lipps's face. I remember treating her for postpartum depression a year or so ago. "How do you know her husband's with the agency?"

"Because when I asked what her husband does, she said he was a lawyer who works for the government. When I asked her which branch, she clammed up. That's when I knew he had to be with CIA."

"Thanks."

I jot Lipps's name on my calendar, then turn to my computer to type out a reply to Traut's letter. I still haven't heard anything about my security clearance, but when it comes through, I'll take a polygraph, endure an interview, and pee in a cup. I'll jump through whatever hoops they hold up and if all else fails, I'll hire a lawyer who's not afraid to confront the CIA on their own legal turf. I start to type:

> Dear Mr. Traut, unless I receive a signed cease and de-
> sist statement from Sarah J. Sims, I'm not going away.
> I'm going to persevere, because that's what family
> does—we stick. If you doubt my tenacity, I suggest you
> broach the subject with my lawyer.

As I watch the letter emerge from the printer, I can't help thinking that if I'd been half as persistent in trying to save my marriage, maybe I wouldn't be spending the coming weekend alone.

Mother's Day at church has always been difficult, especially when the pastor interrupts the service to hand out roses to the youngest mother, oldest mother, mother with the most children, mother who's had the most husbands…

My cynicism is a defense mechanism, nothing more. For not only do I miss my own mother, but on the second Sunday in May, I mourn the children I have never been granted the opportunity to love.

This weekend, however, I will be thinking of Sarah—a young woman who, like me, may be enduring the holiday in the dull haze of nothing to celebrate.

Chapter Twelve

Sarah

At precisely four-thirty—the earliest I'll take a break from work—Judson wheels himself over and asks me to describe the sky. Again.

I glance at the window. "Blue," I tell him, "with a whiff of cirrus clouds in the northwest."

He snorts. "Sarah, baby, you've got to do better than that. Is it a happy sky? A brilliant sky?"

"You expect me to personify an inanimate slice of atmosphere?"

"Actually—" he leans forward in his chair "—I was hoping you'd check my Close Connection account again. Let's see what sort of lovely photos have come in since the last time we logged on."

I inhale a deep breath and glance out into the hallway. "This isn't exactly sanctioned behavior…."

"You're too good, Sarah, you'll never get caught. Just log on and let's see what sort of bait is nibbling on old Judson's line."

After another quick glance out the door, I activate an operating system of my own design and log on to CloseConnection.com, then enter Judson's screen name and password. I keep an eye on the clock. Any discernible lack of activity from my station could arouse suspicion, and I don't want Dr. M breathing down my neck.

I click on Jud's account. "You have one new response."

His chair moves a fraction closer. "Lay it on me."

"From Luscious and Lonely in Dallas. Sent May 20, 7:30 p.m. Shall I read it, or would you prefer to listen in private?"

"Hey, I'm willing to share. Read on, kid."

I lower my voice to a confidential whisper in case the walls are listening. "Saw your profile, Secret Agent Man. Tall, dark, and handsome is just my type."

I stop. *"Tall?"*

"I used to be tall," Judson says. "Now stop complaining and get on with the good stuff."

I sigh and pick up where I left off. "I like skulking on the beach, long moonlit rendezvous, and whispering under the covers. If you'd like to spy in my direction, pick up the nearest sat phone and encrypt my number."

"¡Maravilloso!"

I exhale in exasperation. "You could get in so much trouble for an unauthorized contact."

"What can they do to a dead man? Now, is there a picture? Is she pretty?"

I click on the attached photograph. "Brown hair. Symmetrical features. Big eyes. Lashes, but they look fake."

"Oh, man." He rubs his hands together. "Skin like brown sugar?"

"More like coffee with cream." I log off the account and double-check the clock.

"I want to write her back," Jud says.

"Not from my station, you don't. You can risk your own clearance."

"But you're so much stealthier. They won't even know you've been off the server."

"You need to give up this obsession, Jud."

"Easy for you to say. You're not doomed to stare at the backside of your eyeballs forever."

I can't argue with that, so I push away from the computer. "Don't you have work to do?"

With an adroit move of his left hand he spins to face the door. "Nothing's more fun than pestering you. But I could be talked into going to the kitchen for a snack."

I glance at my computer, where an algorithm is analyzing the responses from one of Mr. Traut's prisoners. I stand and tap the escape key to enable my password-protected screen saver, then nudge Jud's wheelchair away from the desk. "Let's go."

We move out of the operations room and through the second floor hallway, my soundless steps keeping pace with the smooth spin of his rubber-coated wheels. We enter the waiting elevator, which, I notice, is momentarily without a guard. The man must be visiting Dr. Mewton's office or the security station.

"No guard," I whisper, leaning against the wall.

Judson pauses before pressing the button for the first floor. "Did you hear the chopper last night?"

"Yeah, I did."

"Aren't you at all curious about the new arrival?"

I am, but I've lived here long enough to know it's not wise to ask too many questions. Judson grins and presses the button for the third floor.

I cross my arms. "If Dr. M or one of the guards happens by, how are we going to explain what we're doing up there?"

"You left something in the gym—a towel, maybe."

"You know…there are times when I'd like to grab a towel and wring your neck with it."

"Take your place in line, kid." He lifts his chin when the elevator door slides open. "You want to go first?"

"It was your idea."

"Okay, but you're going to have to be my eyes."

"And you're going to have to listen to the lecture if Dr. M catches us up here. I've already heard my share."

We move into the hall and travel soundlessly past the exercise room, the X-ray center, the MRI unit, the visiting doctors' quarters. Quiet lies over the floor like a blanket, which means our new arrival must be sleeping…or drugged.

When we pause outside the surgery, Judson swivels to face the room across the hall. "Well? See if anybody's home."

I creep across the tiled floor and peer through the window in the door. The hospital bed is empty. "No one in there."

"Oh." The word sounds more like a groan. "Do you think he's in 335?"

I tiptoe to the next doorway. This door is always locked and the square windowpane has been reinforced with metal netting. I peer into the padded room and shiver when I realize the space isn't empty. The latest arrival on our island home sits cross-legged in a corner, shaggy head bowed, shoulders hunched.

I crouch beneath the window and whisper to Judson. "Male occupant. He's sitting on the floor, head down, so I can't see his face."

"Tap on the glass. See if he has a greeting for his new neighbors."

Against my better judgment, I thump my knuckle against the windowpane. Resident 335 doesn't move for a long moment, but then the disheveled head rises and a pair of eyes swivels in my direction. The jaw drops, the brows lift, the eyes widen and his hands come up as if to ward off a demon.

I take a quick sidestep and move away from the window. I tell myself that he might have recoiled from *any* stranger's face, but I recognized the horror in his eyes.

He recoiled from *me.*

"So?" Jud asks. "Is he awake?"

"Yeah."

"Smiling, right? Maybe doing a little tap dance?"

I swallow against the lump that has risen in my throat. "Not funny, Jud. Something's gone very wrong."

"How do you know?"

"It's Hightower. I recognize him from the London op. And he's not himself. Not himself at all."

Judson pushes on the armrests of his chair, and for half a minute I'm afraid he's going to jimmy the lock and try to speak to our new arrival. If he upsets Hightower, the guards will come running, and then how will we explain ourselves?

I wrap my palms around the handles on the back of the wheelchair and push it toward the elevator. "When do you think Dr. Mewton will tell us what's going on?"

Judson presses his hands together. "Everything in this place is classified as 'need to know.' So who says she'll tell us anything?"

He has a point, but I've *worked* with Hightower. I'm going to find it difficult to think of him as a classified subject when I know he's locked in a padded room upstairs.

Shelba has two trays waiting on the table by the time we go downstairs and enter the dining room.

"You're late," she says, pulling a sheet of plastic wrap from Judson's plate. "I had these ready at lunch, but you didn't come down. If that sandwich has gone stale, don't you be blamin' me."

I glance at the antique clock on the mantel. "Sorry about that. We got caught up in a project."

"And now you'll have no appetite for dinner." Shelba's gaze falls on me like the quick touch of a raindrop, then retreats to safer territory. "And you'd better not pick at that food. You're too thin, Sarah. I don't want Dr. Glenda fussin' at me because you're as thin as a cattail."

Judson barks a laugh as he rolls up to the table. "Dr. Mewton wouldn't dare reprimand you, Shelba. She who wields the spoon wields the power."

Shelba's narrow face splits in a quick smile, then becomes whole again. "All the same, you two had better be back for dinner in two hours. My corn bread casserole is not as good when it's warmed-over."

As Judson applies himself to his sandwich, I sink into one of the antique chairs and pick up a potato chip. "I'm eating."

"See that you do."

Shelba strides away, her hips swinging in a quick rhythm. I eat slowly while Judson wolfs down his sandwich.

"Hey," he says, his fingers spreading in a search for his fork, "did you watch the baseball game last night?"

"Sorry."

"I thought I heard a game playing in your room."

"You heard *The Natural*. Robert Redford and Glenn Close."

Judson spears a clump of broccoli. "You should lay off the movies and watch some real sports."

"Why?"

"So you'll know what it's like on the outside."

"And why would I want to do that?"

His closed eyelids tremble. "You're kidding, right?"

I bite back my answer when the staccato rap of a pair of high heels intrudes on our conversation. The only nonrubber heels in this facility live on Dr. Mewton's feet.

Judson lowers his voice. "Can you see her yet?"

I glance toward the hallway. Did Dr. Mewton notice my unauthorized visit to CloseConnection.com?

"Judson, if she—"

"Does she look ticked?"

I wait until Dr. M rounds the corner. "We're…fine, I think."

I take a bite out of my sandwich and concentrate on chewing until Dr. Mewton strides over and taps her nails on the table. Judson's head rotates toward the sound.

"Good afternoon, you two. How's the work coming?"

I nod and wonder if she's been listening in on our conversations. Security cameras blink from practically every corner of this facility, and the intercom units function as speakers *and* receivers…not to mention the possibility that even our private apartments are crawling with bugs.

"Listen, I don't mean to hold you up—" her nails click

the polished tabletop again as she stares directly at me "—but I've received a phone call from Mr. Traut's office. Despite my insistence that such contact would be inadvisable, a Dr. Renee Carey wants to visit you, Sarah. She's been told that you can't receive visitors, but she's quite stubborn. She's been pestering the company with calls and correspondence for months, and I don't think she's going to go away."

Judson's hand tightens around his fork. "How'd she learn that Sarah is here?"

"Obviously—" Dr. Mewton's eyes close "—she has connections. But she's willing to back off if Sarah responds with a certified letter stating that she doesn't want visitors."

I shift my gaze to the wide windows that overlook the garden. In twenty years, I've had only five visitors, and all of them were agency-contracted surgeons.

"I'm done with doctors," I hear myself saying. "I've already signed a statement saying I want no more operations."

"Of course, dear. But Dr. Carey isn't a surgeon. She's a psychologist."

Judson exhales in a noisy chuff. "Does this woman think our Sarah is nuts? She should visit when we have someone in room 335."

I want to kick Jud under the table, but since he has no legs, the gesture would be futile. He's said nothing to indicate that we know Hightower is in room 335, but around here it's not wise to notice more than one is authorized to notice.

Dr. Mewton draws a deep breath. "I would simply ignore this woman's requests, but Langley is applying pressure."

"Who is she?" The words slip from my tongue before I can stop them. "If she's not part of the agency, how'd she find out about me?"

"Apparently," Dr. Mewton says, her voice heavy, "she's followed an old paper trail. She doesn't know anything of consequence, but she knows who you are. She doesn't know about this facility, but she knows you're under the company's protection."

She knows who you are. The simple words slip under my skin, warming my flesh with an unexpected sensation that leaves me amazed and unsteady.

I don't even know who I am. So who *is* this woman?

"This is crazy." A flush suffuses even the scars on Judson's cheeks with deep color. "If she's a civilian, she has no clearance. Without clearance, she can't know about Sarah *or* this place—"

"She's applied for a security clearance and a job," Dr. Mewton says, her voice low and level. "And she might get what she wants. Some people in the company believe the rights of family supersede the rights of government."

The skin on my forearms contracts at the word. "But I have no family—"

"Apparently you do," Dr. Mewton finishes. "Renee Carey is your father's sister. She's your aunt—that's why she wants to see you."

Judson turns toward me, his mouth open in a silent gape. But he does not know what Dr. Mewton and I do—that in the twenty years I have lived here, no one has ever really wanted to *see* me.

After leaving Judson in the dining room, I slip down the narrow hallway that leads to the old convent graveyard and the small strip of earth that passes for a wildflower garden. Dozens of ancient nuns are buried here, each anonymous grave adorned only with a carved stone cross. Dr. Mewton refers to this walled patch of grass as our courtyard, but for me it is a sanctuary.

I come here when my heart is too full for words, when my mind is unsettled and my feet are restless. Six-foot walls surround the courtyard, ensuring the nuns' separation from the world even in death, but this is the one place I can roam without worrying that an idle word or gesture will be recorded by a listening device or a concealed camera. I have often wondered if Dr. Mewton has thought of monitoring even this area, but no one comes here often enough to make it worth the effort.

And yet her news has driven me to this place. I have family, she says, an aunt, a woman who *knows who I am* and is trying to find me. If that's true, this woman knows more about me than I know about myself. She knows where I come from, who my mother was. She knows my father.

Maybe she knows why I'm here.

I scramble up the side of the uneven stone wall and peer out over the edge, allowing my eyes to fill with the sight of sun, sea, sky. My hands, resting against the jagged rocks, warm with ambient heat as a long-abandoned yearning seeps out of a locked crypt hidden deep within me.

I close my eyes and hunch forward as an odd pain makes me catch my breath. I can't allow myself to hope, to wait, because I've hoped and waited before. I've searched the night skies for reindeer that never came, for angels that never sang, for saints who never appeared.

Now Dr. Mewton says I have family, an aunt. If only this woman would come; if only she would look at me…and not wince.

If only… I have whispered those words so many times.

If only I had parents.

If only I had been born in America.

If only I had a face like everyone else's, I might be loved.

Chapter Thirteen

Renee

I halt in the parking lot outside Panera Bread and lift my face to the breath of a sweet eastern breeze. Becky, who's keeping an eye on the clock, stops on the sidewalk, a question on her face. "Did you forget something?"

I shake my head. "It's just— Isn't it a beautiful day?"

"Gorgeous," she says, rolling her eyes. "May I remind you that we don't have time to appreciate the weather? You have a patient coming in at one, so we have less than an hour for lunch."

"I'm coming." Reluctantly, I lower my head and follow her into the store, where we stand in line with dozens of other harried Virginians.

Becky and I decide on soup and sandwiches, then take our orders to a table. She's been waiting all day for the opportunity to tell me about her son's problem with his first grade teacher, so I listen, murmur sympathetically, and smile in what I hope are all the right places.

But I can't help watching my fellow diners. We are only a few miles from Langley, which means that anyone in this restaurant could work for the CIA. The fluffy woman struggling to fit a lid on her supersized soft drink might be an analyst; the stubbly man tapping on his computer by the window might be sending a secret message to a Russian spy in the parking lot. The baby-faced guy who just dropped a cup into the trash can might be leaving a message for the Panera Bread employee who is coming over to empty the trash and retrieve the marked cup—

Becky taps my arm. "So…what should I do?"

"Do? About what?"

She rolls her eyes. "You haven't heard a word I've said."

"Yes, I have. Your son's first grade teacher is a bully."

"And?"

"And you want to know if you should go talk to her."

"And?"

"And…" At a sudden loss for words, I drop my chin into my hand. "Maybe you should start over again."

"Renee Carey." Becky slumps against the back of the seat and gives me an incredulous look. "Where have you *been* lately?"

I bite my lip. I want to tell her that since attorney John Lipps has been quietly advancing my case in the intelligence community, I've been reading spy novels and nonfiction books about the CIA. I've been realizing that we live in a part of the country where nothing is what it seems and the Honda salesman next door may be anything but what he appears to be.

Instead, I smile and pick up my cup. "Tell me again about your son's teacher," I say. "I promise to listen to every word."

"Forget it." She digs in her purse, pulls out a tissue, and blows her nose. "Allergies. They drain me. I don't think I have the strength to tell that story again."

"If it's any help," I offer, "I think communication is the key. Go to this teacher, talk to her, and listen. Maybe you're taking two different approaches to the same problem."

Becky tilts her head and smiles. "You know, for a shrink who didn't hear a word I said, that's pretty good advice."

"That's why they pay me the big bucks."

"I'm going to pay you with something different. Here."

From the depths of her voluminous purse, Becky pulls out

a green plastic figure that at first appears to be all arms, legs, and eyes. She drops it on the table in front of me. "Don't you recognize him?"

I pick up the figure and run my thumb over the soft vinyl. "Didn't he used to have a TV show?"

"I think so. Or maybe it was a commercial."

"Gumshoe? Gummy?"

She hits me with a triumphant smile. "Gumby. Remember him? I used to love this little guy."

"And you're giving me this because…"

"Because you need a little laughter in your life, girlfriend. You've been entirely too intense lately."

I lift my hand, about to argue that it's not easy to be the life of the party when you deal with depressed patients all day, but something about Gumby and his little yellow smile chases the impulse away.

I stand Gumby on his legs and walk him over the table. "I can't wait to show Elvis."

"That's another thing," Becky says, her voice deepening with concern. "You need another confidant. Elvis is a wonderful dog, but he's not human."

"But you are. And I have you."

"Yes…and many a time I've worried that we have strayed too far outside a proper psychologist-receptionist relationship."

I glance up, afraid she's being serious, but the light of humor dances in her eyes. "Are you saying I need to get out more?"

"Exactly. It's what you'd tell a patient in the same situation. You need to develop outside interests, tackle a project, maybe take a vacation."

"Funny you should say that." I give her a smile as I drop Gumby into my purse. "I've been thinking along those very same lines."

Chapter Fourteen

Sarah

A light rain is sending long, hesitant runnels down the windowpanes by the time I return to the operations room. When I take my seat at my station, I find an urgent message from Raven, one of my contacts at the DS&T. He wants to see a revised version of the Gutenberg program ASAP, so I create a zip file with the latest incarnation and send it over a secure connection. He should find no problems with it, but I'm not ready to stake my reputation on its reliability.

When I am sure the file has been sent and received, I log on to Intelink and search for "Renee OR Rene OR Renae Carey." No hits, but I shouldn't have expected any if the woman doesn't work for the company.

At his station, Judson begins to chuckle. I ignore him, but after a minute he pulls one of his earphones from his head and turns his face toward me. "Hey, kiddo. I've got an IM here from Raven."

"I've already sent the file he wanted."

"He doesn't want to know about the file. He's asking me if you're good-looking. Obviously—" he cackles with barely-restrained glee "—this guy doesn't have a clue about the Candyman."

I stop scanning my monitor and stare at Judson, momentarily overcome by the irony. "Tell him," I finally say, "that your partner is drop-dead gorgeous."

"What if he wants details?"

I blow out a breath. "Eyes, cheeks, nose—I've got 'em. You have the gift of elaboration. You fill in the details."

"That I can do." Judson flashes me a white smile, then readjusts his headphones and snaps at his keyboard, his fingers flying over the keys.

I draw a deep breath and return my attention to my computer screen. I'll never understand why men are so focused on physical attractiveness, but as long as they are, I'll have no choice but to live a celibate life.

Next, I log on to Intellipedia, a wiki open to officers from all sixteen American spy agencies. If Dr. Carey has done anything of interest to the intelligence community, I might find her name here…but I come up with nothing.

Finally, I log on to A-space, the spooks' answer to MySpace and Facebook. The top secret network allows agencies to share photos, notes, and gossip, but again, I come up with *nada* on Renee, Rene, or Renae Carey.

So I look up the name on Google and discover an absolutely overwhelming number of hits in open-source material. Renee Carey is, according to the Web, a Democratic city council member in Houston, a psychologist living in McLean, Virginia, and a photographic artist living in Boston.

Dr. Mewton says Renee Carey is my aunt…and I have no experience with the word. Scarlett O'Hara had an Aunt Pittypat who proved useless in crisis situations. I've watched *Auntie Mame,* a 1958 movie about a young boy who grows up as the ward of his father's eccentric aunt…and I've found myself wondering what happened to the boy's mother. Was she dead like mine?

An incoming message on the secure server interrupts my musings. Raven is impressed with my progress on the brain scan program, but wonders if I've had a chance to create sub-programs with culturally specific cues. I respond with a question: *What culture did you have in mind?*

The answer appears within seconds: *Islamic. With sub-programs for Sunni, Sufi, Shi'a, and Kharijite sects. Do you like jazz?*

"Your friend," I call to Judson, "is hitting on me."

"Better let him down easy," Jud answers, "or he'll be thinking he can wander through those marble halls until he finds you working in a cubicle."

I'll research those sects, I type. *But I only like jazz on the fifth Tuesday in February. Sorry.*

When the message disappears, I type my father's name into the Google search box. I click Enter and wait as the screen fills with the same links that appeared yesterday and the day before.

Nothing new.

Then I enter my aunt's name again and select the link for the psychologist in Virginia. A professional Web site fills the screen, revealing a picture of a stucco building situated beneath a spreading tree. Under the photo of the office I see a picture of a woman who might be anywhere from thirty to fifty—I'm not good at guessing ages. Like me, she has brown hair and dark eyes.

Nothing else about her face matches mine.

I lean closer and peruse the page. According to the information presented here, Dr. Renee Carey has been practicing psychology since 1997 and specializes in mood disorders, particularly clinical depression and bipolar disorder. She looks prosperous, healthy, and happy.

So…why does this woman want to meet me now? Is she suffering a midlife crisis? Maybe she's stuck at step eight of a twelve-step program, struggling to make amends to all the people she's harmed or ignored during her lifetime…

I activate my screen saver as something thumps against my desk. Judson has pulled off his headphones and wheeled himself over to my station. "Sarah, sweetheart. Want to do me another favor?"

"Can't, I'm busy."

His charming smile disappears. "You okay? You sound uptight."

The man has developed an uncanny knack for reading my voice. I glance toward the hall, then glare at the intercom. Well, let her listen. It's not like I'm about to threaten our national interests.

"Why—" I turn toward Judson "—after all this time, why would my aunt want to see me?"

Jud folds his hands across his chest. "Have you ever met anyone from your family?"

"I didn't know I had family. I never knew my parents."

"They were with the company?"

"My father was."

"What did he do?"

"That…I don't know."

Judson presses a finger across his lips. "I think," he says sotto voce, "that if it's at all possible, you ought to meet this aunt. Everyone has a family, Sarah, and everyone deserves to know where they come from. It's only right that you should give yourself the opportunity. Aren't you even curious about this woman?"

I remain silent as I sort through my thoughts. Judson must sense that I'm confused, because for once he allows me to process without interruption. "I think…it might be nice to meet someone who grew up with my father."

"Good grief, kid, don't you even know your own heart? You're too young to be so detached."

I stiffen. "I'm not so young. And I'm certainly not detached."

"Oh, yes you are." Tremors of mirth fracture his voice. "I know you're smart, kid, but I also know you haven't spent a lot of time in the real world. Sorry, but it shows."

"Dr. Mewton says I'm quite culturally literate."

"Do you *hear* yourself? Normal kids your age don't go around thinking of themselves as culturally literate. I don't care how many movies you watch, until you step out and live your life, you're never going to understand why you're even on the planet."

His broad hands rise to clasp the sides of his head, and though he's wearing a smile, his arms are tense, as if he's in some kind of pain. "I know we're not supposed to talk about certain things, but it's not right that you should stay here, kiddo. I thought only lunatics and NOLs like me ended up in this place—"

"NOLs? Explain the acronym."

"Figure it out, girlie. If you're so smart, you can put the pieces together."

I lower my gaze, unable to bear the pressure of his sealed eyelids and twisted visage. "I've lived here all my life. When my parents died, Dr. Mewton became my guardian. She's been looking after me ever since."

"Ah." Judson lifts a brow. "That explains a lot."

"About what?"

"About why you're the teacher's pet. But let me guess something—this surgery, did it have something to do with your ears?"

Ears, mouth, nose, jaw, teeth, skull…but he doesn't need all the details. "How could you tell?"

"Something in your voice reminds me of this deaf girl I knew once. She could talk and read lips, but her voice always sounded…kind of hooty."

"Hooty? Like an owl?"

He shrugs. "It's hard to explain."

My hand rises to touch the cochlear device implanted in the right side of my head. "I've had good hearing for years."

"Don't get all self-conscious on me. Your voice is fine. It's just different, that's all."

"Different from what?"

"Forget I mentioned anything. You're fine." Judson parks his elbow on the armrest of his chair and drops his chin into his palm. "So…are you going to write this aunt of yours?"

"I want to…but Dr. Mewton doesn't like the idea."

"This one goes beyond Mewton. Sounds like your aunt has a friend or two in high places, so go ahead, invite her to our little fortress. If at any point you feel uncomfortable, you can always send her away."

"I don't know. The Gutenberg project has me tied up—"

"Look, kid, you've got no reason to lay your entire life on the company altar. Live a little, take a chance. Don't push this woman away or you might turn into Spock for real."

I've watched enough *Star Trek* DVDs to understand he's saying I might turn into some kind of emotionless Vulcan. I exhale through my teeth as I consider his advice, then I extend my leg and gently tap his wheelchair with my foot. "Thanks. I'll think about it."

"Course you will. Now—can you find a way to print Luscious and Lonely's picture in Braille? If you were really grateful, you'd find a way to make that happen."

"Keep dreaming, Jud," I tell him, turning back to the computer. I ought to get back to work on Gutenberg, but one of Jud's questions hovers at the edge of my mind: what did my father do for the company?

I log on to Intellipedia and enter my father's name, then click Enter. *Search term not found.* The result doesn't surprise me, because Intellipedia is a relatively new enterprise and my father's been gone more than twenty years.

I bring up Intelink and enter my father's name in the search box. Again, *Search term not found.*

I frown at the screen. Either my father worked under alias…or his records have been cleared from the system.

I lift my chin and scan the room. Judson is back at his station, he's wearing his headset, and the corridor beyond is quiet. If someone at the CIA was merely cleaning house when they deleted my father's records, I have no reason to hide my steps. But if there's some other reason behind the disappearance of my father's information, I should be careful about how I conduct this search.

I glance at Jud to make sure he's engrossed in his work, then I exit the UNIX operating system and move into my own OS. My computer's wireless receiver, now under new orders, joins the network as silently as a virus, then flashes a single word: *Connected.*

I activate Locksmith and type a command, instructing my latest beta to search for "Kevin Sims" in any file and report the location of the search phrase. The code's activity is so surreptitious that not even the keenest packet sniffer will pick up traces of my intrusion.

I tap the edge of the desk as Locksmith begins its work. I didn't ask the program to count searches, but I can't help feeling a ripple of humor as I visualize the thousands of linked machines whose drives are silently being examined for any mention of my father's name. Computers at Langley, the Pentagon, and hundreds of company stations across the civilized world will surrender their secrets—even encrypted secrets—while my little ghost program unlocks the door and retreats without a trace.

KEVIN SIMS: found in SIMSKEVIN.tsp, server forty-seven.

I glance at my watch. Locksmith returned the first result in sixty-five seconds—not a bad result. Now, to physically locate server forty-seven…

I pull out a printed list of all the CIA servers located at Langley. The series ends at forty-five. Server forty-seven must be off-site.

When I hear the clack of Dr. Mewton's heels, I shut down Locksmith and exit my operating system. I glance up as she enters the room, but she moves to Judson's station and bends to ask him a question.

When I place my hands on the keyboard, the acronym I didn't recognize earlier suddenly makes sense.

Judson called himself an NOL—a nonofficial life. Does that designation also apply to my father?

By the time I finish breakfast the following morning, I've decided upon a course of action. I leave the dining room and take the stairs up to Dr. Mewton's second floor office. Because there are no visitors on the premises, there is no guard at the door, so I press my hand to the biometric scanner. A red light scans my palm, then flashes green as the unlocking mechanism clicks.

"Dr. M?" I open the door and see her sitting at her desk, a stack of printed documents spread before her. "You have a minute for me?"

"Of course, Sarah." She peers over the top of her reading glasses. "I'll bet you've come to sign that statement for your aunt."

"Not exactly." I drop into the single guest chair in front of her desk. "I think I'd like to meet her."

Dr. Mewton lowers the document in her hand. "You shouldn't feel pressured, you know. The company can deliver your signed statement, or if that seems harsh to you, they can stall her indefinitely. She has no need to know you, and she doesn't have the proper clearance for this level."

"But she could get clearance, couldn't she? I'd really like to meet her, so if she can't come here…" I let the question hang, implying that I might be willing to visit my aunt at some other location, though Dr. Mewton and I both know that's impossible.

"This facility is closed to civilians."

"But you could arrange it. You transport officers all the time, you rotate medical personnel in and out—"

"They follow procedures. And they have clearance."

"You could see that my aunt gets clearance. Mr. Traut would arrange it, if you asked him to."

My comment is as much compliment as challenge, and she's quick to recognize both aspects. "Don't toy with me, Sarah. I know you too well."

But I know her, too. She's my mentor, protector, and guardian, but I won't let her be my jailer. At one point Baby had to stand up to her father, didn't she? A girl doesn't get to dance with Johnny Castle if she meekly obeys every command.

I return her stare with deadly concentration. "Look, I've given the company every free hour since I finished my schooling. I don't ask for much, but I do want this meeting. Write Dr. Carey and invite her to visit me."

"I fail to see how that would be prudent."

"If you don't write her, I'll contact her myself."

When Dr. Mewton hesitates, I know she's wondering if she could find a way to block me. There are firewalls and safeguards built into every system on this island, but I know how to hack most of them. If given time and the opportunity, I could find a way to reach almost anyone, and Dr. M knows it.

My director taps her fingertips on the desk. "I don't know how long ago this woman applied for clearance, but the process can be quite involved. And it will take time to follow the proper procedures."

I've waited twenty years to hear from a family member, so what's a few more weeks or months? "You said she was stubborn."

Dr. Mewton manages a choking laugh. "True. But no matter how we arrange it, she'll have to come alone."

"Why would that be a problem?"

Dr. M shrugs. "Some women don't enjoy traveling alone, particularly out of the country. I have no idea how she'll react to this stipulation, of course, but she might not be willing to go through such trouble. Still, if she is…I suppose we could arrange a meeting."

"Good. Thank you."

"But don't be surprised if she decides not to follow through," Dr. Mewton warns as I stand. "Not every woman is willing to fly across the Atlantic to visit a place that doesn't exist."

Chapter Fifteen

Renee

During the first week of June, a full fourteen months after I applied for a security clearance, I open a plain white envelope that arrives in the afternoon office mail. The envelope is postmarked with zip code 20205, which, I have learned from my lawyer, is the unique postal code assigned to CIA headquarters at Langley.

Inside the envelope are two pages: the first informs me that my application for employment as a staff psychologist is under consideration; the second advises me to report to CIA headquarters in McLean, Virginia, at 10:00 a.m. on June 27. I must bring an official ID with photograph, my birth certificate, and any information that might help resolve questions about alien registration, delinquent loans or taxes, bankruptcy, judgments, agreements involving child custody or support, alimony or property settlements, arrests, convictions, probation, and/or parole.

I'm tempted to bring a *TV Guide* with my favorite programs highlighted, just in case they ask for more information.

For the first time in my life, I'm grateful I never had children. In the five years since my divorce, my life has remained boring and uncomplicated—no arrests, no bankruptcies, no convictions or parole violations. The only blemish on my record is my penchant for speeding, so if I offer canceled checks as evidence that I've made peace with the traffic court, perhaps I can be forgiven.

I immediately buzz Becky and ask her to clear my calendar for the morning of June 27. "On second thought," I add, "maybe you'd better clear the entire day. I have no idea how long I'll be tied up."

"Something official?" she asks.

"Something...important. And if I tell you any more..."

"I know, you'll have to kill me." She sighs, obviously having heard the joke a few dozen times.

"Speaking of death," I add, "I'm afraid I have bad news about Gumby."

"How's the little guy doing?"

"He's pushing up daisies—and I mean that literally. Elvis took a liking to him when I wasn't looking. Apparently he can swipe things off my kitchen counter. I thought he'd hidden the little man, but a few days ago I was in the backyard and saw Gumby again."

"Ewww." Becky laughs. "How'd he, um, look?"

"Only a little worse for wear. A few tooth marks, a little bleached out, but he was still intact. I left him in the flower bed, where I trust he'll rest in peace."

Becky is still laughing when I sign off.

I'm about to put the mail away, but beneath a flyer from Stein Mart I find another envelope mailed from zip code 20205. This letter, also written on official CIA letterhead, has been signed by a man whose name I don't recognize. But he knows who I am, and he knows of my inquiries about Sarah.

If I am still determined to meet Sarah Sims, the letter informs me, perhaps I can do so in an official capacity, once I am officially engaged as a psychologist. *If* I receive my security clearance, and *if* I agree to the terms of the standard two-year contract, my first assignment "could involve a professional interview" with the person I seek. At that point I should set aside at least two weeks for travel to and from the facility where my niece lives and works.

I'm skilled enough at reading between the lines to understand what the man is really saying: *Call off your lawyer, sign our contract, and we'll let you see Sarah Sims. But on paper, at least, everything must appear official.*

I chuckle as I skim the letter again. No mention at all of where this facility is located, no hint of what kind of clothing I should pack. Tropical whites? Thermal underwear?

I turn to my computer terminal and study my schedule for the next several weeks. My weekdays are filled with patient appointments, but those can be rescheduled with other doctors. My partners in the practice can handle any emergencies; heaven only knows how many times I've stepped in for them.

The CIA contract will ask for two years, but I doubt they'll require my services full-time. They'll probably want me to be on call to consult with officers in the area, and I can do that under the cover of my regular practice. If they have something more intensive in mind, I can take a leave of absence from the office.

When I'm official and cleared for travel, I'll close up the house and ask Becky to take care of Elvis. She and her kids adore my dog, so if I'm gone very long, I'll probably have to pry them apart when I return.

Still…I have three weeks of unused vacation time, so I might as well take every day. Though I've always wanted to vacation on a sunny beach, since I've been single again I've had little inclination to travel alone.

This time, however, I don't think I'll mind.

When I step out of my car and catch my first glimpse of CIA headquarters, I have to admit I'm a little intimidated. I've read enough bad press to know that the Central Intelligence Agency is not universally beloved, so I am prepared to view the institution with a skeptical eye. But when I walk into the marble lobby and stare at the south wall emblazoned with *And Ye Shall Know the Truth and the Truth Shall Make Ye Free,* a surge of latent patriotism catches me by surprise. If someone had offered me the staff psychologist's position at that moment, I'd have snapped it up like a woman trolling for purses at a ninety-percent-off sale.

I walk over a polished floor of gray granite, in which the CIA seal has been inlaid in a thirty-foot circle. A shield occupies the center of the seal, topped by the profile of a fierce eagle. A sixteen-point compass rose decorates the shield, obviously symbolizing the far corners of the planet in which the agency operates. Which arrow points in the direction of my niece?

As I study my surroundings, the north wall catches my eye. There a field of black stars lies on a gigantic block of white marble, one star for each member of the CIA who has died while on duty. Above the stars someone has engraved these words: *In honor of those members of the Central Intelligence Agency who gave their lives in the service of their country.*

I walk toward the wall and see that a case of glass and stainless steel stands below the stars. A book is locked inside—the "Book of Honor" that lists each year a CIA officer died. Some years are followed by names; others are followed only by an anonymous star that represents a covert officer killed on a CIA mission.

I can't help but wonder—does one of those stars belong to my brother?

A pain squeezes my heart as I merge back into the flow of men and women entering the building. Most are moving through a checkpoint, swiping ID badges through a key card reader. Since I have no badge, I walk over to a guard and show him my letter.

"Your appointment is on the second floor," he says, extending his hand. "May I see your ID?"

I hand him my passport, which has a far better picture than

my driver's license. He scans it, checks my face against the photo, then hands me a visitor's key card.

"Any cell phone with a camera must be left at the security station," he says, pointing toward the metal detectors. "Have a nice day."

I join the line of people flowing through the metal detectors, receive a claim check for my cell phone, and move toward the elevators. After getting off on the second floor, I find a guard at the front desk, show him my letter, and am escorted into a small cubicle that reminds me far too much of my obstetrician's exam room, minus the stirrups.

A few moments later, a young woman in a lab coat enters and says she has reviewed my medical records. She is going to conduct a brief physical exam, then I'm to be polygraphed.

As she records my height, weight, and blood pressure, the palms of my hands grow damp. I have nothing to hide, but my blood pressure is higher than usual and I find myself tapping my right foot whenever the examiner turns away. But surely these are normal nervous reactions. I won't be penalized for normal reactions, will I?

"Finally," she hands me a paper cup, "there's this." She points to a hallway and a door marked *Toilet.* "Directions are posted on the wall."

I take the cup and go to the restroom. A few minutes later I return the cup to an assistant, grateful that I was able to urinate on demand.

"Next—" the examiner glances at a sheet stapled to my file "—you're scheduled for a polygraph. Second floor, ask for directions at the desk."

After following her instructions, I find myself entering a softly lit room dominated by a padded recliner. A secretarial chair sits beside a desk at the front of the room, but the computer monitor faces the secretarial chair, not the recliner. The room smells faintly of sweat.

I glance over my shoulder, certain that it would be presumptuous to walk in and stretch out without clearance from someone in authority. Fortunately, I don't have to wait long. An unsmiling young woman steps into the room with a file folder in her hand. She introduces herself as Kathy and explains that the test will measure my physiological reaction to each question.

"I know how a lie detector works," I assure her. "I'm a psychologist."

I also know that polygraph evidence is highly unreliable, but I doubt it'd be in my best interest to introduce that fact into the conversation.

"Please," she says, still unsmiling. "Sit in this chair and extend your arm."

I sit on the edge of the recliner as Kathy wraps my arm in a blood pressure gauge, straps an elastic band around my chest, and taps plastic nodules over two fingers on my left hand.

"Now sit back and relax."

Easy for her to say. I recline in the lounger and am immediately reminded of my dentist's office. Kathy sits in the small chair behind the desk and begins clicking the keyboard. A small box near the computer hums as paper scrolls from the polygraph machine.

"Are you a member of a terrorist network?" she asks.

I almost laugh. "No."

"Is your name Renee Carey?"

"Yes."

"Are you applying for a security clearance through the Central Intelligence Agency?"

"Yes."

"Are you applying for a job with the Central Intelligence Agency?"

I hesitate. Yes, they have my application, but no, I have no intention of working in this place. I choose the obvious answer. "Yes."

"Do you have a cat?"

"I'm allergic."

"Yes or no answers, please."

"No, I don't have a cat."

"Are you married?"

I swallow my first thought—*not anymore*. "No."

"Was Kevin J. Sims your uncle?"

"No."

"Was Kevin J. Sims your brother?"

"Yes."

"Are you a psychologist?"

"Yes."

"Have you ever lied to a patient?"

"Yes, but only if the truth would be—"

"Yes or no only, please."

"Yes."

"Do you intend to answer all questions truthfully?"

"Yes, unless a truthful answer is going to get me arrested."

"Dr. Carey—yes or no only."

"Sorry."

"Have you ever committed a crime that went unreported?"

"I kept the paper graduation cap I was supposed to return in kindergarten. Is that stealing?"

"I wouldn't know."

"It *felt* like stealing. So yes, I suppose I've committed a crime." I also have to go to the bathroom again, because Examiner Kathy and her questions are making me nervous.

By the time we've finished, I'm almost certain I've failed my polygraph. But Kathy unhooks me, prints out my results, and dismisses me without a word.

I've jumped through every hoop the CIA has set in front of me, but I have no idea where I've landed.

On July 9, I receive a notice in the mail. My security clearance has been granted and my application for contract employment has been approved by the Central Intelligence

Agency's personnel department. A position—surprise!—is available, and I will soon receive details regarding my first assignment. If I will complete the enclosed paperwork, my supervisor will contact me about the training required for my assignment….

On the twelfth of July, I find myself back at CIA headquarters, EODing—"entering on duty"—for the first time. I am given my own badge, and this time I am smart enough to leave my cell phone in the car.

I enter a small room where a dozen other men and women are sitting at desks. "Welcome to CIA 101," the instructor begins. "I am here to acquaint you with the designations of different security classifications and the risks and consequences of not handling them correctly." In other words, his tone seems to say, a security clearance is like a loaded gun—useful if handled properly, deadly if not.

On July 16, I receive a telegram. At nine o'clock the following morning, I am to report to Reagan National Airport, Hangar Seven, office 304. I am to bring a maximum of two suitcases and a small personal carry-on. An officer will be waiting with further instructions. I should clear at least fifteen days for my visit and travel, and under no circumstances should I reveal my new employer, my destination, or the purpose of my travel to family or friends.

That final warning makes me smile. How can I reveal my destination when I don't know where I'm going?

Chapter Sixteen

Sarah

Dr. Mewton glances over her notes one final time, then pulls off her reading glasses. "I suppose that's everything on my agenda. Holmes, if you could have your analysis of that Echelon chatter to me by the end of the day, I'd appreciate it. Sarah, those briefs on memory implantation should be considered priority one. I know Mr. Traut would be grateful for a feasibility report ASAP."

"I'll get right on it."

"Good." She stands and picks up her folder. "Oh—I almost forgot. Dr. Renee Carey is scheduled to arrive sometime tomorrow afternoon. Sarah, I'll arrange a private meeting for you. You can reserve this room, if you like."

I blink, stunned by the announcement. I glance at Judson, who shows no reaction at all.

"How long—?" I turn back to Dr. Mewton "—how long will she be staying?"

"Mr. Traut feels she should stay long enough to complete an evaluation of your psychological state. If at any point you feel uncomfortable, however, let me know. I'll see to it that Dr. Carey completes her work in record time."

Judson spins his chair toward the doorway. "Might be nice to have a fresh face in our cozy little nest."

"Officer Holmes." Dr. Mewton presses her hands to the tabletop. "If you would give us the room, please."

Jud takes the hint and wheels out of the conference room, but not before casting a grin in my direction. I wait until the door closes, then cross my arms and look at Dr. M. "You still disapprove?"

"I can't resist you and Mr. Traut," she says, her voice like chilled steel. "Yet I want to know if there's anything I can do to make you more comfortable during this woman's visit. I'm giving her a room on the first floor, and I can arrange for Shelba to deliver her meals to the room as well. She doesn't have to eat with us."

"I don't mind having her around."

"Well…you might also want to consider other aspects of her stay. Since you don't usually have close contact with our visitors, I thought you might be more comfortable if we made special arrangements—something like a veil, for instance. We could divert your aunt in London while the Office of Technical Services creates some kind of concealing mask…"

Something that might be pity flits into her blue eyes. She swallows hard and regards me with a look I haven't seen on her face in years.

"I don't need to hide," I say, surprised to hear a quaver in my voice. "I don't want a disguise."

"But—"

"She's family, right? Aren't people free to be themselves around family?"

Dr. Mewton's face tightens into its usual lines. "You watch too many movies."

Chapter Seventeen

Renee

In the last two days, I have been pushed, prodded, stepped on and frisked—twice. I have traveled aboard a jet, a shuttle bus, and a ship. I have been addressed in British English, American slang, and Castilian Spanish. I think I've been cursed at in French.

Now I am standing on a wharf in La Coruña, Spain, where I have just stepped off an American ship filled with what I suspect are Navy SEALs. But they don't wear uniforms, and they don't talk much—none of them have addressed me with anything more personal than "Yes, ma'am" and "No, ma'am."

I have my passport out and ready, but no one is asking to see it and there's no sign of an immigration office at this port. Not much of anything, really, but shipping containers and a few burly men who are helping secure the ship.

Even though I'm standing next to the sea, this does *not* appear to be a beach vacation.

I slide my passport back into my purse and grip the handle of my rolling suitcase as if I were confident of my next step. Actually, I haven't a clue about what's supposed to happen next. I have no papers to validate my security clearance, and nothing but my passport and my Virginia driver's license to prove my citizenship and identity. I could be mugged and tossed into the sea by one of these longshoremen, and no one would miss me for months, if ever.

All I know is my contact is supposed to meet me here and deliver me to Sarah.

A small black sedan whizzes down the dock and completes a u-turn at the end of the pier. A moment later it pulls up and the automatic window lowers. A man peers out at me from beneath the wide brim of a black hat. "Señora Carey?"

"*Sí. Yo estoy*—" Why didn't I brush up on my Spanish before leaving? Because the ticket I was instructed to purchase took me to Gatwick Airport, outside London. I had no idea I'd be visiting Spain.

"Welcome to La Coruña," the man says, switching to English. He steps out of the car, and I am amazed to see that he is wearing the garb of a priest—an old-fashioned priest, at least by American standards. The black cassock, wide hat, and white collar render me temporarily speechless.

The CIA sent a *clergyman* to pick me up?

My contact bends to give me a hand with my luggage. "Only one suitcase?"

"Yes…that's right."

"You travel light—a real talent. You must teach me that trick."

I bend to peer beneath his hat brim. "And who… What shall I call you?"

"I'm Father Paul."

"Oh." I want to ask if his *real* name is Father Paul, but paranoia bridles my tongue. If this man is an actual priest, I'll offend him with the question. If he's a CIA officer in alias, I'll offend him with my stupidity.

Before I can ask where we're going, he's tossed my bag into the trunk and he's opening the rear door. With one hand, he gallantly offers me the backseat.

"Um…thank you."

In an effort to appear confident and in control, I rummage

through my purse as he strides to the driver's door. I dredge up my cell phone and study the keypad, wondering if I could dial an international version of 911 if this priest turns out to be some sort of renegade, but that idea is as ludicrous as the thought that I might actually have someone to call in Spain.

Father Paul starts the car and pulls away from the ship, ignoring curious glances from some of the dockhands. I shiver as the cool breeze from his window fills the rear seat. "Do you know—" I hesitate, not wanting to create an international incident or an unintentional security breach. "Can you tell me if we're going far?"

His gaze catches mine in the rearview mirror, and his eyes crinkle at the corners. "Not far at all, *señora*. In fact, we are almost there."

I glance around, unable to tell that we have left the port. The sea no longer lies behind us, but is located on my left. We are passing a marina filled with small boats, most of which look like pleasure craft or fishing vessels. My driver pulls alongside a curb, kills the engine, and bounds out of the vehicle before I can gasp another question.

I fumble with the door and let myself out, then step to the back of the car, where the priest is placing my suitcase on the pavement. "We're stopping here? But I'm supposed to go to some sort of facility."

"Sí, *señora*. And this man will take you there."

"What man?" I straighten and shade my eyes from the glaring sun. Another man in a clerical collar is lumbering over the dock, a sheen of perspiration on his wide forehead. No old-fashioned cassock for him, but black pants and a black short-sleeved shirt. He's built like a guy who rips phone books for fun.

"I—I'm supposed to go with him?"

"Sí. Upon his boat, *La Reina del Cielo*."

"The queen…"

"The Queen of Heaven, of course."

I take a step back, not certain I want to go anywhere on a boat dedicated to heaven, but the perspiring priest has reached us. He lifts a questioning brow at Father Paul, who nods and points to my luggage.

I turn and gesture toward the comforting solidity of the city behind me. "Um…"

"This way, Dr. Carey."

The second man's accent is as American as baseball, and he calls me *doctor,* which I take as a reassuring sign. I give him an uncertain nod and follow, remembering at the last moment to wave and thank Father Paul.

He and his sedan have already vanished.

I grip the railing at the side of the boat and brace myself against the pounding rhythm of the waves. The sweaty priest has yelled over his shoulder a couple of times, but I couldn't hear a word over the roar of the outboard engines. Each time I nodded and gave him a tight smile, hoping he wasn't asking if I wanted to stop and pick up a few locals for some suds and a good time.

I'm not skilled at judging distances on land or sea, but we've been jouncing for about twenty minutes when a rocky island rises out of the ocean. A rectangular multistory building of whitewashed stone crowns the summit. Its orange tile roof gleams beneath the sun, and crashing waves enfold the rocky escarpment.

If there's a road leading to that building, I can't see it. I can't even see a dock or a landing.

Mr. Black Shirt cuts the engines to idling speed. "The Convent of the Lost Lambs," he shouts, nodding toward the mountaintop structure. "Built for a group of cloistered nuns in the seventeenth century."

I'm not sure if he's saying this to entertain or enlighten me, but I study the structure and nod as if impressed. "It's beautiful. How did they ever get building materials up there?"

"They used stone cut from the rocks," he says, sighing like a teacher with a slow pupil, "and the island used to have trees. The nuns didn't build it, but no one bothered them once they got up there. As far as the locals know, a couple of dozen nuns are still cloistered in the place."

"So…there are no nuns?"

He snorts with the dry amusement of a man who seldom laughs. "Sister Luke comes and goes with a companion every now and then, but she ain't no mother superior."

He shoves the boat into low gear and steers toward a dark spot in the rock. I focus on the jagged cliffs and am surprised when a closer perspective reveals the dark area as an inlet…no, the mouth of a cave. The opening is no more than twenty feet wide, and not even ten feet tall….

I tighten my hold on the railing. "You intend to take this boat through that *crack?*"

My driver gives me another grin. "It's the most covert approach to the convent in daylight. And we need to proceed, Dr. Carey, because you're expected there for dinner."

I brace myself against the back of my seat and gape in silent horror as my escort launches the boat forward. The sea spits up in white plumes as we near the rocks, and I close my eyes as spray spatters my face. The boat labors up and down the peaks of the waves and I'm certain we're going to crash into the rocks, but somehow my driver manages to maneuver the boat into a channel.

The crashing sounds of the sea retreat as soon as we enter the cave. I open my eyes as the boat rumbles forward, and I see that the mammoth cavern ends at a wall of rock. In front of the rock, armed men in camouflage pants and white T-shirts stand guard on a wide dock, their faces tanned and grim.

I don't know where they picked up their tans, because this cavern is as dark as the grave and illuminated only by a few electric lights. I can't shake the feeling that we have entered some mythical kingdom set in the bowels of the earth.

One of the guards calls a greeting to the pretend priest, while another tosses a rope over a cleat at the bow of the boat. A moment later Mr. Black Shirt stands and moves toward me. I instinctively sink lower in my seat as he grabs my suitcase and sets it on the dock.

"Dr. Carey." The first guard removes a toothpick from between his front teeth and extends his hand. "Welcome to the Convent of the Lost Lambs."

Somehow I gather my wits and allow myself to be hauled onto the dock. Once there, I smooth my damp blouse and thank the guard for his help.

"No problem," he says, a faint light twinkling in the depths of his eyes. "I'm to show you directly to your room. Dr. Mewton wanted you to have a chance to rest before she meets with you."

Like a dullard who's always the last to get a joke, I look at Mr. Black Shirt. "Let me guess—Dr. Mewton is Sister Luke?"

He winks and gives me an impenitent grin.

"And Sarah? My niece?"

The young guard interrupts. "You'll have to speak to Dr. Mewton, ma'am. We're not authorized to discuss other personnel."

I am too tired and overwhelmed to argue, so I follow the guard pulling my suitcase, which bumps in an uneven rhythm over the stone floor. We enter an elevator, an unexpected convenience, and ride in silence to the first floor.

In the elevator, I study my escort more closely. The young man is probably in his late twenties or early thirties, with a clean, military look about him. He wears no wedding ring, but an eagle tattoo peeks from the bottom of the shirtsleeve over his upper arm. He must be fond of body art, because he also sports a tattoo on the back of his right hand.

I study his face last. I've made a living from reading people's thoughts and feelings in their expressions, but though this man's ruggedly handsome face reminds me of every young male TV star, dignity and concealment have made a mask of his features. His mouth is clamped, his eyes are fixed on the elevator door, his expression is locked and guarded.

Obviously, I'll not be exchanging convent gossip with him any time soon.

I exhale in relief when we exit the elevator and step into sunlight. A door stands at my right, though it is barred, and a window looks out on what might be a lovely garden, if anyone cared enough to tend it.

My escort approaches another door that looms straight ahead. After sliding his key card through a scanner, he leads me into a narrow corridor that looks just as it might have when the nuns lived on this mountaintop. Several rough-hewn doors stand in this simple hallway; he opens the first and reveals a surprisingly spacious room with a large window, narrow bed, antique wardrobe, bureau, desk and chair. I'm surprised to discover that the room also contains a modern bathroom, complete with toilet, tub, and shower. Apparently the CIA believes in the value of home improvement.

The guard sets my suitcase beside me. "Do you need anything else, ma'am?"

I glance around. A pitcher of ice water waits on a stand, along with a pair of crystal glasses. "Thank you. Everything looks…fine."

"Good. Someone will page you on the intercom when Dr. Mewton is ready to see you. Until then, she'd like you to relax and refresh yourself."

The guard closes the door, and silence descends as his heavy steps fade from the hallway. When I am completely surrounded by quiet, I try the handle of my door…and am startled when it turns in my hand. I half expected to find myself locked in.

I peer into the hall, glance right and left, but no one else moves in the corridor. Later I might explore my surroundings, but I need to pull my clothes from the suitcase and let the wrinkles fall out. I need a glass of water, and I need to wash twenty-four hours of grime from my complexion.

Before unzipping my suitcase, however, I cast a longing look at the bed. It is covered with a thick white comforter and a lush mix of colorful pillows.

More than anything, I need ten minutes to close my eyes. I crawl under the comforter and let my head sink into an oversize bolster. Before I can even kick off my shoes, exhaustion overpowers me in a warm, irresistible wave.

Chapter Eighteen

Sarah

Judson and I monitor my aunt's arrival on the computer in my apartment. Dr. Mewton doesn't know that I've tapped into the intercom and the security cameras, but I doubt she'd be surprised to discover that I've been snooping.

Though I remained quiet and pretended to be nonchalant as I watched the woman disembark, my pulse quickened as she passed a guard and moved toward the elevator.

I switched to the elevator cam. The guard stood in front of the camera, blocking my view of all but the tip of a perfect nose.

I muttered beneath my breath and clicked to a security cam on the first floor. I forced the camera to zoon in on the elevator door and caught my breath as it opened. The woman passed by the lens in a blur of motion, far too quickly for me to get a good look.

But then she paused outside the door of her room. I adjusted the security cam, and while the guard carried her suitcase inside, Renee Carey glanced up and I snapped her picture.

Enlargement of the image reveals a perfectly symmetrical combination of two eyes, a slender nose, two lips, two cheeks, two ears, one chin. Skin as smooth as porcelain; large eyes rimmed by lush lashes. An arresting dark spot above the corner of the mouth, reminding me of the intentional mistake

Amish quilters reportedly sew into their creations to remind themselves that only God is perfect. Still, whether mole or freckle, this spot deserves to be called a beauty mark.

"So…" Judson says as I watch Renee Carey step into the hallway for a quick look around. "Can you see inside her room, as well?"

"That's classified." I watch as the door to my aunt's room closes, leaving me fixated on an empty corridor. "If I did have a camera in her room, I don't think I'd use it. A woman's entitled to some privacy."

Judson laughs. "Not here, she isn't."

"As long as she's not under investigation, she can close her door. I wouldn't want anyone snooping on me without cause."

"Girl, what do you think we're doing here at the convent?"

I ignore him. If he can't understand the vast difference between monitoring crucial communications and peeping into someone's bedroom, he's being deliberately obtuse.

"So." Judson's smile widens. "You've planted cameras all over this place, haven't you?"

"A girl has to keep busy. Besides, Dr. Mewton wants me to sharpen my skills."

"Have you bugged the conference room? The chapel?" He lowers his voice and leans closer. "Don't tell me you've even bugged Mewton's office."

"If I had, I wouldn't tell you."

Jud slaps the armrest of his wheelchair. "I can tell you didn't come up through the system. Somebody forgot to drum a healthy fear of the brass into you. So what are you going to do if she finds one of your little cameras?"

I exhale in a sigh he'll be sure to hear. "Passive transmitters aren't detectable until they transmit. I'm not even sure a bug *is* a bug if it's not doing anything. Maybe it's just a bit of unobtrusive decoration."

"That kind of decoration is going to get you into trouble if it's ever discovered."

"I doubt it. Dr. M will probably congratulate me on my ingenuity."

When it becomes clear that Dr. Carey is not going to come out of her room again, I lean back and lock my hands behind my head. "So…what do you think, Jud?"

He snorts. "About your camera work?"

"About my aunt."

"You're the one who saw her. You tell me."

"What do I know about other women? Besides, I described her to you."

"'Short hair, medium height, and symmetrical features' doesn't do it for me. If you're going to be my eyes, you've got to start sprucing up your adjectives. Add a little pizzazz to your descriptions."

"I have no idea what you're talking about."

"I was afraid of that. Okay, tell me—did she have a pleasant face?"

"What's a pleasant face?"

"Did she have a *nice* face?"

"Do you mean was she nice-looking, or did she look nice?"

"Good grief, you're frustrating. You've got to give me something useful."

"Give me a minute." I shift my gaze to the photograph still displayed on my monitor. I could try to describe this woman, but words like *symmetry* and *purity* cannot begin to describe the aura of loveliness surrounding this face.

And I'm not sure I can speak of it without my voice breaking.

So I close my eyes and remember details of what I saw on the dock. "She brought one suitcase. And she had a handbag on her shoulder."

"What about her face?"

"I told you, she had eyes, ears, a nose—"

"Her *expression.* Did she look nervous? Excited? Happy?"

"I have no idea."

He sighs heavily. "Okay. Let's go back to the luggage. What does one suitcase and a purse tell you?"

"How should I know? I've never packed a suitcase in my life."

Judson pinches the bridge of his nose. "Well, at this point it'd be convenient to have a camera in her room because everything depends on what's inside the suitcase. Did she bring lots of clothes? Then she's a fashionista and possibly self-centered. Did she bring a couple of family photo albums? That would tell you she's considerate. If you opened her bag and found bottled water, protein bars, and packages of sunflower seeds—meet your aunt the health food nut. But only one bag? That means she's not planning an extended visit." He chuckles. "My wife never went anywhere with only one suitcase. Juanita would have packed one bag with nothing but shoes—stilettos, maybe, sandals, a pair of loafers, and something suitable for dancing. She had a real thing for shoes."

His voice softens, and so does his face. I watch, fascinated, as a tear seeps from his sealed eyelids and falls onto his dark cheek. "If you miss her," I whisper, "you could contact her."

"No, I can't." He swipes at the tear, then jerks on his wheels, edging the chair backward over the tile floor. "I died, she mourned, my son has a new daddy. I can't go back."

"But you didn't die." I feel like a moron pointing out the obvious, but Judson won't hear it.

"I might as well be dead." The tendons in the backs of his hands stand out like a bas-relief as he grips his wheels. "Scarred up, legs gone, blind, half a man—even if the agency had been able to come up with a reasonable cover story to explain why I was at that warehouse, I wouldn't want to face Juanita like this." He lowers his head. "No, she's better off thinking I died in that bus crash. Better for my kid to visit an empty grave in Lubbock than learn I'm living like this."

Because his voice has gone all jagged and hoarse, I remain quiet and wait for the storm to pass. I pull my keyboard closer and deactivate the screen saver so I'm again looking at the symmetrical features of Dr. Renee Carey, who has traveled across an ocean to see me.

Would she be better off thinking I died with my mother?

Chapter Nineteen

Renee

I awaken to the sound of insistent knocking. For a moment I don't remember where I am or what day it is, but then the sight of my waiting suitcase sends a jolt of adrenaline through my bloodstream.

"Just a moment," I call, struggling to move legs that feel like deadwood. I glance at the nightstand, wondering why no one has called, then I realize there's no phone in the room. No alarm clock, either. Only an intercom panel on the wall, and it's silent.

I open the door, expecting to see one of the guards, and am startled by the sight of a woman in white: white hair, white blouse, white slacks, white smile. She's holding a white book, and for an insane moment I'm certain my imagination has conjured up Sister Luke, Mother Superior of the Convent of the Lost Lambs.

"Dr. Carey? I'm Glenda Mewton." The vision extends a hand, the white tips of her nails gleaming in the space between us. "I'm sorry—did I wake you?"

She's real; I feel the warmth of her skin when I shake her hand. I give her a dazed smile. "I'm sorry. I only meant to close my eyes a few minutes, but I must have dozed off."

Dr. Mewton takes a step back and gestures down the hall. "I wanted to speak to you before you meet Sarah. There's a small chapel at the end of this corridor. Will you join me there in a moment or two?"

Apparently I'm in no condition to join her now. I run my hand through my hair and wonder if I have a trail of dried saliva at the corner of my mouth. "Let me splash my face and change clothes, then I'll be right out."

"Thank you."

She moves away, her figure casting a regal shadow on the wall. I retreat to my room and hurry to unpack my toiletries bag. After a less-than-efficient encounter with toothpaste, hairbrush, and deodorant spray, I toss my travel clothes onto the bed and pull on a yellow blouse and navy slacks. This place could use a little color.

I head for the hallway, but hesitate at the threshold. My hands feel empty, but I can't think of any reason to carry a notebook or my purse. Finally, I grab my wallet and step into the hall. I carry a picture of Kevin in my wallet; perhaps Dr. Mewton would like to see it. If that doesn't prove my connection to Sarah, I can always flash my passport and birth certificate.

The chapel stands at the end of the hallway, just as Dr. Mewton said. The narrow room, which still contains an altar and four pews, looks as though it hasn't changed since the last nun vacated the premises. A carved crucifix hangs above the altar, and though the bowed head of Christ is fuzzy with dust, I can feel the pressure of those unblinking eyes as I walk forward to meet Dr. Mewton.

She stands when she hears me approaching. "We thought about turning this room into an operations center," she says, taking in the entire chapel with a sweep of her hand. "But on the off chance we'd need to maintain our cover, we decided to keep it."

"Along with a chest filled with habits and cassocks, I suppose." I smile, but Dr. Mewton must not see the humor in my statement, because she doesn't smile. She has a politician's face—almost anything could be going on behind that facade of bland cordiality.

I step into the pew where she stands and notice that she's still holding the white book, which appears to be an album of some sort.

"I wanted to meet you here," she says, a small smile playing at the corner of her mouth, "because it's one of the few rooms not monitored by surveillance cameras. When we're in here, I can be reasonably sure Sarah isn't watching us."

I drop my jaw. "She could be watching?"

"I'm sure she's already checked you out. The girl is exceptionally bright, and I've never known her to remain stymied by anything for long."

"Really?" I force a laugh. "Her father would be so proud."

"Would he?" Dr. Mewton lifts a brow and gestures toward the pew. "This may feel a little awkward, but since Sarah's already seen you, I don't feel it's unfair to let you learn about her before you meet her. If you'll have a seat, I'd like to show you these pictures."

We sit. But before opening the book, she smiles and gives me a sidelong look. "I must apologize for what might seem like overprotectiveness on my part. But Sarah has been in my care since infancy, and I have resolved to protect her as best I can."

"Protect her from what?"

"Anyone who would harm her. Those who would persecute her because she doesn't fit into a predetermined and artificial mediocrity." The woman's face bears a look of deep abstraction, and for a moment I'm not sure she's even aware of my presence. Then she stares directly at me. "Why don't we start at the beginning? I understand that officially you're here to report on Sarah's well-being."

I smile and shrug. "We both know that directive is pretty much smoke and mirrors. I'll write a report, of course, but my primary purpose is to meet my niece. The psychological evaluation is a secondary priority unless—" I hesitate "—I'm not going to find a problem, am I?"

"With Sarah?" A faint trace of humor slips into the woman's expression. "The girl is probably better suited to her job than either of us. Very well, then, let's review the basic facts of Sarah's case. What do you know of your brother's assignment in Spain?"

I spread my hands. "I don't know anything. I didn't know Kevin worked for the CIA until I discovered a letter from you in my mother's storage unit."

Dr. Mewton nods. "That's how it should be. Extended family members rarely know about NOC personnel."

"You'll have to explain; I don't speak acronym."

"Nonofficial cover officers. Everyone on the outside thought your brother worked for a chemical company. In reality, he had been trained and placed by the CIA. His mission remains classified, but I can assure you we were sorry to lose him."

"His wife, Diane—did she know what he really did?"

Dr. Mewton tilts her head. "I can't say. Some spouses are fully informed. Others make it clear they'd rather not know the entire truth. But I suspect Diane knew something."

"Did you know my brother?"

Amusement flickers in her eyes. "We took out his appendix not long after he was posted. I remember him as a charming young man, devoted to his wife and his work."

"I didn't—I didn't know he'd been sick."

"He wasn't, not really. We had him in and out in a matter of days. Most of his friends thought he and Diane went away for a brief vacation."

I glance at the wallet in my hand and remember the many steps I've taken to reach this point. "At Langley, as you enter CIA headquarters, there's a marble wall with stars on it…eighty-three, I think, when I was there. Does one of them represent my brother?"

The woman caresses the album on her lap. "Thirty-five of those stars are unnamed. One of those belongs to Sarah's father."

"So he *didn't* commit suicide. Kevin died on a mission."

The woman's lips compress into a thin line. "I can't discuss details with you, Dr. Carey. I am eager, however, to tell you about Sarah."

I hesitate, torn between pursuing news of my brother and wanting to know about the girl I've come so far to see. "Fine, let's talk about Sarah. Why weren't we given more information? We would have taken her in. My mother or I would have—"

"We did contact your mother with news of Sarah's condition. At birth she had severe disfigurement caused by Treacher-Collins—"

"Your letter said her prognosis was poor, and you asked for power of attorney. I'm assuming my mother gave you that."

"Your assumption is correct."

I lift my hand and close my eyes, stumbling over the problem that has troubled me for months. "I don't understand why she did that. I've researched Treacher-Collins, so I know Sarah was a normal child."

"Mentally normal, yes, but she suffered from significant facial defects. The craniofacial surgeon we brought in said he'd never seen such a severe case."

"How bad could it—"

"Why don't I show you Sarah's first pictures? They speak for themselves."

Dr. Mewton slides the album onto my lap and lifts the cover. On the first page, beneath a protective plastic sheet, is a photograph of a healthy baby with strong arms, chubby legs…and a head shaped like a matchstick. I can see no hair, no ears, and no discernible forehead. A mouth occupies the center of the shape, and three bulging sacs protrude above a lolling tongue.

"How on earth?" The exclamation slips from me before I realize I have spoken.

"Most babies," Dr. Mewton says, her voice gentling, "are born with the features people consider attractive—big eyes, long lashes, oversize pupils, chubby cheeks, small noses. Falling in love with a baby is as easy as two plus two. Loving a genetic mutation doesn't come as naturally."

I look up, the muscles of my forearm tightening beneath the book. "Are you saying my family didn't love this child?"

"I have no idea what your mother and brother felt, but I know your family faced a definite challenge. As you can imagine, the physicians' immediate concern was maintaining the child's airway—with no developed nostrils and only a small mouth, she needed a tracheotomy immediately. The feeding tube was another necessity, so the agency airlifted the baby and brought her here. We flew in a British surgeon from London who probably saved Sarah's life. We know he saved her eyesight."

She turns the page and shows me another picture of the same baby. In this shot, a stiff collar surrounds her neck, and dark lines of stitches mark two of the bulging sacs above the flat tongue.

"The eyelids had not formed." Dr. Mewton taps the page with a fingernail. "The doctor had to cut an opening to admit light, or Sarah's eyes would never have functioned properly."

I stare at the photographs in stunned silence. I have seen pictures of other children with Treacher-Collins, but none of them looked like this.

Somehow I draw enough oxygen into my lungs to speak. "Was Diane—was she aware of this?"

Dr. Mewton shakes her head. "Unfortunately, your sister-in-law began to hemorrhage. She died at the Spanish hospital before the doctors could stop the bleeding. Your brother remained with her while I took charge of the infant."

I close my eyes, unable to imagine what Kevin must have endured in those awful hours. And where were Mother and I during that time? At home, blithely watching *Cosby* and *Family Ties*?

"We didn't know," I whisper. "I can't believe we didn't know about any of this."

Dr. Mewton's eyes soften. "You couldn't have been old enough to do anything."

"I was fifteen. But Mother could have done something. She *should* have done something."

Even as I say the words, I know I'm not being completely truthful. A sudden heart attack took my father six months before Kevin died, and Mother wasn't herself in those days.

Even before my brother's death, I remember looking at mother and thinking that she was like a helium balloon that had lost its buoyancy. She went through all the motions of daily life, but she appeared slightly shrunken, and all her energy had drained away.

"While the baby was recovering from surgery," Dr. Mewton says, lowering her voice, "your brother had to complete a task on his covert assignment. I'm sure that seems extreme to you, but I suspect he pressed on because it was easier to live in alias than to deal with his grief. Something went wrong, though, and he died two days after Diane. That's when I wrote your mother about the power of attorney. I also sent her a picture of the child."

A lump rises in my throat, a knot born of certainty. I know how my grief-stricken mother must have responded, but still I have to ask. "And Mom said?"

Reluctance struggles with indignation on the doctor's fine-boned face as she looks toward one of the sunlit windows. "She wanted us…to let nature take its course. She asked us to withdraw the feeding tube, but after some consideration, I decided I couldn't do it. Legally, ethically, morally, it would be wrong to starve that child. So, because I had custody and power of attorney, I approved the surgeries Sarah needed to live and to function more like normal people."

When Dr. Mewton looks back at me, I see no pride or judgment in her eyes. She is simply stating the facts.

"Sarah had those operations here?"

"Don't let our rustic appearance mislead you. For more than twenty-five years, the Convent of the Lost Lambs has served as an emergency hospital for CIA officers and allied contacts. We're a black site, so we keep a low profile, but we have contract surgeons and other medical personnel on staff. Though most of them live in Britain or France, we can usually assemble a surgical team in a matter of hours." Her eyes flash. "Of course, you can never divulge any of this to anyone."

"But why has my brother's daughter been kept in a hospital all these years?"

"Because she needed several surgeries…and many months to recuperate between them. We brought in a maxillofacial surgeon to work on her mouth and teeth because we knew she'd need a functioning jaw in order to eat and talk. That surgery had to be accomplished in stages, of course, because a young child grows so rapidly. A craniofacial surgeon used pieces of her rib to shape her skull; a plastic surgeon fashioned a rudimentary pair of ears. Another surgeon implanted the cochlear device that allows her to hear—"

"Wait—she's deaf?"

Dr. Mewton lifts her hand. "Not when she's wearing her headset. She had no ears at birth, no auditory canals. The microphone of her implant picks up sound, the speech processor arranges the sounds, and a transmitter converts those sounds into electric impulses. The electrode array sends those impulses to different regions of the auditory nerve, allowing Sarah to hear."

"I'll take your word for it. I've heard of such things, but I've never known anyone who uses one."

"Sarah was one of the first people to have a Nucleus multichannel implant—she received hers when she was eighteen months old. Her current model is state-of-the-art. In fact, I'm quite sure she's received better care at our facility than she would have received anywhere in the world."

Dr. Mewton doesn't elaborate, but I can read between the lines. I don't know how much money is funneled into the CIA's off-book operations, but with no one to look over the division's shoulder, who limits their budget? As a civilian, Sarah would have had medical decisions made by insurance companies and HMOs; here her needs have been met without question.

I flip through the pages of the album on my lap. The little girl changes from picture to picture—the bulging eye sacs recede, the lump that was meant to be a nose is shaped with tubes, the forehead becomes defined, the jaw descends.

In one picture, I see a much younger Dr. Mewton holding the baby in a rocking chair. She cradles my niece's head as chubby arms cling to her.

"She couldn't cry, not for months," the woman says, her voice only a shade above a whisper. "Oh, she'd try to, but she couldn't because of the trach tube. When she was in so much pain after the surgeries, I would rock her for hours. I cried for her." A rueful smile quirks her mouth. "It's so hard. When we get an officer who needs plastic surgery to alter his appearance, he understands that a few days of suffering might save his life. A baby can't comprehend why we sometimes have to hurt her."

I swallow hard and turn another page. With a potato-sized lump in my throat, I flip through the remaining photographs, marking the progress of years and additional operations. Sarah grows hair, Sarah learns to walk, Sarah has her trach tube removed, Sarah gets her first tooth.

The last page in the album features a photo of a child who appears to be five or six. The eyes are firmly seated in the head, a nose is apparent, and I can even see the hint of a smile on that face. But the skin is quilted and scarred, the nose pinched, and the little girl lacks eyelashes and brows. The lips are thin and malformed, and something about the dimensions of the face remains noticeably unbalanced.

"What do you think?" Quiet pride shines in Dr. Mewton's

eyes. "Sarah can now hear, breathe, eat, and smile. She's exceptionally bright and has demonstrated a remarkable aptitude for computer programming. Her intellect has always been above normal, and even though our surgeons have had to manipulate the skull, she has suffered no brain damage. You'll find her a remarkable young woman."

I bring my hand to my mouth, afraid to say what I'm thinking. "She— This is what she looks like now?"

"She's grown-up, of course. She has her father's height and slim build. And despite being confined to this facility all her life, she's remarkably conversant in American culture. We've imported every book, DVD, and recording she's requested. She probably knows more about American movies than you do."

"I don't get out much," I answer, vaguely disturbed by the woman's pride in Sarah's accomplishments. "Dr. Mewton— did Sarah have any surgeries after this last photograph?"

The doctor's mouth spreads into a thin-lipped smile. "Sarah was eight when that photo was taken…old enough to tell me she didn't want any more operations. We discussed it and I agreed."

"But surely you might have tried to convince her to consult with a plastic surgeon. Knowing that one day she would need to live in the real world…"

"Sarah has never expressed a desire to leave this facility, so I saw no need to push. Besides, where would she live? She had no family in the States, nowhere to go."

"She had me."

"Did she?"

I stare at Dr. Mewton. I have no answers, no excuses that can make up for twenty years of silence. But I do know one thing—my brother was such an adventurer that I can't imagine any child of his being content to remain on an island barely large enough to contain a football field.

But I have not met the girl. All I know is what Dr. Mewton

has told me, and the woman is far from unbiased. She has developed a relationship with my niece…and I suspect it's an attachment that must be severed if Sarah is ever to live a life of her own.

"What can you tell me…about who she is?"

"I've just given you a history."

"I don't want a history, I want to know *her.* What's she like?"

Dr. Mewton tilts her head as a smile plays at the corner of her mouth. "She loves cherries. She has a real talent for mathematics, but she's slow with foreign languages. She's brilliant and logical, but even now she sleeps with a lamp burning. She'd never admit it, but I think she's afraid of the dark. The fear probably stems from something in her childhood, but I'll leave the psychoanalysis to you."

When it becomes apparent that she will say nothing else, I close the album and offer it to Dr. Mewton. She shakes her head. "Why don't you keep it awhile? It might help you to remember how far Sarah has come."

I hug the album to my chest and stand. "As the only remaining member of the Sims family, I owe you our deepest thanks. But I've come a long way to meet my niece and assure her that she's not alone in the world."

Dr. Mewton rises and walks me to the doorway of the chapel. "I'll send her to you soon. Is there anything you need? A snack, perhaps? Something to drink?"

"I'm fine." I meet her smile with one of my own, but mine feels tight on my face. "Just send my niece to me as soon as possible. I've waited long enough."

Chapter Twenty

Sarah

Fixated on the computer monitor, I watch without speaking as Dr. Mewton walks through the first floor hallway and my aunt returns to her room. When our guest moves beyond the range of the cameras, I rewind the security footage, zoom in, and study the flickering muscles of my aunt's perfect face.

According to the Virginia Department of Motor Vehicles, Renee Carey was born in March 1972. Though she is thirty-five, I can see no signs of age in her skin. She wears her dark hair short, like mine, so I suspect she also lacks the patience for elaborate hairstyles. Wispy bangs fall across her wide forehead, and laugh lines radiate from the corners of her eyes, but only when she smiles. Her lips are full and round, her teeth are even, and her chin is square.

I think she's as pretty as any actress I've ever seen in a movie, but she must be intelligent, too. I'm amazed that she's able to hold Dr. Mewton's gaze without flinching.

Renee Carey, whoever she is, is nothing like the nervous, weepy woman in one of my favorite movies. For the past few days I've been imagining her as *The Shining*'s Wendy Torrance, trying her best to protect her child in that forsaken old hotel. I was wrong, though—Dr. Carey is more like Ripley in *Aliens,* who glares at the razor-jawed creature as she thrusts the innocent child behind her and makes a desperate plan to escape.

I flinch as the intercom buzzes. "Sarah?"

"Yes?"

"Your aunt is ready to see you. She's in room 101 on the first floor…in case you didn't know that already."

I wait, wondering if Dr. Mewton plans to join me, but she says nothing else.

"All right. Thanks."

Judson must have heard the squawk of the intercom, because he rolls past my open door and pauses. "You want me to go downstairs with you?"

"Um…thanks, but I should probably go alone."

"I could wait in the hall and provide a diversion if you give the signal."

He's such a spy. I laugh. "What kind of signal?"

"You could cough. Shoot, you could just yell for help. I'd be at your side in a flash."

"Relax, Jud, this isn't a mission. She's not the enemy, and I shouldn't need extraction."

"Then go on in and wow her with your charm and good looks. I'd go with you, but my social calendar is overcrowded these days."

My voice is strangled when I stand and reply, "I'll do my best."

He scoots out of the way and lets me pass, but I can feel his anxiety following me as I head toward the stairwell.

They say that when an individual loses one of his senses, like Jud's eyesight or my hearing, the other senses improve to compensate for the impairment. I know Judson's hearing is excellent and his sense of touch keen.

Yet I don't understand how he can be my best friend and not realize my chief handicap.

Chapter Twenty-One

Renee

When a knock interrupts the quiet, I brace myself and prepare to meet my niece. I open the door and see a slender figure dressed in sneakers and baggy surgical scrubs. The hand on the door frame is long-fingered and the arm lightly freckled, like Kevin's.

But the face—

Despite Dr. Mewton's effort to prepare me, I am shocked into silence when I lift my gaze. If this girl appeared at my door on Halloween, I would congratulate her on finding such a delightfully original fright mask.

It's not that her features are missing—I can see two brown eyes, a nose, and a mouth. But there are no proper lips, there is no delicate cleft between nostrils and upper lip, no rounded chin. The cheeks are too compressed, the hairline's uneven and jagged. The eyebrows are missing and so are the eyelashes. My niece may have functional features, but this is not a face. It is a random and incomplete collection of facial parts.

"Sarah." The name catches in my throat as I focus on the wall behind her and extend my arms. "I'm your aunt Renee."

She comes forward and clasps my shoulders, offering a stiff sort of shoulder-squeeze instead of an embrace. That's all right; the girl doesn't know me at all. I step back and gesture toward the only chair in the room. "Come in and have a seat, will you?"

She strides forward and drops into the chair with adolescent ungainliness, then crosses her legs. "So," she says, speaking in the slightly hollow voice I've heard other deaf children employ, "you are my father's sister?"

"That's right." I sink onto the corner of the bed and cross my legs, mirroring her posture to put her at ease. "Kevin was quite a bit older than me, but we were close when he lived at home…I think he thought of me as a pet. Do you… How much do you know about your mom and dad?"

She lifts one shoulder in a shrug. "I know his name was Kevin Sims. My mother was named Diane. My father worked for the company and he died two days after my mother. My mother died when I was born."

"*After* you were born." I look her in the eye, stressing the importance of the chronology. "Your birth didn't hurt her, but something went wrong later. You need to understand that."

She draws an audible breath. "I know I didn't kill her, if that's what you're worried about. These things happen sometimes."

"Yes, they do." I reach for my wallet, grateful for the opportunity to do something with my hands. "Let me show you one of my most precious pictures. Your dad was a handsome young man—people always said he looked like one of the Kennedys. Personally, I've always thought he looked *better* than any of the Kennedy kids, but maybe I'm biased."

I unsnap the wallet and show her the first picture—me and Kevin, sitting side by side, crowded into the photo booth outside the local drugstore. Kevin is thirty-one, auburn-haired and lanky; with my hair cut short, I am a scrawny fourteen-year-old replica of him.

Sarah takes my wallet and stares at the photo for a long moment. "You've changed," she finally says, her eyes not leaving the picture. "But you're just as pretty."

In any other circumstance, I would have said, "You're pretty, too," as casually as I'd follow a sneeze with "God bless you." Today, however, the words catch in my throat, and I

wonder if mentioning Kevin's attractiveness was a thought-
less gaffe. I can see nothing of him or Diane in this girl, but
maybe I'm not looking hard enough.

"You have his build," I offer in a rush of words. "Kevin was
tall and slim, just like you are. He could eat anything he
wanted and never gain an ounce. Even as a kid, I always
envied him for that."

Something that might have been a smile lifts a corner of
the slit that functions as her mouth. "You're not exactly slim."

I turn my startled gasp into a cough. "No, I'm what most
people call 'curvy.' I have to watch every bite."

"Too bad." She looks up and notices the album on the bed.
"I see Dr. Mewton has brought out my baby pictures."

"Yes. They were…fascinating."

"She wanted to prepare you for the freak show." Her voice
is flat and calm, but an involuntary muscle quivers at the
corner of one lashless eye.

I am careful to keep my own face composed in straight
lines. "I think she wanted me to see how well you've done.
She said you are a remarkable young woman, and I can see
she was right."

"Are you surprised?"

Once again I'm startled by her candor. "Well…yes and no.
I was astonished to find out you were alive—I'd been told you
died with your mother. That's why you've never heard from
me through all these years. I'm so sorry about that."

She shrugs. "I don't blame you for anything."

"Still, I feel terrible. I'm not surprised to find out you're
remarkable—I didn't know your mother very well, but Kevin
was the light of my world. He could make a party come to
life just by walking into the room. He was smart, witty,
clever—all the things I'm not."

Sarah shifts in the chair and curls her legs beneath her.
"Did he like the sea?"

"Kevin liked *everything*. He was a real 'don't fence me in' kind of guy." I stretch out on the bed and prop my head on my hand, relaxing in the security of my memories. "What else can I tell you? He was seventeen when I was born, but I adored him. He'd come home from college and take me to high school football games, showing me off like a little mascot. I'd ride on his shoulders… Mom always said I was too young to remember that, but I *do* remember feeling like a princess whenever I was with him."

Sarah looks at the photograph one more time, then sets my wallet on the corner of the bed. "You must not have had much time with him."

"But the time we had was good. After college, Kevin came home and worked, so I saw a lot of him in those years. I remember giving him a hard time when he started dating your mother."

"Didn't you like her?"

"I didn't really know her. I was thirteen, Kevin was my hero, and Diane didn't have any family, so she sort of wrapped herself up in my brother. It was childish, I know, but I hated her for taking him away from me. I was a junior bridesmaid in their wedding, but I didn't smile in a single wedding photo. I think I sulked through the entire reception."

I glance at Sarah, hoping for some expression of sympathy, but her face is like a mask. I've made a livelihood out of reading human expressions, but none of the usual markers are present in Sarah's features. How am I supposed to know what this girl is thinking?

Mewton may be right about Sarah being well equipped for her job. But she's not so well equipped for ordinary conversation.

"I'm sorry, is this what you want to hear? Would you rather talk about something else?"

"Please…" She wraps her arms around herself. "Please go on."

I run my hand over the comforter as I search for some other

conversational nugget. "Kevin was always entertaining…and kind of restless. My mom was surprised when he decided to go to college right after high school. She kept thinking he'd take a year off to backpack through Europe or some other kind of freewheeling gig. But he went through school, got a job, and got married. My brother the free spirit went the traditional route. Or at least we thought he did. Turns out we didn't have a clue."

"What did he study in college?"

"Political science, I think. And chemistry. Mom wanted him to be a doctor, but he found a job with a chemical company and took off for Spain with Diane. Now I realize, of course, that the CIA sent him to Spain, so he must have applied for a job or been recruited by the agency soon after he finished school."

"You didn't know he worked for the company?"

"That's what you call it, right?" I shake my head, tracing the subtle pattern on the comforter. "I would never have dreamed that anyone in my family worked for the CIA. No one gave us any details when he died, either. I was fifteen when we got the news, and all I wanted to do was curl up and die, too. I felt so bad—I had barely spoken to him since he moved away. I kept thinking that soon he'd get homesick and come back. I was just a kid, you see. Now I would give anything to know Kevin as an adult. I still miss him."

"It's hard to miss someone you never knew."

"You're right, it is." I force myself to look directly into Sarah's face. "Now that I know about you, I'd give anything if we could make up for lost time. If I'd known you were growing up here alone, I'd have brought you home and adopted you. I'd have done anything to see that you got the help you needed."

"It's okay." She looks away and squares her shoulders. "I don't think I've missed out."

"Oh, sweetie." I bite my lip, wanting to say that she's

missed out on *everything*—family, friends, a social life. She's never been to a reunion, never sung in a school choir, never belonged to a church. But that's probably the last thing she wants to hear.

"So," I begin again, "tell me about yourself. What do you like to do for fun?"

She blinks. "Fun?"

"Do you have a hobby?"

If anything, her expression becomes blanker than before. "I like to read. And watch movies."

"I like movies, too. And books, though I don't have nearly as much reading time as I would like."

"I understand. There's always some project to work on around here."

"I'm sure there is." What I'm not sure about is what Sarah's free to discuss and what is verboten. "Who are your friends? Do you get enough social interaction out here?"

She looks at me as if I've just suggested that she's not eating enough lead. "I talk to people every day."

"Friends?"

"They're certainly not enemies." She lifts her shoulder in a stiff shrug. "How many friends is a person supposed to have?"

I laugh softly. "Maybe you have a point. I'm not sure I have more than a handful of close pals."

"I have Dr. Mewton and Judson and Shelba, the cook. And I talk to a couple of the guards from time to time."

That's not much personal engagement...and humans are such social creatures. I sit up, well aware that the psychologist in me is overpowering the inexperienced aunt. "Tell me about your relationship with Dr. Mewton. Are you close?"

Sarah shrugs. "Close enough."

Her response is vague...deliberately so? "Well," I answer, fumbling for words, "while I'm sure Dr. Mewton has been kind to you, she's not your mother."

"Neither are you." She utters the words calmly, without

rancor or bitterness. "People come through here all the time. They get patched up, they convalesce, they go away. Sometimes they stay, but I don't spend a lot of time getting to know people who are going to leave."

"Why don't you tell me more about your friends here?"

She opens her hands and begins to count on her fingers. "Judson has been here over two years. He lives in the room next door and he helps with op tech. He's blind, but he types like a madman. I modified a text-to-speech program that allows him to hear anything on screen, so he's quite capable."

"What brought Judson to this place?"

"That's classified—need to know only."

"Oh." I know it's silly, but I feel as though I've just had my hand slapped. Maybe the information is classified, or maybe Sarah harbors romantic feelings for this friend. In any case, I'd better watch my step.

"How old—" I approach the question carefully "—is Judson?"

The corner of Sarah's mouth dips. "Old. At least forty."

Well, no romance on *that* horizon. "And the others who live and work here?"

"Shelba, the cook, is probably Dr. Mewton's age. She's always fussing at me about not eating enough, but I love her."

"Good."

"Hightower—he's back with us, but he's not talking right now. I've run op tech for a couple of his missions, but I'm not sure why he ended up here this time." She stares into space for a moment, then lowers her gaze. "The reason is probably classified, so I haven't asked. Chip and Mitch are the guards who met you on the dock. There's a six-man team assigned here, but they rotate on and off the island. They're all nice guys."

"You know them well?"

"Well enough—sometimes they work at different posts. We talk every now and then. Mitch and I talk more than most."

"Wait a minute." A slow smile creeps across my face as my feminine intuition sounds an alarm. "How do you know who met me at the docks? Were you peeking…or is that classified, too?"

Her eyes dart toward the intercom, then she looks at her hands and lowers her voice. "Security camera feeds. I hack into them all the time, but don't tell Dr. M."

I laugh, as amused by her honesty as by the fact that Dr. Mewton knows Sarah is prone to eavesdropping. "Don't worry, I'll keep your secrets to myself. Your father would have commandeered the system, too. Remind me to tell you about the time he set up a video camera in our neighbor's backyard."

I search her features for a trace of humor, but what passes for a face remains as motionless as stone.

"Can we talk at dinner?" she asks. "Shelba will be serving in half an hour."

"Let's do it. I hope I'll be able to meet Judson and Shelba. I'd like to meet all your friends."

She stands, and her voice is light as she steps toward the door. "I think that can be arranged."

Chapter Twenty-Two

Sarah

Beneath the hum and flicker of the dining room's fluorescent lights, I watch as my aunt laughs at one of Judson's tired jokes. His face positively glows when she talks to him, and his smile spreads when she places her hand on his arm—something she often does when she speaks. I never touch Judson, and neither does Dr. Mewton. Neither of them routinely touches me. Is this practice peculiar to my aunt, or do other people casually touch when they talk?

I can't deny that her presence has cast a spell over our little threesome. I felt her power the moment she opened the door to her room. I saw her standing there, framed by the doorway, and for a moment I couldn't speak. Though I had watched her on the monitors, the pixelated two-dimensional image could not convey the full reality of who she is. Her presence—her texture, her warmth, her vitality—could not be conveyed on the screen.

Only after we began to converse did I realize that she is only the fifth woman I have seen up close. I have known Dr. Mewton and Shelba for years, and twice we sheltered female officers who came to the convent—one for plastic surgery, the other to recuperate from serious chemical burns. Neither of those women behaved anything like Dr. Renee Carey.

Other women visit this facility, of course. They rotate in

and out with the medical teams, but they tend to remain isolated in the upstairs hospital unit. On more than one occasion a visiting female has caught a glimpse of me near the workout room, and she has always turned her head and hurried away. Not one of them has ever come forward to talk to me. The reason may have something to do with security, but I suspect it has more to do with the natural human tendency to avoid monsters.

Dr. Renee Carey, on the other hand, has no monstrous characteristics. I've decided that she looks a bit like Audrey Hepburn in the post-*Breakfast at Tiffany's* years. Even though he cannot see her, Judson certainly seems to find her attractive. She must have what others refer to as *charm*.

During a break in the chatter between Judson and my aunt, I jump into the conversation. "Do you like Audrey Hepburn?"

My aunt blinks. "*My Fair Lady's* Audrey Hepburn?"

"Good grief, Sarah," Judson says, "where on earth did that come from?"

My neck burns with humiliation, but my aunt laughs. "I do like Audrey," she answers, "but Katherine has always been my favorite Hepburn. I love those old movies with her and Spencer Tracy."

I make a mental note. "I must have missed those."

"They're oldies but goodies." Dr. Carey folds her hands over her now-empty plate. "I love old movies, but I prefer the theater. Have you ever seen a play, Sarah?"

Why is she asking? She knows I don't leave the island, but maybe this is a probe, like those I've developed for the Gutenberg program. My aunt the psychologist is trying to discover what experiences I have in my brain.

"I've seen plays on DVD," I tell her, glad that I can answer in the affirmative. "One weekend I watched all ten hours of *Nicholas Nickleby*."

"Did you enjoy it?"

"Very much."

"I'm sure it was good," she says, picking up her water glass, "but there's nothing quite like being in the theater, right down front. When you can hear every gasp and see every drop of perspiration on the actors' brows…that's a unique experience."

I lift my chin. "The DVD version was exceptional."

Judson leans in my aunt's direction. "Last time I was in New York, the wife and I saw—" he scratches his shaved head "—you know, the play about the French Revolution."

She smiles at him. "Musical?"

"Yes."

"You must mean *Les Miserables.*"

"That's it!" Judson snaps his fingers. "That show lasted nearly three hours, but it was unbelievable. I'll never forget it."

If they're trying to make me hunger for new experiences… they're doing a better job than they realize.

I turn the focus of our conversation back to our visitor. "Do you have children, Dr. Carey?"

She widens her eyes and takes a quick sip from her glass. "Unfortunately, I spent the first five years of my marriage establishing my practice. By the time the business was strong enough for me to think about maternity leave, I had managed to lose my husband."

"But why does a woman need a husband to have a baby? In *Baby Boom, The Natural,* and *One Fine Day,* women prove to be perfectly capable of raising children alone."

Dr. Carey lowers her glass and gives me a direct look. "Listen, Sarah, films can be wonderful entertainment, but they're rarely realistic. I talk to unhappy people all day, and I can't help noticing that a lot of unhappiness stems from homes where children felt neglected because their parents were absent or too busy. I didn't think it would be fair to offer a child one distracted mother when he deserved two committed parents."

Shelba enters the dining room, a freshly starched apron

tied around her waist. She smiles at my aunt and gestures to the table. "The dinner was good?"

"Delicious," Dr. Carey says, setting her napkin on the table. "Thank you very much."

I watch, amazed at the graceful ballet between her words and gestures. Without being told, she has placed her napkin to the left of her dinner plate, exactly where Judson has left his. Now Jud is wheeling away as the doctor stands, both of them perfectly in sync with some music I can't hear…

I drop my napkin onto my plate and stand, too, not willing to be left behind. "Dr. Carey, would you like to see my apartment?"

"Yes," my aunt says, hesitating only an instant. "I'd like that very much."

Chapter Twenty-Three

Renee

Sarah's use of the word *apartment* to describe her one-room living space is about as accurate as the real estate agent's description of a fifth-floor walk-up as "a fitness lover's dream." A twin bed rests against the plaster wall, covered by a fuzzy afghan and several throw pillows. Two pairs of sneakers are conjoined in tumbled comradeship at the base of an antique armoire, while a lamp, a hairbrush, and a half dozen flash drives lie scattered over the top of a dresser. Movie posters adorn the walls, the largest of which features Gloria Swanson's luminous face in *Sunset Boulevard*.

A computer desk dominates the business end of the room. Two monitors, a keyboard, a laptop, a mouse, and an external hard drive crowd the top of the desk. I spy other pieces of equipment, but to my technologically untrained eye they look like a jumble of wires, cables, and boxes.

"Impressive." I slip my hands into my pockets as I jerk my chin toward the mess. "Obviously, you know more than I do about computers."

Sarah drops into the desk chair, sitting on one bent knee. "This is just…stuff. It's what we do with the stuff that's important."

"I'm sure it is." I glance around for another chair, but apparently she doesn't entertain many guests.

"Did you…" she begins, her voice tentative. "Did you happen to bring a photo album or something? I'd like to know more about my dad, maybe see pictures of him when he was my age."

"I'm sorry, Sarah, I didn't bring pictures. But I did bring something else." I reach into my purse and pull out a small plastic trophy—a gold loving cup that must have cost forty-nine cents at some cheesy gift shop.

I sink to the edge of her bed and smile at my distorted image in the cup. "When I was thirteen, Kevin joined me, Mom, and Dad at an old-fashioned church dinner on the grounds. They had a three-legged race after lunch, and Kevin and I won this for first place. It's nothing, really, but I think that was the happiest moment of my life."

Sarah leans forward in her chair. "What's a three-legged race?"

"You've never seen one? Not even in a movie?"

"No." Her tone has soured.

"Two people," I explain. "They stand side by side and bind their inside legs at the thigh, knee, and ankle. So when the race begins, they have to work together or they fall together." I meet her gaze and hold out the trophy. "Kevin's not with me anymore, but sometimes I can hear his voice in my heart. I think he'd want you to have this. And I think he'd want you and me to work together."

She takes the little trophy and studies it as if it's a price-less treasure. "Work together in what way?"

I gather up my courage and bend to peer into her face. "I didn't bring a photo album because I thought I was coming only for a short visit. And, to be honest, I was hoping I could convince you to visit me sometime. There's no reason we have to remain apart, you know."

She swivels her chair toward the wall and sets the trophy on a corner of her desk. "Come on, Dr. Carey. You know I can't leave the convent."

"I don't know that. You can do anything you want to do."

"Like this?" She turns and points to her face. "I know how people will respond to me. I saw how you reacted this afternoon, and you'd been prepared." She shakes her head. "I've read about people like me—burn victims who end up committing suicide, and cancer patients who would rather stay in their homes than venture out and show the world how tumors have eaten away at their faces. So thanks for the invitation, but I think I'm better off staying here."

What can I say? She *will* be more sheltered here, but behind these walls she'll never have a chance to experience life in all its fullness.

"I don't know, Sarah." I keep my voice light as I stand and move to her dresser. "Everyone is born with virtually unlimited potential. I think we're meant to spend every bit of it and die without a smidgen of promise left."

I run my fingertips over the edge of the bureau, where behind the jumbled cords and a hairbrush I spy a plastic case filled with mounted coins—British guineas, crowns, and gold sovereigns. American pennies, nickels, dimes, quarters. The Canadian two-dollar coin known as a "tooney." The miniature portraits of Washington, Lincoln, Roosevelt, and Queen Elizabeth wink at me in the lamplight.

"You like coins?" I ask, delighted to have found that she has an interest in something outside this facility.

She shrugs. "I used to collect them when I was younger. Dr. Mewton would bring them to me."

I pick up the plastic case and examine it in the lamplight. "I don't recognize this big piece—the one with the two men on it."

She rises out of her chair to glance at the case, then settles back down. "That's Juan Carlos of Spain and his son, Felipe. That's two thousand pesetas."

"Ah." I set the case back on the dresser, taking care to avoid hitting the lamp. "I don't know much about foreign coins, I'm afraid. I suppose it'll be easier now that so many countries are using the Euro."

"Those coins aren't as nice," she says, "but I do like the Spanish Euro. It features Juan Carlos and Sofia on the face."

I grip the edge of the dresser as the truth crashes into me. Every coin here features a portrait—not a building, a monument, symbol, but a human *face.*

My brother's daughter has spent a lifetime collecting faces—first on coins, then on movie posters. She may never have admitted the truth to herself, but she has yearned for the thing that makes us most human, the thing she doesn't have.

Instinct tells me that in all that face collecting, she's been longing for something else she lacks. A father. A mother. A sister. Anyone she can call *family.*

In the silence of the room, I catch my breath and hear my heart break—a clean, sharp sound, like the snap of a pencil.

I am going to help her. I'm not sure how to proceed, but Sarah will let me know what she needs.

"Sarah." I spin around and squeeze her shoulders, bending until our eyes are only inches apart. "Sweetheart, I think I understand some of what you've been feeling. There's a wonderful world out there, and I'd love to help you experience it. Say you'll at least think about coming to visit me, okay?"

She hesitates. "Yeah, sure. I'll think about it."

"Good." I close my eyes and press my lips to her uneven hairline. "On that note, I'll leave you so I can get some rest. I'll see you in the morning."

And as I walk down the stairs that will lead me back to my room, my thoughts drift to *Sunset Boulevard* and the radiant Norma Desmond. In the musical version, Norma's former director sings an aria about the moment he first saw the young actress and knew he'd found his perfect face….

In Sarah Sims, I've found an imperfect face. But I might have also found my heart.

Chapter Twenty-Four

Sarah

When my aunt has gone, I pull a random DVD from my favorites drawer and pop the disc into my computer, not caring what might appear on the screen. Whatever it is, the movie is bound to carry me away from troubling thoughts and unanswerable questions.

I settle into a nest of pillows on my bed as Jack Nicholson appears on the splash screen for *One Flew Over the Cuckoo's Nest*. Within a few minutes, I am involved in the movie, wrapped up in the triumphs and challenges of Randle Patrick McMurphy as he faces the despotic Nurse Ratched.

As the familiar plot unfolds, however, for the first time certain aspects of Randle's environment strike me as familiar. The hallways of his insane asylum are wide and empty. Guards patrol the halls of his home. A thin-lipped woman in white rules his world. Nurse Ratched gives every indication of being friendly until pushed, then she pushes back with unyielding force…just like someone I know.

On a whim, I minimize the movie player and open the program that allows me to cycle through the security cameras—obvious and hidden—throughout the facility. Within five clicks, I am watching Aunt Renee's first floor room; another click brings me into her bathroom. Aunt Renee is standing in front of the sink, her hands lathered, her eyes closed as she splashes her face with water.

I prop my elbows on the desk and lower my head into my hands as I study the screen. She is wearing a T-shirt and a pair of baggy pajama bottoms, not at all what I would have imagined for her. Her short hair has been pushed back from her forehead, and the bangs are damp from the water she's splashing over her face and neck.

She grabs a towel and gently pats—not rubs—her face dry. I blink as she hangs the damp towel on a rack. She leans toward the mirror and peers at her reflection, her eyes wide as she tilts her head and checks her face for…what? Imperfections? Signs of age?

Apparently satisfied with what she's seen, she pulls a bottle from a little zippered bag and squirts some sort of lotion or cream into her palm. The bottle goes back into the bag, then she touches her hands together and begins to rub the lotion into her face and throat. After smoothing the liquid over her cheeks, she uses her pinky finger to delicately pat the area under her eyes. She smoothes lotion over her brows, then grimaces into the mirror and checks her teeth. Finally, she wipes her hands on the towel and gives herself a smile before turning out the light.

I lean back in my chair and bring my own fingertips to touch my neglected cheek. Does my aunt perform this loving ritual every night?

The thought brings back a memory of Dr. Mewton dropping onto the edge of my bed with a tube in her hand. I was young, probably no more than four or five, and she said the ointment would help my skin heal after surgery. I still remember the astringent smell of the cream, the pressure of her hand on my ragged skin, and the sharp tone of her voice. "This is about as useful as rubbing skin softener on a crocodile," she said, her words slicing through the haze of pain surrounding me. "Still, one has to follow procedures."

At a sudden sound in the hall, I bring *Cuckoo's Nest* back up on my screen. And later, as Chief Bromden breaks through the bars and escapes through the open window of the asylum, I find myself wondering what it might mean to live free. How would it feel to walk down a street and stop to look at anything I pleased? What would it mean if I could make plans for a trip to Alaska…or decide to have lunch at a mall?

I punch my pillow and rest my chin on my fist. Is Disney World really a magical kingdom? Is the Lincoln Memorial as majestic as it looks? What does a McDonald's hamburger taste like? If they've sold billions worldwide, they must be the best things on earth.

"*Cuckoo's Nest* again?" Judson rolls into my apartment as the closing credits scroll. "Don't you ever get tired of watching the same movies?"

"No." I sit up to greet him. "It's late. Can't you sleep?"

"Wanted to talk to you about our guest before I turn in. So…what'd you think?"

I pick up the remote and power off the monitor. "You certainly seemed to like her."

He laughs. "Hey, I've always gotten along with the ladies. But you…do you think you'll end up living with her?"

"What?"

He grins. "Don't play innocent with me, kid—these walls aren't as thick as you think."

I drop back onto my pillows. "I'm not living anywhere else."

"Why not? How many times have I told you this isn't the right place for a girl of your age."

"And I've told you that you don't understand. I don't fit out there."

"And why don't you fit?"

"Because I'm a freak."

Judson snorts. "Every kid feels that way at one point or another. I used to think I was a freak because I wore size fourteen sneakers. Now I *know* I'm a freak because I have two fourteen-inch stumps. But life is flowing by out there, kid, and you need to jump in."

I pound my pillow. "I can't swim."

"It's never too late to learn."

"Oh, yeah? Then why don't you dive back into the real world?"

"I told you, I can't."

"I can't go, either. I can't leave my work."

"Are you kidding? You're not the only techno-genius on the payroll. Within a week, Mr. Traut will be assigning impossible tasks to someone else."

"How can I leave Dr. M? She depends on me."

"Mewton depends on this place. As long as it's here, she'll be fine."

I glare at him, hoping he can feel the heat from my stare. He may never understand. And I may never hear the end of his blustering.

Fortunately, I have a remedy for it.

"I'm going to bed," I tell him, punching my pillow again.

He laughs. "You think that's going to shut me up? Darkness means nothing to me, kid."

"I'm taking off my processor," I say, pulling the mechanism from my ear. "So talk all you want, Jud, but know that I can't hear you anymore. Good night."

Silence swallows up his ranting as I switch off the device and set it on the nightstand. Then I close my tired eyes and lie on my left side until unconsciousness claims me.

Chapter Twenty-Five

Renee

A note slipped under my door during the night informs me that breakfast will be served at eight o'clock in the dining room. I'm grateful for the relatively late hour. Jet lag and the shock of meeting Sarah have left me feeling a bit unbalanced.

I begin my first full day in this top secret institution by walking in the wrong direction as I look for the dining room. When I reach the chapel and realize that Shelba isn't likely to be serving pancakes on the altar, I turn and make my way to the vestibule. I thank the guard on duty there for not shooting me on sight and smile as he points me down another hallway. The dining room, he reminds me, is the last room on the left.

I lift a brow as I examine the young man, who's probably only a few years older than Sarah. "Have you already had your breakfast?"

"Sorry, ma'am," he answers, a reluctant grin tugging at his mouth. "But we don't eat with the residents."

"Too bad," I murmur, thinking about Sarah.

I enter the room in time to see Shelba setting trays before my niece and her friend Judson. Sarah is eating a bowl filled with something mushy.

"Good morning." I take the empty chair at the head of the table. "Did everyone sleep well?"

Judson grins. "Like the proverbial log. You?"

"Very well. I was so tired I could have slept standing in the closet." I glance at Sarah, who is silently putting butter on the mush in her bowl. "How about you, Sarah?"

"Good." She offers me the butter, but I wave it away as Shelba brings me a tray of toast, scrambled eggs, and sliced melon.

After thanking the cook, I spread my napkin in my lap and smile at my niece. "What shall we do today? Would you like to walk through the gardens? Maybe take a ride around the island? I've never driven a boat, but I'll bet we could convince one of the guards to take us for a spin."

A palpable silence falls over the table, and even Shelba's cart stops rattling in the hallway. Sarah's expression remains inscrutable, but Judson gapes as if I've just suggested we jump off the cliff for a little bodysurfing.

"We don't *do* pleasure boating," he says in an exaggerated whisper. "We don't roam around the island, either. It's not safe."

Not safe from what? I'd ask, but the answer to my question is probably classified.

"What Jud means," Sarah says, "is it's not nunly. All kinds of fishing boats pass the island during daylight hours, so we don't do anything a group of nuns wouldn't do."

"Well, then—" I pick up my fork "—I suppose we could have a time of prayer and *then* go for a boat ride."

Again, my attempt at humor falls flat. Sarah regards me with a perplexed expression, as if she were wondering whether or not it'd be rude to ask if I just fell off a turnip truck.

"I had planned on working today," she says, stirring the buttered mush in her bowl. "But if you really want to do something together, we could watch a movie."

I wave her idea away. "I love movies, but I don't think that'd give us much of a chance to get to know each other. It's hard to carry on a conversation when you're trying to concentrate on a plot."

When Sarah falls silent and keeps stirring her hot cereal, I realize I've made her uncomfortable. Dr. Mewton may have taught her about international espionage and computers, but apparently she's spent little time learning the social skills necessary to entertain guests.

"Don't you worry about me." I pat Sarah's hand. "You go ahead and tackle your work. I'll find a way to keep myself busy until lunch, then maybe we can catch up some more. I think I'll take some time this morning to chat with Dr. Mewton."

If Sarah is curious about what the director and I might discuss, she doesn't show it.

The guard in the vestibule directs me to Dr. Mewton's second floor office, and another guard stops me at the door. The director of this CIA pseudo convent has no secretary or assistant, but I don't suppose the administrator of a top secret facility in the middle of the ocean gets many drop-in visitors.

"I'd like to see Dr. Mewton when she has a moment," I tell the unsmiling young man outside her door. "I'll be in my room, so she can let me know when she's available."

I have barely entered the nearby stairwell when I hear a door open behind me. "Dr. Carey," Mewton calls, her voice bright. "Come in, please. If we don't take this opportunity to meet, I'm not sure when I'll be free again."

I turn, tempted to ask what could possibly keep her busy in a place this remote, but what do I know of spy operations? For all I know, I could be standing atop a nuclear weapons cache or some other hazardous national secret.

"Please, come in and have a seat."

She gestures to a white leather chair with steel legs—a chair as sleek and modern as the woman who sits behind a leather-and-chrome desk. I take the seat she offers and lean toward her, determined not to waste her time. "Dr. Mewton, while I appreciate everything you have done for Sarah, I need to know if there's any reason why I couldn't take her away from this place."

The woman's forehead crinkles. "Sarah would never leave. This is her home."

"But if she were convinced to go—if she *wanted* to go— is there any reason she couldn't?"

"Of course. Quite simply, Sarah can't function on the outside."

"How do you know? She's never had the opportunity to try."

She smiles a grim little grin. "One needn't try stepping on a land mine in order to know the experience would be lethal."

From somewhere deep within, I summon a measure of polite patience. "Surely you exaggerate. Sarah has come a long way from those photographs you showed me, but I know she could go further. Plastic surgeons are doing amazing things with facial reconstruction."

"Dr. Carey, you don't have to tell me about the marvels of plastic surgery. I work with doctors who are on the field's bleeding edge."

"Then you know Sarah could benefit—"

"Sarah is content the way she is. She had a rough childhood, a painful childhood, and at one point she decided she'd had enough surgery. I respect her decision, and I will continue to honor it."

"You respect—" I blink in dazed exasperation. "How old was she when she made this decision? Seven? Eight? You can't mean to honor the wish of an exhausted child who had no idea what she'd be missing."

"What is she missing, Dr. Carey? A society where beauty is prized above intelligence or virtue? A world where she'd be ostracized because she doesn't look or sound or think like everyone else?"

"Sarah could adapt. It would have been easier if you'd let her adjust while she was young, but there's no reason she has to remain here. I'm sure you've heard about the partial face transplant performed by French surgeons. Sarah's condition could be markedly improved—"

"Of course I've read about it. But the changes you're suggesting are merely physical. Even if she looked as normal as you or me, she would have a terrible time adjusting."

"Why?"

"Because she is as vulnerable as she is brilliant. I have done my best to challenge Sarah intellectually while protecting her socially. You can't possibly mean to suggest that I toss her to the wolves."

"But if she wanted to try… Tell me you wouldn't stand in her way. If she wanted to leave, she could go, right?"

Dr. Mewton lifts her chin and meets my gaze straight on. "Sarah Sims is an adult. She can do whatever she likes."

I clasp my hands. "Good. Tonight I'd like to take her to dinner in La Coruña."

Mewton laughs. "The devil you say. She won't go."

"I think she will. I think I know how to convince her, but I'll need your help."

Dr. Mewton regards me with a narrowed gaze, then dips her chin in an impersonal nod. "I think you are asking for trouble, Dr. Carey. But if I can help you, I certainly will."

Grateful for this reluctant promise of support, I leave her office and trot down the stairs. A question strikes me, though, when I turn at the landing—who are the "wolves" Dr. Mewton is so intent on keeping from Sarah?

Chapter Twenty-Six

Sarah

I am analyzing an anomaly in Judson's latest brainprint readouts—apparently he spent several minutes clicking his tongue, a movement that dramatically skewed the results—when I hear a knock on the open door. Dr. Carey stands in the hallway. She's smiling.

"I spoke to Dr. Mewton," she says, entering the operations room, "and she's agreed to arrange transportation for us."

I lower the printout. "Transportation? To where?"

"I thought it might be nice for the two of us to have dinner tonight in La Coruña."

A dozen objections surface in my mind—it's impossible, it's a security breach, we don't speak the native language, we'd have to mind the tides, we don't have a boat or an escort—but all I say is "I can't go."

"Why not?"

I decide to spell out the obvious. "Look, Dr. Carey, you're not a fool. Can't you tell why it's impossible for me to go anywhere?"

She comes closer and leans on the edge of my desk. "Call me 'Aunt Renee,' please. You're not my patient; you're my brother's daughter. We're family and I love you."

"You don't even know me."

"I'm beginning to. And I want to know you better."

I don't have an answer for that.

"I understand that you're frightened," she says, running her hand through her hair. "I'd be terrified at the thought of leaving if I had never traveled outside a place like this. In fact, you should have seen me trembling when I got off the boat to come here. But you won't be alone like I was. I'll be with you."

"Dr. Mewton would never allow—"

"Dr. Mewton has agreed to help us. I think she is eager for you to spread your wings."

Ripples of astonishment swell from an epicenter deep in my stomach, sending shock waves to the tips of my fingers and toes. "She *wants* me to leave the island?"

My aunt releases a short laugh. "It took me a while to convince her, and she says you'll have to travel 'in alias,' but yes, she wants you to go."

My mind clicks like a metronome, shifting from terror to delight with every heartbeat. I am terrified at the thought of leaving, but what a thrill it would be to walk free like other people. Most of the time I feel as though I'm living at the center of the planet, but I would love to experience whatever lies beyond these stone walls and rocky cliffs.

"What sort of alias did she have in mind?"

My aunt smiles again. "Since Spain has so many Muslims, she suggested that you wear a burka. You'll be covered from head to toe."

"A Muslim woman leaving the convent? I don't think so."

"We'll wait until there are no boats in the vicinity. That shouldn't be too difficult."

This information brings relief…and sends a tremor rippling up the back of my neck. Dr. M really does mean to allow it, then.

"We'll go ashore, find a nice restaurant, and have a quiet dinner," my aunt continues. "Then we'll walk around and see some of the town. Don't worry, though—like a good fairy godmother, I promise to have you back before nightfall."

I glance up, almost afraid to speak the words that have bubbled up from someplace deep within me: "Do we have to come back so soon?"

Just before lunch, I step down the hall, nod at the guard on duty—it's Mitch—and feel the back of my neck burn when he smiles.

"Hey, Sarah," he says, relaxing his rigid pose. "How's everything today?"

He shouldn't be so familiar with me, at least not outside Dr. Mewton's office, but his smile sparks an electric tingle at the base of my spine.

"I'm fine." I lower my head and knock on the door.

"Enter."

Dr. M is sitting at her desk, her hands folded atop a stack of documents.

"You wanted to see me?"

"Yes." Her gaze flits over my form. "I suppose you've heard about your aunt's proposed excursion into La Coruña."

I drop into the guest chair. "She said you approved it."

"I had to, or she'd think I was holding you prisoner."

"So you don't want me to go?"

She releases a heavy sigh and gives me the look that tells me I've disappointed her. "Don't you know I only want what's best for you?"

I shrug to hide my confusion.

"Dear girl." Dr. Mewton steps out from behind her desk and moves to stand directly in front of me. Her hand floats up and traces the air, outlining my eye sockets, cheek, and chin. She does not touch me, but closes her eyes and sighs. "Sarah, dear heart, the world is cruel to those who are different. I've done my best to shelter you, but if you go out there I'll be helpless to protect you."

"Why should people be cruel to me? I've never hurt anyone."

"People are vicious to those who are different…especially

those who *look* different. Did I mention the film I watched the other day? A documentary about a poor Haitian girl who had a tumor so large it overtook her face. The other children called her *devil child* and ran screaming every time she went out to play."

I look away from Dr. M's burning gaze.

"I don't want you to be hurt, Sarah. Your aunt has come, and I'm happy that you've had this chance to meet her, but she will never know you like I do. I don't think she knows the world like I do, either, because only someone with no regard for your feelings would even suggest that you leave a safe place and subject yourself to the cruelty of others."

A sough of wind rattles the windowpanes, followed by the soft tapping of blown rain.

"I'm not going to forbid you to go," Dr. Mewton continues, "but remember what happened to John Merrick, the Elephant Man. Think of the poor hunchback of Notre Dame. Why do you think they produced movies about these poor souls? Because what I'm telling you is true—society does not make allowances for those who do not fit the norm. The world offers little kindness for people like us."

I lift my head, startled by her last admission. Dr. Mewton is not deformed, ugly, blind, deaf, or dumb.

"What do you mean?"

"Hmm?" She looks at me, but I can tell she is no longer listening. It is as if she were hearing something that happened in another place, another time.

"Dr. Mewton?" I wave my hand before her wide eyes. "Are you all right?"

Her eyes clear. "Of course. And now there is this." She turns and picks up a package on the desk. "This is for you," she says, sliding it onto my lap. "The choice is yours, Sarah. Go or stay, but if you go, I insist that you follow the security protocols. Take a radio and return before sunset and high tide. If you decide to stay overnight, there'll be no coming back until morning." She shrugs. "I know you won't make things difficult for me."

I clutch the package and feel the soft weight of fabric within its wrapping. The burka. My ticket to walk free for a few hours.

Without speaking, I nod my thanks and leave Dr. Mewton's office.

Chapter Twenty-Seven

Renee

After eating lunch with Judson and Sarah—who doesn't say a word about our upcoming excursion—I walk back to my room while they go upstairs to the operations room. Both of them seem to have an uncommon devotion to duty, and I can't tell if that devotion stems from patriotism, a strong work ethic, or pressure from their superiors.

As I reenter my monastic room, I tell myself none of that matters. Sarah and I will be together tonight, and I will give her a taste of the life Kevin would have wanted her to enjoy.

If Kevin were here, I know, he'd do anything to free his daughter from this place. He'd make sure she had whatever surgeries were necessary for her best chance at a normal life. He might not have access to the "bleeding edge" physicians Dr. Mewton referred to, but he would cart Sarah to hearing specialists and speech therapists. He would invest in orthodontia for her teeth and plastic surgery to improve her appearance. If necessary, he and Diane would have taken out second and third mortgages to cover the expenses.

He would *not* leave Sarah in this isolated facility. My extroverted brother would have hated living in that solitary room upstairs. I'm terrified by the possibility that Sarah might hate it, too…if she had a choice in the matter.

I can't stand this. I can't stand back and watch my brother's daughter function as a lackey for the U.S. government. I also can't see myself leaving this island under a promise not to tell anyone about her. But how can I expose her plight without jeopardizing our relationship? Sarah probably fears change… but she has no real idea what waits beyond this remote island.

If all goes well, I hope I can instill in her a real hunger for life and all its experiences. If I'm successful, she'll press for the help she needs to accomplish her goals.

Feeling restless, I move to the window and look out on the grassy graveyard studded with stone crosses. If I leave without doing anything, Sarah may one day be buried in that field. She deserves more than that—and she deserves to live before she dies.

Off to the west, malignant masses of dark clouds advance toward us, promising an afternoon thunderstorm. I hope the rain moves off before we take the boat to the mainland. I do *not* want to miss this opportunity.

Now that I've found my niece, I'm not going to miss the opportunity to demonstrate that she can live a normal life. But if I'm going to help her, I must approach the situation with caution. Despite all her talk of support and concern for Sarah, Glenda Mewton has profited from my niece's skills. She won't want to see the girl leave.

Maneuvering around Mewton won't be easy. One thing is certain—if I allow myself to become overly emotional, I'm going to end up ranting at that woman, an action that would almost certainly result in my ejection from this facility. They might even cancel my contract and revoke my security clearance. Without those, I'll never be able to help my niece.

I pull my suitcase from beneath the bed and take out my leather folio, then sit cross-legged on the bed and write the date at the top of the page. With the discipline that comes from habit, I set out to record my thoughts and observations. The CIA has hired me to be a psychologist, so that's exactly what I'll be.

I write *S. Sims: Clinical Impressions* on the chart and then stop to think. Because she lacks an expressive face, Sarah has been deprived of one of the chief tools of communication. How has this damaged her emotionally? I have seen evidence of primitive emotion, but her feelings seem to be held in check—whether by natural reserve or by physical limitation, I can't yet say.

The fact is, Elvis has a more expressive face than Sarah.

But even if she possessed normal features, Sarah might still be emotionally handicapped, because she hasn't been exposed to the ordinary trials and lessons children face. Glenda Mewton may have served as a maternal figure in Sarah's childhood, but the woman now maintains a definite distance from her employees. I've seen no evidence of tenderness between her and my niece, heard no endearments. Sarah seems to feel more affection for Shelba and Judson.

I glance at my watch to remind myself of the date. My plan is to stay here less than two weeks, but I'd be willing to extend my stay if I could help Sarah become better equipped for life in a less sheltered environment. Kevin would want me to.

And Becky and her kids will take good care of Elvis.

I believe I can help my niece prepare for interpersonal encounters in the outside world…as long as I can convince her that a new life waits outside these walls.

Without so much as spitting in our direction, the growling thunderheads blow over us and push toward the mainland. When I'm sure they've moved inland, I step outside and walk in the graveyard I was admiring earlier. I'm sitting on a bench near the wall, enjoying the warmth of the sun on my face, when I hear a door slam. I open my eyes, expecting to see Dr. Mewton or Sarah, but instead I find Judson Holmes wheeling toward me.

"Dr. Carey?" he calls, his face lifted to the sun. "You're out here, right?"

Like a fool, I wave. "Over here."

He focuses on my voice, his motorized wheelchair humming as it bumps over the stone pathway edging the grassy graves. "Shelba said she saw you come outside. I wondered if you had a few minutes for me."

"I seem to have an abundance of free time." I shift on the bench in order to face him. "Would you be more comfortable if we talked inside?"

"No, this is nice. I like the fresh air."

He stops just short of the bench and leans forward, his elbows on the armrests of his chair. Unlike Sarah's, Judson's face is a map of human emotion. Though injury has permanently closed his eyelids, they flutter like the heartbeats of baby birds as thought lifts his brows and twists his mouth.

The man is searching for words. Maybe I can help.

"Something you wanted to talk about?" I ask. "Maybe something about Sarah?"

His smile widens, confirming my intuition. "I can't tell you how relieved I am that someone in the real world has taken an interest in the kid."

"I only wish I'd known about her sooner. My heart breaks to think about her being alone all those years."

"Well…she's had Dr. Mewton."

For the first time, I'm grateful this man can't see the expression on my face. "Hmm. She has."

He lifts his chin. "So…do you plan on making a career out of this gig with the company?"

"What's that?"

"Sorry, but I looked up your file. Psychological services, a two-year contract, right?"

"That's right. But I don't think it's going to be long-term."

"I suppose you need to discuss the matter with your husband."

"I have no husband. I might, however, discuss the job with Elvis."

He accepts this with a "Hmm" and a polite nod, then rubs his chin. "Speak often with Elvis, do you?"

"Every day. He's my dog."

The grooves beside his mouth deepen into a relieved smile. "I was beginning to worry about you, Doc."

"I could see that."

"But now that I know you're okay, I wonder if I could ask you a philosophical question?"

"Wouldn't you be more comfortable speaking with Dr. Mewton?"

He barks a laugh. "Would you?"

The man has a point. I cross my legs and smile. "What can I do for you?"

He turns his face to the stone wall. "I know you're not technically with CIA, but you still adhere to the doctor-patient confidentiality rule, right?"

"I won't repeat anything you say—not to anyone."

"Okay." He draws a deep breath. "Do you believe it's possible for a man to atone for his sins?"

The query catches me by surprise. "Don't you think that's a question for a priest or a minister?"

"Haven't you noticed there's a shortage of both around here?"

I laugh. "That sounds odd coming from a man who lives in a convent."

"Ironic, isn't it?" He smiles. "But you haven't answered me. Do you, as a psychologist, believe a man can make things right after living a life filled with wrongs?"

"Do you?"

"I'd forgotten that you shrinks like to answer every question with a question. Is that what they teach you in school?"

"I think, Mr. Holmes, what we try to do is help you sort through your own beliefs."

"If we're going to be friends, you should call me Judson."

"All right…Judson."

"That's better. Okay—so if you're not going to give me your opinion about my past sins, maybe you'll tell me what you think a person has to do in order to be damned forever. I'm pretty sure Hitler qualifies, along with Stalin and some of those other evil characters. I was wondering…if maybe I qualify as well."

Every nerve in my body tingles with alarm as I stare at the edge of the protective wall and listen to the sounds of the sea. I'm not sure I want to hear what Judson is trying to tell me.

"I don't think my opinion is what matters," I begin. "A more pertinent question is why you feel the need for atonement. What is making you feel so guilty, Mr. Holmes?"

His lips thin. "As you said, you're not a priest."

"No."

"And I'm no saint. But because I'd like to be a friend, maybe we shouldn't discuss the gory details of my past. After all, we've only just met."

I tilt my head. "Fair enough."

"Let's just say we break a lot of rules in this business. Lying is at the top of the list because we're trained to deceive. It's all for a good purpose, you understand, and common sense dictates that you can't let your enemy know what you're doing, especially in a time of war."

I laugh softly. "I suppose a covert operation is illegal by definition. After all, if an operation were legal, it wouldn't be covert."

Judson clasps his hands. "Not necessarily, though it might appear that way. But after a while you find yourself lying to your family—still for good reasons—and then you find yourself encouraging other people to lie. And we steal—state secrets, vehicles, weapons, documents, whatever we need to accomplish the goal. And then… Suppose you find yourself watching an agent die…someone who wouldn't be dying if you hadn't brought them into this business."

"Wait a minute. I thought all agents signed up voluntarily—"

"No offense, Dr. Carey, but you watch too much TV." He tosses me a good-natured grin and scrubs his bald brown scalp with his knuckles. "The goal of a CIA officer…almost all officers in the clandestine service…"

"Spies."

"Right. The goal is to recruit foreigners to spy on their countries. The agent is the *native* who has been recruited by a CIA case officer."

I digest this news. "So James Bond…"

"Fantasy."

"And Sydney Bristow…"

"More fantasy—but some of Marshall's technological references came close to the real thing." He leans forward, his face pulling into earnest lines. "So I ask you—given the laundry list of offenses I've committed, do you think I stand a chance of wiping the slate clean?"

"By living and working here?"

"That's right."

"By spending the rest of your life in service to your country?"

"That's the idea."

"But how is this different from what you were doing before?"

The corner of his mouth twists. "Is that a trick question?"

"Not at all. I'm merely trying to understand your thought processes."

A line appears between his brows. "I've given up my family and left everything behind."

I settle back and cross my arms. "Tell me about your family, Judson. Was your mother supportive?"

"When she wasn't working, sure."

"And your father?"

"Don't remember much about my dad. He walked out on us." He sits motionless a moment more, then grins at me. "Caught you shrinkin' me, didn't I?"

"Maybe. Why'd you sign up for the CIA?"

"Saw too many James Bond movies, I guess. I enlisted in

the Air Force straight out of high school and applied to CIA when my hitch was up. That's when I learned that being a spy didn't mean I'd be climbing buildings, stealing secrets, and having drinks with beautiful enemy spies—no, my job would be living for months in foreign countries while I convinced poor local schmucks to steal intel and hand it off to me so I could hand it over to analysts at Langley. And even though I was risking imprisonment practically every day I lived overseas, I couldn't tell anybody back home what I was doing. I had to live my cover, hiding my work even from my wife and kid."

"So why'd you do it?"

"Because I wanted to be a better man than my dad. Wanted to serve, do my duty, tough it out, no matter how hard it was. Wanted to be a big man in front of my boy. An American hero."

His voice takes on a faraway quality as he turns his sightless eyes to the western horizon. "Three years ago, I recruited an agent, Alberto Herrera, who worked for a Spanish pharmaceutical firm. He had a wife and five sons, and he worried about his sons' future. Wanted them to go to university, wanted them to eventually move to America. As I'd been trained, I bribed him with promises of money and visas for his entire family. All he had to do was monitor a shipment from his firm and let me know when it was leaving the country. Simple enough."

He falls silent, and all I hear is the steady crashing of the waves against the rocky cliffs.

"Maybe I should have arranged a dead drop, but I wanted to get the intel and get out of there, so I told Alberto we'd do a brush pass outside a local warehouse. He completed the pass, but he didn't know he'd picked up a tail. Long story short, a couple of bad guys snagged both of us and hauled us to a shack on the beach. Alberto, they killed right away. Me, they tortured. Shot me in both kneecaps, destroyed my eyes with some chemical they'd developed. They said I'd never see my family again…and they were more right than they realized."

Despite my resolve to listen calmly, my stomach shrivels. The flat tone of Judson's voice tells me he's shared this story more than once, but it has not lost its power to move him…or to terrify a listener.

"I thought," I whisper, "you were going to spare me the gory details."

Judson chuffs. "Give yourself some credit, Doc. Not many people could make me spill my guts after ten minutes of small talk."

The silence stretches between us until I ask what happened next.

"I never told them a thing," he says, a hint of satisfaction returning to his voice. "And they left me for dead. I might have died on that beach, but some children found me after a few days. The police put me in a Spanish hospital, where I spent months in a coma as 'John Doe.' Because I'd been in a hurry and sloppy in my protocol, my handler didn't find me until after the hospital had amputated both legs. By that time, CIA had told my wife and son I was missing, presumed dead, and washed out to sea. For a while, I wished that were true."

I force words over the lump in my throat. "The agency brought you to this place?"

He nods. "I've been here ever since. While I was in the coma, my wife badgered the company to make my death official so she could marry my cousin. I'd been stationed overseas so long, I suppose our marriage died long before I did."

"But…don't you want to go back?"

He folds his hands across his chest. "My life insurance is going to pay for my son's college. My wife is happy. And as far as anyone in Lubbock, Texas, knows, Judson Holmes passed away in a random mugging while he was making big bucks in Europe. Now I'm content to be the Candyman and do whatever I can to bring down some very bad people. And I hope—I hope that counts for something."

I wait, recognizing that significant silence in which difficult words are pulled from deep wells of emotion and pains-takingly linked together.

"I do miss my son something fierce. The last thing I wanted to do was abandon him, but that's exactly what I did. And sometimes I wake in the middle of the night and think about Alberto Herrera. Am I to blame for his death? For his kids' poverty? For his wife's loneliness? And if I am, is there anything I can do to make amends? I'm still waiting to feel forgiveness."

"Maybe forgiveness isn't something you feel. Maybe it's something you simply accept."

Easy to say…harder to believe. I understand what Judson is feeling, because lately I've been beating myself up about leaving Sarah alone in this place for so many years.

We sit in the silence, each of us lost in thought, as the wind fills with chimes from the convent bell tower. As I reflect on Judson's story, I can't help thinking about the girl who has brought me to this moment…and the emptiness that compelled me to find her. If I'd been happily married with two or three children of my own, would I have risked so much to get here?

I don't think so. Sarah is all I have in this world, my only remaining relative. Whether or not she's willing to admit it, we are connected by far more than DNA. We share a history and a heritage.

When the bells fall silent, I place my hand on the man's arm. "I don't know what to tell you, Judson. No matter how much we regret it, we can't erase the past. But, at least to some degree, we can determine our future."

"Spoken like a true shrink," he says. "Or a politician."

I laugh softly. "But I'm glad you're the kind of man who thinks about these things. And I'm grateful you're Sarah's friend."

_____

Chapter Twenty-Eight

Sarah

The burka, I discover, is sky-blue, and my aunt laughs when I carry it down to her room and shake it out.

"It looks like a parachute," she says, her eyes wide as she lifts an edge of the billowing fabric, "but it's much more attractive than those black tents I've seen women wearing on CNN."

I lift the burka and turn it, but all I see is a solid wall of fabric. No armholes, no opening for the neck. "How is it worn?"

"Here." Renee plucks at an area of blue mesh not much bigger than the back of my hand. "I think this part goes over your eyes, the band behind it fits around your head. Everything else just…hangs."

"At least the fabric's not heavy."

With Renee's help, I pull the cotton garment over my head and let it fall to the floor. The fabric covers even the laces of my sneakers, and the headband feels tight around my skull.

My aunt's face twists in a strange expression when she settles the strap of her purse on her shoulder. "I hate what these do to women," she says in a voice so low I can barely hear it, "but today, maybe, I'll learn to be grateful."

Imprisoned in my blue tent, I feel strangely light-headed. Because my face is completely covered except for the mesh rectangle over my eyes, I have no peripheral vision. Fabric also covers my speech processor, so every sound seems muffled and indistinct.

Still, I'm excited at the prospect of leaving the convent. My pulse has increased, and so has my respiration rate. If I was hooked up to a polygraph at this moment, I could give the examiner my true name and he'd swear I was lying.

Eager and unsteady on my feet, I keep my eyes fixed on the back of Renee's head as she leads me to the elevator. One of the guards is there—Mitch, I think—and he snaps to attention when he sees us approaching.

"Going down, ladies?"

Renee clings to her purse strap with both hands. "I trust Dr. Mewton has approved our departure?"

"Yes, ma'am, the boat and driver are here. I'll escort you to the dock."

We step into the elevator and I wonder if Mitch can sense my excitement. I must be exuding it like a scent, but he presses the D button as if he escorts disguised CIA employees out of the convent every night.

Mitch glances over his shoulder and smiles…at my aunt. "Nice night for a trip into town. Made any special plans?"

She returns his smile. "I thought we'd be impulsive."

"I hear there's a good Basque-style restaurant in the town center. Pintxos, they call it."

I stare at the two of them, amazed at the ease they display with one another. Mitch doesn't even know my aunt, but he is smiling and telling her about a restaurant without her even having to ask for a recommendation.

Is the entire world friendly, or are things this easy only for beautiful people?

I pause as the elevator door slides open. "Should we—is Dr. Mewton going to see us off?"

Renee smiles. "You don't think they'd have a boat waiting without her approval, do you?"

"No, but—"

"It's okay, Sarah. You're a grown woman. You can come and go as you please."

"In alias."

"However you want to go out."

I step onto the dock. Though I've seen this area many times through the security cams, I haven't been down here in months. The place seems brighter than normal, and far more colorful. The wet wood beneath my feet is dark brown and the water the same color as my burka. The boat at the dock has a bright yellow stripe around its edge and the name *Banana Split* painted on the side.

I feel like Dorothy, who went to sleep in black-and-white Kansas and woke up in Technicolor Oz.

My aunt looks back at Mitch, who is waiting on the dock. "No Father Paul tonight?"

"Father Paul's off duty," Mitch says.

"He's hearing confession," the driver of the boat adds, and I'm not sure he's joking until I hear Mitch laugh.

The man in the boat is not wearing clerical garb, but a short-sleeved shirt and a white cap. He extends his hand to help me into the boat. "Hello, ladies," he says, smiling at Renee. He's holding my hand but looking at her, which makes me wonder if the burka is some sort of invisibility cloak.

I don't mind being invisible—the burka has given me freedom I've never known before. I am used to strangers who look at me and quickly turn away. I usually turn away, too, but behind this mesh wall, I am free to stare back.

When Renee and I are seated, the driver starts the engine and turns in his seat to guide the boat out of the cavern. I don't watch him, but study Mitch instead, grateful for this oppor-tunity to look without anyone—especially Mitch—noticing.

"I had forgotten how small this entrance is," I shout over the growl of the engines. "It's been a long time since I visited the dock."

Because the tide is low, we are able to motor through the

mouth of the cavern without any trouble. Within minutes, we're on the open water, skimming the waves like a rocket. I hang on to the railing, the metal slippery beneath the thin fabric of the burka, and gasp when chilly spray splashes into my eyes. Beside me, Renee smiles and braces herself against the back of my seat. Our driver says nothing, but guides the boat toward a narrow strip of land that rises out of the sea.

Despite the warmth of the late-afternoon sun, shivers track down my spine like melting bits of ice. Judson and Renee keep telling me that the world is a wonderful place, but Dr. Mewton frequently points out horrible stories of cruelty, mayhem, and murder. Dorothy's Oz was a beautiful emerald city, but it was also home to a malignant and treacherous witch.

Which will we discover on this trip? The denizens of a friendly coastal town, or people with malicious intent?

I glance at Renee, who has lifted her face to the sun as the wind streams through her short hair. She is smiling as if she hasn't a care in the world, so I'll try to follow her example.

Filled with anticipatory adrenaline, I breathe in the clean scent of unrestricted air and tremble beneath my blessed blue tent.

As we draw closer to shore, beyond the port I see orange tiled roofs, green terraces, and tan houses with many windows. Several of these buildings are as large as the Convent of the Lost Lambs, and for an instant I wonder if they are hospitals. Surely not. No single city could have so many sick people.

We are heading toward a marina filled with scores of smaller boats, many of them featuring tall masts that rise from their decks like toothpicks. The driver cuts the engine as we approach, then he glides up to a dock. The sun-spangled sea has shifted to the color of celery and is slapping rhythmically against the pilings.

The driver turns to my aunt. "You'll call?"

"I have the number," she says, standing. "And I know the return protocol."

I'm glad she does, because Dr. Mewton didn't tell me anything about how to get back home.

Renee reaches out as the boat sways on the water, and the man catches her hand, giving her a smile. When she looks at him, I sense that unspoken communication is passing between them.

"Miss?" After helping Renee onto the dock, the driver offers me his hand, too, but his eyes do not meet mine as he helps me step onto the dock. When I have safely joined my aunt, he waves at another man on the dock and helps the second man fasten the lines.

"Come." Renee grips my elbow through the folds of fabric. "Let's get away from the smell of saltwater and go into town. We'll hail a taxi."

I follow, but it's hard to walk behind her and take in the sights through a four-by-six-inch mesh window. And there is so much to see—sleek sailing vessels, flat racers, commercial boats, extravagant yachts. Dark-skinned sailors, fair-haired men, and women—not many, but a few, most of them peering out from cabins in the sailboats or sunning themselves on the decks.

With a quick step, my aunt leads me onto a main street, then she drops my elbow and thrusts her hand into the air. I am swiveling from right to left, trying to scan my surroundings and decipher the Spanish street signs. Before I realize what has happened, a car stops at the curb. My aunt opens the back door, nudges me toward it, and bends to tell the driver that we want to go to Pintxos in the city center. He taps a meter, then Renee slides in behind me and we lurch forward.

I can't believe it. I can barely sit still, for there is much to see and absorb, but the cab stops before I have begun to take in the city. My aunt hands the driver some money—euros, I think—and then pulls me from the cab.

I stand on the sidewalk and stare at the cobbled walkway before me, dazzled beyond belief. The slanting street opens to a row of buildings that hunch close together, their orange roofs tilting into one another, their porches festooned with fervid blossoms and bright-hued doors. Tufts of moss and greenery grow between the ancient stones beneath our feet, walkways that have been worn smooth by the passing of so many feet over the years.

Now *my* feet will walk over them, too.

"This way," Renee says, and I allow myself to be tugged down the walkway. My aunt moves forward with fluid strides while I gape at store windows that overflow with colors and twinkling lights and jewels splashed over velvet cushions. Several windows feature statues arranged in awkward poses, their truncated bodies dressed in tunics bordered with sequins and beads and fuzzy feathers that are nothing like the stiff castoffs I occasionally find in the graveyard.

Must we be in such a hurry?

I'm about to ask, but Renee wraps her hands around my elbow, which she has again managed to find through the concealing folds of my disguise.

"What would you like to eat?" she asks, her gaze skimming the storefronts.

I hesitate. "Could I get a hamburger?"

She looks at me and laughs. "You're kidding, right?"

I shake my head.

"Is that a no?" She peers through my mesh veiling. "Well, we can probably get a hamburger…if we find a restaurant with an American menu. Maybe over there."

The restaurant is not Pintxos, and for an instant I'm stunned that she'd be willing to deviate from her original plan. She's frighteningly spontaneous, but if this other place has a hamburger…

She points across the street to a small courtyard filled with tables and potted trees. A chalkboard stands on the sidewalk, but I can't read the language.

"Let's check it out." She drops my elbow and jogs across

the road with a grace that leaves me breathless. Am I supposed to follow? Is she coming back? Did she mean for me to wait, or does she expect me to join her?

I hesitate, confused by the vast array of choices, then I lift my chin and move into the road. I haven't taken two steps when the sharp blast of a horn rattles my speech processor. A car screeches to a halt, its bumper striking my thigh with the force of a blow. I duck to protect my leg, then a man begins to yell at me in a language I don't recognize. A woman is shouting, too. I don't know where all the noise is coming from, but finally I turn and see the man leaning out his car window, his face red, his fist pounding the air.

A woman grabs my shoulders and steers me out of the road. She is jabbering in Basque, which I don't understand. When she releases me, I realize that Renee is awkwardly patting me through the burka. "Are you hurt? Is anything broken?"

I rub my injured thigh. "I'm okay. He only bumped my leg."

"Are you sure? Can you walk?"

By this time the driver has come over. He is still yelling, though I can't understand a word. Renee utters a curt *"¡Silencio!"* then she asks again if I'm all right. I straighten my spine and take three steps, then give an exaggerated nod to indicate that I'm uninjured. "See?" I wave my hands so the burka flaps in the breeze. "No blood. I'm okay."

The driver flips the stub of his cigarette at my feet and stalks back to his car.

"Some men," Renee says, her voice dry, "are still living in the dark ages. I'm sorry about that."

"It wasn't your fault."

"I shouldn't have left you on the curb—I forgot you're wearing a bedsheet. Those things are so unsafe, I can't imagine why anyone believes they're a reasonable idea."

With a firm grip on my upper arm, she directs me toward a courtyard and says something to the waiter in stilted

Spanish. He asks a question and Renee answers, her voice low and measured.

I had been hoping we could sit at a table near the sidewalk, but the host escorts us inside the building and leads us to a booth against the wall. It's not until I slide onto the low bench that I realize what Renee has to be thinking—a burka is a good disguise, but it's not good for eating. How do Muslim women do it?

"I know." Renee catches my eye once the waiter is gone. "I'm afraid you're going to have to take it off if you want to eat. Either that, or take your plate into the tent with you."

"I can wait a while, can't I?"

"Sure."

A waitress comes up, offers us a stiff cardboard menu, and smiles at my aunt, ignoring me.

"Un vaso de agua, por favor," Renee says. *"Dos vasos."*

When the waitress has gone, my aunt asks if I can read the menu.

"Doesn't matter. All I want is a McDonald's hamburger."

She laughs. "I'm sorry, honey, but you can only get one of those at a McDonald's. They might have a regular hamburger, though."

"Okay. That's what I want."

When the waitress returns, my aunt orders *dos consomes de pollo, dos ensaladas verdes, y dos hamburguesas.* I give my menu back to the waitress, content to play the role of non-speaking Muslim friend.

"So," Renee says once the waitress has moved away. "What do you think of the city?"

"I—I don't know. It's a lot to take in at once. But it's interesting."

I say this to be kind, deliberately omitting any mention of the man who hit me with his car and then screamed at me…or the aunt who's dragged me over the sidewalk at a breathless pace. I'm determined to remain optimistic.

"There's a whole planet outside the convent, Sarah. And there's no reason you can't enjoy it."

I nod because I've already heard this speech—and because I've been distracted by a lovely little girl at the table next to us. She can't be more than three or four, and she is everything I'd imagine the perfect child to be—round-faced, chubby-cheeked, and rosebud lipped, with sparkling dark eyes and shiny curls. Her mother has tied red ribbons in her hair, and her father smiles every time he looks at her. The parents are trying to convince the child to drink her milk, but the little girl wants nothing to do with it—

I gasp when she deliberately tips her milk glass, then pushes out her lower lip.

My aunt chuckles from across the table. "Little minx," she says, keeping her voice low. "Your dad was a lot like that as a child. Kevin would do anything for attention, even disobey. He kept Mother on her toes."

I shift my gaze to my aunt. "What about your father?"

Renee looks down at her hands. "Your grandfather died a few months before Kevin did. Dad was a good man, but he was always working. He and Kevin did a lot of guy things together, but he wasn't into girl things, so he wasn't around much when I was growing up." Her voice softens. "Or maybe I just don't remember him being around."

The waitress comes with two water glasses, and this time she glances at me as she sets them on the table. I wait until she leaves, then I begin to gather up the yards of cotton that envelop me. "What are 'boy things'?"

"Baseball, football, camping, fishing—all the things boys like to do with their fathers."

"And 'girl things'?"

She smiles. "These days girls do pretty much whatever boys do. But they also like babies…and clothes."

I pull several yards of blue fabric onto my lap, then cross my arms and pull the burka off in one swift move. After bundling the fabric and squeezing it between my side and the wall, I smooth my hair.

"That's better." Renee smiles again. "I'd rather talk to you than to a mesh square."

I lift the glass and sip my water. My nerves feel electric, as if unfamiliar impulses are traveling up and down my limbs. Maybe this is how Judson and my father felt when they were sent on their first missions. Naked. Exposed.

"You know, you can tell a lot about a person by studying their face," Renee says, sliding a straw into her glass. "Our expressions elicit reactions from others, and often what we say with our face is more important than what we say in words."

I sip my water again, not sure why she's talking about faces while she's looking at mine. Isn't it obvious that the only reaction my face elicits is disgust?

"You like movies, Sarah," she continues. "Haven't you noticed that the best movie stars speak volumes with their expressions?"

"I always thought that was because they're trained actors."

"They are, but on-screen they're only doing what other people do naturally every day. With additional surgery and some training, you could learn how to use your face, too."

I stir my water with my straw and wonder what she's getting at.

"Once," she says, smiling at her glass, "I had a patient with Mobius Syndrome. She couldn't smile at all until she had surgery, and she couldn't afford the surgery until she reached adulthood. Once she was able to smile, she had to learn all the ways she could use a smile to communicate with others."

I stop stirring my water. "So if I had surgery, would I have to learn these things, too?"

"Some things. But you could do it, Sarah, because you're bright and motivated. You can learn anything you want to learn."

Her words give me confidence, but I'm still not sure what

she's proposing. Our conversation is interrupted when the waitress approaches with a tray in her arms.

"Dos ensaladas verdes," she says, placing two small salads on the table. *"¿Quiere algo mas?"* She has spoken to Renee, but her gaze cuts to me as she asks her question. And her face, which had been set in straight, regular lines, twists as her eyes widen and a frightened squeak cuts through the clink of silverware and the chatter of customers.

The guests at the nearest table turn in our direction. The parents frown and the toddler screams. The mother, after casting a disapproving look in my direction, tries to comfort the child, but the little girl is wailing in earnest.

I have terrified her.

I turn my face to the wall and bring up a hand to shield my face. "Perhaps we should go."

"Sarah, you have every right to be here."

"I don't want to cause a problem."

"This isn't your fault. *You're* not the problem, they are. They shouldn't be so judgmental."

"You can't tell me—" my voice quavers "—that the *child* is being judgmental."

Renee closes her eyes and pulls her purse onto her lap. "If you want to go, we will."

"I want to go."

Before she can protest again, I dive back into the burka and slink out of the booth, a silent blue shadow intent on retreat. I make it as far as the restaurant entrance, then I trip on the hem of my concealing tent and fall headlong into the bustling crowd.

And as my aunt and the host help me to my feet, I realize that Dr. Mewton is right. I am a monster and the world is not a safe place for monsters.

Like Frankenstein and Quasimodo, I'll be safer if I'm hidden away.

Chapter Twenty-Nine

Renee

On the bumpy ride back to the convent—in a different boat, and with a different driver—I breathe in the scent of sea salt and search for comforting words to offer Sarah. I had wanted this excursion to be a joyful and intoxicating taste of life, and I had hoped to broach the subject of further surgeries to encourage her to make plans for a life outside the CIA. But our experience in the restaurant ruined my strategy, and the little girl's regrettable reaction damaged Sarah's confidence.

Yet how can I prevent such things? Short of forewarning people of Sarah's condition—an act that would result in a life as phony as the one at Convent of the Lost Lambs—I can do nothing.

We live in a society where nonconformity upsets people and misfortune is frequently mocked. Beauty wins praise and approval, ugliness invites ostracism and derision. I would love to help Sarah improve her life, but I can't change the world.

Five years ago, on a chilly Friday in April, I couldn't even change one man's mind.

I should have known something was wrong in the weeks before that night. Charlie had begun to grow distant, but I attributed his silence to problems at work. I understood career pressure, and as the head of an architectural firm, he had several big projects under development.

But even when I came home to find Charlie's suitcases standing in the foyer, I didn't consider the obvious explanation. I saw him sitting in his overcoat in the dining room with his keys on the table. "You have a trip?" I asked, dropping my purse to the carpet. "Did I forget to put it on the calendar?"

"Renee." His faint smile held a touch of sadness. "I'm leaving."

"Do you need a ride to the airport?"

As I pulled my scarf from my collar, he reached up to catch my hand. "I'm not going on a trip. I'm leaving *you*."

The emphasis on that last word was like a dagger to the heart. Quick, sharp, sudden. No drawn-out fights or probationary period for us, no undignified arguments or public brawls. Our marriage would die not gradually, but in a single night.

Unless…

"Charlie—" I clung to the hand he had offered "—I'm sorry. We seem to have neglected each other lately, but we can turn that around. We can take a few days off, make time for each other, do the things we used to enjoy doing together—"

His eyes were damp and filled with pain as he pulled his hand from my grasp. "Too late for all that, Dr. Carey. Time and again over the last five years I've asked you to do one thing or another, but you were always occupied with your work. You've taught me to live without you, and I've learned my lessons well."

My stomach churned in a moment of pure panic—for the first time in months, an aspect of my well-ordered life was slipping out of my control. I hadn't expected this, hadn't planned for it. Charlie and a baby and family time were part of my future, items at the top of the list for next year or the year after.

He stood and slipped his hands into his gloves. "I'll have my lawyer send over the papers next week—everything's been arranged. I think you'll find I've been more than fair."

I sank onto a dining room chair as Charlie crossed into the

foyer, picked up his suitcases, and opened the front door, sending a blast of frigid air into the house.

I didn't cry, not then. My sense of loss went beyond tears, and my wounds had not yet begun to bleed. One thing, however, made sense to my mind: we do teach by example, and Charlie was right…by my neglect, I had taught him to live without me.

What has years of loneliness and isolation taught Sarah?

My niece and I do not speak as the boat takes its loud journey back to the island. By the time we pull into the cavern, my heart is so filled with regrets that I can't remain silent.

"During my residency," I say after the driver cuts the engine, "I once met an adult patient with cherubism—a condition that causes the lower jaw and cheeks to grow to outsize proportions. The patient frequently found herself being stared at—and, yes, some people were shockingly rude to her. But she came to terms with her condition and came to accept it. When I met her, she told me that she considered her uniqueness a gift."

"Is that—" the voice coming from beneath the burka is icy "—because all of mankind's problems can be solved with psychology?"

I meet her cool gaze. "No. My patient's attitude was the product of unusual strength and courage. You have those same qualities, Sarah."

"How would you know that?"

"Because I knew your father. I see him in you. And I know he would not want you to let real opportunities for change slip through your fingers."

Sarah falls silent, not speaking even when the driver offers his hand and helps her onto the dock. She hesitates when one of the guards calls out a greeting, then she strides toward the elevator, leaving me to clamber out of the boat alone.

I can't blame her for being upset. As I thank the driver and make my way across the dock, I realize that I'm failing in all

I came her to do. Since learning about Sarah, all I've wanted is to help her find a new life, but all I've done is demonstrate how painful life can be. Why should she choose to endure suffering when she can remain content in confinement?

I'm afraid she will slip away and go to bed before I can speak to her again, but she waits for me in the elevator. I nod a greeting to the guard. "You don't have to escort us upstairs. I know which buttons to push."

"Sorry, ma'am, but it's protocol."

"Thank you, but we've had a rough night. Please, let us have this elevator to ourselves."

The young man bites his lip and glances up at the security camera, then steps out of the car. When the sliding door has closed, Sarah says, "He's going to be in so much trouble."

"An elevator guard—I've never heard of anything so silly." I pull the confining burka from Sarah's head. "Look," I tell her, grasping at my last hope, "I don't blame you for not wanting to enter a world that can be cruel to anyone who doesn't measure up to whatever's considered normal. But they are doing amazing things in reconstructive surgery today. I'm almost positive you would be a great candidate for a face transplant."

Her expression doesn't change, but her eyes glitter with something that might be interest…or cynicism. "A face transplant…like that Nicolas Cage movie, *Face/Off?* Complete science fiction."

"The movie, yes, but French surgeons performed a successful partial transplant in 2005. The technology is available. If you're willing, Dr. Mewton and I could investigate the possibilities. We could make some calls and get your name on a donor list."

She hugs the crumpled burka to her chest. "It can't happen."

"Why couldn't it? I know you've had your fill of surgery, but the pain would be relatively brief. The result would improve the rest of your life."

She leans against the wall and closes her eyes. The car comes to a halt at the first floor and the door opens.

I step forward, convinced that I've lost her, but her whispered response halts me on the threshold. "I'd like to look different, but leaving here wouldn't be easy. I felt…*lost* out there."

"I could help. I could prepare you for the changes you'll encounter once you leave this place."

She exhales softly and blinks, inadvertently drawing my attention to a trace of wetness on her cheek. "I'll think about it. Good night."

Chapter Thirty

Sarah

I don't know why I told my aunt I'd think about a face transplant. Maybe I did it to get her off my back; maybe I want her to like me. I know she came here because she loved my father, but that doesn't mean she can love someone as ugly and freakish as I am.

I step off the elevator on the second floor and begin the walk down the hallway. The lights are off in the operations and conference rooms, but two guards are seated in the security center, their eyes fixed on the surveillance monitors. They've probably already reported Clint for stepping out of the elevator when Aunt Renee asked him to.

I stop outside the security station and study the backs of the guards' heads. Neither of them, I decide, is Mitch. Since he wasn't on the dock, he must be back in the city, maybe sleeping in his apartment.

I close my eyes as an unexpected wave of yearning rises from some place deep inside me. I know I shouldn't even entertain the idea, but what if—what if I could get in the boat and go to Mitch's apartment? What would it be like to eat dinner across the table from him, or lounge on a sofa with him while we watch a movie? Thousands of women do these things with their boyfriends every day, so why not me? On some days I'd happily surrender my right arm if I could have twenty-four hours of normal life with a man like Mitch.

I shift my focus from the guards to the glass in the door and smirk at my reflection, though I am a long way from genuine humor. I shake my foolish dreams from my head and continue down the hall, tiptoeing past Judson's door until I reach my own. I slide my key card through the scanner and let myself in.

My home is only a small room cluttered with books, computers, and posters, but it is the one space where I feel totally comfortable.

I toss the burka onto my chair and step into the bathroom, where I run water in the sink and pump antiseptic cleanser into my palm. I lift my gaze to the mirror and begin to soap my face, watching my reflection as Aunt Renee watched hers.

In that instant, my surroundings fade away and I see myself as the little girl in La Coruña saw me.

I *am* a freak. A lashless, lipless mask with ribbed and quilted skin. One of my eyes hangs lower than the other, and my nose is far too short for my face. Tracks from various surgeries stretch across my cheeks, and my lower jaw juts too far forward for balance or beauty.

I can't even blame nature for my misshapen appearance. If I'd been left alone after birth, nature would have taken care of her own mistake, but Dr. Mewton and the other CIA doctors stepped in to save my life. Their surgeries gave me teeth, a jaw, hearing, and sight, but my face bears the marks of their tinkering and my nerves will never forget the pain.

As a child, I was helpless to explain how much I was suffering. If I submit to a surgeon's knife again, am I not asking for more of the same agony?

I bend over the sink and splash away suds as I wish I could splash away my confusion.

When I wake the next morning, I suspect that my mind

pondered the possibility of additional surgery even while I slept. My brain feels as if it's made of gelatin, my limbs are heavy with rigor. The eastern sky is delivering a bright new day, but I feel as though I've been grappling with an enemy all night long.

But who, exactly, is my enemy?

I'm not quite sure what to make of my aunt. She's bright, and she seems to care about me, but does she really know what she's talking about? Dr. M doesn't seem to trust her, and I've always relied on Dr. Mewton. Judson, on the other hand, likes my aunt a lot, and he seems to have good instincts about people.

After showering and slipping into clean scrubs, I jog down the stairs and step out into the graveyard. I need a fresh perspective, a neutral place to sort out my thoughts.

The cool air of early morning floats around my arms, which are bare to my elbows. The rising sun resembles a blood-red balloon and its rays have tinted the waters crimson. The day will be warm, for there are few clouds in the sky and not much of a breeze. If only my mind were so uncluttered.

I can't stop thinking about the possibilities. I could have a new face and a new beginning. Do I deserve it? No. Do I have the courage to go through with it? Maybe not. Life would be easier if I stayed here with my movies and my computers, but I would always be haunted by questions of what might have been…

I wander among the dew-drenched gravestones until I reach the stone bench, then I sit and stare at the graveyard, not caring that the seat of my pants will be damp when I go to breakfast.

Did these nuns freely accept their seclusion when they lived at the Convent of the Lost Lambs? Or did they ever need to confess a yearning for another life, even another day, lived beyond these walls?

I stand and plant my feet on the base of the wall, then peer over the edge. The waves in the bay are so high they look like rolling hills. Hills that might be planted with flowers and trees and grass in a little village somewhere else…anywhere else.

Odd, that I never felt the isolation of this place until my aunt arrived. I have watched the world through films; I have tasted it through books. As moving as those experiences have been, they were nowhere as exhilarating as walking through the city center of La Coruña. Despite the confusion and discomfort of the burka, I felt as though I had left my seat and walked straight into a movie.

Could I cope with that level of reality every day? Am I capable of living in a place where I'd be free to do what I wanted? Will I ever know what it means to love?

My questions tremble in the breeze, unasked and unanswered.

In *The Shawshank Redemption,* Red tells Andy about men who have become institutionalized. They get so accustomed to the pattern of prison life that they can't function on the outside.

What if I am one of those people?

My stomach drops when I hear the sound of a door opening. I exhale in relief when I recognize the hum of Judson's wheelchair.

The hum stops. "You out here, kid?"

"I am," I call, sinking back to my bench. "Your instincts are good."

His face turns toward me, like a flower seeking the sun. "When you weren't in your room, I figured I'd find you here. It is a good spot for thinking."

Leave it to Jud to know I'd be deep in thought. Even though he's never seen me, sometimes I think he knows me better than I know myself. I know he understands me better than Dr. Mewton does.

He rolls up next to me, stopping when he feels the brush

of my fingertips. For a long moment we sit in the red rays of sunrise, saying nothing.

"So—are you going to tell me about your trip into the big city?" he finally asks.

"It was interesting," I answer. "Made a baby cry, freaked out a waitress, tripped and fell in front of dozens of people— Oh, and got hit by a car."

"Were you hurt?"

"No."

His face twists in an odd expression, then he shakes his head. "I don't get it, kiddo. Being deaf isn't that big a deal, and though you're a gold-plated genius, I've never gotten the feeling you're too cerebral for public consumption. So what aren't you telling me?"

How do I tell him? I drop my hand to his arm and squeeze.

"Sarah? What's wrong?"

I lift my face to the sky. Only when I open my mouth to answer do I taste the salt of tears and realize that I've been crying.

"Jud…"

"I'm here, kiddo."

I grasp his hands and slip to my knees. As his brows rush together, I place his warm, gentle palms on the wet planes of my face. For a moment he doesn't move, then his sensitive fingers rise to my hairline and flutter down, gently probing the areas where my eyes, cheeks, nose, and lips should be.

"Lord have mercy," he finally says, dropping his hands into his lap. "You poor baby."

I turn and sink to the ground, resting my shoulder against the solidity of one of his sawed-off stumps. His hand falls on my hair, and we sit without speaking until the tower bell chimes the morning Angelus.

When the last chime drifts away on the breeze, Judson's broad hand pats the top of my head. "Thank you," he says, "for being brave enough to show me your scars. But you're a fool, Sarah Sims, if you think you've just shown me your true self."

I turn and gape at him, as surprised by his words as by his unsympathetic tone. "Did you just call me a fool?"

"Turn up your hearing aid, girl, so I won't have to repeat myself. Yes, for a genius you can be remarkably dull-witted."

I scramble to my feet and sputter as I wipe damp gravel from the back of my pants. "Why— And to think I trusted—"

"Calm down, kiddo. So you have facial scars, so what? You're living in a hospital. The agency would do anything for you. Get yourself fixed up and get out of here."

"You're one to talk."

"I'm not the individual under discussion, *you* are. I've lived in the world—I've created a family and left my mark. You haven't even scratched the surface of life."

I seethe in silence, desperately searching for some verbal missile to fling at him.

"Things are beginning to make sense," Jud says. "Your aunt—she's urging you to get help, isn't she?

"How do you know that?"

He snorts. "Come on, kid, give me credit for having learned a few things in my lifetime. Well, your aunt's right. She must have leaped quite a few hurdles to get here, so don't blow her off. Listen to her, Sarah. Whatever she's offering, take it."

I swallow hard and drop to the bench. "She wants me to get surgery. A face transplant."

Jud's brows rise. "Wow."

"But—what if I'm damaged beyond repair? I'm like Brooks Hatlen in *The Shawshank Redemption*. I can't imagine living…out there."

Judson's hand reaches across the empty space between us and finds mine. "Brooks was the inmate with the bird, right?"

"Yeah."

"Then you know that one day that bird's mama pushed him out of the nest. You can fly, Sarah. You only have to spread your wings."

I can only squeeze his hand in answer. He's obviously feeling a lot more confident than I am.

Chapter Thirty-One

Renee

By the time I make it to the dining room for breakfast, Sarah, Judson, and Dr. Mewton are already seated. When I take my place at the table, Sarah puts down her spoon, glances at Judson, and then looks directly at me. "I want to have the face transplant," she says. "I've decided. I'll do whatever it takes to look like a normal person."

Dr. Mewton's face flushes, her mouth pursing into a tight knot. "Sarah, you can't be serious."

"I am. Aunt Renee said she's going to check into the details. I'll have the transplant and whatever reconstructions are necessary to have a normal face."

"But you said you didn't want any more surgeries. You may not remember all the pain you suffered, but I do. When you were in such agony you couldn't sleep, I was the one who rocked you until you stopped sniffling."

"Sure, you helped, and so did the morphine," Sarah quips, and I have to admire her quick wit. "But what did the old mermaid tell the little princess? 'One must suffer to be beautiful.'"

"Hans Christian Andersen." I meet her gaze and smile. "I've always loved that story."

"You want to be beautiful?" Mewton snorts. "Sarah, so many things are more important than physical beauty. You are brilliant and talented and skilled. Plus, the company depends on you. I depend on you. You can't forget that."

Sarah picks up her spoon. "I'll work when I can. But if medical coverage is a benefit of my employment, then the company shouldn't begrudge me the time to finish the job they started years ago."

Glenda Mewton jerks her head in my direction. "What about Dr. Carey? She'll be leaving soon. If you're serious about this, you're going to need weeks of preparatory therapy, a regimen of immunosuppressive drugs, and at least two teams of sophisticated microsurgeons. I don't have time to—"

"I have time," I interrupt, surprising even myself. When every face at the table turns toward me, I know what my next step will be. "This is part of my work for the agency, isn't it? I'll give Sarah all the time she needs."

Ignoring Dr. Mewton's glower, I reach across the table and pat Sarah's hand. "I may have missed your childhood, but I'll be here for you now. I'll oversee the research, talk to the surgeons, whatever you need me to do. We'll get you ready, not only for your transplant, but for your new life."

Sarah elbows Judson, who holds up his hand for her triumphant high-five. And as Dr. Mewton sighs and closes her eyes, I wonder what, exactly, I have promised to do.

But I have no regrets. I've come halfway around the world to assure Kevin's daughter that she is not alone. I will not walk away from her now.

Chapter Thirty-Two

Sarah

I'm working in the operations room when I receive an instant message from Dr. M: *Need to see you at once. My office.*

What could she want? I stand and tell Judson I've been summoned, then head down to Dr. M's office. She's sitting at her desk, obviously waiting.

"You wanted to see me?"

"Come in, Sarah. And close the door behind you, please."

I sit in the chair across from her desk and blink when she lifts a trembling hand to smooth her hair away from her forehead. "I'm so upset I don't know where to begin."

"Dr. Mewton?"

"Give me a moment, please." She leans back and squeezes the bridge of her nose. "Sarah, about your announcement at breakfast this morning…"

"Yes?"

"I wouldn't get my hopes up. The surgery your aunt mentioned is highly risky, still experimental, and fraught with complications. I don't want to see you pin your hopes on this procedure and then be disappointed."

I fold my hands and try to remain calm. "I still want to investigate it."

"But why? Aren't you happy here? Haven't we done

enough for you? We have given you everything you ever needed—food, shelter, clothing, medical care, affection…"

"What about freedom? Choices? A chance to discover that I might have a life apart from the agency?" I struggle to find words that won't hurt this woman who has given me so much. "I'm grateful for everything, Dr. M, but if there's a chance I could live like other people, I want to take it."

"Didn't you learn anything from your experience last night? I heard your trip into the city didn't go so well."

I close my eyes. "I learned that living among other people with this face would be…difficult. So I want a transplant."

"Have you considered what might happen if the transplant fails? You don't have enough spare skin on your body to replace a skin graft."

I swallow hard. "If it fails…I'll cope. I can't be any worse off than I am now."

Dr. M chokes out a laugh. "I don't think that's true."

"How do you know?" I lift my chin and meet her hard eyes. "In a way, I'm already dead to the world. Fewer than twenty people even know I exist. Fewer than ten know me personally. What is living, if it's not knowing and being known?"

She breathes deep and rubs her hands over her arms. "There are worse things than anonymity," she says. "Far worse things."

"Oh, yeah?"

She raises her gaze in a swift, sharp look. "I don't like to speak of the past, but trust me—being used is worse than being ignored. The world is filled with people who will hurt you if you let them get too close."

Chapter Thirty-Three

Renee

Once I reach my room, I launch into preparations for Project Sarah. The restless feeling that has plagued me ever since my arrival has vanished; now that I have a clear goal, a new energy sparks in my blood.

Now…if only I can pursue my goals without upsetting Glenda Mewton's highly important and highly classified applecart.

I pull my laptop from its case and boot it up. I'm relieved to discover that the convent has a Wi-Fi system in place. I may be breaking some kind of federal law by piggybacking off this signal, but Dr. Mewton can arrest me if she wants to. I'm not here to steal government secrets; I'm here to care for my niece.

Ten minutes later, I'm ready to toss my laptop across the room. The internal antenna or receiver or whatever it is absolutely refuses to log on.

I consider throwing a tempter tantrum, but am restrained by the saving grace of second thought. My niece, a computer savant, is working only a few yards away.

I scoop my laptop into my arms and trot up the stairs, happy to see that various guards no longer find it necessary to stop me at every floor. Apparently Glenda Mewton is beginning to trust me…at least a little.

I find Sarah in the computer-filled operations room on the

second floor. She looks up, distracted, when I call her name, and it takes a moment for her to focus on me. "Yes?"

"I'm having trouble accessing the network. The what-chamacallit doesn't seem to be working. Can you help?"

I hesitate at the threshold like a student awaiting permission to enter the teachers' lounge, but she waves me in. She opens my laptop, clears the screen of everything but a blinking cursor, and types in a string of numbers and dots. The computer responds with an even longer string of numbers, letters, and dots, then she hands the machine back to me. "You're in."

"It's fixed?"

"Yes."

"What'd you do? Are you some kind of wizard?"

One corner of her mouth rises in a small smile. "I pinged my computer. See that number?" She taps the string on the screen. "That's my IP address. I told your computer to look for my computer, and it did. The fact that you were able to find me proves we're connected."

"So your computer is found at cyberspace address 172.16.0.0?"

"Something like that."

"That's almost the year I was born...followed by my favorite age. Thanks, Sarah."

"No problem."

Grateful for the help, I leave the laptop open and powered on, then trot back downstairs. Once at my desk, I access Medline with my office password and look up "face transplant." I'm reasonably sure Sarah will need a craniofacial surgeon to correct any lingering bone malformations, so Glenda Mewton will either have to find a qualified surgeon on the CIA payroll or convince someone else to operate for the good of God and country. I find an article about a doctor in Cleveland who has been cleared to do the surgery, so I jot her name on my tablet as a possible candidate for Sarah's operation.

I read about the possible complications—Dr. Mewton has already mentioned the risk of tissue rejection, which means Sarah will have to take immunosuppressive drugs, possibly for many years. These may be expensive and may cause side effects, but won't a life of freedom be worth it?

Finally, Sarah will need a donor. The French patient's transplanted tissue came from a woman who expired from suicide, not disease, so we'll have to wait for a donor from a similar situation. We may be waiting for some time, because not only will the blood and tissue types have to match, but the skin color will also have to coordinate with Sarah's.

I take off my reading glasses and rub the bridge of my nose. The donor issue will be complicated by families' natural reluctance to give up a part of the body that has so much to do with identity. We use faces to recognize each other, and to display almost every possible emotion. I've had patients who had trouble letting go of a deceased husband's favorite shirt or sweater—how could they release something as personal as his face?

I click to another online article and read that out of 120 people surveyed at one hospital, the majority answered that they would accept someone else's face if they needed one. No one, however, indicated that they would donate their own.

That fact dismays me even though I understand it. It's hard to imagine someone else engaging the world behind the face we have worn throughout our lifetime.

My research assures me that the transplant recipient will not look like the donor. Even if some of the musculature and cartilage are included with the transplant, the elastic skin envelope will drape itself over the bone structure of the recipient. The result will be a hybrid, perhaps, but in Sarah's case, definitely an improvement.

Furthermore, the age of the donor is not a primary concern. Skin health has less to do with its physical age than it does with the hormones and blood flow available to nourish it.

I put down my pen as the full weight of this responsibility bears down on me. If I am to do this, I'm going to be here longer than a few weeks. I may need to stay on this remote island for a year or more, depending on how things progress with Sarah.

An entire year…without tending my practice, my regular patients, or my oversize puppy.

I open my wallet and slide out the photograph of me and Kevin. I run my finger over the profile of his face and sort through the loose ends of my life.

I once concentrated on my practice so much that I lost a husband through inattention. I nursed a grudge against my sister-in-law and forfeited every opportunity to get to know her. I pouted at my brother's wedding and missed the chance to share in his happiness.

If I allow my partners or my home or even my darling dog to draw me back before I've seen this through, I'll have missed another opportunity that won't come around again.

So I'll ask Becky to keep an eye on my house and continue fostering Elvis. The big dog may miss me, but at Becky's home he's surrounded by adoring fans. I can ask her to cancel my magazine subscriptions or, better yet, enjoy them herself.

The room swells with silence as I realize that nothing in Virginia requires my immediate return. My neighbors barely know me; my patients will adapt to new doctors. Though some of them may balk, their reasons for resistance will have more to do with the discomfort of reiterating their problems than with breaking an attachment to me.

For the first time in my life, I realize that I may be like the proverbial hand in a bucket of water—pull it out, and no one even knows it's missing.

But Sarah *needs* me. Because while we wait for a donor and a doctor, my niece is going to have to prepare for life beyond these walls. She's going to have to learn how to use a face…and how to handle the emotions she will be expressing. She'll have to learn that the dioramas of American life she's glimpsed in movies are only a shadow of what awaits her.

I don't want Sarah to live her life with a heart full of untapped potential.

I am skimming a summation of body dysmorphic disorder when Dr. Mewton steps into the room, intruding on my space without knocking. "Phone call for you," she says, nodding toward the phone in the center of the conference table. "Just pick it up—the caller is waiting."

I smile my thanks, despite the cold knot that has formed in my stomach. All the other doctors in my practice knew I'd be incommunicado for at least three weeks. No one knows where I am, and Becky is the only person who has an emergency number for me. And Becky would only call if she had a severe problem with a patient…or Elvis.

I wait until Dr. Mewton steps into the hall before picking up the phone. "Hello?"

"Renee?" Becky's voice is breathless. "Listen, I know you didn't want to be disturbed, but—"

"Patient or Elvis?"

I hear that pregnant pause that always precedes bad news. "Elvis. I'm so sorry, Renee, but I was chopping tomatoes. I turned my back for just a minute, and then the darn thing was gone. The kids and I searched the kitchen from top to bottom and couldn't find it. I wasn't too worried because Elvis just sat there grinning at us, but—"

"He ate a tomato?"

"He ate a steak knife. One of a matching set."

"Is he *dead?*"

"He's at the vet's."

I sink into a chair as my knees turn to water. "Are you sure he swallowed it? It couldn't be behind the toaster or in that crack between the cabinet and the fridge?"

"The vet took an X-ray, hon. We saw the knife in his belly, clear as day."

I lower my head to my hand and close my eyes. "That doofus."

"I know. But this one's not going to pass. The doctor says the knife has to come out. Surgically."

I press my lips together and nod. "Okay. Have the operation, charge my account. Do whatever you have to do, but save that dumb dog."

"I thought you'd feel that way. The vet wanted me to make sure, though."

"Thanks. Thanks for calling."

"No trouble. And hey—you sound a lot farther away than D.C. Where are you hiding yourself these days?"

For an instant I'm confused, then I remember that the CIA gave me a fake phone number with a D.C. area code. Someone at Langley redirected Becky's call.

"Where am I? You wouldn't believe me if I told you."

She laughs. "Don't worry about the dog. He's in good hands."

"Give the doofus a hug from me."

I hang up and press my hands together as I offer a quiet, fervent prayer for the success of Elvis's surgery. When I open my eyes, Dr. Mewton is standing at the end of the conference table.

"Why," she asks, her eyes dark and brooding, "are you doing this?"

For an instant my head swarms with confusion, then I realize that she has to be talking about my promise to help Sarah. "Why does it matter to you?"

"Sarah matters to me."

"She matters to me, too. I'm her family."

"I'm her guardian. I've looked after her for twenty years, and I only want what's best for the girl."

"Then why do you want to imprison her?"

The woman shows her teeth in an expression that is not a smile. "Imprison her? I'm protecting her."

"You've stifled her. You're *using* her."

"I'm employing her."

"Only now. Why were you so keen on keeping her here before she was old enough to be employed by the CIA?"

"Somebody had to take care of the girl. No one in your family seemed interested."

I draw a deep breath and try another tack. "I don't know why you're so set against this, Dr. Mewton. Maybe you're gaining power or prestige from the work Sarah's doing. Maybe she's fulfilling your minuscule maternal instincts. I don't know why you're holding her back, but clearly you are."

She sends me a glare hot enough to singe my eyebrows. "Don't make assumptions, Dr. Carey. They can be dangerous."

"I might say the same thing to you. Don't assume you know what's best for Sarah. She deserves the opportunities she should have been granted as a child."

"What, opportunities to be mocked? Scorned? I don't know what you've told her, but she will never be a beauty queen. Frankly, compared to the mess she was at birth, I think her face is a vast improvement."

"She may not be a beauty queen after additional surgery, but she deserves a chance to speak to people without seeing them flinch or avert their eyes."

"You think I want to protect her only because of her *appearance?* You misjudge me, Dr. Carey. I'm trying to protect her intellect, her very soul."

"What sort of intellect flourishes in confinement? What soul finds its full expression in seclusion? We are social creatures, Dr. Mewton, so if you care for Sarah as much as you say you do, you'll support her in her desire to be free. You and I ought to work together to do what's best for her."

Beneath the frozen surface of my adversary's countenance,

I see a suggestion of thawing and flowing, as though a submerged spring were trying to break through.

"It won't be easy." She steps forward to place her hands on the table. "I can foresee a dozen major risks."

"You have resources—far more than I do. If you help us, you'll earn Sarah's undying gratitude…and her affection."

I am guessing, of course, that Sarah's affection is what this lonely woman craves. When a trace of wistfulness steals into her expression, I'm sure I've guessed correctly.

"I do want to help her," Dr. Mewton says, lowering her voice. "And I have read about facial transplants. But the risks are so high."

"Such as?"

"Rejection, of course. Some of the immunosuppressive drugs can lower a patient's resistance to other illnesses. Sarah could be trading a cloistered life for a considerably shorter one."

"Not necessarily. A researcher in Cleveland has managed to induce long-term tolerance to hind-leg transplants with a drug regimen lasting only seven days."

"In rats. Sarah is human."

"Sarah is an adult. Shouldn't we let her make her own choices?"

The doctor presses her lips together. "I'm going to help you, even though I'm afraid I'll be picking up the pieces when your grand experiment fails. But that's what we do here at the convent—we patch up and repair people when missions go awry."

"This mission isn't going to fail." I speak the words out of hope and faith and optimism, even as I realize I can offer no guarantees.

Mewton's eyes narrow. "Let's hope it doesn't. But if it does, Sarah will be in a worse situation than she is now. Then she'll need a safe place to recover…so I'll stand by, waiting to offer it."

I draw a deep breath, fully aware that I have suggested an

incredible feat. We will be engaging in an experiment that, to my knowledge, has never been attempted, and I have a less-than-enthusiastic support team. Mewton doesn't like me, Sarah is quietly terrified, and no one at home even knows where I am. The haunting isolation of this place has made me feel completely alone, but if I feel bereft after being here two days, how must Sarah feel after twenty years of seclusion?

But with Mewton's assistance—and grudging support—we'll have access to personnel and technology we might not have otherwise. I'll stay here to support Sarah emotionally. And I can't help feeling that when all this is over, somewhere, somehow, Kevin and Diane will look down on us with approval, and maybe even gratitude.

Before leaving, Dr. Mewton turns to me. "I think this operation is a mistake. But Sarah's mind is made up, and she'll manage to convince Traut to okay the procedure. Anything she wants, he eventually gives her."

She extends her hand. "So if we're going to be in this together, I suppose you should call me Glenda."

Chapter Thirty-Four

Sarah

For the next three days, I don't see much of my aunt except at meals. She spends most of her time in the conference room, scribbling notes on a legal pad or gathering information from Web pages. Occasionally I glance out the window of the operations center and see her wandering in the graveyard, her arms crossed and her head down, as if she's deep in thought. Sometimes she sits on the bench and reads, her hand spread protectively over the pages of a book.

At lunch on Tuesday, she tells me she's spent the morning in Dr. Mewton's office, ordering things we'll need for our pre-transplant therapy.

I glance at Judson, whose head is bent over his soup and sandwich. He's not going to be any help.

"Who says I need therapy?" I ask.

Aunt Renee puts down her spoon. "Anyone who is facing a major life change needs time and tools to make the adjustment. Dr. Mewton agrees that you and I should have a few sessions together."

It's all been decided, then. Like Randle Patrick Murphy, I'm to be treated to a mental health checkup whether I want it or not. I can only hope they forgo the lobotomy.

And what *things* could she be ordering? Cases of stage makeup? Burkas in every color in case the face transplant fails?

I pick up my egg salad sandwich and swallow my dissatisfaction with this latest wrinkle in my routine. Dr. Mewton may be tolerating my aunt's therapy plans, but I know her well enough to sense the reticence behind her grudging approval.

I've also seen what they don't want me to see—the two of them arguing in Dr. M's office. Occasionally, when I know they're together, I hack into the surveillance feed and watch them snipe at each other across the desk. Keeping the volume low so Jud won't hear, I watch their heads bob back and forth like players in a heated tennis match. It's almost comical.

When Aunt Renee and Dr. M aren't arguing, they go about their work and I try to apply myself to the Gutenberg project. Every message from Mr. Traut is more terse than the one before, but my hands are tied when it comes to the testing stage of the program. I don't have a pool of test subjects at the convent, so I have to rely on data from Langley.

One disturbing fact has come from that data: it's impossible to distinguish between brain signals produced by actual memories and those produced by *imagined* memories. Unless a programmer knows exactly what cues to include, the clever criminal who imagines the perfect alibi might convince a brain scanner that he was nowhere near a crime scene.

Meanwhile, Judson has been pulled off Gutenberg and assigned to investigate Hightower's situation. The officer I once thought infallible is still confined to room 335 and still suffering some sort of mental disconnect. Dr. Mewton even asked Aunt Renee to examine him. She did, and came out of that room saying that she'd never seen anything quite like Hightower's condition.

Dr. Mewton asked for my assistance next. With help from the guards, she got Hightower into a straitjacket and managed to strap him to a gurney. Then I hooked him up to the EEG, but his brain waves were all over the place.

"Fried frontal lobe," Dr. M said, glancing at the printout. "This isn't the typical result we see with injury or disease, which leads me to one conclusion—a designer drug. But something new, a combination we haven't seen before."

I'm not supposed to inquire about cases I'm not assigned to, but my professional disinterest only extends so far. I've worked with Hightower; I like him. So occasionally Judson rolls over to my desk and pretends to read over my shoulder— ha!—while he taps out a message in Morse code: *Hightower condition definitely associated with Saluda.*

Then, fully aware of the security cameras, packet sniffers, and hidden microphones, he'll ask me to check out the pictures of women who've responded to his Close Connection ads.

I've always admired the subtlety of Judson's approach. By openly appearing to disregard Dr. Mewton's protocols to engage in harmless infractions, he deflects suspicion from more serious security breaches.

In the graveyard one afternoon, Judson shared more detailed information about Hightower's case. After scanning pages and pages of publicly available materials—European newspapers, Web sites, even online hospital reports—he found only three cases similar to Hightower's, and all occurred in Spain. In each of these situations, the affected young adult was confined to a mental ward while doctors tried unsuccessfully to determine what had caused his altered state. The local cops focused on illegal drugs, as well they should, but none of the police thought to investigate Saluda Industries.

I think I smell a few rats in the Spanish police.

"What's Saluda?"

The question comes from Aunt Renee, who shouldn't be familiar with the name. I kick at Judson's wheelchair under the table, knowing he'll feel the vibration.

"Saluda?" He lifts his head and crinkles his nose. "That's Spanish, right?"

Aunt Renee nods slowly. "*Salud* is Spanish for health. But I asked about *Saluda*."

Judson swings his head, doing a fair imitation of Stevie Wonder. "Um, let me see. Did you hear that somewhere? Because I'm not sure I've heard that word used that way."

"Yes, you have." My aunt gives me a small smile. "I was in my room with the window open. I heard you and Sarah talking about Saluda. Now…is that some deep, dark secret, or can you tell me what it is?"

Judson shakes his head, but I'm tired of playing dumb. "Saluda Industries is a Spanish company, Aunt Renee. It's one of the few international firms allowed to grow, manufacture, and sell poppy products—namely opium—for commercial use."

She lifts a brow. "That's legal here?"

"Of course. Where do you think morphine comes from? Codeine, Methadone, Demerol, Vicodin—and heroin. They all come from opium. Poppies."

She looks from me to Judson. "Surely it's not legal to sell heroin."

"No, not that. But where there's a poppy field…"

"There's a heroin trafficker," Judson finishes. "So we help the DEA keep tabs on 'em. We've been trying to keep up with Saluda—and its big man, Adolfo Rios—for years."

Again I kick Judson's chair. "Too much information. The walls?"

He shrugs. "Your aunt has clearance, right? Besides, I didn't give her details. She could learn that much about Saluda from Google."

He has a point. I reach for the pepper and sprinkle my soup, then offer the container to Aunt Renee. She shakes her head, smiling, and ladles up another spoonful of steaming broth.

I often wonder what she's thinking. She might think Judson and I are a good team. If so, she'd be right.

Dr. Mewton has assured me that Jud will help keep Mr. Traut at bay while I'm in therapy with Aunt Renee, but he and I both know that's Cinderella talk. We're both swamped with work on urgent projects the director wants wrapped up ASAP.

The good thing is that even though we're involved with different projects, we know enough about each other's work that we could cover for each other in a pinch.

But even friends, I hope, are allowed to have some secrets between them.

Chapter Thirty-Five

Renee

In the ten years I've been a practicing psychologist, I've never been so challenged by a case. I've spent most of the past week trying to decide how best to proceed with Sarah, and I've realized that I might as well begin with basic interpersonal relations. Though my niece is a brilliant young woman, her development has been hampered by isolation and a lack of social contact. She will learn as she begins to venture outside the convent. My job is to prepare her for her first day of independent living…and the many that will follow.

Sarah seemed startled to learn that we will be having sessions together, but maybe the word *therapy* made her skittish. I can't be sure, but I imagine she heard the word many times as she recovered from various surgeries during her childhood. No wonder doctors have negative associations for the girl.

As part of my preparation, I have done a bit of research on Dr. Vincent Kollman, the surgeon who'll be overseeing the transplant team. From Dr. Mewton I learned that Kollman is a contract surgeon who often works at the convent hospital. His British neighbors think he's an American doctor who volunteers at an AIDS hospice; in reality, he routinely patches up CIA officers at the Convent of the Lost Lambs.

Dr. Kollman was scheduled to arrive yesterday morning,

but at the last moment he was detained by some emergency. I swallowed my disappointment, but made a mental note: I would not miss his arrival.

Now he's expected today, in late afternoon, so after a long interval of reading I take the elevator down to the dock. Glenda Mewton isn't likely to send a welcoming committee to meet anyone who's been here before, but I want to personally greet the man who will be taking care of my niece. I hope he can handle the delicate microsurgery Sarah's case will require.

The two guards at the dock straighten and give me a cursory once-over as I step out of the elevator. "Can I help you, ma'am?" the first asks.

I shake my head and wonder if this is Mitch, the guard Sarah often mentions. "I've come down to meet the boat."

He glances at his companion, making me wonder if I've committed some sort of faux pas, but the second guard only shrugs. "Why don't you wait over there?" With a jerk of his head he indicates an alcove in the rock. "You'd be more comfortable."

I blink when I see a bench hidden behind a wooden railing and so cleverly camouflaged I'm surprised I didn't noticed it before. Perhaps the guards sit here when no visitors are expected. Surely they don't stand at attention and hug their weapons all day.

I sit and wait in silence, my thoughts drifting over my to-do list, until the first guard steps forward and glances at his watch. At that moment I hear the roar of a motor, which subsides to a dull gurgle as a boat cruises beneath the rocky portal.

The vessel is *La Reina de Cielo*—the *Queen of Heaven*—and the driver is my friend the broad-shouldered pseudo priest. Beside the priest is a handsome man in a white dress shirt, navy tie, and dark pants. He leaps out of the boat before the guards have even attached the mooring lines, and calls his thanks to the driver, who tosses out a rope, then hands over a suitcase and a briefcase.

Feeling suddenly shy, I stand and walk forward, hoping

to catch our most recent arrival before he gets in the elevator. "Dr. Kollman?"

He stops, one bushy brow lifting. "You're new."

It's unprofessional, but I feel a rich blush stain my cheeks. "I'm Dr. Carey. I don't know if Dr. Mewton has told you, but we're going to be working together on Sarah Sims's case."

Kollman's tanned face brightens as he extends his hand. "Call me Vincent."

"And I'm Renee." I gesture toward the elevator and lead the way. "After you've had a few minutes to settle in, I'd love to talk to you about Sarah. My interest in her is far more than professional. She's my niece."

"Really?" At the elevator panel he punches in a code, waits a moment, then presses his thumb to a pad. A light blinks red, then green.

"Look at that," I say, impressed. "The man even has his own key."

To my surprise, Kollman laughs and holds the door open. "Tell you what," he says as I pass under his arm, "why don't I ring Shelba and ask her to serve dinner in my office? We can talk there without an audience—seen or unseen."

"We don't have to eat in the dining room?" My spirits rise at the thought of a change in surroundings. "Tell me where and when, and you've got a date."

Dr. Kollman's "office"—a loose description at best, he tells me—is located on the third floor. Instead of taking the elevator, I climb the uneven stone steps in the stairwell and hesitate at the third floor landing. There's no guard here now, but I've never been able to predict when or where I'll run into a young man with a gun.

I've only been on this level one other time, when I came up to see the man they call Hightower. On the wall opposite the landing I see signs directing me to the surgery, medical offices, a pharmacy, an exercise room, and an imaging center.

Below those markers, a handwritten sign on green paper says *Kollman* and points to the right.

I grip my folio and follow the corridor, noticing that the arched window at the end of this hallway has been blackened. A wry smile twists my mouth as I imagine boatloads of Spanish fishermen heading out before dawn and wondering why the nuns at the Convent of the Lost Lambs have every light blazing while the rest of God's creation sleeps.

Another handwritten sign on a door catches my attention: *Dr. Carey's destination.* I smother a smile as I knock. A moment later, a masculine voice bids me enter.

I open the door and am surprised by the room beyond. The space looks more like a loft apartment than an office, and even though a desk occupies one corner, I feel as if I've been temporarily transported to London or even New York. A low sofa and a modern chair occupy the nearest area, and beyond that stands an attractive dining set. The room is tall enough to enclose a spiral staircase that must lead up to the sleeping area.

I whistle softly. "Nice digs, Doc. How long have you been living here?"

The doctor smiles and tugs at his tie. "I'm not sure I'd describe it as *living,* but this work does keep life interesting." He pulls the tie from his collar and pauses. "Sorry—this must seem rude, undressing in front of a guest. Truth is, I've had this thing on for hours and I'm about to choke on it. Cover, you know. I'm supposed to be a businessman come to consult with Sister Luke."

I cough to cover a laugh. "Please, be comfortable."

"I love a woman who's flexible." He tosses his tie onto the desk and gestures toward the sofa. "Have a seat. We can chat until Shelba brings our dinner."

I sink onto a plush leather cushion. For the first time in six days, I wish I'd taken my usual pains with hair and makeup. In this isolated, windswept place, such things didn't seem to matter…until now.

"So," the doctor says, sliding into the chair across from me. "Tell me about this patient of ours."

I'm grateful that the conversation is veering back toward business. "Sarah Sims—have you met her?"

He shakes his head. "You may have noticed that Glenda 'Need to Know' Mewton runs a tight ship. She's given me free run of this third floor, but strongly suggested that I keep to my place while I'm in the convent."

I lift a brow. "You don't eat in the community dining room?"

"I didn't know there *was* a community dining room." He settles back and props his chin on his hand. "Congratulations. Glenda must trust you implicitly."

I laugh. "I think it's more likely that she believes in keeping her friends close and her enemies even closer. I've been a thorn in her side since before my arrival. Sarah has been under Glenda's care more than twenty years, so I think I'm a bit of a threat."

"She doesn't trust you?"

"We don't agree on what's best for Sarah. I think she's a viable candidate for a face transplant, but Glenda would prefer that Sarah remain as she is, staying here and doing whatever she does with computers. It hasn't been easy, but I've managed to convince Sarah that she needs to give herself a chance to experience the world outside this place."

Kollman nods. "Sounds reasonable. I've had to do skin grafts on burn patients who told me that living with severe facial disfiguration isn't easy. The word *suicide* often creeps into the conversation."

I lift my hand, warding him away from that topic. "Sarah's not suicidal. I thought she might be suffering from body dysmorphic disorder, but she's not obsessing about an insignificant physical defect, because her defects are real and major. On the other hand, she's had no real opportunity to live in a heterogeneous society. She's spent her entire life within these walls."

"How old is she?"

"She turned twenty-one a few weeks ago."

"And she's spent all that time *here?*" Kollman whistles and then folds his hands. "Glenda said I might be doing some facial reconstruction even before we find a donor. Was the girl in an accident?"

"Didn't Glenda tell you anything?"

"Glenda will speak no word before its appropriate moment. She did e-mail me a file, but I haven't had a chance to read it."

I sigh. "Sarah was born with Treacher-Collins Syndrome—a severe case. She has a working mouth, she can eat, she sees and breathes and hears with a cochlear implant. But her features—" I look directly into his eyes and hope he can see into my heart "—she looks out on the world through a pitiful excuse for a face. If she's ever to leave this place and find happiness outside this facility, she'll need our help—yours as a surgeon, and mine as a psychologist."

"Does she want to leave?"

"Now she does. For years I think she believed she had nowhere to go, and Dr. Mewton has been kind to her. Sarah's been well-educated, she watches movies and reads books. She's not a recluse, but her social skills are limited."

"You're convinced she can adapt? If we change the circumstances of someone who's not capable of coping, we might not be performing an act of kindness."

"She wants to move forward—and with an improved appearance, I think she can put the past behind her. If you can give her a new face, I can teach her how to read visual cues and how to respond to people. If you can help her become physically normal, I can help her become socially adept."

"I wonder." The surgeon laces his fingers. "Is it possible to teach someone to live behind someone else's face? We may be stepping into uncharted waters."

Kollman's eyes have gone soft and distracted, but they clear when he looks up at me. "I will do everything I can to help your niece, Dr. Carey. Because while Glenda Mewton is extremely capable, I don't think there's a comforting bone in her body. For the girl's sake, I'll sail these waters with you."

"But—"

"Something else?"

"Something I have to know before we go any further."

He straightens and sits on the edge of his seat. "Ask."

"Are you a good surgeon?"

The question is tactless, faithless, and blunt, but he doesn't seem to mind.

"Dr. Carey, put your mind at rest. I'm the best Uncle Sam can buy."

"Yes, but doesn't Uncle Sam always go with the lowest bidder?"

He tilts his head back and roars with laughter, not stopping until he's progressed from crowing whoops to teary spasmodic squeaks. "Not…in…this…case," he manages to say. "Do you know why I came in a day later than expected?"

I shake my head.

He wipes tears of mirth from his cheeks, then leans forward until I can feel his breath on my hair. "Emergency operation," he whispers. "In Washington. Reattached a right little finger. The president got it caught in the limo door yesterday—it's all very hush-hush. But you should be glad to hear that the First Pinky is bending and waving just as it should."

My throat tightens and my eyes sting in a sudden surge of gratitude. Fortunately, I am rescued from a potential blubbering incident when Shelba knocks on the door. A moment later she brings in our dinner on a cart, so the doctor and I adjourn to the dining room to talk about less secret matters.

But I am deeply impressed with Vincent Kollman.

Chapter Thirty-Six

Sarah

By quarter past six, I can't help but notice that my aunt has not come out for dinner. I glance across the table at Judson, who is calmly eating his salad as if he hasn't noticed our missing guest. Dr. Mewton hasn't come down, but she often eats in her office. Where is Aunt Renee?

I know I shouldn't worry—after all, this is a beautiful July day and she's in a secure facility. No one in this place would harm her. But I can't help but feel a twinge of unease on her behalf.

Wherever she is, she's out of her element. She's among savvy intelligence professionals in a facility that doesn't officially exist. She's not with the company, she has never been field trained, and as bright as she is, there's so much about this place she's not allowed to know....

The empty chair to my right seems to vibrate with emptiness.

I blurt out the uppermost thought in my mind: "Have you heard anything about my aunt? Where is she?"

Judson lifts his head as if scenting the air. "She's not here? I thought she was just being quiet."

I want to smack his hand. "Stop fooling around. I haven't seen her since lunch."

He spears a hunk of lettuce with his fork. "Maybe she's taking a nap."

"Then she'll be hungry later. I should have Shelba make up a tray."

"She's a grown woman, Sarah. I think Renee can take care of herself."

I pick up my fork and glance toward the hallway. Shelba is usually hovering near, waiting to hear if we want anything else, but there's no sign of her, either.

I eat a tomato and force myself to calm down. It's not like me to be nervous, but I've been anxious ever since Aunt Renee arrived. Maybe she's put ideas in my head that shouldn't be there.

I nibble at my salad and wonder if life on the outside would be one long chain of worries. What would I do if I lived alone in an apartment and had a medical emergency? What if I choked on a piece of cheese or had a reaction to a bit of bad salami? Who would help me? Who would know I needed help? Here I am constantly surrounded by friends, staff, and guards, but who would keep watch over me if I lived on the outside?

My belly fills with cold, as if I've swallowed an entire cup of ice.

"Jud," I ask, scarcely daring to breathe. "When you lived on the outside, were you frightened?"

He stops chewing. "Of what?"

"Of…the unexpected. Of being alone."

A line creeps between his brows. "You can't think like that, Sarah. You'll drive yourself crazy."

"But were you?"

"You learn not to worry about things you can't control. Life is bigger than us, anyway."

I bend my head and watch as he goes back to eating, his fork moving up and down in an automatic pattern. Anything could be in his salad bowl—a bug, a button, a dust bunny— yet he doesn't hesitate, because he trusts Shelba.

After a moment, he looks up again. "Saluda's henchmen put me in this chair. I have to accept that."

"And that doesn't make you bitter?"

"What good would bitterness do me?"

I consider the question as I pick up my own fork. "No good, I suppose."

"Eat your dinner before Shelba comes in and starts to fuss."

I shovel salad into my mouth because I know it's good for me. While I eat, I wonder if Aunt Renee is working. A new fear rears its head: What if she left the island? What if after poring over all those research articles she decided to bail because my case is hopeless?

I glance up when the clack of heels alerts us to Dr. Mewton's approach. She appears in the doorway a moment later, a stack of folders in her arms. Shelba trails behind her, pushing a cart with our entrées.

"Dr. M," I call before she has a chance to speak. "Is my aunt all right?"

"I suppose so." Dr. Mewton glances at Renee's empty chair. "Is she not eating dinner?"

"She and Dr. Kollman are eating in the apartment," Shelba remarks, moving in to remove Judson's salad plate. "I took their dinners upstairs."

Dr. Mewton looks at me with a strange little smile on her mouth. "I wouldn't worry about her, dear." She slides into my aunt's empty chair. "How are you feeling tonight?"

"Fine."

"Good. Your aunt and I have arranged for your therapy to begin tomorrow. But if at any point you want to withdraw from this, all you have to do is let me know. You could have the procedure we discussed without participating in your aunt's therapy program. I could give you the tools you need."

"Don't you think she has good ideas?"

"I'm against anything that pulls you away from your work. Your aunt, however, seems intent on delving inside your psyche."

"Maybe she wants to know me better."

"And maybe she wants to use you for a behavioral study. Who knows? In any case, know that I'm not requiring this of you. I've always thought you were perfectly fine just the way you are."

I dip my head in a slow nod. "Understood."

Across the table, Judson clears his throat and taps his finger on the tablecloth. I glance at his hand, but I can't stop to decipher Morse code while I'm talking to Dr. Mewton.

"I must say, after investigating what will be involved in the surgery, I am surprised you want to pursue this," Dr. Mewton continues, playing with the strand of pearls at her throat.

I swallow hard. "I want to be able to walk down a street without people staring. I want to look normal."

Dr. Mewton casts a swift glance at Judson.

"It's okay," I say, my voice flat. "You don't have to talk around the truth. Jud knows about my face. And he agrees with my decision."

"So be it, then." Dr. Mewton gathers her folders and stands. "I actually came down here," she adds, "to tell you that Mr. Traut wants you to call him as soon as you get back to your desk."

Judson waits until Dr. Mewton's heels have clacked out of range before he leans toward me. "What do you think? Good news or bad from Traut?"

"I have no idea."

"Whatever he wants, don't let him talk you out of your decision. If they can fix you up, they need to do it."

I draw a deep breath that catches on the lump in my throat. "I want to leave…and yet I don't. I'd miss you something terrible, Jud."

"That's sweet, kiddo, but don't let me stop you from conquering the world." His hand slides across the table and catches mine. "I've always thought you were special. And no matter what you look like a year from now, know that you're right up there with Halle Berry and Catherine Zeta Jones in my book."

My eyes fill with water as I squeeze my friend's hand. His

skin is warm, and I'm beginning to understand why Aunt Renee enjoys touching people. "You're a crazy old man, you know that?"

But I can't deny that something in his smile has made me feel better.

Chapter Thirty-Seven

Renee

I slice into Shelba's baked chicken and try not to be too obvious as I study the man across the table. Vincent Kollman, handsome as he is, wears no wedding ring. His thick brown hair is going gray at the temples, and the parentheses around his mouth give him a look of determined resolve—definitely a good quality in a surgeon.

I ask if he's looking forward to his next assignment.

"Of course," he says, pausing to take a sip from his glass. "The entire idea of a face transplant—it's a welcome challenge, but it's incredibly complicated."

"Could you explain in more detail?" I pause, fork in hand. "Unless the surgery is classified."

He laughs. "Several surgeons around the globe are preparing to embark on facial transplants. We're simply the first to find a viable candidate. Sarah's surgery has nothing to do with national security."

"I want her to have a new face, but I'm not sure I like the idea of her being a guinea pig."

"You don't have to worry. The procedure will be worked out long before we pick up a scalpel."

I cut another piece of chicken breast. "Would you mind walking me through it?"

He shrugs. "No problem. Once we find a donor, I'll

prepare Sarah by excising all the fibrous tissue that has formed on her face. Once her old skin and some of the underlying muscles have been removed, I'll examine her skeletal structure to be sure the bones will be a good fit for the donor's skin."

I glance up in alarm. "That's a little late, isn't it? What if the new skin doesn't fit?"

He smiles. "It's only a precaution—we'll have made thorough measurements before we accept a donor." He pauses to swallow a bite of chicken and closes his eyes. "I hadn't realized how hungry I was. I didn't have a chance to eat lunch today."

I look down at my plate and smile, realizing that not many people would enjoy a gourmet meal along with a discussion of state-of-the-art surgery. "What happens next?"

"Well," he says, still working on his entrée, "I'll have to bring in several surgeons to help with the next step. Using microsurgical techniques, we'll suture the blood vessels in Sarah's face to those of the donor tissue. We'll then connect the nerves and muscles. We'll stitch in the lining of the mouth. Finally, we'll attach the donor face by sewing a complete circle—starting beneath the chin, moving behind the ears, across the forehead, and down the other side." He gestures with his fork, drawing an oval in the air. "You see?"

"I do. And I'm thrilled for Sarah, but—"

"But what?"

"She won't be terribly scarred, will she? She's already been through so much."

"The stitches will be hidden in the hairline, behind the new ears, beneath the chin. Other scars will be inside the mouth and nose. Maybe a small scar in the neck. But nothing obvious, and nothing a light application of makeup wouldn't cover."

"Will she be able to speak? To chew?"

Vincent nods. "The nerves will regenerate. It may take four to five months, but they will work again. If all goes well, within a year no one meeting her on the street would ever guess she'd had any type of work done."

I lower my fork as a blush of pleasure warms my cheeks. "I'm so thrilled for Sarah. I only wish she were as excited as I am."

"It will be a tremendous change. She has to be anxious."

"I'm sure she is...but she's coping remarkably well, don't you think?"

Vincent breaks into a friendly smile. "I think she comes from good stock."

I swallow the compliment and turn the conversation back to my niece. "That all sounds wonderful, but I want you to be honest with me—exactly what are the risks? Glenda Mewton makes them sound awful."

He spears a clump of broccoli. "Sarah's going to be fine."

"I didn't ask for comfort, I asked for honesty. What's the worst that could happen?"

He hesitates, the broccoli dangling from the end of his fork. "Do you really want to know?"

"No, I only asked because I enjoy hearing the sound of my voice." I lower my head and scowl. "Tell me everything."

He bites the broccoli and watches me as he chews, his eyes vaguely appraising. "Complications—" he swallows "—might include tissue rejection, in which case the skin might slough off. We'd have to replace it with donor grafts or skin from elsewhere on Sarah's body."

Something inside me shrivels at the painful thought. "Anything else?"

"Infection. The new face might turn black or mottle in color. If so, we'd have to do another transplant or replace the skin with grafts. The result would be an appearance even more pieced-together than Sarah's present face."

"Anything else?" My voice sounds strangled in my own ears.

"That's the worst of it."

"I preferred hearing that Sarah's going to be fine."

"She is."

I pick up my knife and fork. "I'm not sure Sarah needs to know about the complications."

"She's an adult. I'm ethically bound to tell her."

"You've told me. I'm her aunt."

"Renee." His voice softens. "I know you want to protect her, but not telling her the truth is not protecting her. It's shielding her, and Sarah's been shielded far too long."

"But not by me." I look up, a little surprised by the sound of steel in my voice. "I wasn't there for her, don't you see? When she needed my family, when she needed me, I wasn't around. We should never have left her in this place."

"She could have been abandoned in places far worse than this. She had care, she had the necessary surgeries…"

"But did she have *love?*" I lower my fork as my throat tightens. "I can't help feeling that I've let her down."

"You're here now, aren't you?" His hand reaches across the table and catches mine. "Didn't you crack a few skulls together in order to find her?"

"How did—?"

"Dr. Mewton and I go way back. She filled me in."

"Oh." I press my lips together and feel my heart slip toward him.

Uh-oh.

Chapter Thirty-Eight

Sarah

It's seven o'clock by the time I return to my desk, which means it's 2:00 p.m. in Washington. Mr. Traut is in the middle of a conference and waiting for my call. He patches me in and puts me on speakerphone.

"We've been waiting to hear from you, Sarah," he says, his voice tight. "We've come up with a new wrinkle we'd like you to incorporate in the Gutenberg program."

Not knowing who else is listening to this call, I respond carefully. "Yes, sir?"

"The other day you sent us a memo about how imagined alibis can leave verifiable traces on a brain scan."

"I remember."

"Would you mind explaining that for the people in this room?"

I glance at the printed copy of the report on my desk. Can't the people with Traut *read?*

"Functional MRI," I begin, "or brain fingerprinting, is based on the idea that the brain releases a recognizable electric signal when processing a memory. Unfortunately, we've discovered that it's nearly impossible to distinguish between brain signals produced by actual events and those manufactured by the imagination."

"Are you trying to say—" a rough voice interrupts "—that

we've wasted hundreds of hours pursuing a technology that is never going to be useful?"

"I don't think we've wasted anything, sir. We've simply learned that we need to work with well-defined, specific cues. If we probed a murder suspect, for instance, we might determine that he had the victim's face, address, and a gun in his memories. But it'd be difficult to know if he actually committed murder or only *thought* about committing murder without definitive details available only from the crime scene."

"So we're going to have to work with local police departments?" The tone of the man's voice suggests that this is not a desirable prospect.

"Perhaps," I answer. "Whether we do or not, we'll need details. For instance, an imagined murder might reveal knowledge of a gun in a suspect's brain. But the real murderer's brain scan might reveal knowledge of a Rohrbaugh R-9. The key to success will lie in specificity."

"That's excellent, Sarah." Mr. Traut's voice brims with approval. "What we'd like you to do now is consider the possibility of reversing the process."

"Sir?"

"Could we plant certain explicit memories *into* a subject's mind? For instance, if we put together a code that fed electronic signals into a human brain, could we not program a subject with detailed, specific memories?"

While the people in the conference room murmur in hushed whispers, the question hovers before me like a hallway with a dozen locked doors.

I clear my throat. "I fail to see a useful application for this, sir."

"You don't have to see the application. I want to know if it's possible."

"I suppose so. Information flows in two directions."

"Excellent. Thank you, Sarah."

The line clicks, and the receiver in my hand goes dead. I set the phone back on its base, then lower my head into my hands and mentally replay the conversation. I picture myself slipping the device we've developed on Judson's skull, I see myself taking Dr. Mewton's EEG and feeding her memories into my friend's brain….

In a barely comprehendible flash, I understand. Mr. Traut wants to create sleeper agents. They have been the subject of dozens of spy films, including the 1977 classic *Telefon,* staring Charles Bronson. The movie was pure fiction in its day, but now the idea is plausible. Possible.

We could implant specific memories of a mission in an agent's mind, memories that could be buried deep and resurrected by a code word. In *Telefon,* the trigger was a line of a Robert Frost poem, today it might be a single word, a name, a number, even a scent. Upon activation, the buried memories could become as real as a direct command, and the officer could be compelled to complete the mission he thought he had been given.

Gutenberg…the world's first printing press.

Now I understand. From the beginning, Mr. Traut has intended to imprint something far more powerful than words on paper.

My aunt is still AWOL at breakfast the next morning. But before I have finished my cream of wheat, Dr. Mewton stops into the dining room to tell me that Aunt Renee has been given one of the small rooms on the hospital floor for her use. "She's expecting you this morning," Dr. M says, "so don't disappoint her."

When I jog upstairs, I find Aunt Renee in a transformed examination room. The elevated exam table has been pushed against the wall and covered with a sheet. The center of the room has been filled by a table on which rests a computer, two monitors, two cups of coffee, and two mirrors.

I try not to look at the shiny ovals as I greet my aunt. "Good morning."

"The same to you." She smiles and props one hand on her hip. "Are you ready to begin?"

"I suppose."

"Good. Since I skipped breakfast, I brought coffee." Aunt Renee gestures toward the steaming mugs as she pulls out a chair on the far side of the table. With nowhere to sit except across from her, I pull out the other chair.

"I'll be right with you," she says, picking up a book and thumbing through it. "I just need to find a certain page…"

I fold my hands and avoid the freestanding mirror as I wait. I'm actually *more* than ready to begin whatever procedures she has planned. Last night I watched *The Bourne Identity,* and as the scenes played on my computer I couldn't help wondering how it would feel to be Jason Bourne or the girl, Marie. At one point Marie crossed a crowded street, and my skin contracted into gooseflesh as she moved into traffic. *I've done that.* I've stepped into a busy street and felt the smack of an automobile bumper against my hip.

A week ago, I wouldn't have felt that frisson of familiarity.

"Tell me," I say, watching as she flips through her book. "when you move among people all the time, do the things you see in film and read about in novels—do they come alive for you?"

She stops flipping and looks at me. "Come again?"

"Do you begin to identify with everything?"

Her lips curve upward. "Not with everything, especially not with some of the things you see in films these days. But identify? That's what books and film are supposed to do— through vicarious life experiences, they help readers and viewers understand the world we live in. This kind of learning helps us empathize with people we might never meet or understand."

I shrug. "I wondered."

"That's an astute observation, Sarah." She flattens her book on the table and smoothes the page. "I wanted to share this quote with you: 'The face is the mirror of the mind, and eyes without speaking confess the secrets of the heart.' That's from St. Jerome, and it applies to what we're going to talk about today."

"We're going to discuss poetry?"

"No, reading. Face reading." She looks at me—more intently than anyone has looked at me in a long time. "The ordinary human face—the kind of face you will soon have—can create over seven thousand different facial expressions. Forty-four different subdermal muscles help us send signals with our mouths, eyes, cheeks, and noses. Far more is communicated through body and facial language than through words."

I cross my arms, not certain why she's telling me this. "I've seen people smile and frown. Do you think I don't know what those things mean?"

Before she can answer, someone raps on the door. A man steps into the room, an older man who looks me square in the face and smiles as though he's genuinely happy to see me.

I'm so startled I can barely speak.

Chapter Thirty-Nine

Renee

"Good morning, ladies."

I sit back and cover my smile as Dr. Kollman greets his startled patient with an outstretched hand. "I'm Vincent, and I'm going to give you a new face."

A blush creeps up Sarah's neck as she stands. As he continues to talk to her in a relaxed, calm voice, I wonder how many men my niece has known over the years. Doctors and patients frequently rotate in and out of this place, but I doubt Sarah's had much interaction with them. She's noticed the guards, and she frequently mentions Mitch, but I've seen how she scurries away when he glances in her direction. She's never known a father, and I doubt that Jack Traut spends much time here.

The only real male friend Sarah has is Judson, and he's blind. So who has served as her male role models, Mel Gibson and Tom Cruise? Or has she, like so many other orphaned children, created a fantasy father?

I jot a note in my folio as Dr. Kollman pulls a plastic tape measure from the pocket of his lab coat and teasingly touches one end to Sarah's chin. When her flush deepens, I suspect this may be the first man who has ever looked her in the eye and held her gaze. She is fortunate, then, that the doctor who will be handling her case is as kind as Vincent Kollman. I've only known the man a few hours, but I've been impressed by his compassion and gentleness.

"Excuse me for interrupting, but I need to take a few measurements," he says, pulling a chart from beneath his arm. "I need to calibrate the machine so we can do an MRI later this morning. With a clear picture of your facial bone structure, I'll know exactly what we're looking for when we begin our search for a donor."

Sarah glances over her shoulder at me. "I meant to ask about that.... Am I going to be stealing someone else's face?"

Dr. Kollman shakes his head. "You won't be stealing anything, Sarah—you need to consider the donation a gift. And you won't look like the donor when we're done. You'll look like the woman you were meant to be."

When Sarah bows her head and doesn't respond immediately, I'm afraid the doctor has somehow offended her. But when she covers her face and her shoulders begin to shake in slow, silent sobs, I realize he has touched something within her, something too deep for words.

He's touched me, too. His attitude will help Sarah feel that her new face is a restoration, not something she took from someone less fortunate.

"While we're waiting for a donor," Dr. Kollman continues, gallantly pretending not to notice her reaction, "Dr. Carey will help you learn to use the face you'll soon be enjoying. So...does all of that make sense to you?"

Sarah pulls herself together and lifts her head in a teary nod. "Is it possible...after the donation, I mean...is it possible to thank the family?"

Vincent pulls a packet of tissues from his coat pocket and presses it into her hand. "These things are usually kept anonymous. You can write a letter, perhaps, and we'll make sure it's delivered to the family. But you will never know the donor's name."

A tear slips from her lashless eyes. "Why?"

He glances at me. "Dr. Carey may be able to explain this better, but I think anonymity is guaranteed so families can heal. The donor's relatives will want to know that the gift was helpful, but after that, they'll need to grieve and move on."

"He's right, Sarah." I give her a smile and gesture to her empty chair. "And if you'll sit down, we'll let the doctor take his measurements. We have a lot to do before we're ready to think about thank-you letters."

Sarah sniffs, wipes wetness from beneath her eyes, and sits, a willing student at last.

Chapter Forty

Sarah

I know I shouldn't be upset, but the MRI is proving to be an unpleasant experience. Lying on this imaging platform isn't painful, nor can I feel the magnetic waves scanning my brain. But my palms are perspiring, because something in this process has unleashed a horde of memories that keep battering their boundaries and threatening my composure.

These are sharp-voiced, needle-toothed recollections I'd rather forget. Despite my determination to keep them pent up, my heart has begun to pound and my teeth are threatening to chatter. I'm supposed to lie still and not move, but I'm doing everything I can to keep from leaping up, scrambling off the table, and canceling the entire procedure.

Why am I doing this? Am I doing it for my aunt? Am I doing it because I was so idiotically happy to meet someone who knew my father that I'd agree to walk across hot coals if she wanted me to?

Come to think of it, hot coals might be less painful than the surgery I've agreed to. I haven't gone under a knife in years, but I remember lying in a bed with my arms strapped down so I wouldn't touch my stitches. I remember whimpering because it hurt too much to cry.

As if she's read my mind, Aunt Renee's voice drifts over the intercom. "I know this might be uncomfortable for you,

Sarah, but close your eyes and try to relax. Think of the future. Think about how glad you'll be a year from now. Think of what you have to gain."

I grit my teeth and try to do what she says. My final result will depend on the skill of my surgeons and the characteristics of the donor, I suppose, but I could walk out of here looking like an impish pixie, a sloe-eyed beauty, or the all-American girl. I could be given a turned-up nose or a broad-through-the-nostrils model. I could have bee-stung lips or a narrow mouth. My complexion could be pocked or as smooth as silk.

I snort softly as I imagine the future of facial transplantation. Might there one day be a catalog of features from which a prospect could choose? If I had a catalog, I don't know what features I'd pick. I'd feel like an impostor making any choice at all. I'm not a pixie or a beauty or the girl next door. I'm me. For better or worse, I'm a facial junkyard who stands in dire need of a clean-up.

Isn't that why I'm on this table?

I force myself to compose a mental list: a year from now, I should be able to leave this place. I could go to New York, where I could walk through Central Park, which must be ten times as big as this island. I could ride around the park in one of the famous horse-drawn carriages. I could go to the Boathouse Café, where Harry met Sally, or stop into Tavern on the Green, where they filmed a scene from *Ghostbusters*. I could splash in Bethesda Fountain, where Mel Gibson lost his son in *Ransom*. I could go to the top of the Empire State Building, where Sam Baldwin met Annie Reed in *Sleepless in Seattle*.

I could walk down Fifth Avenue without people staring at me. I could sit in a diner without seeing those quick, surreptitious looks people cast at freaks when they think no one is watching. I don't get many of those here, but I've seen *The Elephant Man*. I know how people treat the odd and ugly.

If I persevere with this, I could have a new life. A *real* life.

I could go to any city on the planet. All the places I've read about and seen in movies…I could visit them. I could touch the hot desert sand and feel a cool wind blowing through the redwood forest. I could smell the muddy Mississippi and hear waves crash on the Pacific shore. I could hear Texas twangs and see snow on Alaskan mountaintops.

I could visit my aunt's house and sleep in her guest bedroom. I could pet Elvis and see if a 200-pound dog is as big as I've imagined.

I could walk into CIA headquarters and talk to Jack Traut in his office. I could meet those people gathered around the speakerphone and put faces with their voices. If I learn my lessons well, I could watch their eyes and mouths and eyebrows and understand not only what they're saying, but what they're *thinking*.

Best of all, I could look at a man…one who will smile and call me *cute* or *beautiful* or *darling*. I'll know he's not only saying that because he loves me, but because it's true—because I'm no longer freakish, ugly, and repulsive.

That alone makes this struggle worth the effort.

Chapter Forty-One

Renee

By the next morning, Sarah seems to have moved past her anxiety about the MRI. She comes into our makeshift therapy room and drops into a chair, tucking one leg under the other.

"Don't have too much time this morning," she says, her hand moving to turn the freestanding mirror away from her face. "Mr. Traut's breathing down my neck about adjustments to this project I'm working on."

"Then let's not waste any time." I open the program I've installed and pull up several photographs.

"Social researchers," I begin, "have identified seven universal emotions and corresponding facial expressions. I'm going to show you photographs of people exhibiting those emotions. Your job is easy—just tell me what emotion the person in the photo is displaying."

Sarah shrugs. "Doesn't sound too hard."

"Trust me, it's easier than computer programming."

I tap a picture on my computer and send it to her monitor. "What do you think about the man on the far right? What emotion is he expressing?"

The photo, a black-and-white candid, was snapped during a tavern brawl—probably during the seventies, if the clothing and hairstyles are reliable indicators. The man on the far right is striding forward, his hands fisted, his teeth bared in an unsmiling grimace. His eyes are nearly closed, and his brows are lowered.

Sarah studies the picture. "I can see all his teeth," she says, "so he must be excited about something. So…maybe he's excited about going to a party. Right?"

I make a note on my notepad: *Limited recognition of anger.* "Let's look at the next shot." I click the second image on my screen and send Sarah a picture of a young woman cowering in a closet. The girl's eyes are wide, and the corners of her mouth are pulled back into a fearful grimace.

"She's hiding," Sarah says, "and her eyes are wide. So she must have been startled when the door opened."

"That's possible." I tap the tip of my pencil on my notepad. "But a startle is more of a reflex than an emotion."

"Then she's surprised," Sarah says, her voice matter-of-fact. "She's surprised to be discovered in her hiding place."

I make another note on my pad: *Patient does not recognize fear…does she feel it?*

I tap my pencil against my chin. "Living here must be one surprise after another. After all, with injured spies and government big shots landing at a moment's notice—doesn't all this cloak-and-dagger stuff ever frighten you?"

She blinks at me. "Why should it?"

I falter in the silence. "Well…if I knew that a—"

"I *don't* know," she interrupts, "unless I need to know, and I don't need to know about most of the things that go on upstairs. Dr. Mewton handles everything in the medical ward."

Of course she does.

I draw a deep breath. "Maybe I wouldn't strictly need to know, but if I lived here I'd be constantly asking questions. With so much going on, how could I not be curious?"

The corner of Sarah's mouth twists. "Curiosity…isn't that what killed the cat?"

"Well. Yes. Let's move on."

I send her a picture of a teenage girl holding a plate of

worms. The girl's nose is crinkled, her upper lip slightly raised, and her eyelids relaxed, not tense.

"Disgusting," Sarah says, and I'm not sure if she's talking about the worms or the girl's expression. Since the expression is one of disgust, however, I give her credit for the answer.

The fourth photo is a well-known image from 1972, taken when Vietnamese officials released several American prisoners of war. This photo shows a soldier walking toward his family. We can't see his expression, but we can see the faces of his son, daughters, and wife. All three wear broad smiles, and the first daughter has her arms spread wide in greeting.

"They're happy," Sarah says. "They've missed their father."

Something in her tone tears at my heart.

"How about this one?" I click on the photo of a smiling female tennis champion who is leaping in the air, arms raised, to celebrate her victory.

"She's angry," Sarah says. "She's about to run over and hit someone with her stick."

I peer more closely at the image. The racket is tilted and the picture one-dimensional, so perhaps the racket does resemble a stick. "Are you sure she's angry?"

Sarah crosses her arms. "I see teeth."

"Some people show their teeth when they smile."

"Not that many."

Okay… *Subject does not recognize jubilation.*

I show her a photo of a grief-stricken woman cradling the body of her lifeless child.

"She's sad," Sarah says. "She's crying."

I show her a photo of Richard Nixon the day he left office—his lips are curved in a smile, but his eyelids are tight and not a single tooth is showing.

"He's…" Sarah hesitates. "I think he's just smelled something bad."

I snort softly. "That's apt. Can you put a word to the emotion?"

Sarah studies the picture again. "He's definitely not happy. Do you know this man?"

"That's Richard Nixon, our thirty-seventh President. He was forced to resign during the Watergate scandal."

"Oh." She looks at the picture with renewed interest. "I remember reading about him for my history course."

"I lived through it—but I don't remember much, because I was a toddler at the time." I exit the computer program and watch my photos fade away. "That's it. Our little test is finished."

"Did I pass?" Her voice is dry.

"You did better than I expected. But we still need to do some work."

"If that's as hard as it gets, this therapy will be a breeze." Sarah stands and pauses at the edge of the table. "I'll be going, unless Dr. Kollman needs to see me."

"He didn't mention anything, so you can go on to the operations room. I wouldn't want your boss to think we're not doing our part to keep the world safe for democracy."

I am finishing up my notes when Dr. Kollman steps into the room. "How'd our girl do today?"

I lower my pen. "Our girl has just confirmed that she is deficient in three abilities—recognizing universal facial expressions, making those expressions, and feeling the emotions behind those expressions. The art of communicating with a face is a three-pronged approach that most of us take for granted. Instead of three solid prongs, Sarah is operating with three little stubs."

Dr. Kollman's eyes narrow in thought. "Prognosis?"

"Excellent, because she seems eager to learn. I can teach her to read faces, and we can begin to work on manipulating the facial muscles she has. The emotions themselves will come in time—they're a natural by-product of the process."

He leans on the edge of the table. "Good. She's a nice kid, and *nice* isn't a word I'd apply to most of the people who come through this place. Half of them are crazy or completely paranoid by the time they arrive here. Too many years of living in alias, too much lying to their friends and family. After I fix 'em up, the lucky ones get transferred to another assignment. The smart ones go home and quietly retire. The majority, though, are loners, so they return to the field. The strain of living a double life means that one life—usually the real one—ends up in the trash bin."

I listen with rising dismay, wondering if that's how Kevin felt in those last few months. I can't help him now, but I can make sure his daughter doesn't find herself in the same position. "Sarah's been protected from having to live a life of deception—once you get past the fact that she's living in a place that's anything but a convent. But even in her case, protection has come at a price."

"How can it be otherwise?" The surgeon drops into the chair Sarah vacated a few minutes ago. "She grows up with Glenda Mewton, who's not exactly nurturing, if you know what I mean. Nearly everyone in this place is transient, so she forms few friendships and meets no other children. The people she does meet are either crazy, maimed, or transferred before too long."

"Don't forget paranoid," I add. "I keep feeling that the plaster is listening to every word I say."

Dr. Kollman laughs. "True. Information doesn't exactly flow around here. At the convent, if you don't *need* to know, you don't *get* to know. All that had to affect Sarah while she was growing up."

I drop my chin onto my hand. I haven't thought much about Sarah's immersion in the CIA mind-set, but the man has a point. Since these people work for a top secret agency, they can only talk freely with other agency people…while they treat everyone else with suspicion. How normal is that?

"Dr. Kollman—"

"I asked you to call me Vincent."

"All right. Vincent." I meet his gaze. "Why are you being so open with me?"

He smiles, setting a dimple free to wink in his left cheek. "If I were trying to charm you, I would say it's because I feel completely comfortable with you."

"Since you're *not* trying to charm me?"

"Who says I'm not?"

"You wouldn't do it on company time…unless you simply couldn't help yourself." I lift my pencil and point to the surveillance camera discreetly tucked into the corner of the ceiling. "Mama is watching."

The dimple winks again. "Then I could say I'm being open because we're partners in the same project. Sarah is within her rights to ask for the agency's help, but altruism is not their only motivation for helping her. Certain people are also interested in the outcome of her procedure. Face transplants, after all, could be a foolproof way to defeat facial recognition technology."

"Always putting the company first," I whisper, my thoughts drifting again to Kevin. "My brother must have been a company man to the bone. Two days after his wife died in childbirth, he went on a mission for the CIA."

Kollman shifts in his seat and eyes me with a calculating expression. "Where did you hear that?"

"Why? Do you know something different?"

He shakes his head in a barely perceptible movement. "Need-to-know, remember? I don't know anything about your brother, but I can tell you this—don't trust anything you don't read in an official file."

"And where would I read an official file?"

He gives me an apologetic smile. "That, my dear, I don't know."

Chapter Forty-Two

Sarah

For more than two months, I've been using my alternate operating system to troll the Internet as a script-kiddie, one of the thousands of unsophisticated young hackers who test random IP addresses for weaknesses. But I'm not unsophisticated, and the IP addresses I'm pinging aren't exactly random.

In my calculatedly haphazard search, I've discovered that CIA servers forty-six through fifty are stored at a server farm in London—an arrangement, I suspect, much like the agreement that supports the covert work of Echelon, a classified program that allows five English-speaking nations to monitor electronic communications. Since the United States has no authority to spy on its own citizens, the nations involved in Echelon have reportedly entered an arrangement that allows them to monitor the other nations' phone calls, faxes, and e-mails.

For all I know, the Brits could be storing some of their top secret information at the Lincoln Memorial or the Washington Monument. What does it matter? All I care about is my father's file, which I have finally located.

The British server farm holds primary and backup servers allocated to a single task. Server forty-seven, therefore, exists in two places. I only need access to one.

As the quiet of evening steals over the convent, I say good-

night to Judson, Aunt Renee, and Dr. Kollman, who has
joined us for a game of cards after dinner. Pleading a stom-
achache, I hurry up the stairs, close the door to my apartment,
and enter the server farm's network.

Once I'm inside server forty-seven, I type *ls* and wait for
the contents of the directory. The command *setfacl* allows me
to modify the access control list, so I grant myself permission to continue unimpeded. Finally, I type *locate Kevin Sims,*
knowing the command will list any file in the archived
database containing my father's name.

Two file names appear on my screen. I open the first and
am about to skim the contents when my speech processor
picks up a strange sound—the *whompa-whompa-whompa* of
whirling chopper blades.

I glance at the clock—11:30 p.m. Too late for ordinary
activity, so something unusual is afoot. I hesitate, not sure
whether I should print or save the file, then decide to close it
and log off. Printing or saving would leave an electronic trail
I don't have time to cover.

When the secondary OS has shut down, I stand and peer
out my window, but I can't see anything but the star-filled sky.
So I go to my door, open it, and look into the hallway. No
one stirs in the shadows, no light burns in Dr. Mewton's
office or the conference room.

The chopper must be transporting an injured officer or
asset. This medical emergency has nothing to do with me,
but I can't help thinking about what Aunt Renee said earlier.
Why am I not more curious about the things that go on
around here?

Since no one is moving on the second floor, I slip into the
hallway and tiptoe to the stairwell, then tilt my head and
listen for sounds from above. I hear voices, and they are
enough to entice me up the stairs.

I reach the landing and see no one, but the door to room
335 is ajar. I push on it, expecting someone within to slam it

shut at any moment, but the door swings slowly on its hinges, allowing a stream of light into the padded room.

It's empty. Hightower has vanished.

I turn, about to tiptoe back down the stairs, and nearly bump into Dr. Mewton, who stands behind me in a blood-stained surgical gown, cap, and soft-soled shoes.

"Oh! Dr. M. You startled me."

She frowns at me. "What are you doing up here?"

"I heard the chopper. I was…curious."

She frowns and takes a deep breath as her gaze drifts toward room 335. "He—" she points to the empty room "—suffered a ruptured brain aneurysm. We had to bring a neurosurgeon from the mainland."

"But Dr. Kollman's here."

"He diagnosed the problem and recommended the neuro-surgeon. We've done the best we can, but I don't think High-tower's going to make it." She swallows hard and points toward the stairwell. "It's not something you need to worry about, so go downstairs. We'll talk more in the morning."

But I know we won't.

Even as I walk back to my room and climb into bed, I know we won't ever mention Hightower again. Dr. M has already told me more than she would have if she weren't tired and stressed. If Hightower recovers his cognitive functions, she'll send him to a facility where he can be useful and content. If he dies, she'll have room 335 cleaned and set aside the knowledge that our enemy destroyed a wonderful man's brain. Life will go on at the convent, and people who don't need to know about our tragedies never will.

In all my dealings with the officer, I never learned the man's real name.

I wake before sunrise and stare into the lamp-lit gloom, trying to pin down the startling thought that slashed my sleep like a knife. Hightower? I'm still sad about his condition, but no, it was something else…. *My father's file.*

I spring out of bed, grateful for the early hour. Mr. Traut keeps demanding further progress on the Gutenberg program, but these predawn hours are not his. They belong to me.

I log on to the network and enter the rehash command. If anyone wonders what I was doing on the computer at this early hour, they'll think insomnia drove me to take care of computer maintenance. While the system is recomputing the internal hash table of my directories' contents, I open my secondary operating system and hack into the London server farm again. Within five minutes I'm back at server forty-seven and opening my father's file. It's encrypted, but one of my decryption programs makes short work of decoding the twenty-year-old report.

I am startled when a familiar word leaps out of the text: *Saluda.* Before reading another paragraph, I walk across the room and lock my door, then return to my computer.

The information here is rudimentary, but it's far more than I've ever been given. According to the record, Kevin Sims joined the CIA in 1979 and trained for two years. He served in several stateside positions, but in 1985, shortly after his marriage, he was assigned as a NOC to the Crescent Chemical Company in Valencia, Spain. While working under nonofficial cover, he was tasked with aiding the DEA in monitoring Saluda, one of two Spanish pharmaceutical firms authorized to cultivate opium poppies to produce narcotic raw materials, or NRM.

I glance toward my locked door when I think I hear footsteps in the hall. I wait, half expecting to hear a knock or a voice, but the only sound is the faint whistle of my own quickened breathing. I'm not wearing my speech processor, so I'm probably imagining things.

I return to reading. Saluda used the NRM to produce CPS-M, or concentrate of poppy straw rich in morphine. The production of Morphine, Codeine, Methadone, Demerol, and Vicodin is a legitimate enterprise, but heroin is a combination of morphine and acetic acid. DEA officials suspected that Adolfo Rios, president of Saluda, was trafficking in heroin and using his company as cover.

My mouth goes dry as I continue reading. While living in alias, my father was tasked with offering a formula for a more addictive heroin to a Saluda contact. On July 1, 1986, he met with his contact and explained his formula. On July 5, he was to meet the contact again and provide a sample of the drug. He was also supposed to tag the contact's vehicle with a tracking device. After the meet, DEA agents were planning to follow the contact, find the heroin processing plant, and expose Saluda's underground operation.

I was born—and my mother died—on July 3.

My father, who had to have been distracted with grief and worry, went to Valencia on July 5, but didn't check in with his handler after the meet. Neither, apparently, did he plant the tracking device on his contact.

On March 7 Kevin Sims's car was discovered nose-down in a gorge outside Valencia, his body sprawled across the shattered windshield. After learning of my mother's death, local police investigators ruled my father's death a suicide.

Though the investigation into my father's death has been closed, Saluda is still under investigation and Adolfo Rios remains at the head of the firm.

My mind shifts abruptly to Judson, whose scarred body lies in the next room. He was investigating Saluda when he was tortured and left for dead. Hightower is only the latest in a string of officers who have sacrificed their lives in our efforts to stop this drug lord. Who will be next?

I glance out the window, where a faint glow on the horizon signals the sun's approach. Jud will wake soon, and Dr. Mewton, and my aunt. Do any of them know the truth about what happened to my father?

I shut down my connection to the server farm and cross to my dresser. I slip my speech processor behind my ear and power on the device, then creep to the door, half expecting to hear the sound of breathing from the other side. All is silent…until I hear the groan of aging plumbing in the walls. Judson's awake.

I give him a minute to finish whatever he was doing in the bathroom, then step into the hall and rap on his door. "Jud?"

"Sarah?" His voice is muffled.

"Can I speak to you?"

I hear the creak of the leather in his wheelchair and the click of the latch. The door opens and he leans toward me. "You're up early."

I bend to whisper in his ear. "We have to talk. But not here."

He lifts a brow and grins. "Meet you outside, then. In twenty minutes."

A loud wind howls in my earpiece as I stride across the graveyard. Judson is already waiting by the wall. He lifts his head as I approach, and I know he recognizes me by the sound of my steps on the gravel.

"Is this about the choppers last night?" he says.

I stop and shove my hands into my pockets. "I know about the medical emergency. I heard the team arrive."

"Choppers coming and going all night," Jud says, scrubbing his head with his knuckles. "Last one arrived at four and woke me up. I'm betting it was Traut."

My stomach drops. "Traut's here?"

"I thought that's why you wanted to talk."

I shake my head. "No, it's something else. Did you know my father was working on the Saluda case when he was killed?"

Judson releases a low whistle. "What was that—twenty years ago?"

"Twenty-one. I'd like you to fill me in. Everything you know about the organization."

"Wait." His brows flicker above his closed eyes. "Why do you want to know?"

"Doesn't a girl have a right to know about her father?"

"I suppose she does." He draws a deep breath and opens his hands. "I don't know that any of this is going to help you understand what happened to your dad. Okay…we know Adolfo Rios is manufacturing illegal drugs and using Saluda as a cover, but no one's been able to find his manufacturing plants or uncover any proof of his operation. Twenty years ago, his black market op focused on heroin, but these days he's into other chemical concoctions—powerful drugs that are far more dangerous."

I sit on the stone bench. "Dangerous…how?"

"Dangerous enough to fry your brain. Think about Hightower. We don't know what happened, but I'd say Adolfo Rios got wind of what he was up to."

"Who were his contacts? Besides Espinosa, I mean."

The corner of Jud's mouth pulls downward. What kind of expression is that?

"Mewton would kill me if she knew I was telling you this."

"Why? It's not like I'm going to tell anyone."

"It's classified."

"But we're partners. Besides, I've been involved in the Saluda investigation. The more I know, the more I can help."

Jud blows out his cheeks. "Remember the op where Hightower first met Espinosa? For over a year the bookkeeper fed us paperwork—details about Rios's income, production profits, shipments and destinations. We were expecting great things, but none of it was useful. Saluda was moving a lot of poppy products, but all of it was legit."

"Hightower must have been ready to strangle the little twerp."

"The feeling was mutual. Espinosa kept demanding cash and a visa; Hightower wouldn't give him anything more than pin money until he got something worthwhile. So last May, Espinosa promised details on the development of a new drug. I had Hightower wired—everything went according to plan. Espinosa gave Hightower an envelope, Hightower gave him a package with ten thousand U.S. dollars and the promise of another ten thousand if the information paid off. Espinosa walked away and Hightower went to his apartment. But on the way, he's talking to me on coms and he suddenly cuts out. I send an officer to check on him. Ten minutes later, he finds Hightower curled up and hiding behind a garbage can, shivering like a baby and scared spitless."

"And that's when Hightower arrived here."

"Yeah, you saw him. He never recovered. And we haven't been able to figure out how Saluda got to our man."

"Wait a minute—we went upstairs together. You were surprised to see Hightower in room 335."

He shakes his head. "I was hoping to find him in a bed, not in a padded room."

"So you know—you *knew*—what happened to him?"

"Some of it."

"And you didn't tell me?"

"Sorry, kid, but you didn't need to know. Besides, you had other things on your mind."

I snort softly, but I don't argue. This place is rife with secrets, even between friends.

I rub the rough patch of skin between my mouth and my nose. "The envelope Espinosa gave Hightower—did you retrieve it?"

"It was gone when our agent arrived."

"Do you have video of the meet?"

"We do. Dr. Mewton and I have been over it a dozen times."

"Any contact between the two men? Any touch at all?"

"None."

"Any way Hightower could have been hit with an airborne toxin? Something he inhaled?"

"Someone else would have been affected. The exchange took place on a public street corner."

"Maybe the toxin was on the envelope." I blink as a scenario forms in my head. "On your surveillance tape, what was the accountant wearing when he met Hightower?"

Judson snorts. "You forget, kid—I can't *see.*"

"Can you show me?"

"What are you getting at?"

"If the toxin was on the envelope and Espinosa knew it, he might have been wearing gloves."

Judson shakes his head and leans forward in his chair. "You're bright, kid, but so is Dr. Mewton. If Espinosa had been wearing gloves, don't you think Mewton would have noticed and said something?"

I press my hand to my temple, where a headache is beginning to pound. He's right, of course. He and Dr. M always are.

Chapter Forty-Three

Renee

"Dr. Carey?"

Glenda Mewton's voice on the intercom startles me so completely that I nearly drop my glass of water. "Yes?"

"Could you attend a meeting in the conference room in half an hour? I'd like your professional evaluation of a newcomer we'll be introducing."

I smother a snort of surprise. "I'm supposed to evaluate someone on the spot?"

"I need a summary opinion, that's all."

I sigh. "All right, I'll be there."

I wait until the hum of the intercom stops, then roll my eyes and return to my reading. Until now, Glenda Mewton has seemed intent upon ignoring my status as a CIA employee, so either she's run up against something she can't handle or she's been instructed to make use of me.

Probably the latter. I heard helicopters last night, which means officers and/or assets were coming and/or going. For all I know, the President of the U.S. of A. could be having an emergency face-lift upstairs.

I check my watch, finish the article I was reading, and step into the bathroom to brush my teeth. After popping two pain relievers for an incipient headache, I pick up my notepad and stroll to the conference room.

Judson is sitting alone at the table. He acknowledges me before I speak a word. "Morning, Renee," he says, continuing to tap on his laptop.

"Morning, Jud." I slide into an empty seat. "Is Sarah coming?"

"I don't think she was invited to this little parley. We got a bigwig in residence, though."

"How big a wig? Should I be nervous?"

He chuffs. "Not hardly. It's Jack Traut, our boss. I smelled his pipe when I came through the hallway."

Despite his assurances, my nerves tense when I hear footsteps in the hallway. I look up in time to see Glenda Mewton enter, followed by a man carrying a cup of coffee. "Sorry to hear about Hightower," the man was saying. "A terrible thing."

Glenda moves to an empty chair and shakes her head. "I don't know what those fiends hit him with, but he didn't stand a chance. Even if he'd pulled through the surgery, his brain was gone."

"Did he have family?"

"A wife and daughter in Portugal. They think he's been on an extended business trip."

"Make the arrangements. Full burial with honors, the whole nine yards."

The man takes a sip of his coffee, then looks at me for the first time. His brow shoots skyward. "You must be Dr. Carey."

I stand and offer my hand. "I am."

"Jack Traut. Nice to have you on the team, Doctor." He shakes my hand, then lifts his coffee cup. "Can I get you something before we begin?"

"No, thank you. I'm fine."

I sink back into my seat as he sits next to Judson. I glance around the table, acutely aware of the two empty places. Glenda wanted my impressions of a newcomer. Did she mean *Traut?*

The boss wastes no time. He settles in his chair and glances at Glenda. "I'm assuming we've had no success with the Mona Lisa. No one from Saluda took the bait?"

Judson shakes his head. "I checked first thing this morning. Even though we mailed over two dozen copies to employees, no one's activated the program. My guess is that Saluda's people have been threatened with dire consequences if they install any nonapproved software on the company system."

Glenda sighs. "If only government employees were as conscientious. I'll never forget what happened when that 'I Love You' virus was unleashed. Langley had computers down all over the network."

"People have learned a lot since then," Jud answers. "And people who have a lot to lose are naturally suspicious."

I find myself wishing I'd accepted Traut's offer of coffee when a tanned, mustached stranger enters, a steaming mug in his hand. His eyes rove around the room without so much as a flicker of interest.

"Hola," he says, moving to an empty seat. "Good morning."

"About time," Traut says, nodding at the man. "Glenda, Judson, Dr. Carey, I'd like you to meet Oscar Espinosa. Since no one picked up the Mona Lisa, I thought it'd be a good time to call on one of our assets. Espinosa is a bookkeeper at Saluda, and he's provided information over the past several months. He's willing to help us again."

Judson, Glenda, and I murmur polite "nice to meet yous," but I can't help noticing Glenda glancing at Judson as if she'd send him a message if she could. What's that about?

Espinosa nods at me and Glenda and stares for a moment at Holmes. Though the man's gaze darts from face to face, his mouth never moves—likely a sign of anxiety. But who wouldn't be nervous in this situation?

"Oscar's been at Saluda three years," Traut continues, pulling a pipe from his pocket, "so Adolfo Rios and his men are accustomed to seeing him. Espinosa has also developed a friendship with Rios's secretary, a woman named Felicia Vargas."

"I'm assuming this is a romantic relationship." Glenda meets Espinosa's gaze without smiling. "Those relationships can be…unpredictable."

Espinosa gives her a smile as thin as rice water. "I have everything under control."

Of course he does. He's oozing machismo.

"Espinosa's computer is monitored, of course," Traut continues, "so our plan is to send him out on his lunch break. He'll talk to Ms. Vargas and distract her long enough to plant the Mona Lisa on her computer."

"Why her computer?" Judson asks. "Why not use someone a little lower down the food chain?"

Espinosa's mouth shifts just enough to wriggle the mustache on his upper lip. "Felicia must have constant contact with the boss, no? She will have access to files that are off-limits to other departments."

Traut nods. "With any luck, we'll have copied and uploaded all the files on Saluda's servers by the time they close their offices for the day." He glances around the table. "Comments? Let me have them."

Holmes twiddles his fingers over the keys of his laptop. "I'm not sure I'm comfortable with this approach. Saluda's henchmen don't stop at warning those who are caught betraying the organization. Your computer is monitored, Señor Espinosa, so you don't want to risk your neck. What makes you willing to risk Señora Vargas's?"

Espinosa's mouth curls in a one-sided smile. "She is a woman. No one will believe her capable of planting a sophisticated program."

"Why not?" The words zip out of Glenda's mouth. "She's obviously bright enough to be the big man's secretary."

The newcomer's hand rises to tweak the end of his thin mustache. "Maybe it is different here, but the women at Saluda are not clever. Felicia is, however, a feast for the eyes."

A disgruntled sound rises from Judson's throat. "What if you're seen at her desk?"

"I will improvise. Don't worry, I am good at it. Your people have trained me well."

I glance around the table and study my companions' expressions. Traut seems content, but something about the plan doesn't agree with Glenda.

She turns to face Espinosa. "How can you be sure this woman isn't setting you up? She may not be as thickheaded as you think. I'd bet my last euro that she isn't."

Traut shuts her down with a stern glance. "If Espinosa trusts this woman, we'll trust her, too. When he's ready to proceed, I want to bring Sarah in to provide satellite surveillance."

Judson clears his throat. "Isn't that overkill? If it's as simple a matter as Señor Espinosa proposes…."

Glenda shakes her head. "It won't be simple. Even if he succeeds in loading the Mona Lisa onto Saluda's network, the files we want will certainly be encrypted."

Espinosa lifts a hand. "I need to know—what exactly does this Mona Lisa do? If they find the program on Felicia's computer, it might be helpful if I could deflect their suspicion—"

"They won't find it," Judson interrupts. "The Mona Lisa plants a half-dozen innocent files, all of them with random creation dates and .doc, .jpeg, or .pdf extensions. Only by breaking the files apart and analyzing every string would anyone find the code that's siphoning off information."

Espinosa leans back and whistles. "Genius. Did you write the program?"

"It's one of Sarah's," Jud answers, grinning. "A little ditty our steganography whiz kid whipped up in an afternoon. And if you think that's impressive—"

"If there's nothing else—" Glenda cuts him off, her voice dry "—we should get back to work."

I exhale in relief when Traut grips the arms of his chair.

"I think that takes care of it," he says. "Espinosa, we'll give you a flash drive loaded with the Mona Lisa before you go."

Traut and Espinosa stand. They pause to exchange smiles and claps on the shoulder before moving into the hallway. When they've gone, Glenda turns to me. "And your impression of Señor Espinosa is…?"

I blink. "Based on a ten-minute encounter?"

"I'm not asking for a case history, only an impression."

"Okay…chauvinistic and strong-willed, but anxious. And at least partially deceptive."

"Based on what?"

"His mustache. He kept grooming it."

One of Judson's brows rises. "He was lying to us?"

"Or he was thinking about the lies he'd have to tell in order to pull off his assignment. He seems capable and willing…but I can't be more definite than that."

Apparently my professional opinion counts for less than nothing, because Judson shuts his laptop and turns to Glenda, his closed eyes holding her as firmly as if he'd been a sighted man. "Do you feel good about this one, Dr. M?"

"No." She peers into the hallway. "No, I don't."

"Me, either," Jud admits. "But I can't put my finger on why."

Chapter Forty-Four

Sarah

Aunt Renee knocks on my apartment door and asks if I want to have a session while Judson and Dr. Mewton have their meeting. I don't open the door, but beg off by telling her I have stomach cramps. I'm stretching the truth only a little because my gut has been tied up in knots all day.

While Judson and Dr. Mewton meet with Mr. Traut, I hunker at my desk and consider the new information I've learned this morning. My father was killed while trying to expose Saluda. Judson was maimed while following the same case. Hightower was—what, poisoned?—while trying to get the goods on Adolfo Rios.

I have no way of knowing how many people have lost their lives while trying to expose Rios and his henchmen, but I don't think I'll be able to rest until I know who killed my father. The CIA knows he was murdered, but Aunt Renee says everyone back home thinks he committed suicide.

How could my country allow such a travesty of justice? It's not right; it's not fair. We should have exposed Rios and his thugs long ago.

For an aching instant I wish I could unlock the door and let Aunt Renee in to share all my secrets. I would love to have a partner in what I'm about to do, but I can't tell anyone.

Judson has already paid for his involvement with Saluda, and Aunt Renee didn't sign on for this kind of venture.

I must take this next step alone.

I want the world to know the truth; I want the murderers exposed. So how can I, a faceless girl, succeed where so many agents have failed?

I can only do what I do best.

I line up my fingers on the keyboard and close my eyes. I've already hacked into the agency's server farm, surely a federal offense. I've pried into every corner of the convent. I've rifled through networks at Langley without being detected. If I'd left a trail, they'd already have enough evidence to hold me in prison forever, but they've never detected my snooping…and in my skill lies my only hope.

I set my jaw and open my basic steganography program, then pull up a photo of one of Judson's Internet bimbos. The blonde is big-haired, sleepy-eyed, and wearing a red dress so tight every microfiber must contain a full strand of her DNA. Any man with eyes in his head would pause if this picture flashed across his computer screen.

It's perfect.

I input the .jpg file path, then open a new file and save a simple message as plain text. The program asks for a pass phrase and I type *HOLA*.

When I click the F5 key, the program replaces random pixels of the photo with my text file. I double-check the finished picture to be sure the blonde's eyes have not been crossed or her cheeks misaligned, but the bimbo's face is still flawless.

I attach the jpeg to a blank e-mail and type Adolfo_Rios@Saluda.com in the "To" window. I tab down and type: *Para destapar mis secretos, digas hola.*

I'm not certain of the Spanish, but I'm confident my message will be noticed.

I save the e-mail to a flash drive, delete the file from my system, and enter the defrag command. While the largest portion of my hard drive gets busy wiping and reorganizing files, I enter the partition with my alternate operating system, access the e-mail through the flash drive, and bounce it through a dozen trap doors.

By the time Adolfo Rios opens the message, not even the hacker with the patience of a spider could trace it.

Chapter Forty-Five

Renee

When Sarah finally arrives in our therapy room, she gestures toward the computer, where a colorful splash screen brightens the monitor. "What's this?"

"A game," I say, coming around to stand beside her. "It's all the rage in the States. People of all ages enjoy it."

"The Sims? I think I've heard of it."

"Ever played it?"

"Apparently I'm about to."

Oh, yes, you are.

On the flight to London, I read an article claiming that many little girls were surrendering their Barbie dolls in favor of the Sims. The computer characters were more interactive than dolls, providing a more enriching and imaginative experience.

I hope the article was right.

I fold my arms and smile. "The object is to create characters and keep them happy. They'll let you know what they need."

"How?"

"Oh, they talk. They don't speak English, but you'd be surprised how well they communicate through sound, facial expression, and posture. They also give you pictorial hints whenever the situation becomes especially dire."

"And what would they consider a dire situation?"

"Being tired, hungry, or lonely. Or desperately needing a toilet or shower."

Sarah exhales heavily, a clear look of disbelief on her face, but she grabs the mouse, sits, and clicks on the screen.

She must be feeling better.

I step back and try not to hover as Sarah sets up her make-believe family. I'm not surprised when she figures out the mechanics of the game intuitively. The operation of the program shouldn't give her problems, but I wonder how she'll handle the social aspect of the Sims.

She names her female character Sarah and giggles. "Sarah Sim. How perfect."

I laugh. "Isn't it? I ordered the game especially for you, but I wasn't thinking about the name. That's purely a coincidence."

"I know," she says, clicking on the next screen. "Believe me, there have been days when I felt more like a simulation than a person."

She's reached the screen where the game offers several female faces and body shapes to choose for the female character. Sarah clicks through the options, finally settling on a combination that looks like a curvy storm trooper. I can't help noticing that the avatar wears a helmet with a face shield; like Sarah, she has no face.

Sarah investigates the male character options more slowly, finally choosing the head of a man with brown hair with gray streaks at the temple. I lift a brow, recognizing the similarity between her character and the newest man in her life. Does she realize that she's created a Sim who resembles Vincent Kollman? Frankly, I expected her male Sim to look more like Mitch.

She clicks on the Done button. "What next?"

"You buy furnishings for your Sims' new home. Keep an eye on the budget, and try to purchase things they'll really need. If they don't have a bed, for instance, they will complain."

Her mouth twists in a grimace I've begun to interpret as

an expression of concentration. Within a few minutes she's furnished her make-believe home with what she considers essentials: a shower, toilet, sink, desk, bed, and computer.

"Your Sims need beauty, too," I point out. "A picture on the wall, a potted plant. Something to spruce up their lives a little. If they don't have it—"

"They'll complain," Sarah finishes for me. "Good grief, what's the fun of playing a game where the characters complain all the time?"

I move to the opposite side of the table and take a seat. "Just give it a try. I think you'll soon see why the game is so popular."

I pick up a book and skim the pages while I listen to various sounds coming from the speakers. The roar of a car engine assures me that Sarah has found jobs for her Sims; the noise of doors opening and closing indicates that her Sims have survived their first day. I hear tender Sim voices cooing to each other, then the heavy sighs of disappointment.

"Was that you?" I peer over the top of my book. "Or is someone unhappy in Sim city?"

"How are you supposed to get points in this game?" Sarah is too busy clicking to look up. "How do you win?"

"The game isn't about winning. It's about keeping your Sims happy and helping them lead productive lives."

Sarah makes a faint sound of derision. "Fat chance of that. My girl keeps moping, and there's a heart in her thought bubble."

"She wants love." I soften my voice. "Select the male, then right click and tell him to hug her. Or dance with her, or kiss her. Whatever you think she'd enjoy."

Sarah gives me a glance that clearly says she thinks I've lost my mind. I make a mental note—either her face is becoming more expressive or I've grown more adept at reading it. Either way, we're making progress.

I close my book, content to let Sarah enjoy this virtual taste of the outside world. In fact, I think I'll let her take the game with her for solo play. She might be more spontaneous if I'm not in the room.

"I'm going for a cup of Shelba's coffee," I say, standing. "Would you like some?"

"No." She doesn't glance up, but flinches when an outsider, Sim Neighbor, walks up to Sarah's female and begins to talk in Sim language. "What am I supposed to do with *him?*"

"Right click and smile," I tell her. "Be friendly. Invite him in for coffee. Turn on the radio."

"But we don't have a coffee machine or a radio."

"That's the nice thing about Sim world—as long as your Sims are working, you can always stop the game and buy one. But if they get too unhappy to work…that's when things get difficult."

With that, I slip out of the room and leave my niece to further her emotional education on her own.

Chapter Forty-Six

Sarah

I drop my arms from the keyboard when I hear the door open, then I glance at the clock on the computer. Twelve-thirty? I can't believe I've been dealing with Mr. and Mrs. Whiny Sims for more than *two hours*. Even more unbelievable is the fact that I've played through lunch.

"Did Shelba save me a plate?"

"Yes, and Judson wondered where you were." Aunt Renee's voice is light as she strides toward me with a tray. "I brought you a sandwich and a bottle of cranberry juice. Thought you might be getting a little hungry and dehydrated up here."

"Thanks." I take the juice and twist off the cap, then take a long swallow. "In a minute, I might start making those gestures that mean I need a toilet."

"Outside, first door on the left," Aunt Renee quips, dropping a napkin in my lap. "Seriously, if you want to take a break—"

"I'm fine. I just need to stretch." I pull the napkin from my lap and stand, then walk toward the wide arched windows. At this moment, I'm sorry they blackened the glass on this floor. It would have been nice to see sunshine on a bright day like this.

When I return to the table, Aunt Renee has spread several photographs over the surface. Each picture features a different person, but all of the subjects are smiling.

"They're happy," I say, unwrapping the sandwich she's brought. "Right?"

She folds her arms. "Have a seat. We're going to have a brief lesson in Smiling 101."

I drop into my chair. "You mean these people *aren't* happy?"

"Not exactly. That's the thing about a smile—sometimes it's trustworthy, sometimes it's not. You have to know the subtle signs that indicate the difference."

I take a bite of my chicken salad sandwich and shrug, but I am interested. These people have all the appropriate parts—nice lips, straight teeth, oval faces. If they can't manage a genuine smile, who can?

Aunt Renee taps the first photo. "Look at this picture and tell me what you see."

I swallow. "A man. He's smiling."

"How do you know?"

"The corners of his lips curve upward. And I can see his teeth."

"Right, and that's a good indicator, but we smile with more than our lips. Examine his eyes—what do you see there?"

I set my sandwich down and peer more closely at the picture. "His eyes seem small. There's a little bulge beneath his lower lashes. And his brows…they're kind of low."

"You have good powers of observation, Sarah. That little bulge and the lowered brow are caused by the tightening of a muscle known as the zygomatic major. When a person is truly happy, the lower eyelid rises, the brows lower, and the corners of the mouth turn up. Now look at this picture."

She taps another picture of the same man.

"Same man, same smile." I take another bite of my sandwich. "You havth a duplicath."

"Don't talk with your mouth full," she says, tapping the photo again. "And no, it's not a duplicate. You're getting lazy."

I tighten my mouth and look at the picture again. On closer examination, I can see that the man's head is tilted in a different direction, and there's a small shadow on his jacket. His eyes are different, too.

"His eyes." I swallow and look to Aunt Renee for confirmation. "They're big and flat now."

Her eyes crinkle at the corners when she smiles. "They are indeed. The man is smiling, but his smile isn't genuine. Maybe someone told him to smile for the camera, or maybe he's pretending to be happy about something. But if you look closely, you can see the difference."

"He's also not showing as many teeth."

"Right. You can't always count on teeth because mouths come in all shapes and sizes, but usually the more teeth displayed, the more enthusiastic the smile."

She stands and pulls a plastic shopping bag from the examination table against the wall. "This was Dr. Mewton's idea," she says, lifting a stack of magazines from the bag. "I'll bet the newsstand owners got a kick out of seeing Sisters Luke and Shelba buying fashion magazines."

She spreads them over the table so I can see the glossy covers. Most of them are unfamiliar to me, but one looks familiar.

"I recognize this one." I tap the cover of *La Hora del Rezo*. "Dr. M buys it all the time."

Aunt Renee picks up the magazine. "*The Hour of Prayer?* Dr. Mewton buys *this?*"

"Sister Luke does." I shrug. "I've never seen any of the others, but I did learn a few things about magazine publication by watching *13 Going on 30*."

Aunt Renee smiles, but she's not showing any teeth.

"I'm not going to be able to read these," I tell her. "My Spanish isn't so great."

"I don't want you to read them. I want you to go through these magazines and examine smiles. Tag them with these—" she slides a stack of Post-it notes across the shiny surface of a gossip magazine "—and tell me what kind of smiles you see. Are they genuine smiles, insincere smiles, hesitant smiles, reluctant smiles. If you're not sure, guess. You need to develop your intuition, as well as your powers of observation."

I set the sticky notes aside and pick up a fashion magazine. "Is that my only assignment?"

"There's one more."

When she blinks rapidly, I wonder what *that* expression means.

"I want you to practice smiling in every way you've learned. Use the mirror, and do your best."

I glance at the oval standing at the end of the table. For two days, I've done my best to ignore the reflective glass. "What if my results are nothing like the pictures?"

"Doesn't matter. I'm not even sure your facial muscles are capable of some of the expressions we'll be discussing in the days ahead, but for now we're focusing on smiles." She drops her hands into her lap. "I thought it might be nice to begin with something easy."

I flip through the magazine and nod. "Okay, teacher. But I have to go back to work soon. Mr. Traut and the CIA don't care much about smiling."

"I know, and that's a pity. If you have any questions, I'll be in my room."

"I'll be fine." I open the magazine on the table, pick up my sandwich, and turn the pages as if I'm going to be a good girl and look for pictures while I eat. The moment the door closes behind me, though, I flip to the table of contents and skim through the titles. A headline on the cover caught my eye: *La cara perfecta. The perfect face.*

I find the page number and fast forward to the article. The bright pages feature a face with smooth skin, large brown eyes, delicately arched brows, a slender nose, and full, perfectly shaped lips.

The opposite page features photos of assorted beauty *cosméticos*. A block of text follows the pictures, but I don't bother trying to translate it.

Despite the promises of this article, I know that achieving the perfect face is impossible with cosmetics alone. Someone like me needs professional help to present even a passable face to the world. I don't want to be breathtakingly gorgeous; I wouldn't know how to handle perfection.

Still, to have *la cara perfecta*... Some things might be worth dreaming about.

Dinner turns out to be a festive affair. Since Mr. Traut is present, Shelba prepares a feast—onion soup, steamed vegetables, roast duck, and a chocolate soufflé. Aunt Renee, Dr. Kollman, Dr. Mewton, Mr. Traut, and Judson have all been seated by the time I arrive, but they wait until I take my place before picking up their spoons and tasting the soup.

As they eat, I sip from my own bowl and study my companions. Though I've spent the entire afternoon grappling with the problem of how to turn brain signals into memories, I can't help but think of my aunt's lessons as I look around the table. What are these people saying to me with their faces?

Judson's face, broad and brown, is the most flexible of the group, continually twisting into a smile, a gape, or an exaggerated grimace. I suspect this is not only part of his personality, but something he does to compensate for his missing eyesight.

My aunt's face is more delicate, and tends to be still when the others are talking. Yet her eyes frequently flash unspoken messages, which I try my best to decipher. Does her uplifted brow mean surprise or alarm? When her eyes widen, is she pleased? If only one corner of her mouth rises, is she intending a half smile or an expression of doubt? Is the expression intentional or unconscious?

Dr. Kollman's face seems most at home when nestled against his palm. Except when his hands are occupied with silverware, his napkin, or his glass, he likes to rest his elbow on the table and prop his chin in his hand. His blue eyes are usually soft, and the creases at the corners are deep, as if they've existed for years.

Mr. Traut is hard to read. Unless he's talking, he tends to look at the edges of other people's plates or study the wall behind their heads. He rarely smiles and he never looks at me. He's nice to my aunt and friendly with Dr. Mewton, but he maintains a professional distance from everyone else.

I know Dr. Mewton's face best, but I've never studied it analytically. Though she is sixty-one years old, her skin is remarkably unlined. She wears her gray hair as short as a soldier's. Her teeth are perfectly white and perfectly spaced; her blue eyes can prick and deflate a lie even from across the room.

Dr. Mewton guards her face, I think. I study her as she watches the conversational exchanges between Dr. Kollman and Aunt Renee. Whenever one of them looks at her, Dr. Mewton smiles, but the zygomatic major, my aunt would say, is not tensing, so those smiles are insincere. But I do not believe them malicious, for Dr. Mewton is always polite to our guests.

My gaze drifts back to Dr. Kollman's face as I ponder what I've learned over this dinner's first course. An insincere smile, then, could be a good thing.

It is here, in this unexplored territory, that I realize how I can make Gutenberg more reliable as a truth detector. By connecting the computer to a camera, I can train the program to identify the key facial movements and micro expressions that signify deception, embellishment, and mood alteration. The research already exists; scientists have been hard at work on programs to help people with Asperger's syndrome and other types of autism. Aunt Renee will know how to help me access it.

"Oh, my." I drop my spoon and look at Mr. Traut, who looks at me and then turns away.

I switch my gaze to Dr. M. "I know how to do it. Gutenberg needs a camera."

Dr. Mewton lifts her upper lip and makes the quick *tsssst* sound that means I've said too much to the wrong people.

But that's okay. The best-attended dinner of my life has also been the most productive.

Maybe even the most enjoyable.

I'm pushing in my chair when Shelba stops to clear away my dessert plate. "Miss Sarah, a word?"

"Sure."

She casts a quick glance at the departing diners as she bends to pick up another set of dishes. "What I hear—is it true?"

I lean on the back of my chair. "What have you heard?"

"I hear you're leaving us." She sets the dirty dishes on her cart and looks at me without even the hint of a smile. "Things wouldn't be the same around here if you left us."

"I'm not going anywhere for a long time." I watch the others as they file through the doorway—especially Judson and Dr. Mewton. "Who told you I was leaving?"

She bends to reach for Mr. Traut's coffee cup. "It's not a secret, is it?"

"I suppose not."

"Then Dr. Mewton told me. She would hate to see you go."

I cling to the back of my chair and wonder what Aunt Renee would do in this moment. She would probably touch Shelba in some way, maybe pat her back or squeeze her arm. I lift my hand, then grip the chair again. "Shelba, would you be happy if you had to spend all your time here at the convent?"

She straightens, the creamer in her hand. "*All* the time?"

"What if you were never allowed to go ashore to shop, pick up a newspaper, or visit your family on vacation. How would you feel about that?"

I watch as her face flutters with tiny movements. "I—I wouldn't like it one bit. Those trips…they keep me sane."

"Then you understand. If the doctor can fix my face, I want to be able to leave this place. I'm not planning to abandon my work, but I'd like to have options."

She draws a deep breath and bends to retrieve the centerpiece from the table. "All the same, I will miss you when you're gone."

"I'll miss you, too."

I slip past her and exit the dining room, but a question follows me out the door: is Dr. Mewton so intent on keeping me here that she'd enlist Shelba to talk me out of having the transplant?

After dinner, Judson catches me in the hallway and asks me to ride upstairs with him. Once we're safely inside the elevator I cross my arms and turn. "What's up?"

He lifts one shoulder in a shrug. "Nothing, really. Sounded like you had a nice epiphany at dinner."

"I did. I'm excited."

I slip my sweater from my shoulders and toss it over the security camera in the corner of the car, then I kneel and whisper in Judson's ear. "The camera's blocked. Why the private conference?"

He turns his head and it all comes tumbling out. "You didn't seem like yourself tonight," he says, his voice a rough whisper. "Are you okay? How are things going with your aunt?"

I prop my hands on the armrest of his wheelchair. "Epiphanies aside, the work is harder than I expected."

"You mean the whiz kid has found something she doesn't comprehend right off the bat?"

"You should *so* be a comedian." I pause to pull my thoughts together. "You know what I had to do during my lunch today? Flip through magazines and look for smiles. After I found a few, Aunt Renee wanted me to imitate those expressions in a mirror."

"What's so hard about that?"

I blow out my cheeks. "If you had my face, you wouldn't ask."

"Honey." Judson's tone is slightly reproving. "I've known you for what—two and a half years? In all that time, you've never seemed anything less than lovely."

My eyes fill with sudden tears. Judson turns, waiting for a response, but my throat's too tight to speak.

"Sarah? You okay?"

Somehow, I manage to squeak out an "Uh-huh."

"Baby girl—" Judson reaches for my hand "—I don't know what happened to you, but I believe you're ready to grow up. So even if the going gets tough, you keep going. Don't let anything get in your way, you hear?"

He's a huge encouragement, but he didn't see me attempting to bend my lipless flesh in the mirror this afternoon. I tried to smile like a movie star, and ended up scowling like a freak.

"You hang in there," Judson says, rubbing my hand. "You're going to do just fine."

Chapter Forty-Seven

Renee

After a long, rainy weekend, most of which I spend helping Sarah gather research on micro expressions and deception analysis, I decide to begin the new week with a walk in the garden.

I step outside and lift my face to the sun, then realize I am not alone. Vincent Kollman stands about ten yards away, his hands in his pockets and the slanting rays of sunrise on his face.

"I thought I'd have this place to myself," I call. "Apart from the chapel, I think it's my favorite place on the island."

He squints at me through the bright orange beams and steps closer. "Didn't know there was a chapel. Then again, until I started hanging out with you, I didn't know there was a graveyard."

"A garden," I correct him. "The beauty of this place depends entirely on your perspective."

He smiles. "Spoken like a true shrink. Tell me, Dr. Carey, do you ever turn it off?"

"I don't know what you mean."

"Sure you do. But that's okay—I find your insights charming."

He jerks his head toward the bench against the wall. "Care to sit and talk?"

"Do we have something to talk about?"

"Indeed we do—our patient. And since this is one of the few places we can talk in private…"

"Lead the way, sir."

I follow him, my arms crossed against the chill, and we sit together on the bench. For a long moment, neither of us says anything. Then I elbow him. "So…how goes the work of finding our donor?"

He grips the edge of the bench with both hands. "That's proving to be a challenge. Last night I thought I'd hit the jackpot—an accident victim in Kentucky was a match in all the crucial categories, and she had agreed to be a donor. They harvested her kidneys, her heart, and her eyes, but the family refused to even consider donating her face. The face is so…personal."

My heart shrivels. "You didn't mention this to Sarah, did you?"

"Not a word. I didn't want to get her hopes up."

"Smart thinking. And that's okay—I'm not sure she's ready. But she will be. I've been praying that everything will fall into place just as it's supposed to."

Vincent raises a brow. "You pray?"

"All the time, these days. I'm trying to reconnect with my faith."

He snorts softly. "Not a bad idea. Especially when you're involved in a case like this."

"It's tough, but I can't give up. I knew it'd be tough."

"Maybe not as tough as you think. After all, there are over six billion people in the world. And we only need one face."

I like the way he says *we*. As if he, Sarah, and I are in this together.

"Speaking of surgery," he says, leaning into me, "how's your dog?"

"You know about Elvis?"

"Sarah mentioned something at lunch yesterday. Said he had a tendency to eat inappropriate materials."

I laugh. "I managed to get a call out Friday afternoon, and Becky says he's fine. Too fine, in fact. I don't think he misses me at all."

Vincent leans forward and turns his head so I can see his face. His eyes are serious, but one corner of his mouth curves upward. "I'm glad the dog is okay, but don't take his fickleness to heart. If I were wherever he is, I'd be missing you something fierce."

I blink, not sure how to react. I study him, and he studies me back. From the corner of my eye, I see a seagull land on a nearby grave marker and twist his head, his black eyes bright with curiosity.

Vincent gestures to the bird. "Have you been feeding them?"

"Not a crumb."

"Then this guy must think you have a kind face."

I smile, liking the curve of the surgeon's mouth, the compassion in his eyes, the graceful strength of his hands. I'm a little confused by his easy charm—is he like this with all women?—but I'm willing to sit on this bench a little longer.

Maybe a month or two.

When a door slams, my first reaction is regret. But Sarah steps out and strolls down the narrow strip between the building and the graves, her head bent, her eyes downcast. She's nearly to the bench before she lifts her head and sees us. "Oh! Sorry." A flush colors her scarred cheeks. "I didn't know you two were out here."

Vincent twiddles his fingers in a playful wave. "No need to apologize. Maybe you're the one the birds have come to see."

"Me?" She glances around and spies the sharp-eyed gull on the cross. "Oh. Yeah." She pulls the round end of a loaf from her pocket and tosses a few crumbs to the bird. Almost immediately four or five others join the scout, all of them circling and begging for a handout.

"I think," I say, ducking, "this'd be a good time to go in for breakfast."

"I'll come with you," Vincent offers. "Sarah?"

She shakes her head and tosses another handful of bread to the birds. A shadow has filled her eyes, and the sight of it gives me pause. Have I said something to upset her? Has Vincent? Or is this one of those inexplicable moods that often plague young women?

I reach out and touch her arm as I pass. "I'll save you a seat at the table."

Chapter Forty-Eight

Sarah

I don't go in for breakfast. Not because I'm not hungry, but because I don't want to sit beside Aunt Renee and pretend that nothing is wrong while she smiles at Dr. Kollman and he grins back at her.

He's my doctor. He works for my agency. So why has she suddenly become so interested in him?

They were sitting close together in the courtyard, shoulders touching. People don't sit that close unless they're attracted to each other or there's no room on the bench.

There was plenty of room on the bench.

I jog up the stairs to the second floor, then stride into the operations center and wake my sleeping computer. They'll probably ask about me at breakfast. Aunt Renee might even ask Shelba to set aside a bowl of oatmeal for me, but there's nothing worse than coagulated mush.

Unless it's cold toast. Or cold coffee.

I hate cold food almost as much as I hate the dark. Maybe because the two are forever linked in my mind, the link forged back when I used to curl up in my bed with my eyes covered in bandages. I was always cold as a child—either shivering because they kept the room cool or pulling away from the startling chill of the stethoscope and the iron bars they planted in my face. I remember darkness and the cold splash of Betadine across my cheeks, chest, and neck.

I've seen *Forrest Gump.* I know some kids wear braces on their legs or on their teeth. But I've never seen a movie in which a kid wore a metal band around his head and had bars poking through the skin above his jaw. That's what I had. That's what I knew.

I've heard Dr. M talk about my past with Aunt Renee and Dr. Kollman. She drops those years into the conversation as if they were nothing but a minor difficulty, but pain and agony were all I knew for months at a time. For her, those days were a means to an end, but I didn't know the pain had a purpose. All I knew was agony, manipulation, darkness, pricks, blood…and cold.

Other children come out of childhood with memories of Easter egg hunts, bright Christmas mornings, and festive birthday parties. In movies I see kids dancing on Daddy's feet and riding on his shoulders; they go shopping with their moms and fight with their siblings over who gets first dibs on the Nintendo.

I have none of those memories. I participated in no neighborhood high jinks like *Dennis the Menace,* no silly holiday gifts like those in *A Christmas Story.* And though Dorothy Gale was an orphan, at least she had Toto, Uncle Henry, and Auntie Em. She got a trip over the rainbow, but all I got was months of agony while Dr. Mewton adjusted screws on an apparatus implanted in my jaw.

I'd be happy to trade places with Dorothy…or any other American kid. Sometimes I look at Jud in his wheelchair and think that I'd gladly endure the frustration he feels now if I could enjoy the life he had before.

I draw a deep breath and watch a slanting sunbeam shorten, withdrawing by centimeters over the worn floor tiles. An unformed thought teases my mind, hiding like a shadow among my wishes and regrets.

I need to focus on work. I click on my in-box and delete a

couple of unimportant e-mails. Raven has sent another message, wanting to know how I'm coming with the memory implantation module for Gutenberg. He'll be glad to hear that I've made progress.

I click Reply and place my hands on the keyboard, then freeze as the teasing thought blooms into realization. Why not give myself the childhood I've always wanted?

If I can implant details of an imagined mission into someone's subconscious, why can't I plant memories of a happy childhood into my own head? Instead of transfusions, I could remember Popsicle ices. Instead of recalling endless hours of pain, I could remember idyllic days of walking on a beach or making sand castles.

I could lock my actual past in a drawer, choosing instead to remember things that bring pleasure, not pain.

Now that we have the technology, why shouldn't I?

Chapter Forty-Nine

Renee

At breakfast, I tell Vincent and Glenda that Sarah reminds me of a night-blooming cereus. "It's the homeliest plant you can imagine," I say, spreading jam on my toast. "Looks like a cactus—scrawny and flat-leafed—until it puts out this bloom that hangs like that droopy bud in *The Little Shop of Horrors*."

"Sarah loves that movie," Glenda interrupts. "She and Holmes went through a phase where they watched it every weekend."

"Go on." Vincent smiles at me over the rim of his coffee cup. "Why does she remind you of this plant?"

I glance at Glenda. "Because the plant never seems to change, and then, boom! It flowers. But it blooms in the middle of the night, and the blossom only lasts for a few hours. But it's one of the most beautiful and fragrant flowers you can imagine—large, pure, and completely unexpected."

Vincent lowers his cup. "If it opens only at night, how does anyone ever see it?"

I laugh. "Well, you have to keep an eye on it, and when it gets ready to bloom, you have to camp out and wait for it. I've spent a couple of nights out on the back porch with candles, a book, and my camera. I consider it an adventure."

Glenda abruptly stops chewing. "I fail to see how that relates to Sarah."

I draw a deep breath. "It's a metaphor. I meant that Sarah is a bit of a slow bloomer. We've been working together every morning, and most of the time I think we're making no progress at all. And then—bingo! She'll say something, or look at someone, and I suddenly realize she gets it. She's experiencing an emotional awakening, but it's coming in fits and starts."

"You'll be interested in her proposal, then," Glenda says, pressing her napkin to the corners of her mouth. "She wants to meet with the three of us later this morning. In the conference room at eleven—she said she needs to talk to all of us."

My gaze drifts to Sarah's empty chair. "Is she preparing something for us now?"

"I don't know what she's doing," Glenda answers, her tone clipped. "She's kept her head down all week, but her logs show that she's been working on the Gutenberg project. I have no idea what she wants to tell us."

I look at Judson's empty place, then glance at Vincent. His eyes warm when they meet mine, and his hint of a smile acknowledges the success of my mind reading. Wherever Sarah is, Judson is with her.

I'm glad she's not alone.

At eleven o'clock, I slip into the conference room and take a seat with the others. As I might have predicted, Sarah and Judson are sitting on one side of the table, while the three chairs on the other side are clearly meant for Glenda, Vincent, and me.

"Thank you for coming," Sarah says once we have all taken a seat. "I wanted you all here because I value your opinion…and because you have supported my desire to have the face transplant."

My heart thumps against my rib cage. Has she changed her mind about the surgery?

"Aunt Renee," she says, her flat mouth spreading in a thin

smile, "without giving you too many details, you should know that I've been working on a program that probes the brain for specific memories. It also has the potential to *deposit* memories into a patient's consciousness."

"Wait a minute." I glance around the gathering, not certain where this is going. "This doesn't sound like computer code."

Sarah folds her arms on the table. "The computer's a tool we use in conjunction with an EEG. I've devised a program that will help us learn if a certain memory is in a patient's head."

I give her a wry smile. "Sounds like science fiction."

"Not really. You know how people say, 'I'll recognize it when I see it?' They say that because they know they have a memory tucked inside their brain. When they receive the proper stimulus, that area of the brain lights up. My program links various stimuli to the 'hits' in a patient's brain and interprets the result."

"Dr. Mewton—" she turns to face Glenda "—you'll be pleased to know that I've solidified the procedure in which we implant memories into a subject's subconscious. I'm sure Mr. Traut will be pleased."

Glenda lifts a brow. "Hypnosis?"

"Partly. As you know, Dr. M, memories are called up via activation of the entire network across multiple regions of the brain. In order to plant memories, we'll have to stimulate several regions—the process will be a combination of hypnosis, electrical stimulation, audiovisual feedback, and adrenaline injection. But it's possible. We can do it."

"Wonderful." Glenda claps her hands, startling me with this unexpected display of emotion.

"I don't understand," I break in. "How are you supposed to internalize something that didn't happen to you?"

"Adrenaline is the key," Vincent says, nodding at Sarah. He looks at me. "As you know, our memories are a bit like gelatin— they take time to solidify in the brain. A memory reinforced by adrenaline becomes rock solid. Almost unforgettable."

"Because I'm sure the process will work," Sarah continues, looking from Glenda to Vincent, "I'd like to be the first to have memories implanted—memories of the childhood I was never allowed to enjoy."

Sarah looks at Judson as silence sifts down like a snowfall. "Told you they'd be surprised."

"Sarah," Glenda says, confidence fading from her voice, "I don't think we can sanction any sort of experimentation on one of our own."

"I'm not talking about implanting a mission," Sarah says, "but something completely innocuous. While I'm waiting for a donor, I can put together my own memories. Aunt Renee can help me. She could send for photo albums so I could compile memories of my father and mother…maybe even a pet."

I am too startled by this suggestion to offer any objection.

"But Sarah," Vincent says, bringing his hand to his cheek. "So many changes at once! A new face, new feelings—"

"Why shouldn't I have new memories?" Sarah's eyes widen. "I won't be obliterating my real past, I'll just be filing it away. But when I think about my parents, instead of drawing a blank, I'll be able to enjoy memories of being with them."

"Wait a minute." I hold up a hand. "Sarah, you can't pick and choose what happens to you in life. Everything that happens, good and bad, *is* your life. Your experiences are what shape you into the person you become."

"You urged me to ask for a new face, didn't you? How is that different from asking for new memories?"

"It—it just is. To a certain extent we can direct our present and our future, but we're not all-powerful, only God is. The good and bad things in our past are uniquely ours. You can't change the past without changing who you are."

Glenda raises a brow. "Many people would disagree with your last statement."

"You know—" Vincent presses his hands together "—they are now giving propranolol to people suffering from post-traumatic stress disorder. Unlike adrenaline, which solidifies a recollection, propranolol seems to cut the cord between memory and emotion."

"Cut the cord?" I gape at him. "By eliminating the links between memory and emotion, wouldn't we be creating zombies? Children who can't weep for dead parents, abused women who can't vent their anger or fear—"

"You're overreacting. If I had a daughter who'd been brutalized in a rape or a mugging, you bet I'd give her the drug. I'd do it in a heartbeat to spare her the memory of such pain." He looks at me, one bushy brow quirked in a question. "Wouldn't you?"

My mouth goes dry as all of them turn to me—Vincent, Glenda, Sarah. Even Judson, who has not offered anything to the debate, seems to stare at me through his sealed eyelids.

"I would give anything to prevent my child from suffering," I say, my voice heavy. "But who can say that a painful experience wouldn't serve a purpose in my daughter's life?"

Glenda turns her head, waving my opinion away. "Spoken like a fatalist. Everything has a purpose in your world, right?"

"Well…yes."

Vincent shakes his head. "While I respect your opinion," he says, his voice warm with regret, "I have to admit that I agree with Sarah. What's the harm in giving her a better childhood than the one she's known? Why not let her have a handful of pleasant memories she can enjoy?"

"I—I need to think about it." I look around the circle and struggle to explain my resistance. "But if we give Sarah a past that's not real…isn't that worse than keeping her in a pretend convent? She may not have enjoyed many experiences here, but at least those experiences were *hers*. Her life is her own."

"Your illogic astounds me." Glenda eyes me as if I were a bad smell. "You want to take our Sarah and send her away with a fake face. Yet when Sarah volunteers to use her own program to give herself a happy childhood, you balk."

"I have to say, Aunt Renee," Sarah adds, "I don't understand, either. Of all people, I thought you'd be happiest for me."

I look to Judson, hoping for a word of support, but he
remains silent, his face tilted in my direction, his brows lifted
in an unspoken question.

Apparently my answer is unacceptable to everyone in
the room.

Chapter Fifty

Sarah

For the next two weeks, I spend far more time in the past and future than in the present. I've begun to fill a notebook with recollections I want to create and store in my memory. When I'm not dreaming up new memories, I have been enthusiastically applying myself to Aunt Renee's lessons—studying photos, watching faces, and sitting in front of that nasty oval mirror while trying to imitate Dr. Kollman's uplifted brow and Dr. Mewton's curled upper lip. I am determined to face the future well equipped.

Though Aunt Renee does not agree with my decision to adopt a new past, she does not criticize me during our sessions. Still, there are times when I catch her looking at me in unguarded moments, and now I am better able to read the shadow in her eyes, the sadness in her smile.

She would change my mind if she could.

"It's strange," I tell Judson one afternoon. "Dr. Mewton is against the face transplant but she supports my plan to implant new memories. Aunt Renee is in favor of the transplant and opposed to the memory transfer. They disagree about almost everything."

"And yet they manage to avoid coming to blows," Judson quips. "Admirable women, both of them."

I leave him in the hallway and jog up the stairs to the third floor. Dr. Kollman didn't come down for lunch, and I want to be sure he's feeling okay.

As I turn at the third floor landing, I slow my step and consider my approach. I know he is much older than I, but we have spent time together nearly every day. He has measured my face "inside and out," as he likes to joke, and sometimes I think he knows me inside and out. We laugh and talk at breakfast every morning. Judson and Aunt Renee eventually join us in the dining room, but Dr. Kollman and I are nearly always the first at the table.

I'm not sure I understand why my heart has begun to thump every time his gaze meets mine, but lately I've been drawn to him like a butterfly to a flower. Though I used to get nervous every time Mitch came into view, Mitch never asked about my favorite poet or recited lines from *Moonstruck* as he took my blood pressure.

After Dr. Kollman told me "Snap out of it!" was his favorite line in any movie, I hurried downstairs and ran into the garden, so filled up with feeling that I thought I might burst. I had to do something—run, jump, dance, or turn cartwheels—so I stepped onto the flattened grass covering a grave and then hopped to the next on one foot. I had never played hopscotch, but suddenly I *had* to. I owed myself this opportunity to hop in a flood of happiness.

So I bent one leg, held my foot behind my back, and jumped from grave to grave, laughing myself silly. If Aunt Renee or Dr. Mewton had glanced out a window, they would have thought me crazy, but I didn't care. I hopped the entire width of the graveyard and collapsed next to the wall in a gale of giggles.

What is it about Dr. Kollman that makes me happy? I don't know. Why does his smile make me feel warm inside? I don't care. Let Dr. Mewton call me silly or stupid or even insane. It doesn't matter.

What I felt for Mitch, I've decided, was a silly crush. What I feel for Dr. Kollman…must be love.

At the top of the stairs I draw a deep breath, smooth the wrinkles out of my cotton shirt, and knock on his door. From within, I hear a deep greeting that increases my pulse rate.

I open the door and step into the room. The doctor is seated at his desk, but he smiles—with teeth showing—when he sees me. "Sarah!" He stands, a polite gesture I never see in modern movies. "Can I help you with something, or are you playing hooky from work?"

I shrug and lock my hands behind my back. "I wanted to stretch my legs, so I thought I'd come up to see you. Do you mind?"

"Mind? I'd find your company a welcome diversion. Please, pull up a chair."

I pull up one of the chairs next to the desk and sit down, grateful that he's not going to put his medical journal aside on my account. I like to watch him work. "What are you reading?"

"Preparatory materials."

"Preparatory for what?"

"For you." He pushes his reading glasses back to his nose and runs his finger over a column. "I've been lining up the team we'll need when we do your transplant. The operation will require specialists in two operating theaters—one here, of course, and one in the city where your donor is located."

"Why can't they bring the donor here?"

"Too much time, too many permissions required. The donor face will be degloved and shipped in a cooler, but don't worry, it will last up to eight hours. While it's en route, we'll prepare you—" He hesitates, his eyes searching my face. "Does discussing this bother you at all?"

I wave my hand, dismissing his concern. "Are you kidding? I'm the queen of surgical procedures."

"All right, then. I'll make a long description short and say that we'll remove your damaged tissue, then reattach your clamped blood vessels and nerves to the donor face. It's complicated microsurgery, but I'm confident our team will be able to handle it."

"Nothing but the best for America's team."

"Something like that." H abruptly closes his periodical. "Can I get you something? Water? A soft drink?"

"No, thank you. I'm fine." A brittle silence falls between us, and I look up, wondering what has changed. I study his face, but he has lowered his gaze and seems reluctant to meet my eyes.

Has talking about the transplant reminded him of how repulsive I am? Did I say something to embarrass him? Or…could he be feeling some of the same emotions I am?

"Dr. Kollman—"

"Sarah, I—"

"Please. Can I tell you something?"

Before I can explain the emotions that have been battering my heart, someone raps on the door.

Aunt Renee's face appears in the opening. "Hi, you two," she says, her voice as sunny as her smile. "Am I interrupting something?"

Dr. Kollman lifts a brow at me—his shorthand for a question—but I'm not about to spill *this* secret in front of Aunt Renee.

"Not a thing." I pull myself out of the chair. "And I'd better get to work."

And as I leave the room, I hear him greet her, and a note in his voice that wasn't there a moment ago…or was it? Love is so confusing.

I don't want to be hurt. I don't want to love anyone who doesn't love me back. But once you open your heart to someone, how can you stop feeling?

Only three of us show up for dinner that night—Dr. Kollman, Aunt Renee, and me. Judson comes down late, and when I lean over to ask him what's up, he gives me a terse response: "Espinosa is stalling. And Mewton's not happy."

When Shelba comes in to clear the table, we stand and compliment her on a delicious dinner. She thanks me when I stay behind to help her stack dishes on her cart.

I hand her the set of salt and pepper shakers. "Is Dr. Mewton eating?"

Shelba shakes her head. "The doctor is on an urgent call and cannot be disturbed. She may come down later for a bite, but who can say? The woman works too hard."

As Shelba pushes her cart toward the kitchen, I linger at the bottom of the stairwell and wonder what I should do with my evening. I could go upstairs and get in a couple of hours of work, I could go to the therapy room and stare at pictures of facial expressions, or I could roam around down here and hope to bump into Dr. Kollman, who has not yet gone upstairs. I'm not sure where he is, but if I wander in the right passageway…

I stroll through the hallway and try to imagine the building as it was a hundred years ago. Fewer than thirty or forty nuns worked and ate in these rooms, living on charity while they passed their lives in prayer and meditation. They spent hours on their knees, developing thick calluses, no doubt, while they waited for a word from God.

These walls have witnessed a lot of waiting.

I pass my aunt's room and then glance into the chapel. The sight of Dr. Kollman's figure in a pew catches me by surprise. I didn't know he was a religious man. Has he been coming here every night?

I creep into the chapel and slide into the pew behind him. He is sitting quietly, his head bowed. After a little while, he turns and glances toward the door.

And sees me.

"Sarah." His voice is both powerful and gentle. "I didn't expect to see you."

"Surprise."

He gestures toward the altar. "I find this one of the most

peaceful rooms in the facility. Coming here helps me focus my thoughts."

"On your work?"

"On everything."

I look up at the face of Jesus while I weigh his words. This may be the opportunity for which I've been waiting. Like Scarlett in *Gone with the Wind,* sometimes a woman has to gather her courage and say what's on her mind.

"Dr. Kollman, I need to tell you something."

He shifts on the pew to better see me. "Having second thoughts about the surgery?"

"No—if anything, I'm even more determined to go through with it. But during these last few weeks, I've...I've begun to feel things I've never felt before."

He tilts his head. "Your aunt told me this would happen. I was surprised by the data, but apparently there's a real physiological connection between facial expression and corresponding emotion. You've been concentrating on creating expressions, so it's only natural that you should begin to experience a corresponding increase in emotion." His face creases in a smile. "I hope the emotions have been pleasant."

"They have...mostly. Sometimes a bit unpredictable, though."

"That's what emotions are...unpredictable. The trick is learning how to keep a rein on them."

"Even love?"

He lifts a brow and takes a wincing little breath. "Love? Some would say it's more an action than an emotion. Love is what we do, not necessarily what we feel."

"But I do feel it...for you."

The doctor blinks, his strong mouth opens in a look I've learned to recognize as honest surprise.

His look fills me with a painful feeling of emptiness. Something rushes up from the pit of my stomach, sucking the air from my lungs, from the room, from the world.

I cling to the seat of the pew as the room begins to spin.

"Sarah…while I appreciate the compliment—"

"You don't love me."

"I didn't say that. I am fond of you, quite fond. And I'm honored you should feel…anything for me. But really, I think your feelings are probably more like those of a daughter for a father."

He can't look me in the eye, but seems intent on delivering his speech to a spot beside me on the pew. "I suggest—" he clears his throat "—that you talk to your aunt about these emotions. She will help you understand them, sort through them."

I lower my gaze and try to swallow the lump that has risen in my throat. Ten minutes ago I was facing the future with hope, not resignation. Now my mouth fills with the bitter taste of ashes—the ashes of my dreams.

What good is a new face if the man I love knows what a fake I am? He can't love me because he knows I am a misshapen monster. Even if I look like Miss America by this time next year, he will never be able to forget what I truly am.

I stand, keeping my head lowered. "I'm sorry if I embarrassed you."

"I'm not embarrassed. I'm honored, really."

Sure you are.

I nod a brief farewell and walk toward the door, blinking back tears as an odd line—is it from an old movie?—comes to mind: *Beauty may be only skin-deep, but ugly goes clear to the bone.*

Chapter Fifty-One

Renee

I am waiting outside Sarah's door when she comes up the stairs. She seems surprised to see me, so I flash the DVD case in my hand: "It's a classic—one I know you'll like. *Sunset Boulevard.*"

She glances uneasily at Judson's door, and she does not look happy.

"Did you have plans?" I ask, ready to retreat. "I only came up because it's Friday night, and nobody likes to sit home on Friday night. I thought it might be fun to watch a movie, maybe see if Shelba can scrounge up some popcorn."

"Popcorn?"

"Or hot dogs."

"But we just had dinner."

I laugh. "That's not the point. The point is to stuff yourself with junk food while you watch the film. If the movie's good enough, you won't even notice the resulting tummy ache."

Sarah draws a deep breath and opens her door. "Come on in."

As she takes the DVD and sets it up on her computer, I glance around her room. Nothing has changed since the last time I was in here, but maybe she's finding new meaning in the faces on the movie posters on her walls.

One can only hope.

We start the movie and climb up on the bed, bracing our

backs against the wall and surrounding ourselves with pillows. Joe Gillis has just parked his car in Norma Desmond's garage when Shelba knocks and brings in two buckets of popcorn, complete with dripping butter and napkins.

I thank her with a smile and invite her to stay for the movie.

"No, thank you," she says, waving us off. "I have bread in the oven."

Joe is watching Norma bury the dead monkey when Judson sticks his head into the room. "Do I smell popcorn?"

I wave the bowl in his direction. "Want some?"

"Naw." He shakes his head. "But boy, does that bring back memories."

"You're welcome to watch with us," Sarah says. "This film's at least as old as you are, so I'm sure you've seen it before."

"You're a heartless thing," Judson answers, rolling backward. "Keep your popcorn and your ancient movie. I'm going to bed."

Soon Sarah and I are alone again. I've seen the movie several times, so I watch my niece as much as I watch William Holden and Gloria Swanson. I ordered the film because I wanted Sarah to see the power of an expressive face…and because I assumed she liked it.

"Look." I point to Ms. Swanson, who's in full-on diva mode. "See how her eyeliner exaggerates the width of her eyes? She's playing a silent film actress, who would have had to exaggerate every gesture and expression. Contemporary actors don't do that because dialog helps carry the emotion. But by watching Ms. Swanson, you can see exaggerated emotional tells."

"They didn't need words," Sarah says, "because they had faces. Isn't that what Norma says?"

"You've seen this one before."

"About a dozen times. But it never grows old."

She falls silent and takes another handful of popcorn, leaving me to speculate on why she likes the movie so much.

Does the theme of communication resonate with her, or does she relate to the doomed loves of Norma and Joe, or Joe and Betty Schaefer?

"Do you think," she asks, "that Joe loves Norma?"

I glance at her, surprised by the question. "Do *you* think he loves her?"

"He sleeps with her, doesn't he? He laughs with her, takes her money, comes when she calls."

"He feels something for her," I admit, "but I'm not sure it's love. More like concern, maybe. Or responsibility."

"But Norma loves him."

"Maybe. I think Norma *needs* him. She needs someone to adore her, and Joe happened along at the right time."

Sarah remains silent, except for an occasional sigh. Her eyes, when I glance at them, are wide and unfocused, as if she's thinking of something else.

I point to the screen. "There…what expression do you see on Joe's face?"

Sarah's lashless eyelids blink at the screen. "Anger—but he's not furious. Temper, maybe."

"Look at his hands."

"They're clenched. Okay, so maybe that's frustration?"

"I think so. He wants to leave Norma and go with Betty, but he feels trapped. Norma depends on him, and she's already proven that she'll hurt herself if he tries to leave. So even though Betty's waiting—"

"He can't go."

I reach over and squeeze her hand. "You're getting good at this."

"Well—" her head tilts in what might be an attempt at a winsome expression "—I do work for CIA. We're supposed to be good at what we do. Someday I'll use all this in the field."

I exhale a quiet sigh. So…she has begun to think seriously about leaving this place.

I follow up on her thought. "When you're in the field,

you're going to depend on your ability to read facial expressions. I think you're going to be exceptionally good at it. You've had to work at what other people take for granted."

She grabs another handful of popcorn. "I don't think I'm so good at it. Lately I've been feeling like I've lived my entire life in a place where people are speaking a foreign language. I picked up a few words, but I missed a lot more than I picked up. With what you've been teaching me, I'm beginning to understand the language I missed."

She might have said more, but the cell phone on her desk rings. Grimacing at her butter-coated fingers, she gingerly pulls her phone out of its cradle. "Yes?"

I can hear Dr. Mewton's voice from where I'm sitting.

"I'll be right up."

She snaps the phone shut. "Sorry, but Dr. M needs me."

"Urgent meeting?"

Sarah wipes her fingers on a napkin. "It's—"

"I know, it's classified."

"You know, you're getting pretty good at this." Leaving me with that, she saunters out of the room.

Chapter Fifty-Two

Sarah

Dr. Mewton greets me with a perfunctory nod and leads me past her desk and through the doorway that opens into her apartment.

I hesitate at the threshold.

"It's okay." Dr. M tosses the words over her shoulder. "I know it's late. I was going to let this go until morning, but—"

"Let what go?"

"—I just can't."

She turns and waits until I step into the apartment. I glance around, taking in the sofa, the overflowing bookcase, the narrow bed against the window.

"Dr. Mewton—" my voice trembles "—what's wrong?"

"Have a seat, Sarah." She gestures toward a guest chair, then lowers herself onto the sofa. "I wanted to speak to you in private. This has gone on long enough."

Unable to imagine what she means, I stare straight ahead, one hand grasping the chair's armrest.

"Dr. Kollman pulled me aside a few moments ago. He told me about your meeting in the chapel."

I close my eyes. Heat floods my face, and my shoulders slump as something inside me crumbles. "Dr. Mewton—"

"This is why you should put all thoughts of leaving out of your mind, Sarah. You think you were hurt and embarrassed this evening? You haven't felt anything yet. You haven't been publicly scorned or shamed. But here you've been protected, nurtured, given the best education money could buy. You've had every advantage—"

"You call being locked away here an *advantage?*"

"You've never been locked away. You're free to come and go anytime you please."

I lift my hands so all ten fingers point to my face. "Like *this?*"

"Count yourself blessed." Dr. M leans forward and lowers her voice. "You think I don't understand what you're feeling? I do. Oh, I was never ugly, never misshapen. But I was every bit as different. It didn't matter so much in high school, but in college, when all the other girls were concentrating on getting their marriage certificates, I was studying brain and cognitive sciences. I was brilliant, Sarah, as smart as you are, and I paid a price for it."

I cross my arms, determined not to listen.

"It doesn't matter *why* you're different," she continues. "Some women are ugly, some are stupid. Some are smart, some are talented. Men hate the latter two groups most of all, because most men are insecure and they feel threatened. And when they feel threatened, they react…often with violence."

Unwillingly, I lift my gaze to meet hers. "I don't know what you mean."

"Don't you think I know how love can hurt?" She flushes when her voice cracks. "I loved a young man once. I gave him everything, and he gave me nothing but grief. And then, after he'd used my brain and my body, he turned on me—he and his friends."

She pins me with her gaze. "They attacked me, Sarah. Violated me. When it was over, I knew I'd been a fool…and I knew I could never let myself be vulnerable again."

She reaches toward me, her hand trembling. "Ever since you were born, I've only wanted to protect you. If you get this transplant and leave the convent, you may look like everyone else, but you'll always be brilliant. People will want to use you. That's why I urge you to call off the surgery. Stay here where it's safe. Stay here where I can protect you."

I stare at her cheeks, which are shiny with tears. Dr. Mewton…*cries?* She reaches for me again, but I scramble out of the chair and back away, not certain I can deal with both her emotions and the feelings burgeoning in my own chest. "If I stay…will you help me find out the truth about my father?"

"Your *father?*"

"I know he was working on an assignment when he died. I know he was tasked to investigate Saluda."

"That's classified."

"I have clearance."

"Not for that. It's need-to-know, and you don't—"

"But I do need to know, because he's my *father.*" I underline the word with a ferocity I've never used with Dr. Mewton. "I wouldn't exist without him, and he allowed me to be brought here. I want to know about my dad, and I need to know who killed him. Since we're still investigating Saluda, we could find someone who knows details about how he died."

She looks away and exhales as if I'm testing her patience. "Is this what's behind your talk of leaving? You think you can learn something about your father out there?"

"I'm certainly not learning anything here!"

"I hate to tell you this, but the world has a very short memory. Those who knew your father have been scattered or are dead. Didn't your aunt say she's the only one left in the family? And she's here, not out there."

"She won't be here long."

"Then ask your questions and tell her goodbye. But don't listen to her, Sarah. Don't listen to her promises of a brave new world—trust me, I've lived in the world and it's neither brave nor new. It's the same old mess, and people are as depraved and grasping as ever."

"Aunt Renee says people are good."

Dr. M rolls her eyes. "Like you, she watches too many movies. Well, dear heart, movies have to have a plot that makes sense. Real life doesn't. People are born, they die, and sometimes you can't understand why evil triumphs and good people suffer. But that's the way life is…out there."

I straighten my spine. "I don't believe it's as bad as you say."

"Really? Then ask your aunt about the little ones who die because their crack-addicted mamas leave them out in the snow. Ask her about the child rapists who get their jollies from watching innocent ones suffer. Ask her about the children who are shuffled from foster home to foster home because no one cares. Ask her about the child soldiers who are rewarded for murdering their family members. That's what the world is like, and if you don't believe me, ask your aunt. Ask Holmes. He knows the truth."

My chin trembles as she returns my glare, then I spin on the ball of my foot and stride out of the apartment.

"Sarah!"

I don't answer, but break into a run, slamming her office door behind me.

Chapter Fifty-Three

Renee

I'm alone in the therapy room, reviewing Sarah's comments on a series of facial photographs, when I hear her voice: "Aunt Renee?"

I look up, glad to see that she must be feeling better. The girl refused to leave her room all weekend, so Judson, Dr. Kollman, and I heard several renditions of Shelba's speech about how the girl works too hard. The cook and her cart made regular trips upstairs, however, delivering trays with Sarah's meals.

"I'm glad to see you," I say, setting my reading aside. "I was beginning to be concerned—and I *know* Shelba was worried."

Sarah rolls her eyes and sinks into her chair. "Shelba loves to grumble that we're not eating enough. Sometimes I think she's only happy when we're stuffing ourselves in the dining room."

Sarah glances at the photos spread over the table. "Did you have plans for us today?"

"Actually, no. I thought I'd catch up on some reading. You can play the Sims game or evaluate more pictures, if you like—"

"I think I'd like to take a walk. Want to join me?"

The abrupt question, coupled with the way Sarah tilts her head toward the wall, raises my suspicions. I lift my gaze until

I see the tiny camera mounted in the corner, then I shrug. "A walk outside might be nice. Shall we go downstairs?"

"You bet."

Sarah says nothing as we trot down the stairs. When we step into the ancient graveyard, I wait for her to bring up whatever subject is on her mind, but she doesn't speak until we have reached the bench beside the wall. She sits on the edge and hunches forward, tucking her fingers beneath her thighs. As she jiggles her feet like an overanxious schoolgirl, I sit next to her and scan our surroundings. I know the CIA has clever eavesdropping devices, but I have no idea what to search for, especially out here.

Sarah waits until a hard gust blows her bangs into her eyes, then she squints at me. "I did something that could get me into a lot of trouble. I think I need advice."

I am about to gape at her, then I remember that someone could be watching from a camera or one of the windows. I'd better guard my own expressions.

I force myself to relax my shoulders and smile up at the sky. "Care to explain that comment?"

She clears her throat. "A couple of weeks ago I sent a query into cyberspace—and today I received a reply. Trouble is, the reply is from an enemy. And I made him an offer I wasn't authorized to make."

In my years as a psychologist, I've heard many patient confessions, but never one with such serious implications. "What did you promise, Sarah?"

She stares over the wall, where a thin film of clouds is sudsing the horizon. "A copy of the Guttenberg program—not all of it, but the lie detector module. I thought this person might be interested in knowing if his people are loyal. As it turns out, he is."

My mind spins with confusing thoughts. I am grateful that she has come to me, that she's trusting me with this, but I am out of my element. I know nothing about national security, but I know Sarah is devoted to her country. I also know treason is a serious offense.

"Sarah." I resist my impulse to turn and grip her hands. "Why did you contact this person? What could possibly induce you to offer something so important to an enemy of the United States?"

The corners of her mouth have gone tight, and her eyes are shiny. "The truth, Aunt Renee. The truth about how and why my father died."

My niece is chock-full of bombshell announcements this morning. Even as my blood floods with adrenaline, I remain perfectly still, rooted to the old bench like a witness to a fatal accident. "Why? Why would you do that?"

She looks at me, her eyes large and fierce with pain. *"Father of the Bride,"* she says. *"Father Knows Best, I Never Sang for My Father, Honor Thy Father, Father was a Fullback. Ghost Dad, American Dad, Major Dad, My Dad the Rock Star."* When she drops her gaze to her hands, sounds of the sea rush in to fill the brief silence. "I had Dr. M, so I knew what mothers were like. But I've never been able to imagine my dad. I watched so many movies…but none of them seemed to fit."

I want to protest that Glenda Mewton is nothing like Sarah's mother, but this moment is not about Mewton. It's about Sarah and her yearning for someone who would protect her, comfort her, and love her unconditionally. Her desire to know about the man to whom she would always be acceptable and worthy and precious. Her father.

I understand. Lately I've found myself wanting to curl up in a safe nest with someone strong to watch over me.

Sarah's sniff brings me back to the present. My niece has taken some very real risks. "Sarah…have you received the information you wanted from this party?"

"Not yet—but if I provide the program, he'll give me what I want. And I'm pretty sure I can deliver it without being discovered."

I close my eyes, torn between wanting to urge her forward and wanting to throw myself between my niece and oncoming disaster. "Sarah—"

"The program I'd give him is really not much better than the standard polygraph. And maybe the exchange is fair—after all, it's almost like mutually assured destruction. If both sides have the same weapon, the odds are more favorable for détente, right?"

I shake my head. "You're rationalizing. You don't bring about peace by giving opponents an equal number of guns."

"But Gutenberg's not a weapon, it's a tool. I don't even see how he could use it against us. He'd use it to vet his own people."

"But what if his people include one of our agents? What if we manage to send someone in undercover?" I meet her eyes. "You don't have to use code around me. You're talking about Saluda, right? Adolfo Rios?"

She nods as she pulls windblown hair out of her eyes. "That's the case Dad was working on when he was killed. He was undercover, meeting someone from Saluda."

"How do you know this?"

"I accessed a file."

"One of Dr. Mewton's?"

"One…on a top secret archive stashed on a server in London. I don't know if Dr. M even knows about it."

I turn away and resist the urge to clap my hands over my ears. I shouldn't be hearing this, I shouldn't encourage her, but she's talking about *Kevin*.

I brace my arms against the cold stone beneath us and lower my voice. "Tell me everything you know."

She straddles the bench to face me, but I'm sure she's also trying to frustrate anyone who might be watching or trying to eavesdrop. "Kevin Sims was assigned to the Crescent Chemical Company under a nonofficial cover—and that's dangerous, because NOCs have no diplomatic immunity, so they can be arrested and imprisoned for spying. Dad was tasked with offering Saluda's black market operatives a new formula for heroin. Apparently the mission objective was planting a tracker for DEA agents to follow."

I nod. "That fits with what I know. What happened?"

"They set up a meet, and my mother went into labor. After Mom died, Dad had me airlifted to the convent, and two days later, he was on his way to the meet. But that's all the agency has on him. The last entry in his file says the local police found his car in a gorge and ruled his death a suicide."

I swallow hard as tears brim in my eyes. My head is full of them, and each breath tastes of the salty sea. "Not for a minute," I say, gulping oxygen, "do I believe that Kevin killed himself. He may have been heartbroken over losing Diane, but he still had you. He wasn't the type to walk away from his duty. That's why he didn't walk away from that meeting. And he wouldn't have walked away from you."

When I look up, I see tears flowing down Sarah's face, an overflow of emotion that has bubbled up and splashed onto her cheeks.

Every day she plumbs new depths of feeling. Maybe I do, too.

I drape my arm across her shoulder. "These bad guys— do they know who or where you are?"

She shakes her head. "Their security guys are good, but they're not that good."

"Then maybe you should let them stew a few days before you decide how to respond. Maybe Dr. Mewton knows what happened to Kevin."

"I asked her. If she knows anything else, she's not telling."

"And that file you found—"

"Apparently it's the agency's last word on the subject. The investigation of Saluda continues, but the chapter on Kevin Sims has been closed."

I pull a tissue from my pocket and wipe the wetness from her face. "I can't say I approve of what you did, Sarah, but

I'm glad you did it. But don't do anything else—don't tell Dr. Mewton what you've done, and don't risk your future for the past."

"Not even to—"

"Not even," I finish for her. "Your father wouldn't want you to spend the rest of your life in prison. He'd want you to live free."

Chapter Fifty-Four

Sarah

Aunt Renee and I are stepping back into the building when the cell phone in my pocket rings. I pull it out and glance at the ID, then flip it open. "What's up, Judson?"

"We need you, kiddo. Operations room."

"Be right there."

Aunt Renee nods. "I know. Your duty calls."

"Thanks...for listening."

"Anytime, Sarah. That's why I'm here."

She walks away, going back to her room, and I pause before heading up the staircase. My aunt walks so easily, so gracefully. I don't think she realizes that she possesses the same kind of grace I see in so many movie stars. What gives her that kind of beauty? It's more than having a good face, because not all beautiful women have that queenly quality.

I don't have time to ponder the question because my phone rings again. This time Dr. Mewton's ID flashes on the screen, so I take the stairs two at a time and hurry into the operations room.

Judson is already at his desk; Dr. Mewton is standing behind my station, one hand on her hip. "Where were you?"

"In the courtyard." I slip into my chair and log on to the network. "Why didn't anyone tell me we had a mission scheduled for this morning?"

"Need-to-know," Judson says, his voice flat. "Dr. Mewton figured you didn't need to know until the last minute."

I'm sure he's being sarcastic, and the look in Dr. Mewton's eye—narrow gaze, lowered brows—confirms it. I feel a sudden surge of gratitude for Aunt Renee's lessons as I pull up the sat grid. "Anybody want to tell me who we'll be surveilling today?"

"Espinosa," Dr. Mewton says, exasperation in her voice. "He's finally worked up the nerve to plant the Mona Lisa."

Judson snickers. "What a weenie. Maybe his girlfriend dumped him and he's been trying to find another high-ranking secretary to butter up."

"I don't care what his reason is," Dr. Mewton says. "Just line up a KH 12 satellite and let's keep an eye on the streets while he makes his move."

"Where's he planting it?"

"Saluda headquarters," she answers. "The Valencia office."

Something cold slides down my back, leaving a faint trail of unease in its wake. "You want infrared?" I ask, my voice cracking.

Jud turns in my direction, but Dr. Mewton doesn't seem to notice the brittleness in my voice.

"Shouldn't need it," she answers. "The man is supposed to walk over to a secretary's desk and distract her while he uploads the program from a flash drive. A baby could do it."

I locate the nearest KH 12 satellite and feed it the coordinates of the Saluda headquarters. "For the record—" my voice is far too loud, but I can't help it "—let me say that I think this is a bad idea. If no one installed the Mona Lisa when we shipped out free copies to Saluda employees, why do we think Espinosa is going to be able to install it now? I'm thinking Saluda must have supertight network security. He's going to get caught."

When Dr. Mewton looks my way, her expression is far from pleasant. She's not frowning, but from the way her brows have lowered, I'd say she's edging toward fury.

"When I want your opinion, Sarah," she says, her voice clipped, "I'll ask for it."

She pivots toward Judson. "Is that satellite in position yet?"

He taps on his keyboard. "Sarah, you ready to receive images?"

"Ready."

My screen fills with a black-and-white photo of Valencia's downtown, courtesy of a camera aboard the keyhole satellite and a Milstar relay.

"Espinosa?" Dr. Mewton speaks into the microphone dangling from her earpiece. "You're clear to proceed."

I pick up my own headset and loop it over my ear. I hear a hiss of static, followed by Espinosa's voice: "I've patched a transmitter into the security system. Approaching the main lobby now."

Dr. Mewton leans on the back of my chair. "Are you getting those shots from the security system?"

"Give me a minute." I home in on Espinosa's frequency and capture the images from the Saluda security cameras. Four cameras have been set to cover the exterior entrances, with an additional two cameras aimed squarely at interior doors. I send the satellite photo to my backup monitor and zoom in on the streets surrounding the office building. Between the two monitors, I ought to be able to keep an eye on everything moving in and around the office complex.

Dr. Mewton stands behind me. "There." She points to the camera in the lobby. We see Espinosa cross the vast empty space, his hands in his pockets, an exaggerated swagger in his walk. He pauses at the front desk and is pointed toward the elevator. He takes a side step, but the guard responds by pushing a clipboard across the desk.

I snatch a quick breath. "He's been stopped," I say, translating for Judson's benefit. "Why is the security guard making him sign in?"

Judson sighs. "Not a big deal. A lot of bookkeepers work from home."

"But the transmitter at the security feed—where'd he apply the patch?"

"Probably a junction box outside the building." Judson's brow furrows as he taps a message to me on his desktop. I glance at him, then watch his tapping from the corner of my eye as I pretend to study the monitors. *Why so jumpy today?*

"I'm fine." I answer aloud, not caring if Dr. Mewton hears. "It's fine, I mean. Everything's a-okay."

Judson shakes his head and drops his fingertips to his keyboard. "How's the sat picture?"

"Five by five. Thanks."

We watch as Espinosa signs his name and the guard hands him an ID badge. Behind me, Dr. Mewton makes a clicking sound with her tongue. "Can you believe it? Even organized crime bosses make their employees wear ID."

"Saluda is a legitimate business," Judson reminds her. "They have to keep up appearances."

We watch Espinosa step into an elevator. "Do they have a camera in that car?" Dr. M asks as the doors close.

I cycle through the available cameras on the security system. "Apparently not."

"Do we know where he's going?"

"My money's on the top floor," Judson says. "That'll be where the boss has his office. And you can bet there's a camera aimed right at Rios's door."

Sure enough, a moment later Espinosa enters the frame of another camera. "Got him," I call, zooming in on the shot. Dr. M and I watch as Espinosa walks up to a desk stationed in front of an impressive pair of double doors. He talks to the pretty secretary and leans against her desk. The woman shakes her head in answer to some question he's posed, but he leans toward her and gestures more fluidly.

"*¿Qué pasa?*" Judson whispers.

"He's talking to the woman," I say. "What do you think he's saying?"

"Don't ask me," Jud says. "My last good pickup line was 'Hi, I suffer from amnesia. Do I come here often?'"

I smother a smile as I continue to watch the monitor. Apparently the secretary doesn't want to go along with whatever he's suggesting. Then Espinosa leans forward, bringing his lips closer to the woman's ear. She raises her gaze to his face in an oddly keen, swift look, then he drops his hand to her shoulder.

"If that's his big move," Dr. Mewton says, her voice dry, "I've seen smoother."

I cover my mouth with my hand as Espinosa pulls back and looks at the señora. For a moment I'm sure she's going to agree to his suggestion, but then another man, an older man, steps out of the double doors and approaches the desk. He hands the secretary a folder and looks at Espinosa, his eyes narrow and disapproving.

Dr. Mewton makes a sound deep in her throat. "That's trouble. That's Adolfo Rios."

Espinosa lifts both hands and backs out of the picture. Rios retreats, too, leaving the secretary sitting alone in her chair.

If we could see her face, I think we'd see a look of disappointment. What'd he ask her to do, meet him in the custodian's closet for a quick kiss?

"Is that all he's going to do?" Dr. Mewton snaps.

Without warning, the security camera pictures begin to flash in a regular rhythm. I lean forward as my uneasiness swells into alarm. "Something's up. Maybe security detected interference on the line. Someone is manually cycling through the cameras."

"Wait, what was that?" Dr. Mewton points to another screen, where we see Espinosa slide into a chair at an unoccupied desk. The computer on the desktop is in screen saver mode—

The image flashes, replaced by a shot of the lobby foyer.

"The secretary must have stepped away," I say. "But she'll be back."

"There." Dr. M points to another window in my split screen. "We've got him again."

An almost palpable tension fills the operations room as we watch Espinosa slide the flash drive into one of the computer's USB ports. I tense, almost certain the screen saver will ask for a password, but before the computer can respond Espinosa yanks the drive and rushes away from the desk.

Dr. Mewton's hand falls on my shoulder. "What just happened?"

"I—I don't know. Maybe the secretary came back, or the system detected an intrusion."

"How is that possible?"

"Anything's possible if Saluda's security guy knows his stuff. Obviously, something raised their suspicions. That's why they were cycling through the monitors."

Dr. Mewton falls silent and the hair at the back of my neck rises with premonition as we study the flashing image on the split screen. Finally we spot Espinosa again. My heart sinks as I point him out—he's walking between two men in uniform and his hands have been cuffed behind his back.

"This is not good." Mewton crosses her arms. "Not good at all."

Judson draws in a breath, between clenched teeth. "They snagged him?"

"Yes," I whisper.

Judson curses softly under his breath, and I watch the dark image of Espinosa's retreating figure.

We have lost too many people to Saluda. Are we about to lose another one?

For the next three hours, I monitor shots from the geosyn-chronous KH 12 satellite, searching for any sign of Espinosa being led out of the building or driven away from the site. We have dispatched an agent to Valencia, hoping to track Espinosa, but so far we've seen no sign of anyone leaving the complex in custody.

"I have a vehicle exiting the property," I tell Judson. "Dark sedan."

"Any way to see the license plate?"

"Sorry, the angle's wrong."

Judson grinds his teeth and I feel his frustration. Espinosa could be in any vehicle, in the seat or in the trunk, and we wouldn't be able to see him unless—

"Do you think he has his cell phone on?"

I have no sooner asked the question than Dr. Mewton's cell phone rings. She unclips it from her belt and shows me the caller ID.

I look at Judson. "Speak of the devil. It's Espinosa."

"How'd he get my number?" Dr. Mewton presses her lips into a thin line and hands the phone to Jud. "Why don't you answer it?"

Without missing a beat, Judson snaps the phone open and presses the button for the speakerphone. *"Hola."*

"Listen to me." Espinosa is breathless, his voice heavy. "I've slipped away," he says, "and I need immediate extraction."

Dr. Mewton braces her hands on the desk and leans toward the speaker. "Where are you?"

"Somewhere near the beach, I think. But they'll be looking for me, so you need to come immediately. And you should bring Sarah. I've stumbled across a problem only she can solve."

Judson twists his head so sharply that I hear the pop of a joint in his neck. I stare at Dr. Mewton, whose face has gone blank with shock.

"Whatever you want to show Sarah," she says, her voice as smooth as oil, "it'll wait. The important thing is getting you out safely."

"But it won't wait, it's urgent. I've found this device, but I can't access it until I break an encryption code on the front panel."

"All right," Dr. M says, injecting her voice with iron. "Keep your cell phone on. We'll triangulate the signal and send Sarah with the extraction team."

"When?"

"ETA in one hour."

She gestures for me to disconnect the call, which I do. Then I stare at her in a paralysis of astonishment. "Why did he mention me?"

"He's lying," she says, sinking into a chair. "He would never ask for you if he'd met you, no agent would. But he's heard your name."

Judson groans. "He knows you wrote the Mona Lisa program. We talked about your work in our meeting with Traut."

I prop my chin on my hand and stare at the monitors. "Do you think he's under duress? Do you think they're hurting him?"

Judson reaches out to pat my arm, then turns toward Dr. Mewton. "So why does Saluda want our girl?"

Dr. Mewton shakes her head. "Hard to say, but I'm guessing they've either examined her work on the flash drive or Espinosa has told them about her."

Or maybe they've realized that I've sent an offer to Adolfo Rios.

I shiver as an icy finger touches the base of my spine. I glance from Dr. Mewton to Judson. "So what do we do?"

"We track his cell phone signal," Dr. Mewton says, crossing her arms, "and we have our agent scout out the area for possible extraction. While we wait, we hope Espinosa is strong enough to endure…or clever enough to escape. "

I turn back to the monitors, but I keep thinking of Judson, his missing limbs, the scars on his face, his blinded eyes. Is Espinosa being tortured for information about me?

As I focus on the image of the streets surrounding the Saluda building, I am glad my face is stony and blank. I wouldn't want anyone to read the fear behind my eyes.

Chapter Fifty-Five

Renee

"**Y**ou two must have had a busy day yesterday. Dr. Kollman and I couldn't believe how quiet this place was at dinner last night."

I am addressing Sarah and Judson at breakfast, and though they respond with quick, almost automatic smiles, it's not hard to read the worry on Judson's face. Even Sarah seems guarded. She finishes her cereal and boiled egg without a single attempt at conversation, then stands and leaves the dining room without glancing back.

When she has gone, I reach across the table and tap Judson's arm. "Are you going to tell me what's going on, or am I supposed to guess?"

"Aw, Doc," he says, "you know I can't say anything."

"I know it's classified, but I also know something's not right with my patient. Sarah doesn't upset easily."

Judson's mouth curves in the faint beginnings of a smile. "I'll bet you're a darn good shrink."

"I am pretty good," I answer. "But it doesn't take a genius to figure out when something's out of kilter around here. Since you're all obviously worried, why should I pretend not to notice? Tell me what you can, please, so I won't think I've overstayed my welcome."

"We are worried." Judson leans toward me and lowers his

voice. "We had an operation go south yesterday. The details are classified, but something odd happened—someone on the outside asked about Sarah."

"Sarah! Whatever for?"

Judson shrugs. "I'm guessing someone applied pressure to our agent. In any case, apparently her reputation is spreading…among people who shouldn't even know her name."

I swallow hard as the memory of my last conversation with Sarah rises in my consciousness. Did she underestimate her opponents? Or is Jud right about the agent mentioning her name?

Suddenly I feel exposed and frightened…for Sarah's sake. Someone needs to move her, place her in a safe American fortress.

Like Fort Knox.

"I have a friend," I tell Judson, "who's a brilliant psychiatrist, one of the best in the country. But ever since I've known her, she's refused to publish and has never granted an interview—and she's had plenty of offers, believe me."

"Don't shrinks like publicity?"

I manage a hollow laugh. "Far too many love it. But my friend is always saying that evil can't find you if it's never heard your name."

Judson grunts in affirmation. "Your friend must have pals in the intelligence business. We spies know only one prayer— 'Lord, let me never, ever be noticed.'" His mouth compresses into a thin line. "I wish Espinosa had prayed that prayer before they nabbed him."

We fall silent as the door opens and Dr. Mewton steps into the room. Her face is tight, and the color has drained from her cheeks. She walks straight toward Judson, bends to whisper in his ear, and leaves the room.

When the door has closed behind her, Judson makes a fist and uses it to cover his mouth. "Bad news from the wire," he says, speaking in a rough whisper. "Spanish police found our man dead in an alley this morning. Single gunshot to the head. Looks like a robbery, but we know better."

I stare at him, panic swelling like a balloon in my chest.

Chapter Fifty-Six

Sarah

By the end of the day, I am so tired that my corneas burn with weariness. I press the heel of my palms against my eyes and apply pressure, then check a mirror to be sure I haven't bruised the skin. Fatigue has settled in pockets under my eyes, making me look more disfigured than ever.

A long sigh escapes me, a cascade of exhaustion that ends only when I drop my head onto my folded arms.

At his station, Judson hears and understands. "For what it's worth," he says, "I thought we were going to reach him in time. If we hadn't lost the cell phone signal—"

"Put it in the report," I tell him. "I don't want to talk about it anymore. I *can't* talk about it."

"Mr. Traut isn't going to like this."

I lift my head, but Judson appears to be addressing his keyboard.

"Mr. Traut isn't going to like this at all."

I push back, lifting my feet until the back of my chair smacks the filing cabinet against the wall. "You hungry?"

Judson's head hangs a moment more, then his mouth twitches. "What'd you say?"

"Are you hungry? Are you going downstairs for dinner?"

He tilts his head from side to side as if working out stiffness in his neck, then he shakes his head. "I'm going to bed.

Too tired to eat. Too tired to care. But you're a growing girl, so you go on downstairs."

A dull laugh bubbles up from my chest, but I clear my throat rather than release it. "You sound drunk, you know that?"

"Whatever." He backs his wheelchair away from his desk. "I'll catch you later, kiddo."

I log off my computer and head for the stairs, where the scent of dinner rolls and roasted meat floats on the air. My stomach gurgles, reminding me that all I've had to eat today is a candy bar and a package of Spanish potato chips.

I leave the stairwell and turn the corner, then halt just before I reach the dining room's open door. Aunt Renee is speaking, her words running together in a soothing tone.

"But surely," she says, "you can see the danger if such a practice becomes widespread. Suppose a man gets drunk and makes a fool of himself at an office party on Friday night. Is he supposed to take a pill and forget all about his mistake?"

"No one's suggesting that propranolol be used for such things," Dr. Kollman answers, his voice rumbling through the hallway. "It's supposed to be used for traumatic events."

"Perhaps trauma lies in the eyes of the beholder."

"Okay, suppose it does. I still think your example is a little extreme, but let's say that event is traumatic for him. What's the harm in helping him forget it?"

I step to the side of the hallway and lower my head as I listen. I know I shouldn't eavesdrop, but how often do I get this kind of opportunity? They're discussing something that will affect me.

"Wouldn't he be better served if we helped him learn how not to make the same mistake twice?" Aunt Renee says. "You seem to forget that we learn from our mistakes—our breakups, our failed relationships, our overindulgences. We learn from pain. We learn how to avoid it."

"But what about the pain we can't avoid? What about Sarah? What has she learned from being shut away in this place?"

I lean against the wall, holding my breath as I wait for my aunt's response. "She's learned how to be strong. To be independent. In fact, she's going to have to learn how to occasionally be dependent if she's going to survive on the outside."

"Those lessons aren't going to evaporate. So what's the harm in letting her have a few pleasant memories to share with people she meets for coffee? When she and her husband are gathered with the neighbors around a friendly game of cards, what's she supposed to say when the topic of family comes up—'I grew up on an island of freaks?'"

"Sarah would never say that."

"But it's the truth."

My aunt releases an exasperated sigh. "Perspective, Dr. Kollman. That's not Sarah's perspective."

"Let me get this straight." I hear the chink of silverware as Dr. Kollman pauses. "Let's suppose I have a patient who's just been badly beaten. He has broken bones, maybe a pierced lung. He's in intense pain. It hurts to breathe."

"So?"

"So—" he chokes on a laugh "—if I followed your principles, I would withhold morphine in order for him to fully enjoy his suffering."

"I never said suffering was enjoyable." Her voice contains a note of irritation.

"Implication, dear lady. You implied it was beneficial."

"That's better. Beneficial, yes, but only in certain circumstances. There's a point where physical pain becomes insurmountable."

"Couldn't we say the same thing about emotional pain?"

"Of course—and that's why we have psychologists!"

Dr. Kollman laughs, but his laughter is sharp and edged. "Spoken like a devoted practitioner of the mental arts."

"Would you expect less from me? And while we're engaging in hypotheticals, let's take your approach and follow it to its logical conclusion. If, for a moment, we could resurrect Anne Frank, would you advocate giving her a drug so she could forget all about the unpleasantness of the Holocaust? All the people whose lives have been changed because of her story—can you honestly believe mankind would be better off if we'd eradicated Anne's trauma with a handful of pills?"

Enough—in a minute they'll be yelling at each other. I take a deep, quivering breath to calm the leaping pulse beneath my ribs, then I step into the dining room, flashing the widest smile my muscles will allow. The tension is even more evident here; it hangs in the air like toxic gas. Dr. Kollman and Aunt Renee turn startled eyes on me and lapse into silence when I drop into the empty chair at the head of the table.

"I'm so hungry I could eat a horse," I say, amazed that my voice can sound so artificially bright when I'm practically running on fumes. "Where's Shelba? Umm, that dish looks wonderful. Is it beef?"

I stand and move to the intercom on the wall, then call for Shelba. And as I wait for her response, I peek at my shrink and my surgeon. Their gazes meet and hold, and in that instant some sort of silent truce is negotiated and accepted.

Someday, somehow, I will learn how to read the hidden language of the human heart.

Chapter Fifty-Seven

Renee

I have never been directly involved in life-threatening work, but I have counseled police officers, firefighters, and soldiers. I thought I understood how the pain of a bad mission haunted survivors, but today I witnessed the scenario as it unfolded before my eyes.

After dinner—which proved to be an exercise in subtext, since after Sarah arrived, no one at the table said what he or she was really thinking—I retire to my room, put on the cotton pajamas decorated with dozens of dancing sheep, and curl up with my journal. I make a few notes about Sarah's exaggerated reaction to the discussion she must have overheard as she came down the hallway, and conclude with a summary thought: *Though S. was obviously upset, she maintained an artificially cheerful demeanor throughout the meal. I count this as a solid victory—she is experiencing and reacting appropriately to emotions she would not have felt several months ago. She is on her way to becoming a fully emotive person.*

After finishing the entry, I turn out the lights and pad into the bathroom to wash my face. The hour is early—ridiculously so—but with no television, no radio, and no company, I have nothing to do but sleep.

A wry smile curls on my lips as I peer into the mirror and

wash the day's grime from my face. When I finally return home, I'll be so rested Becky will swear I've had a face-lift.

I turn out the light and crawl into bed, then lie beside the open window until the restless sounds of wind and waves lull me to sleep.

I am awakened by noises in the night. I sit up, thinking I've heard a helicopter, but the night is windy, so perhaps I was dreaming.

A breath of chilly breeze touches my cheek and lifts the hair above my ears. I hear nothing but the howl of the wind and the steady beat of the surf until I hear the tinny sound of something metallic skittering across a solid surface.

I know that sound. I've heard it in movies—after someone ejects a cartridge from a gun.

I roll out of bed and drop to my knees. Moving on all fours, I crawl to the open window and look out on the graveyard. Night has fallen, and a thousand pinpoints of diamond light decorate the canopy of the sky. The moon has gilded the stone grave markers with silver, and shadows lurk among the crosses…yet some of the shadows are shifting. I see three men, dressed in black. One is peering into the dining room window, one is checking a weapon, and one is kneeling on one leg, doing something with a box that sits in a rectangle of silver moonlight.

My heart begins to thump almost painfully in my chest. I rise and run for my bedroom door, then open it and peer into the hallway lit only by an emergency exit sign. Nothing moves down by the chapel, so I close my door behind me and sprint toward the vestibule.

I have to warn the others.

The three men in the graveyard will not want to alert anyone to their presence, so they're not likely to use the elevator. After entering the building—if they *can* enter the building— they'll creep up the staircase. But why? What do they want?

The answer comes to me in a rush: *They want Sarah.*

My heart knocks in my chest as I pound on the elevator call button. According to the indicator above the door, the car is on the second floor. As I watch, the light blinks and the car descends.

I glance over my shoulder, afraid that I'm going to see intruders coming through a door at any moment. Though there are sensors at every exterior opening, I know that pros can defeat almost any security system. And there are always fools like me who sleep with the window open—

I pound on the call button again. The elevator lands; the door slides open, retracting at its unhurried pace. I whirl into the car, press the button for the second floor, and cower behind the instrument panel.

For the first time since my arrival, I'm beginning to think the idea of an elevator guard isn't so silly after all.

The elevator rises at a glacial pace. I brace my arms against the wall and steel my nerves for the strident sound of an alarm, but nothing happens. So…either the intruders haven't found a way into the first floor, or they've already disarmed the system and are now climbing the stone stairs.

Finally the elevator stops. I spill out of the opening and stagger down the hall, remembering that Judson's room is the first I'll reach. In the dim glow of security lighting I spy the plastic nameplate marking his door. Afraid to scream, I rap on his door with the staccato knock of a frenzied woodpecker. A moment later, I hear a click. I try the handle, the door opens, and I lurch through the darkness, nearly tripping over his wheelchair as I struggle to reach his bedside. "Judson," I call in a hoarse whisper. "I think we're under attack."

His voice, low and steady, cuts through my panic like a knife. "Calm down, Renee. What's going on?"

"I saw men in the graveyard—I don't know how they got there. They're armed. And like a fool, I was sleeping with my window open. They can walk right in."

"Not likely." I hear clinking as he reaches for the suspended bars that help him maneuver in his bed. "Even with the window open, they'll break a beam if they enter when the system's armed."

"But what if they disarm the system?"

"Then we have a problem." Jud's voice isn't much above a whisper, but the effect is as great as if he'd shouted in my ear. "Don't turn on the lamp," he says, "but behind you, in the nightstand. My pistol is in the drawer. Get it."

With trembling fingers I pull the drawer open and find the gun. It's cold and heavy in my hand, but I'm grateful for its solidity as I offer it to Judson.

"Here. Take it."

A ripple of mirth warms his voice. "Not for the blind man, Doc. Not tonight. I want you to hold it."

The gun feels suddenly colder and heavier. "But I can't—"

"Get down on the floor, out of the way. Slide under the bed if you can. And keep the pistol in your hand."

"I can't shoot a gun!"

"It's child's play." He takes the weapon from me, and I hear a click, then he drops it back into my palms. "Meet the Judge. This pistol is loaded with five .410 shotgun shells, so all you have to do is point at the enemy. When he's close enough that you can hear him breathing, pull the trigger until the gun runs empty. Just make sure your target isn't one of us."

I swallow hard. "What are you going to do?"

"I'm going to the security station to check on the guard who's supposed to be monitoring the cameras. If he's not there, I'll raise the alarm."

"What if I'm mistaken?"

A smile crosses his lips. "Better safe than sorry, Doc. If you're wrong, we'll chalk this up to bad dreams and indigestion."

As Judson uses the suspended bars to lower himself to the

floor, I lie flat and slide beneath the steel bed frame. I'd melt into the linoleum if I could, but I do feel safer in this position.

Even though Judson is blind and missing his legs, I'm happy to cower in the dark and let him check things out. At least he's experienced.

I close my eyes and whisper a fevered prayer—*Please, God, let everything be okay*—then my eyes fly open.

Judson was remarkably unruffled when I woke him. Is his calm a result of his clandestine service training, or was he anticipating trouble?

The truth strikes like a blow between my eyes. This team has just lost an agent. Like Judson, Espinosa might have been tortured before he died. But unlike Judson, he talked. He must have told them how the convent can be accessed, where the guards are stationed, described the layout of the building. Espinosa must have told them everything, and now they want Sarah.

At least three of them are here, armed and deadly, but Sarah won't hear their approach because she's sleeping…and not wearing her speech processor.

I shimmy out from beneath the bed frame, my bare feet thumping against the vinyl as I pull myself along the floor. I pause at the threshold, but Judson is nowhere in sight, which means he must have found something amiss in the security center. Perhaps he's trying to wake Dr. Mewton or alert the guards at the dock. But nothing he's doing is going to help Sarah, so I push myself upright and step into the hallway.

I am surrounded by rooms—Judson's room, Sarah's, the security center, Dr. Mewton's apartment, the conference room, the operations room, the empty apartment across from the stairwell. Acting on impulse, I run to Sarah's apartment and slide her nameplate out of the holder on the wall. I dash to the empty room at the far end and slip her name into the holder. Then I open the door and run toward the empty bed.

The mattress is covered only with a folded blanket and a

pillow, but it'll do. I grip Jud's pistol with one hand and shake out the blanket with the other, then lie down and pull the covering up to my shoulders. I close my eyes and struggle to control my breathing as I hold the cold weapon between my hands, muzzle pointed toward the door.

Deep breaths. They'll come up the stairs; they'll check the names on the doors. Even if they don't, this is the first room, so maybe…

My skin contracts when I hear movement in the hallway. I hope—please, God, let it be!—I'm hearing two of the guards, coming up to talk to Judson and have a laugh at my expense.

I hear a murmur of voices and the quiet chirp of a pass card as it slides through a nearby electronic lock. If this is Judson or the guards, they're being unnaturally stealthy.

With my face pressed against the stale pillow, I feel each thump of my heart like a blow to my chest. I'm trying to remain motionless, pretending to sleep, but my forearms pebble with gooseflesh when the door creaks. I see the bouncing beam of a flashlight, followed by two shadowed hulks.

The flashlight plays over my face and touches my eyelids. *"¿Como se llama?"* a rough voice demands.

I keep my right hand on the pistol and squint into the light, my left hand rising to shield my eyes. *"¿Que pasa?"*

"¿Como se llama?"

"Sarah," I whisper. "Sarah Sims."

"Sí," another man answers. *"La Americana."*

The light clicks off; a rough hand grips my hair and jerks me into an upright position. I lift the gun and fire twice at the dark shape, but I'm unprepared for the recoil, the noise, the wet splatter in my face. The man falls and I fling the frightful gun away, but before I can scream a second shadow looms up and something hits my temple, sending a shower of fireflies sparking through my head.

I should have kept firing that pistol.

I taste blood as someone slaps a piece of duct tape over

my lips. I try to scream, but there isn't enough air in my lungs to nudge the sound out of my throat. While I struggle for clarity in a haze of violence, the second man binds my wrists, then tosses me over his shoulder and carries me into the hallway.

A shot cracks through the hall, but the man carrying me doesn't stop. He jogs down the stairs, jostling my ribs against his shoulder blade with every step. The elevator is waiting at the first floor vestibule, along with the third man in black. We enter the elevator, and I blink in the sudden brightness as the two strangers escort me into the belly of the mountain.

When the elevator door finally opens, the third man leads the way, firing at the waiting guards. Though it's obvious that the guards have been alerted to the trouble, my presence prevents them from opening fire. One of the young men— Mitch, I think—wounds the third man, but doesn't stop him.

A moment later, both American guards are on the ground and I am shivering in horror. My abductor lowers me and I fall hard on the wooden planks. I tug at the restraints on my wrists and terror blows down the back of my neck as the third man pulls a small scuba tank and swim mask from the pack on his back. I glance around, searching for some clue that will help me make sense of all this, but my kidnappers persist in dressing up for a midnight swim.

I roll onto my side and groggily remind myself that they want Sarah alive. As long as they think I'm Sarah, I'm safe…and so is she.

After putting on his own mask, the third man walks to the edge of the dock and jumps into the sea, feet first. My captor bends to lock me in a one-armed embrace, then pulls me to my feet and sidles toward the water in an awkward dance. He rips the duct tape from my lips. With one arm locking me to his chest, he adjusts his mask, looks into my eyes, and issues a command: *"¡Respires!"*

What? *Respire—respire—respiration.* Breathe!

While he slips a mouthpiece in place, I inhale one deep breath, then exhale and gulp another.

The man wraps me in a bear hug and steps off the dock, dragging me with him into cold darkness.

Chapter Fifty-Eight

Sarah

I awaken as a faint thread of an acrid scent invades my sleeping senses. I sit up in the darkness, certain that something is wrong, and fumble for my earpiece. I put it on, and immediately hear the pulsing alarm, underscored by muted sounds of panic from the hallway.

Is the convent *burning?*

I scramble out of bed, flatten myself against the wall, and run my palm over the door. It's cool to the touch, so I summon up my courage and peer out. The security lights are flashing with a strobelike effect, illuminating the hall at half-second intervals. Dr. Mewton, clad in white silk pajamas, is standing in a shooter's crouch, her eyes wide and vacant as she stares at the elevator. Judson is lying on his stomach outside the security station, his stumpy thighs protruding from a pair of boxer shorts. Perspiration has dampened his T-shirt between his shoulder blades. One of the security guards stands behind him, his gun drawn as well.

I lean against the wall as my knees go weak. "Jud, are you okay?"

"I'm fine, Sarah." He lifts his sightless eyes as the elevator opens at the end of the hallway. Someone steps forward, Dr. Mewton tenses, and in the dim light I recognize another guard from the security squad. Jeff Prather, I think, though I've only seen him a few times.

"Stop right there," Dr. Mewton commands, her voice as brittle as glass.

"Hey." I step forward and place my hand on top of hers, forcing her weapon down. "He's one of ours." I look at him. "You're Jeff, right?"

The guard nods in a brief acknowledgement and taps the radio receiver on his collar. "We've got an all clear on the second floor."

"Not quite," Judson says, his face swiveling in the guard's direction. "I gave Dr. Carey a gun, and I'm pretty sure she used it."

Distracted by a sudden thought, I walk down the hall and stare into the security center. I see two chairs, the banks of monitors, one guard, one computer—so who is Jeff talking to?

He steps forward, his weapon drawn, moving from room to room. I step aside when he gets to my apartment, but he only glances inside before moving on.

"Where was Dr. Carey?" he asks.

Judson pushes himself into a sitting position. "In my room at first. But then…" His brow furrows. "Try the room across from the stairwell."

The guard and Dr. Mewton hurry to the empty room. Dr. M's shoulders slump as Jeff checks the stranger's pulse, then taps his transmitter again. "We've got a dead tango on the second floor."

"Where's my aunt?" I shiver as gremlins of fear nip at the backs of my bare knees. "Where's Aunt Renee?"

Dr. Mewton blinks at me, but Judson answers. "Dr. Carey heard them first," he says, seeking me with his face. "Smart lady, your aunt. She figured they were coming for you."

"What?" I glance again at Dr. Mewton, but the woman who has had an answer for my every question now seems unwilling to answer anything. She opens the door to her office and leaves it open as she walks inside, drops her weapon on her desk, and picks up the phone.

I kneel by Judson's side, my pulse racing. "Suppose you tell me what you know."

"I don't have proof—only assumptions. They might be worthless."

"Still…let me hear them."

"Okay." He pauses to wipe a sheen of perspiration from his forehead, then swipes his hand on his T-shirt. "Espinosa must have told them about you, your program, this place."

"How did Aunt Renee know about Espinosa?"

Judson winces. "Traut introduced them. She knew about his mission, so when she heard the intruders, she must have figured they wanted you. She knew they were coming up the stairwell—the elevator would be too obvious."

Nothing he's said makes any sense, but when I stand and run to the empty staff apartment, I see blood-spattered walls, a rumpled blanket on the floor, and a man, his face gray and flaccid with the life drained out. The pillow still bears the imprint of a human head…and my nameplate is in the holder by the door.

I lean against the wall and slide to a crouch. Why would Aunt Renee pretend to be me? If Judson is right and Saluda's men are behind this, she has nothing to give those people. She may be able to fool them for a little while, but she can't maintain the charade for long. And when they discover that she knows nothing about computer programming, they're not going to let her live.

I close my eyes as an even more astounding thought penetrates the fog of uncertainty: My aunt is a bright woman. Surely she has realized these things, too.

I race toward my computer.

Chapter Fifty-Nine

Renee

I'm coughing and shivering like a frightened puppy as strong arms pull me into a boat waiting outside the cave. The diver gives me a shove, sending me headfirst over the railing, and another man grips my arm so roughly I know I'll be bruised tomorrow.

Wet and cold, I sit on the floor of the boat and breathe in the scents of fish and motor oil. One of the men shines a flashlight in my eyes, forcing me to squint. He says something in Spanish; the diver responds with a grunt and what sounds like an explanation.

I lean forward, my hands still fastened behind my back, and cough up seawater. Twice during our underwater swim the diver took off his mouthpiece to let me breathe, but in my panicked state I inhaled water along with the air.

The diver picks me up and pushes me into a seat. I open my mouth to protest, but my voice is only a hoarse gurgle, stopped a moment later by another slap of duct tape. The boat lurches forward, and we ride through the darkness for at least fifteen minutes, bouncing hard over the waves, until I see a blinking light on a distant shore. The driver heads for the light, and a few minutes later we pull up to a dock. I'm hauled up like a bag of potatoes and carried to a paved area where a cargo van waits. The two men from the boat push me into the back of the van and climb in behind me. The doors slam and the vehicle roars away.

The back of the cargo van smells of gasoline and damp burlap. I shiver, my pajamas wet and cold next to my skin, and lean against a canvas bag. Despite the steady shivering that now has more to do with nerves than the cold, I'm glad I'm here in Sarah's place. I don't know what Espinosa told Saluda about my niece, but apparently he didn't mention her appearance. In light of Glenda Mewton's protectiveness, it's possible he never met her.

I close my eyes in an effort to make the time pass more quickly. Somehow, despite my terror, exhaustion overpowers my fears and I drift into an uneasy doze.

Chapter Sixty

Sarah

Driven by frustration and fear, I run to my room, lock the door, and log on to my cloaked operating system. I task the nearest satellites to give me real-time images of the island and the surrounding waters, then switch to infrared. There's nothing in our immediate vicinity, but I see several possibilities near the shore.

I pick up the phone and try to ring Mewton's office. She should be calling in choppers, alerting Langley, talking to Traut. We have been compromised and one of our own has been abducted—

Dr. Mewton doesn't pick up the phone. I grit my teeth and slam the receiver against the edge of my desk, then force myself to breathe deeply and calm down. I am not alone here. We all have jobs to do, and we will do them; we will find Aunt Renee.

With a deft series of keystrokes, I hack into the closed-circuit feeds and activate the passive camera in Dr. Mewton's office. Within a minute I'm peering into the inner sanctum itself.

I'm sure she never dreamed I'd dare this intrusion—I'm a little surprised at my own chutzpah. Not even the security station has a feed into her private rooms, but one afternoon when she and Shelba went ashore for supplies, I installed a tiny camera in the ornate frame of an oil painting behind her chair. Now it's registering the back of her head and the blank expression on Jeff Prather's face.

No wonder she isn't picking up the phone. She's busy.

"You may go," she says, her voice dull and lifeless in my headset. Prather nods and withdraws, closing the office door behind him. Dr. Mewton then reaches for the bottom desk drawer, rummages through whatever's stuffed inside, and pulls out a package of cigarettes.

What the—?

Her fingers tremble as she crinkles the cellophane wrapper. She turns, bringing the package to her nose and breathing deeply, then shakes out a cigarette. She holds it between her pursed lips while she bends and searches through her drawer again.

Finally she pulls out a lighter, flicks a flame into existence, and touches it to the end of her cigarette. She tosses the lighter onto her desk and inhales.

I watch, horrified and fascinated. I don't think Dr. M has smoked in years, though her clothing used to smell of nicotine when I was young. She must be operating in panic mode if she's smoking again.

But we have no time to waste. My hand moves toward the phone.

Dr. M exhales in a steady stream, then closes her eyes and presents me with an expressionless profile. None of Aunt Renee's lessons are helping me now; Dr. M's face is as still as death.

What is she thinking? Does she see the dead man imprinted on the backs of her eyelids? Or is she seeing Aunt Renee trussed up and crammed into the trunk of a European car?

Maybe she's seeing Mr. Traut's face, his features tight with disapproval and scorn. Or maybe she's seeing me…and wondering why Saluda is so desperate to reach me.

I search that exposed slice of a face, desperately seeking

some sign of anger or fear or desperation, but the woman offers no clue.

I'm about to dial her extension again, but Dr. M takes another drag from her cigarette, then tips an empty coffee mug and sets the stick inside the mug to smolder. She reaches across her desk for the intercom's broadcast button. "May I have your attention," she says, her message entering my room in a brittle stereo. "I'd like all employees to gather in the dining room ASAP. We're going underground."

Chapter Sixty-One

Renee

When the sounds of life abruptly cease, I sit bolt upright, as awake as if I'd just been given an intravenous dose of pure caffeine. The van has stopped, and when the side door slides open, I realize we must have traveled a considerable distance. I can no longer hear the sea, and this place lacks even the barest breeze. The air is cool and still, and stinks of garbage.

Could this be Valencia?

We are in a sleeping city. The streets are dark; the surrounding buildings seem deserted. A few lights gleam in windows, and silence covers the street like a mist. The eastern sky glows faintly with the promise of dawn, and when one of the men stubs his toe and curses, a dog begins to bark.

The driver of the van shoves me toward a small building with a glass door. I'm amazed by the ordinariness of the place—this could be an accountant's office or a repair shop. Another man opens the door, and we walk through a nondescript front room filled with a sun-faded sofa, an uneven card table, and the stench of cigarette smoke.

"*Vamanos,*" the driver says, thumping the space between my shoulder blades.

I continue walking through a paneled hallway that opens into a larger room. The man behind me flicks a switch. The overheated air pulses with fluorescent light and the hum of computers—at least a half dozen, set up on folding tables scattered throughout a room where the air has been breathed far too many times. What is this, a tech support center for drug dealers?

I am shoved again, so I step over a tangle of cords and walk toward the nearest chair. When I turn to ask if I'm supposed to sit, a pair of muscular arms pushes my shoulders down and turns my chair toward a desk covered with computer towers, keyboards, and monitors.

The driver of the van bends and examines me, the corner of his mouth lifting in a smirk. I'm not sure if he's reacting to the prancing sheep on my pajamas or my bedraggled appearance, but something about me elicits a crinkled nose and a curled upper lip—elements of the universal expression for contempt.

Someone stirs behind me, then another man steps into my peripheral vision and nods at the driver. The driver inclines his head in a respectful gesture and steps away, leaving the space open for the newcomer.

The short, white-haired man who stands before me wears wire-rimmed glasses. A thin gray mustache barely clings to his upper lip, and his dark eyes narrow when he focuses on me. I have no idea who this man is, but he is obviously a person of some importance. Perhaps Sarah or Glenda would know him on sight. I only know he's well-dressed, well-groomed, and probably well-armed.

"So this is the brilliant computer programmer," he says, speaking in heavily accented English. "Not so smart today, eh? Not smart enough to outfox Señor Adolfo Morales y Rios."

He strips the duct tape from my mouth in one rough gesture, but I hold my tongue, convinced that the less I say, the less likely I am to reveal my identity. By now the people at the convent have realized the intruders' intention. I need to give them time to do whatever they must to protect Sarah.

The short man turns my swiveling chair to face a computer keyboard and nudges the mouse with his index finger, waking the hibernating machine. The monitor flashes to life, reveal-

ing lines of numbers. I may not know much about computers, but I've seen enough movies to recognize the strings of
zeros and ones.

Determined to play my part, I lift my chin. "You want me
to do something special with that binary code?"

"Show me," the man says, bending close enough for me
to smell bacon on his breath, "how you hid that code in a
.jpg file."

The events of the past few days collide in my head like the
bits of glass in a kaleidoscope. He wants to know about concealing code…so does he know about Sarah because of the
agent Espinosa or because she sent Adolfo Rios a message?

I have no idea, so I shoot him a withering glance. "Am I
supposed to type with my nose?"

He glares at me, eyes hot with resentment, and cuts the
plastic restraints on my wrists. I swing my stiff arms back to
their natural position, wincing as I stretch.

He points to the screen again. "This is your code, *señora*.
Explain it."

I return his glare and flick a glance at the gibberish on the
screen. "I shouldn't have to explain something so elementary."

"Do not be funny. I am an impatient man."

"Then perhaps you are in the wrong line of work."

The blow arrives without warning, a strong backhand that
snaps my head to the side and fills my vision with pulsating
blobs of color. I blink, trying to focus, and somehow manage
a grimace. "If that was meant to motivate me, I'm afraid it's
the wrong approach. I've always responded better to positive
reinforcement. Chocolate, perhaps. Or the promise of a
bubble bath." I glance at the two goons leaning against the
wall. "Alone."

Another blow, from the same direction, and this one fills
my mouth with the metallic taste of blood. I let my head fall
forward and offer him only the top of my skull for a target.
If he wants to smack me again, he's going to have to manually

lift my chin—I'm not about to do it for him. If he keeps this up, my face will look like a bruised grape in no time.

I think I'd like to preserve my face.

I close my eyes, inhale a deep breath, and struggle to think of my training. Any good hostage negotiator would try to enter the mind-set of the perpetrator, but how can I do that? This man wants something I can't provide, but I can't let him know he's grabbed the wrong woman. So I need to stall. I need to give him something, and I need to ask for something.

I swallow the blood in my mouth and lift my head high enough to catch his eye. "You want one of my programs, right?"

His mouth curves like a snake. "Why play coy with me? I got your message."

I smile, glad that at least one question has been answered. "You are Adolfo Rios? I'm sorry—I thought you'd be a bigger man."

He bends his arm, preparing to backhand me again, but I hold up a warning finger. "Stop—no more hitting. I will not tell you a blessed thing if you hit me again."

His squint tightens, but then he lowers his arm and pushes my chair closer to the keyboard. "Show me." He picks up my hand and drops it on the keys. "Show me how you hide code in such pretty pictures."

"Not so fast." I remove my hand and deliberately set it back in my lap. To play this game, I must remain in control; I have to ask for something, even if it's only a glass of water. "Before I tell you anything," I say, licking my dry lips, "I want—"

"I know what you want." He jerks his chin upward and gestures to a thug in the back of the room. The man comes forward and unfolds his massive arms, revealing a folder clenched in one hand.

My interrogator takes the folder and drops it in my lap. "What's this?"

He snorts. "See for yourself."

My fingers tremble as I lift the stained manila cover,

exposing several black-and-white photographs of a bare-chested man stretched out on a table. His bare arms are dotted with dark circles, his hands have been fastened to the table by the sort of metal clamps I've seen supporting two by fours at a construction site. Blood has turned his face into a glistening mask, and only when I flip to the fourth picture do I recognize the profile—

Kevin.

A hoarse cry escapes my lips as I hunch forward, my body bent by a sorrow that the passing of twenty years has not healed. "They told me," I gasp, "that he died in a car crash."

Rios sits on the edge of a desk and folds his arms. "Do you believe everything you are told? That man died in this room, under torture. Your superiors know this. They have known it for years."

The CIA has known all along about my brother…Sarah's father. The secret Sarah has been seeking has been entrusted to me.

I lower my head into my hand and weep…for Kevin, for Sarah, and for all the years we will never share.

Chapter Sixty-Two

Sarah

I ignore Dr. Mewton's announcement and go to my desk in the ops room, where I can concentrate on the work of finding my aunt. Now that the sun is rising, I type in coordinates to direct another keyhole satellite to shoot photos of the Spanish coastline, desperately trying to find some clue—a car, a boat, a convoy—that might tell us something about where the invaders have taken Aunt Renee. Judson has been busy at his computer, too, sending inquiries to officers in the field and searching the Web for any leads on who might have led last night's attack.

"Got a couple of CSAR choppers flying up and down the coast," he says, his mouth tight. "Hopefully the search and rescue teams will pick up something we can use."

I run down the checklist of procedures we're supposed to follow. The security guys should be examining the surveillance tapes; Mewton should be alerting Traut; I should be tasking satellites and listening for electronic signals....

I activate our system's listening protocols, adjusting the diagnostic tools so that any pings to our server will be noted and identified. If anyone is still trying to infiltrate our base, I want to gather as many details as possible.

Jud pulls his headset from his ears and snaps his fingers for my attention. "Didn't you hear Mewton?"

"I heard."

"So? Are we going downstairs?"

"Maybe she's speaking metaphorically," I answer, adjusting the angle of the KH 12 satellite I'm using to photograph the coastline. "Go underground? What else could she mean?"

"Right." Jud settles his headset on his ears and gets back to work. He is monitoring reports from the NSA, looking for any terms that might refer to a kidnap victim or the convent. He has added my name and Aunt Renee's to the Echelon intercept list, though my aunt's captors will probably not be stupid enough to refer to her by name.

Jud has also contacted Britain's MI6, asking for help in the investigation. They've been monitoring Saluda, too, but without success.

The dead enemy commando has been no help. He carried no identification, and the Polaroid Jeff Prather snapped has not resulted in a hit from our facial recognition software. I am sending a copy to several European field stations, but it's too early to expect a response.

Even though I'm trying to concentrate on my work, I can't help feeling as if there are tiny hands on my heart, slowly twisting the life from it. Not only is my aunt gone, but Clint and Mitch are dead. We can't even watch the surveillance tapes to see what happened at the docks. Apparently some sort of electromagnetic-pulse device knocked out our cameras during the attack.

I pause to skim a quick e-mail from a contact in London, but I have to look away when my eyes fill with unexpected tears. I can't help it. Sorrow is like an oozing knot inside me, and I regret the day I told Dr. Mewton to invite my aunt to the convent.

Wasn't I better off when I lived from day to day and didn't care a fig about what other people were thinking? In the last few weeks I have begun to understand people, to love them, and everyone I loved, even Mitch, has met with trouble.

Now that I have learned how to read expressions, I see fear all around me...even on Dr. Mewton's face. As for me, I'm living in a state of near panic, my feelings quick and razor-sharp.

I didn't really understand joy before Aunt Renee came into my life, but neither did I know this kind of fear. Or guilt. If anything happens to my aunt, I will never be able to forgive myself.

At his station, Judson removes his headset and drops it on his desk. "We were hit with a well-planned operation," he says. "The EMP took us off-line, but the on-duty guard thought it was only a glitch in the system. The three tangos had to be dropped in by zip line from a chopper. Only men with military training could do that."

"Excuse me."

I look toward the doorway as Jeff moves into the room. "Dr. Mewton specifically asked you to move out."

"We're busy," I tell him.

"I don't think you understand," he answers, hooking his thumb on the edge of his belt. "We're transferring all operations to a secure level. No one is to spend another hour up top without an armed escort."

I glance at Judson, who appears as startled as me.

"Up top?" Jud emphasizes the two words. "What secure level?"

"Make backup copies onto the network and come with me," Jeff says. "Now. Dr. Mewton wants everyone underground by 1300 hours. You have five minutes."

I freeze in position, waiting for Jeff to leave. He must sense my hesitation, because he back steps and leaves the doorway.

I open my automatic backup program. "Underground?" I keep my voice low. "Do you know what he's talking about?"

"I only work here, kid," Jud says, running his own backups. "I didn't build the place."

Two minutes later Jeff is back, one hand on the door frame as he waits for us to shut down programs and gather our laptops. I glance at Judson, who has tossed his laptop and a stack of DVDs into his lap. He is already wheeling away from his station and moving toward the door.

I swallow and pick up my own computer. I fall into step beside Jud, and together we allow ourselves to be escorted into the elevator. Jeff moves to the corner and presses a button, then reaches inside his white T-shirt for something that looks like a dog tag. He slips the tag—a pass card—into a narrow slot beneath the call buttons. The elevator groans and begins to descend, traveling past the first floor.

"You know," I say, thinking aloud, "I always wondered why it took so long for the elevator to go from the first floor to the dock. I assumed we were traveling through solid rock— I had no idea we were traveling through a classified area."

Jeff says nothing, but locks his thumbs in his belt and waits for the door to open. Judson's face swivels toward me, and in his uplifted brows I think I see surprise…and maybe a trace of pride.

In me?

The door slides open. I stand stock-still as my suspicions are confirmed, then step out of the car and enter a hallway illuminated entirely by electric light. Off the hallway are several reinforced doors, each fitted with a small square window. Dr. Mewton is standing beside an open door, a sat phone in her hand.

"Why," I ask, not caring that I'm interrupting, "does a hospital facility need jail cells?"

Dr. Mewton's silver brows shoot up to her hairline. "I'll call you back," she murmurs into the phone.

She disconnects the call, then crosses her arms and fixes her glare on me. "What are you talking about?"

"I used to think that Jeff only worked the night shift because I didn't see him very often. But I didn't see him because he works down here, isn't that right? All those choppers that come and go—they're not all patients, are they? Some of them are prisoners."

Dr. Mewton holds out her hand. "You need to calm down, Sarah."

"How can I? We're not safe here, not anymore. My aunt is missing because someone knew about this place."

"That's enough," Dr. Mewton snaps, using the tone she used to employ when I didn't want to settle down and work on my studies.

But I am no longer a child. I spin on the ball of my foot and walk back to the elevator, but Jeff stands in front of the door, his arms crossed.

"You can't go up," Dr. Mewton calls, a silken thread of warning in her voice. "Not without an escort. It's not safe."

"But all my things are in my apartment—"

"Later I'll send you up with Jeff and you can bring down a few items. Until then, you can sleep in one of the cells. We're all sleeping down here tonight. Take a look around. You'll find it's not such a bad place."

I grip my laptop and materials and walk back down the hallway, peering into the reinforced square windows in every door. This area contains five or six small cells, each equipped with a bed and a toilet. Beyond them are two interrogation rooms, beyond that, a computer area with several workstations. Beyond that, a medical examination room with an X-ray illuminator on the wall.

"To check for broken bones," I whisper.

"What?" Dr. Mewton calls.

"Nothing." I turn and walk back to the narrow cells, then select one at random and step inside.

When Aunt Renee spoke of the convent as a prison, I thought she was being melodramatic.

She was more right than she knew.

Chapter Sixty-Three

Renee

When my sobs have quieted, Adolfo Rios pulls a chair from beneath another desk and plants his knee firmly in the seat. "So," he says, gripping the high wooden back, "I have given you what you wanted. Now you must give something to me. I want the lie detector program."

"What?" I glance at the computer screen, still covered with strings of numerals. I don't know when we changed the subject, but I know less than nothing about Sarah's current project.

I close my eyes and try to remember everything she's told me about Adolfo Rios's operation. "Saluda has a computer guru," I say, glancing at the man across from me. "Perhaps it would be better if I explained it to him."

A small smile puckers the man's lips. "He is not here. And I do not need an explanation—I need the program."

"Well, then, what can I say?" I lift my shoulders in a shrug. "I didn't exactly have time to grab my briefcase before I was jerked out of my room last night."

Rios tips his head back and laughs. "You are...how do you say? A comedienne? A funny lady."

"I try, you know. A good quip comes in handy at office parties."

His smile vanishes. "I am not so stupid as you think,

eñora. You can get into your network and download the
*p*rogram. And you will do it now."

I shake my head. "Because of your little venture, my
*n*etwork is in lockdown. I can't get in."

"You can. You undoubtedly have—how do you say?—a
*b*ack door."

"Why should I give my secrets away?"

"Because," he says, his smile almost friendly, "I have
*g*iven you what you wanted—and you do not want to end up
*l*ike the man in the pictures."

I blow out my cheeks and place my fingers on the keyboard.
"I'll try," I say, "but my back door isn't easy to slip into."

"You have a password?"

"Well…yes and no." I am improvising, relying on conver-
*s*ations with Sarah and memories of *Alias* and James Bond
*m*ovies. "The password changes every twelve hours—and
*a*fter every intrusion. It's probably changed twice since I left,
*s*o I'll have to unlock the encryption key. If I can't unlock it,
I'll have to create one."

He frowns at me, his dark brows knitting above his eyes,
*b*ut eventually he relaxes. I am spouting gibberish, but it must
*b*e decent gibberish, or by now I'd be spitting blood.

I straighten my spine and tap the enter key. "If I'm going
*t*o work for you," I say, "I'm going to need food. A paper and
*p*en. A bottle of water."

His upper lip curls. For an instant I'm sure he's going to
*t*hrottle me again, but then he looks toward the door and snaps
*h*is fingers.

If only he'd leave, maybe I could think.

I hunch over the keyboard and struggle to remember what
*S*arah has taught me. I hit the enter key twice, and am relieved
*t*o see a blinking cursor appear beneath the lines of code. I
*h*ave no way of knowing if I can reach Sarah through this
*c*omputer, but if it's connected to Saluda's network, it must
*b*e hooked up to the Internet.

I wait and listen as Rios leaves the room. Apparently the big boss has decided to give me some space, though he's positioned a burly guard by the door. Apart from the unsmiling muscleman, I am alone.

I close my eyes and try to visualize the numbers Sarah recited when she had me ping her computer. It had something to do with my birth year—1972—and sweet sixteen, followed by two zeros.

1972.16.00 doesn't look right.

197.16.0.0? No.

172.16.0.0. I smile as I remember Sarah talking about a light going on in the brain when an old memory is accessed. Right now, some neuron in my frontal lobe is firing in neon.

Again and again I type the sequence, pausing only when the goon at the door steps closer. "What are you doing?"

"Go away, you're distracting me."

He hovers behind me, a disapproving shadow on my right hand. "But what are you doing?"

"If you must know—" I exhale heavily "—I'm inventing a key code. There's no way I can countermand the security perimeter if the integers and pixels aren't congruent with the radii of the hypotenuse. In cryptography, the ciphers must align with the emitted microbursts or the process won't work."

I have no idea what I have just said, but apparently my bodyguard doesn't, either. He sinks into a creaking chair and watches me, satisfaction evident in the relaxed line of his brows.

After pinging Sarah's computer several times, I throw up my hands in mock exasperation. "How am I supposed to decrypt the algorithm in my head? I asked for paper and a pen."

Slowly, the mountain of a man pulls himself out of the chair and moves toward the door. When he has gone, I type Sarah's IP address again and again and again and again—

"*Aquí lo tiene.*" He sets paper and a pen on the table. "Now get to work."

I write out several lines of mathematical nonsense, then

tap the pen against my chin and pretend to agonize. A glance behind me reveals that my guard's chair is now leaning against the wall. A night without sleep has taken its toll, and he is dozing.

I begin to write in earnest, jotting down my thoughts, wishes, and fears. The pen keeps threatening to slip from my trembling fingers, but I cling to it and scrawl out my feelings until nothing remains to be said. Then I fold the paper into a small square and slip it into the pocket of my pajama pants.

I return to the keyboard and send another series of pings. From somewhere deep in my memory, I recall a couple of random DOS commands that might rewrite or reformat the hard drive.

Since I'm not going to be able to give Adolfo Rios what he wants, maybe I can at least fry his computer. But I don't dare do anything irreversible as long as there's even a slight chance I might be able to reach Sarah.

I am about to send another ping when I hear raised voices from the front of the building. A new arrival stomps forward in heavy boots, and several men greet him in Spanish. One of the guards laughs, and the unfamiliar footsteps draw closer. "*¿Que pasa?*" a new voice calls. "*¿Que tal?*"

A sense of foreboding descends over me with a shiver as a man in jeans and a cotton shirt moves into my field of vision. His brows lift and his face shifts into an expression of surprise.

I am undoubtedly wearing the same expression, because I am looking at a dead man.

Chapter Sixty-Four

Sarah

What Dr. Mewton calls our "secure ops center" is little more than a damp, dingy room with tables, chairs, and computers. The place has been threaded with secure phone lines, power cords, and Internet connections, but it doesn't feel like home.

Still, the computer is my only link to the world and my only hope of helping find Aunt Renee.

I am tasking a satellite in geosynchronous orbit to sweep over La Coruña's city center when a security alert flashes across my screen—my computer has received a series of direct pings. For an instant the notice irritates me—what maniacal script kiddie could be that determined to hack into our network?—then I realize that this is not a typical ping sweep. The intruder hasn't targeted our network block, just my specific computer.

My breath catches in my lungs. Any computer connected to the Internet will receive random pings, but it's rare to receive so many at once. I memorize the originating address and go to the IP locator at geobytes.com. Unless someone is using a proxy to spoof the origin, this signal is coming from a European computer and originating from the RIPE regional Internet registry. This could be Aunt Renee.

I enter the IP address in the search box, click Submit, and wait. Within seconds, my screen has filled with details and a map of the area where the intruding computer is located: Sagunto. It's a small town a few miles north of Valencia, but something tells me we won't have to search every house.

"Judson?" I raise my voice. "Roll yourself over to the phone and find Dr. Mewton."

"You got something there?"

"I think I've found Aunt Renee. After you get ahold of Mewton, see if you can get us a list of any and all Sagunto properties owned by Saluda. I'm thinking they would take her someplace quiet, maybe on the outskirts of town. A small office complex or a storage facility. Maybe near the beach."

Judson picks up his cell phone and talks to Dr. Mewton, then returns to his station. Within two minutes, he has sent a list of Saluda-owned properties to my monitor.

"Do you see anything?" he asks, one hand on his headset. "It's taking too long for me to listen to this list."

"Got a likely prospect." I focus on an address on the beach. "A Saluda-owned commercial building, but no tenant listed."

I glance up as Dr. Kollman strides through the door with a distracted look in his eye. "Dr. Kollman?" I try to contain my excitement as I wave for his attention. "Did you hear? I think we may have found her."

"I know," he says, reaching for the briefcase he dropped earlier on a table. "I'm going with the rescue team."

And as he broadens his shoulders and hurries toward the elevator, I realize that I am not the only one who has been touched by love at the convent.

And I am glad for it.

Chapter Sixty-Five

Renee

The man staring at me is no stranger; two weeks ago I met him and his skinny moustache in the convent's conference room. Only yesterday I heard he'd been murdered.

The man I know as Espinosa retreats as abruptly as he arrived. He's not leaving the building, however, because shouts fly thick and fast as he rails at the men in the next room. I don't have to understand Spanish to know that he's accusing them of being stupid and they're proclaiming their innocence. How were they supposed to know they grabbed the wrong woman?

How were we supposed to know Espinosa was double-crossing us?

When he has finished berating the thugs in the front room, Espinosa stomps down the hall and curls his hand in my hair. I wince as he yanks my head back and bends low to breathe in my face. "I never expected to find you here, *señora*. Why are you playing this dangerous game?"

I meet his glare head-on. "I can't hear you. You're in the morgue."

"I would not joke about such things. As for what you heard about me—" a self-satisfied grin sneaks onto his face "—a little fake blood, a quick photograph, and a bribe to the local officials makes dead look easy."

When he releases me, I lower my chin long enough to rub my bruised jaw. "I may not know much about the spy business, but I do know that double agents aren't well-regarded by the agency. When the CIA finds out what you've done—"

"They are not going to find out. Agent Espinosa is dead, wiped out of every database, every record. Or he will be, once we get your niece. I have no doubt she can accomplish what I need her to do. She will do many things for us."

"What things?"

He ignores me, but my hulking bodyguard steps forward. From the deferential way he approaches Espinosa, I realize I've been mistaken. All this time I thought Espinosa a scraping beta underling, but in reality…

I wait until the sweaty hulk retreats, then I catch Espinosa's gaze. "Who are you?" I ask, threading my voice with insistence. "Tell me the truth."

His answering smile sends gooseflesh creeping over my arms. "I was born Alejandro Oscar Espinosa y Rios." He tucks his thumbs into his belt, drawing my attention to the handgun tucked inside the waistband of his jeans.

"You are related to Adolfo Rios?"

"I am his son. By a woman he could not marry."

I close my eyes. Sarah once told me something about how Spanish surnames don't correspond to the American pattern. So…some officer of the CIA had the misfortune, or the audacity, to recruit Adolfo Rios's illegitimate son. I can understand how a novice might make this mistake, but how could Glenda Mewton miss the connection?

She wouldn't…unless she'd been distracted. And I've been distracting her for months.

Espinosa glances at the computer screen, where I have done nothing but type the ping command and Sarah's IP address. He lifts a brow. "You have been busy. Did the girl respond?"

I shake my head. "She's probably safe in Washington by now."

"I doubt that. But an extraction team is undoubtedly on its way, so we must wrap things up." He moves to the doorway and shouts an order to the men in the front of the building. Immediately they come into the room and begin to unplug machines.

I pinch the bridge of my nose and try to think clearly. Espinosa seems confident that he can get to Sarah, but surely Glenda has taken precautions by now.

He is back, gesturing to the monitor in front of me. "Why did you do this? Anyone who knows anything about computers would see what you have done."

"Your thugs didn't seem terribly bright. I knew the leader of this group would not be the sort to hire men who would outshine him."

Anger flashes in his eyes. "You risk your life, woman."

I think of Sarah, waiting at the convent. Of Kollman, who will take good care of her. And of Kevin, who died in this room. He died bravely; I know it. Does that kind of courage run in families?

My grandmother had it. She faced cancer and died with a hymn on her lips.

I'd love to follow her example.

"Save your breath," I tell Espinosa. "You have nothing to offer me, and I have nothing to fear from you. My niece is safe."

"You forget, I hold your life in my hands."

A smile tugs at my lips. My life…what is it, really? A daily succession of chores and patients, steadied by the love of a good dog. A friend or two. An ex-husband who hasn't called since the divorce papers were filed. And an unwavering belief in my life's purpose.

I rub my aching jaw and smile. "My life isn't yours."

"But I can take it."

"Not really. You can kill my body, but you can't touch my soul." I squint at him in amusement. "I wish that were original, but someone else said it first."

"You think I am kidding, woman?"

"No…in fact, I'm hoping you're not. I'm counting on it."

Espinosa's hand swings to his belt, and for the first time I notice the oversize bull's head buckle. Compensation, no doubt, for the stature he will never achieve. He wraps his hand around the weapon, withdrawing it, and with pulse-pounding certainty I realize that my faceless life is finished.

Yet the life I've wasted can be redeemed.

Across the room, plastic creaks as one of the men lifts a monitor, but my eyes are filled with Espinosa and the circular barrel of his pistol. How like a toy it is! In my peripheral vision, one of the goons turns his head, probably to escape a spray of gore, and my hand—pale now and forever because I will never take that beach vacation—swings up and catches the gun.

Espinosa's eyes widen. He probably thinks I intend to wrestle the weapon away from him, but instead I lift the barrel, pulling against his superior strength, until the muzzle is aimed not at my chest, but at my forehead. For Sarah's sake, my heart must keep pumping.

Espinosa's finger bends, pulls the trigger. The flash blends with the odor of burning and a sudden surge of light that fills the room, and I am free.

Before departing, I swoop down and study my features— they are calm, almost serene, the lips curved in a slight smile. Aside from a small nick near the right eye, the face is undamaged.

Satisfied, I stretch gossamer arms toward the heavens and ascend to the Light of Love.

_____

Chapter Sixty-Six

Sarah

I want to listen to the rescue team's progress on coms, but Dr. Mewton refuses to allow me to remain in the operations room. With Judson and Jeff at the controls, she orders me to bed. When I tell her I won't be able to sleep, she gives me a sedative and stands in front of me, unyielding and unrepentant, until I swallow the yellow pill.

I go to my secure cell and lie down, fully intending to get up within an hour or so, but four hours have passed when I open my eyes again.

Judson is sitting by my bed, a blank look on his face.

I prop myself on one elbow. "Jud?"

He starts at the sound of my voice. "Sorry—you caught me off guard." He pulls his cell phone from his pocket and presses a button on the speed dial, then drops the phone into his lap.

"Did they find my aunt?"

"Yes."

"Did they bring her back?"

His face twists in an expression I don't think I've seen in any of Aunt Renee's photographs. "Dr. Mewton is waiting to see you."

"Is that who you alerted just now?"

A rueful smile crosses his face as he slips his cell phone

ack into his pocket. "Yeah. We're supposed to go upstairs nd meet her."

I sit up and swipe my hand through my hair, bracing myself or bad news. "Aunt Renee...did they reach her in time?"

When Judson hesitates, I know the news is not good. Almost. Her heart's still beating."

"What does that mean?"

"Come upstairs. The doctors are waiting to explain."

Rather than wait with Judson for the elevator, I run up the airs to the third floor. Dr. Mewton has posted a guard at every anding, but I run past them without slowing. The building eems to have filled with people since I fell asleep—more uards, more personnel, more doctors and nurses. The third oor hums with activity, and the noise fills me with dread.

I find Dr. Mewton and Dr. Kollman outside the operating oom. When I peer through the window, I can see Aunt Renee n a gurney. She's been hooked up to a respirator and her olor is good. A green-gowned nurse stands beside her, aaking notations on a chart.

I stare at my aunt's smooth brow, then turn to Dr. ollman. "Judson said you didn't reach her in time. What'd e mean by that?"

Dr. Kollman opens his mouth to speak, then his expres- ion changes. Something softens his eyes; a thought or motion twists his mouth. He brings his hand up to shield his ace and looks away.

"Sarah." Dr. Mewton tucks a folded surgical gown under er arm and touches my shoulder. "Your aunt was shot. The ullet went through her eye and took out the back of her skull."

Dr. Kollman turns to face me, and in his face I recognize lear marks of grief: lines beside his mouth, shadows in his eyes. lis blue eyes shimmer with threatening tears as he takes my and. "I'm so sorry, Sarah. We got there as fast as we could."

"And you found her."

"Only a little while after the shooting. We were able to

bring her back, and some of the men even confiscated equip
ment. We'll find the people who did this. They won't g
away with murder."

"So…she's dead?"

"Brain-dead, yes, the brain is clinically dead." H
speaks slowly, tonelessly, as if he's channeling Dust
Hoffman as *Rain Man*.

A few days ago, I would have given anything to feel th
man holding my hand; now I'm only sorry that he's not Au
Renee. I squeeze his fingers and pull my hand free, then tu
and walk through the swinging doors of the surgery.

The nurse moves away when she sees me approach.

My aunt looks as though she has fallen asleep. Her rosy fac
is composed and smooth, her hair tousled as though she ju
rolled out of bed. A bruise marks her cheek, and there's a b
of raw skin at the corner of her right eye, but aside from that.

"How—?" The question dies on my tongue when I see th
red stain on the sheet covering the gurney. The area benea
her head is soaked with blood, all of it spilled for me.

I press the thin edges of my mouth together as my ch
begins to quiver. Why on earth did she come here? Whatev
possessed this woman to go with those people? She isn't a
agent; she knows nothing about computers. Any woman wh
could refer to a wireless receiver as a *whatchamacallit* h.
no business even owning a laptop.

But I know why she went with them. I know why she can
to the convent, and I know why she didn't tell her capto
where to find me.

And I've never known that kind of love before.

I stand in silence, my shoulders shaking, until Dr. Kollma
walks up behind me and wraps his arm around my nec
"Sarah," he whispers in my good ear, "I can help you, if yc
want. Do you want me to give you the propranolol?"

The question shimmers on the air in front of me. Take
drug that will dull this pain? For a fleeting instant the wo

es flutters to the tip of my tongue, but then I hesitate. This
an exquisite agony, but if I cut the cord between the
emory and this pain, will I not lose the warmth that comes
ith the feeling of being loved? The pain, the love, the loss
re all braided together, and I don't think I will ever be able
separate them.

I turn to look Dr. Kollman in the eye. "Would you take the
rug?" I gesture toward the lovely woman on the gurney.
Would you take a pill to dull your feelings—and all of your
emories—about her?"

His eyes glaze as he studies Aunt Renee's face, then he
owers his head. "She was right even about this." He gives me
tired smile and slips his hand around the back of my neck,
en pulls me close.

I cling to his arm and fall to pieces as he rocks me back
nd forth, murmuring quiet assurances in my ear.

At some point I look up and realize that he and I are not
e only ones crying. Outside the swinging doors, as she
es on her surgical gown, Dr. Mewton weeps without
aking a sound.

When I am too spent to cry another tear, Dr. Kollman
kes me by the hand and pulls me into his office. "We've kept
enee on the respirator to keep her heart pumping," he says,
is eyes searching mine.

I nod. "I…I suppose I'm the next of kin? Do I have to give
ou permission to pull the plug or something?"

He blows out a breath and takes a folded sheet of paper
om his coat pocket. The page has been folded before; I can
ee several creases in the paper.

"We found this in the pocket of her pajamas," he says, his
oice clotting. "Apparently she found a way to write while
he was being held. Her wishes are quite clear, so we've
lready taken the necessary measures."

For what?

I blink at him. Did Aunt Renee's captors force her to sig
some kind of confession? Was she writing a will?

Dr. Kollman clears his throat and begins to read:

"Dear Vincent:
Sorry to make this short, but I haven't much time and
I doubt I'm leaving this place alive. Even if I could, I've
decided not to, because now I know how I can most
help Sarah.

Funny, how this decision has given me courage. I am
beginning to behave like a Hollywood spy.

I want to be Sarah's donor. Being relatives, we should
be a good match, right? I'll do all I can to make it work.
With much love,
Renee."

"No." I shake my head. "Absolutely not—I won't accept i◼

Dr. Kollman lowers the page. "It's what she wanted, Sarah◼

"But I can't take her face! How could I look in a mirr◼
and see *her?* I can't do it."

"You won't see her, you'll see *you.*" Dr. Kollman lea◼
toward me, his eyes frank and pleading. "She loved you. Y◼
were all she was thinking of in her last moments."

"But I can't, don't you see? I can't, because it's my faul◼
If it hadn't been for me, she wouldn't be dead!"

Dr. Mewton steps into the room, her eyes pinning me lik◼
lasers. Apparently she's guessed what we're discussing, an◼
she must have anticipated my reaction.

"Sarah," she says, setting her jaw, "you can't blam◼
yourself for what happened. Sometimes innocent peop◼
are hurt in our line of work, but we're not the ones wh◼
hurt them—"

"In this case, we are. I am." I lift my gaze and plead wit◼
Dr. Kollman. "Saluda didn't attack the convent becaus◼
Espinosa ratted us out. They attacked because of me."

When Dr. Kollman frowns in confused disbelief, I lower my head into my hands. "I sent Adolfo Rios a message because I wanted to know about my father. He must have tracked it. He came here because I practically sent him a map and a gold-plated invitation."

I turn away from both doctors and hug my bent knees. "I don't want Aunt Renee's face, I don't want the surgery. Tell the CIA what I did. Let them send me to prison. I'll go. I'll do whatever I have to, but I don't deserve a new life, not when Aunt Renee is dead."

Dr. Kollman clears his throat. "Sarah, our time is limited."

I clap my hands over my ears. "I'm not changing my mind."

Overcome by the horror of it all, I close my eyes. When I open them again, Dr. Mewton has pulled off her surgical cap and is motioning to someone in the hall.

Two guards. They look at me, their eyes blank, their posture erect as she gives an order: "Take this woman down to the secure cells. Post a guard. Keep her there until we have a response from Langley."

Something in me is a little amazed to hear the words, but confinement is far less than I deserve. I stand on shaky knees and follow the guards to the elevator, then lean against the wall and keep my face blank as we descend into darkness.

An hour later, Dr. Mewton is staring at me through the tiny window in my cell door, and I'm wondering if I've ever really known the woman. She taught me to walk, to read, and to be self-reliant. She's been everything to me, but I've never felt less connected to anyone in my life.

The door opens with an electronic beep. I lie back on my bed and fold my hands across my chest. I don't want to talk to her; I don't want to talk to anyone. But right now, I don't think anyone cares what I want.

Dr. M lowers herself into the bare wooden chair in the corner and watches me in the heavy silence. Finally, she draws a deep breath. "Tell me how and when you contacte[d] Adolfo Rios. And why. I'm especially interested in why."

I blink up at the ceiling and wonder how long I can sta[ll] this conversation. For a while, perhaps, but stalling woul[d] only postpone the inevitable.

"I contacted Rios because I wanted to know the truth abo[ut] my father. I promised to give him a cutting edge truth detect[or] if he would give me details about Kevin Sims's death."

"You told him about Gutenberg?"

"I never mentioned the name, I only described the capa[-] bility. And I only offered the lie detector module after M[r.] Traut told me it wasn't the program's major objective. A[n] EEG lie detector was new, it had a certain cachet, and [I] figured Rios would want to test the loyalty of his people. A[s] it turned out, I was right."

"Sarah—" Dr. Mewton gives me a brief, distracted glanc[e] and attempts to smile "—did you actually give Rios anything[?] Did you provide him with any part of Gutenberg?"

"I might have, but Aunt Renee told me not to."

"*She* knew you did this?"

Against my will, my chin trembles. "Yes."

"How did you contact Rios?"

"E-mail. I took a photo of one of Judson's Close Connec[-] tion bimbos and planted the code inside it. I wasn't sure Rio[s] would figure out how to find the code, but apparently he di[d.] Judson never knew anything about it."

"He's innocent?"

"Completely. I'd swear it in any court."

"How'd you send the e-mail?"

"Through my own operating system. It runs beneath—"

Dr. M holds up her hand. "Save it for the tech guys. I don'[t] have time to hear a complicated explanation."

She glances through the reinforced window of the cel[l] where I can see the back of the guard's head. "Did you—

ie asks, her voice strangled "—did you tell Rios about the
yout of this facility?"

"No." For the first time I look directly at her. "I never
xpected them to come here. Never."

She lowers her head and pinches the bridge of her nose.
Vhat do I do?" she asks, closing her eyes. "What am I
ipposed to do with this stubborn young woman?"

"Nothing." I direct my gaze to the ceiling. "I messed up,
id I'll pay the price."

Dr. Mewton sits without speaking, and I sense that she's
impted to let me pay the price for *everything*. The CIA might
rgive many things, but it does not forgive collusion with the
iemy. In sending that e-mail, I not only betrayed the agency,
betrayed Dr. Mewton.

Dr. M is many things, but she is not forgiving. I know she
is invested a lot—she would say her entire life—in me, and
have bitterly disappointed her.

I wouldn't be surprised if she turned me over to Mr. Traut
id let him arrest me for treason.

"You won't have to pay the price." She shifts in the chair
id crosses her legs. "We examined the security tapes we
illed from the property where we found Renee. Espinosa
n the place. He shot your aunt."

My mask of indifference shatters in surprise. "But—"

"He's not dead. Apparently he's one of Rios's top men,
:cause we saw both of them on the tape. No audio, so we'll
: a while figuring things out, but one thing is clear—you
dn't lead that commando team to the convent. Espinosa did.
r Traut did—he brought a double agent to our front door
id welcomed him into the house."

I rise up on one elbow. "But he was transported securely,
asn't he?"

Dr. M shrugs. "He and Traut were as thick as thieves by
ie time Espinosa left here. He arrived with a bag over his
:ad, but I'm betting Traut let the bag stay off for the return

trip or Espinosa found a way to track the chopper. Eith[er]
scenario is more logical than Rios tracking your e-ma[il]
You're too good."

I sit up and swing my legs over the edge of the bed. I s[it]
on my hands as I sort through my thoughts. "Rios could ha[ve]
received my message and sent Espinosa to scout ahead."

"That's what I'm thinking."

"And once our location was revealed—"

"You're not to blame, Sarah, and you're no longer und[er]
arrest." She uncrosses her legs and leans toward me, tiltin[g]
her head to look into my eyes. "But you never should ha[ve]
betrayed me."

Chapter Sixty-Seven

arah

lie flat on my back and press my hands to the concave flesh bove my abdomen. Something in my gut hurts, but I don't eed a psychology degree to know that the pain probably has nore to do with the events of the past few hours than with ny internal organs. If I tell the guard I'm sick, he'll call Dr. .ollman, who'll insist on examining me. He'll give me an spirin and tell me to feel better soon.

But he and I will both know that the burning rock of guilt n the pit of my stomach isn't going anywhere.

I stiffen when I hear the swipe of a key card in the canner. The latch clicks, and the door swings wide for a vheelchair.

I let my head fall back to my pillow. First Dr. Mewton, then udson. Are they going to interrogate me one by one?

Judson rolls straight into the room and lets his chair clang gainst the end of my cot. "Time is running out, Sarah. Two nedical teams are waiting. You need to get upstairs for the ansplant."

So…Jud hasn't come to interrogate me, but to bully me. sit up and set my jaw. "Why should the American taxpayer ay for my surgery? I'm as much a traitor as Espinosa."

"Espinosa is a murderer and he will take the fall for the ecurity breach. Let him."

"Easier said than done, when you know the truth. Even Au
Renee knew it. She knew I was guilty when she faced Espinosa

"Sarah. Sweetheart." Jud reaches out for my hand, doesn'
find it, and settles for the edge of my blanket. "Do you thin
she'd have written that note if she didn't forgive you? I sa
the video. I saw her sit in a chair and stare down death wit
a smile. She did it for you, Sarah. Are you going to let her sac
rifice go to waste?"

"I don't deserve it." My voice is flat and final. "I'm
monster and I always have been. I wouldn't know what to d
with a face like hers."

"You'll learn."

"I won't. I can never be the kind of person she was—
charming, funny, sweet. I just don't feel things like she doe
I'm not like her. I'm not and I never will be."

Judson takes the edge of my blanket in both hands, the
wads it up and throws it at me. "Good grief, kid, sometime
I think *you're* the one who's blind. Don't you realize ho
you've been changing? Since your aunt arrived, you'v
been becoming a different person. Like a butterfly emergin
from a cocoon, I've watched you go from diffident t
daring, from impassive to passionate. This pain you'r
feeling now? Two months ago I could have told you tha
your aunt had been kidnapped and killed and you woul
have shrugged it off."

"Two months ago, I didn't know her." I swallow the so
that rises in my throat. "None of this was happening to me.

"But it did happen. Renee taught you how to care—sh
showed you how to *feel*. You may think you can go back t
the way things were, but you can't, not even if you keep you
old face. You're a different person, Sarah, we all are. Like you
aunt said, life is what happens to us. She came here, sh
affected us, and we're different because we knew her. Yo
can't erase her from your life any more than I can pretend
still have eyes and legs."

What does he expect me to do, refute the obvious? I lean against the wall and fold my arms, wishing he'd go away.

Jud remains quiet as I close my eyes and think of Aunt Renee—of her smile, the way the corners of her eyes crinkled when she talked about Elvis, and the way she blushed when he spoke to Dr. Kollman. Even when they were arguing about memory implantation, she never failed to glow when he looked his way. She was so alive, yet she loved me enough to come here to tell me about my father, enough to go away and die in my place.

Judson is right. Renee brought me far more than the promise of family. She brought the hope of a new and better life, the dream of being the person I was meant to be. What was it she said? *I think we're meant to spend every bit of our potential and die without a smidgen of promise left.*

If I don't go upstairs, I'll be allowing her to die with her greatest potential untapped. If I do go…part of her will literally remain alive in me.

"I wish…" Somehow I find my voice. "I wish you could have seen her, Jud. She was more lovely than I'll ever be."

"You're beautiful, too, beneath the skin." He turns his wheelchair toward the doorway. "Let's go upstairs and see about getting your outside to match your inside."

Sarah

Four days after my surgery, I wave the nurse out of the room and peer out of my bandages. Judson is sitting in the doorwa and I've never been so glad to see anyone in my life. Th speech processor that usually hangs behind my ear has bee displaced by bandages, and my jaw has been temporarily wire shut, but I'm determined to communicate with my friend.

"Mmmmmm," I tell him, moving my speech processo into my lap.

"I'm going to assume that's hello," he says, wheelin himself into the room. "I know you can't talk, and I als know you're probably wild with boredom. So I've brough you some entertainment…and something that might prove t be quite educational."

"Hmm?"

He grins as he feels his way to my bedside, then he offer me a laptop. "I know your head probably looks like one bi bandage, but can you manage this?"

"Hmmm."

I raise the bed until my head is elevated, then I maneuve the laptop past the processor and the IV lines. I lift the lid an click the space bar, then blink as the screen brightens.

"Can you seé okay?" Judson asks.

"Hmmm."

"In a lot of pain?"

"Hmmmm."

He grins. "Don't worry. This will take your mind off things."

I look at him, understanding for the first time how much 've missed by not being able to communicate with a face. If y head weren't swathed in bandages, and if he could see, I ould say so much with a single look....

Aunt Renee certainly spoke volumes with this face.

"We've had a field day in your absence," Jud says, folding is hands. "Mr. Traut and I have uncovered all your little ameras, and he's given me his blessing to tune in for an inter- iew he's about to conduct in Mewton's office. He's been usy, too, going through all the data we recovered from the aluda operation. He's reviewing the case with Dr. Mewton ow." He nods toward the computer in my lap. "You know vhat to do, kid. Tune in any time you're ready."

Moving gingerly so as not to disturb the wires and tubes hat surround me, I type in the command that will log me into he subnet surveillance network, then select the proper outlet. 'he camera in Dr. Mewton's office activates and focuses on dark head: Traut's. He's sitting in Dr. M's chair; she's tanding on the other side of the desk. His pipe is smolder- ng in an ashtray; her face is tight and unyielding.

Not wanting to miss a word, I move my speech processor loser to the computer.

"Taking over my desk," Dr. Mewton says, "is premature, ven for you."

"Is it? I think we both know you're overdue for a transfer." Mr. Traut picks up his pipe. "By the way, how is our patient his afternoon?"

Dr. Mewton shrugs and sinks into the chair. "Some welling around the visible stitches, but that will subside vithin a week. We expect the sutured areas to heal com- letely within ten or twelve days."

"Are you worried about rejection?"

"Not at this point. Sarah and Renee shared the same bloo type, so they'll be more compatible than most. We'll still p her on an antirejection regimen, but I don't think it'll l long-term."

Traut tastes his pipe again, but this time the barest ni "Prognosis?"

"Good—she'll not have much feeling in the new tissue for a few months, but as the nerves and blood vessels gro together, any residual numbness will disappear. In a yea eighteen months at the outside, no one looking at Sarah wi know she's had any plastic surgery."

"And, finally—your opinion as to the procedure's fea sibility for our purposes."

Mr. Traut is always thinking of the company.

Dr. Mewton shakes her head. "The procedure should contemplated as a last resort, and only as an answer to injury

"Why not consider it as a permanent means of disguise Once the procedure becomes streamlined—"

"Because the cost is too high."

He harrumphs. "Money is not a factor."

"I was speaking of the emotional and psychological cos Trauma. Even in cases of natural death, the family pays a hig emotional price."

"I'll take that under advisement." Mr. Traut picks up a folde From this angle I can see the cover, stamped TOP SECRET

"Now," he says, tasting his pipe again, "on to the othe matter. You realize, of course, that this facility has been con promised. Langley has given us three months to clean hous and transfer personnel. Until then, unless prevented, yo people will continue to operate from the secure level. Guard at all posts will be doubled."

Dr. M presses her hands together. "We have been operatin under high alert since the intrusion. I only wish we could hav contained the leak. We might be able to salvage the convent

Traut flips through the pages in his folder. "Impossible

When Saluda's lowliest henchmen know that the Convent of the Lost Lambs is really a CIA black site, it's time to move out." He turns another page, then lifts a single sheet. "I believe you'll be interested in hearing what the extraction team discovered in the house where we found Dr. Carey."

Dr. M shoots him a twisted smile. "I'm sure you're going to tell me."

"I assume you saw the video."

"I've watched it several times."

He takes another puff on his pipe, then props it in the ashtray. "Don't think you saw the folder, though."

Her smile stiffens. "What folder?"

"Seems that Rios left a file containing photos and several pages of information on Kevin Sims." He peers at her over the top of the page. "You do recall the name?"

"Of course. Sarah's father."

My body tightens when he nods. "Sims, as you may remember, was tasked with approaching Saluda with a modified strain of heroin. Trouble is, someone tipped off Rios's men before Sims arrived. They were waiting for him...and they weren't happy."

He pulls a glossy black and white from the folder and slides it across the desk. Dr. Mewton pulls her reading glasses from the chain around her neck and peers at the photo, then turns away. "You didn't have to show me that."

"After our officer expired," Traut says, "Rios's men placed Sims's body in his car and drove it off a bridge. After a payment to the proper authorities, the death was ruled accidental. But you already knew that because you had his daughter here in your hospital."

Dr. Mewton pulls off her glasses and uses her sleeve to wipe a smudge from the lens. "Is this supposed to be news? I saw the official report on Sims's death after it came in."

"This isn't the official report—it's a statement from Saluda's files. Adolfo Morales y Rios, you see, runs a tight ship. Everything on Sims's death is here, including the name of the informant who burned Sims. But you don't need me to tell you the name…because it was you, Glenda."

Even in the security of my hospital bed, I feel myself falling as black emptiness rushes up like the bottom of an elevator shaft.

Judson leans closer. "You okay, kid?"

I reach for his hand and clench it as the scene continues to play out on my computer.

"Why'd you do it?" I hear Traut's tinny voice, but I cannot see him through the tears that have blurred my vision. "Why did you betray Kevin Sims?"

I blink and swallow to bring my heart down from my throat. The image on the laptop is hazy, unfocused, and I want to see this—I *need* to see this.

By the time my vision has cleared, I can see Dr. M staring at Traut. "Does the reason matter now?"

"To me, yes. And maybe to those who will hear your case. If there's any hope for leniency…"

"I don't expect leniency…or forgiveness. It's enough that I was able to protect Sarah."

Beside me, Judson squeezes my hand.

"Kevin Sims was going to take Sarah back to the States for surgery," Dr. Mewton says. "He was convinced she should take her place in society, but I knew what a move like that would cost the child. Little girls who are different don't have an easy time of it. Even when they appear to fit in, they know the truth. They know they're misfits." She pushes her glasses back onto her nose and stares at her hands. "I wouldn't wish that on anyone, especially not Sarah. She had no mother to protect her."

"So you had her father killed?"

"I didn't order a hit, if that's what you're implying. But I did arrange for Rios to learn that a certain Crescent Chemical employee was an officer of the CIA."

"So—" Traut's voice tightens "—over the years, how many times have you betrayed our agents? Once Rios knew he had you in his pocket, I can't imagine him letting you climb out again."

Dr. M looks away. "Holding him at bay wasn't easy."

"How did you communicate? If all electronic communications are monitored—"

"Really, Jack." Laughter floats up from her throat. "There's something to be said for old-school tradecraft and coded messages. Every month Sister Luke picked up her copy of *La Hora del Rezo*. The magazine that helped establish my alias also kept me in touch with Rios."

"How many other agents did you burn?"

"I didn't keep score."

"And officers? Were you—" His fist clenches. "Are you responsible for the maiming of Judson Holmes?"

When she glances toward the ashtray, I know she is craving a cigarette. "I've taken good care of Holmes, haven't I? I've taken care of everyone you sent to me."

Judson's hand tightens on mine, and his throat bobs as he swallows hard.

Traut leans back as his voice fills with contempt. "By all that's holy, Glenda, you will pay for this."

She smiles, and I'm grateful Judson can't see her expression. "Do you have children, Jack?"

"Two. Two boys."

"Then you should understand how I felt. When that motherless baby was left in my care, I knew I had to do everything I could to protect her. So I stopped her father from taking her to the States, I brought in the finest surgeons to help her adapt to breathing, eating, speaking. And a few months ago, when she expressed a desire to meet her aunt, I arranged a meeting. Against my better judgment, I've even assisted Dr. Kollman with this plan for a face transplant...all so Sarah can be happy."

Traut picks up his pipe again. "You say you've done it all

for her, but you're the one who benefited. You profited from her work, her genius—"

"Need I remind you of Gutenberg? You've profited, too. But no one here has taken advantage. No one has taken anything Sarah didn't willingly give."

She leans forward and gracefully extends her wrists, holding them together like a dancer. "Are you going to arrest me now?"

Traut pushes away from the desk. "We'll leave in half an hour," he says, standing. "You may take a suitcase of personal items…and count on it being searched."

Almost of its own accord, my hand moves forward and lowers the lid of the laptop. I close my eyes and feel the painful pull of the sutures as my jaw tightens and my skin adjusts to a new position.

My heart is adjusting, as well—to a different perspective. Glenda Mewton, the only mother I've ever known, killed my father, as surely as if she'd aimed a gun at his head. She is responsible for Jud's maimed body and Hightower's death.

I'd like to blame her for Aunt Renee's murder, but I can't. That blood is on my hands.

"No wonder," Jud says, his voice choked with an emotion I can't even begin to define. "No wonder we never made any real headway against Saluda. Hightower's poisoning, Espinosa's treachery, all the slips and false starts through the years—she's been working against us the entire time."

I wince as the muscles around my lips tighten. "Hmm-mmm."

Judson's hand searches through the sheets until it finds mine, then he squeezes my fingers again. "Mewton's freaks," he says, a smile in his voice. "Who'd have ever imagined we'd turn out to be the real good guys?"

Dr. Kollman's smile fades as he reads the digital reading. "Your BP's up," he says, pulling the device from my wrist. "What have you been up to?"

The question is rhetorical; he knows I can't talk. He smiles as he leans on the railing at the side of my bed.

"Listen," he says, peering into my eyes. "I know you've been through a lot, but you need to take it easy. Let Traut and Judson take care of wrapping things up here. Your job is to relax and get better."

We both turn as the door opens. Two guards stand in the hallway, with a single figure between them.

Dr. Mewton.

She looks at Dr. Kollman and attempts a smile. "I wanted to see her before I left."

Kollman glances at me. "Only a minute," he says, gripping the bed railing. "I don't want her upset."

Dr. M nods and steps forward, pulling something from her pocket. For an instant I don't recognize the object, then I see the telltale golden shimmer. It's the plastic loving cup Aunt Renee gave me when we first met.

"I thought you might like to keep this in your room," Dr. M says, moving toward the nightstand. She places it next to the plastic water pitcher and turns it so that it's facing me. "I know your aunt gave this to you," she says, folding her hands. "I thought you might want to have it with you as you convalesce."

And in that moment, Aunt Renee's voice wafts through my memory like the sound of wind on water: *They had a three-legged race after lunch, and Kevin and I won this for first place. It's nothing, really, but I think that was the happiest moment of my life.*

Dr. Mewton's gaze catches and holds mine. "I was listening when she gave you the cup, when she told you the story. That may have been the happiest moment of her life as a child, but she wouldn't say that now. She'd say her happiest moment was when you accepted her gift."

"Dr. Mewton?" Jeff Prather steps into the room. "We have to go."

Like a queen granting a favor, she waves in his direction,

then bends and lowers her voice. "I don't know how to say goodbye to you, Sarah. You may not believe that I cared for you, but I did. I cared for you in the only way I knew."

Jeff clears his throat. "Dr. Mewton, I must insist."

She gives me a smile Aunt Renee would describe as *rueful.* "Goodbye, Sarah. I'm going to miss those brown eyes… They will always be yours alone."

Epilogue

Two years later

"Wait, Peter, you're walking too fast." He turns, tossing a grin over his shoulder, and offers me an elbow. I reach for it gratefully, and hold it close as I snuggle into the space beneath his arm.

"Are you sure this is the place?" Peter pauses and nods toward the bridge that leads away from the student center. "Seems a bit odd, the bloke meeting us out here when we could all be warm inside."

"I'm sure he has his reasons."

I study the bench carved into the toffee-colored stones of the old bridge. The creek beneath the span, not yet frozen, gurgles in a companionable murmur, just as the sea once provided a soothing undercurrent to other conversations whispered among ancient stones and weathered rocks.

"I like this place." I sit on the bench and pull Peter down beside me. "And I think you'll like Vincent."

"I shall reserve judgment," Peter proclaims, "until after I've met the man. If he's one of your old sweethearts—"

"Not mine." I lower my gaze as unexpected tears sting my eyes. "He was close to my aunt, though. If things had been different, I think they might have gotten married."

"Oh?" Peter slides his hands into his pockets and shivers in the frosty air. "What happened?"

The question jerks me from an old memory of a dining room debate about my welfare. "Hmm?"

"What came between them?"

I hunch deeper into my coat and blink tears from my eyes. "Another love."

I stand as a familiar figure alights from a black London cab and approaches from the road. Dr. Kollman's hair is lighter now, threaded with strands of silver, and his walk is a little less smooth than before. But his face lights when he sees me, and his smile is wide when we meet. A toothy smile, Aunt Renee said once, is almost always sincere.

"Dr. Kollman!" I leap up to wrap my arms around him.

"Sarah." He returns my embrace and rhythmically bestows a few paternal pats on the back. "How are you?"

"I'm good. And you?"

"Busy running here and there. Still patching people up, but operating out of a new clinic these days. Always glad to visit London, though."

"Still working for the company?"

"Of course, but the division is under new management. The work, as you might imagine, is always interesting." When we pull apart, Dr. Kollman nods in Peter's direction. "Is this the young man you mentioned?"

"Vincent Kollman, meet Peter Stillman." I step back as Peter stands and shakes the doctor's hand.

The men exchange "good to meet yous," then Peter clears his throat. "Sarah talks about you all the time. She says you're a brilliant surgeon."

"Sarah's always been prone to exaggeration. But I must say it's wonderful to meet the man who's made Sarah so happy."

"That—making Sarah happy—has been my pleasure."

Embarrassed, I grip a sleeve of each man's overcoat. "I'm delighted to have both of my favorite men within reach."

"Better not let Judson hear you say that," Peter says. "He thinks he has a firm grip on the number two position."

"What Jud doesn't know won't hurt him. Oh! Did I tell you e big news? Judson's son arrived a few weeks ago. After dson left the company, he sent Darius a letter. They've nally reunited."

"How did Darius take the news?"

"Surprised, of course, but he was thrilled once he got over e shock. They've done a lot of catching up, and I think arius will be going to school here next term." I beam up at r. K. "You're looking really good, sir."

"So are you." Dr. Kollman slides his hands into his ockets. "How's school these days?"

I roll my eyes. "Judson's as happy as a lark in his class-oom, but that applied calculus class is still giving me trouble."

"The lads keep asking her out," Peter says, grinning, even though I tell them it's not proper for a student to date e professor."

Dr. Kollman lifts a brow. "Is that all you tell them? You ust be a man of remarkable restraint."

"Well, no." The tip of Peter's sweet nose goes pink. "If ey press, I inform them that Dr. Sims is unavailable. She's marry me in two months."

"Really? That's wonderful news." His eyes sink into nets f wrinkles as he smiles. "Congratulations, both of you."

"Actually, sir—" I tug on his sleeve "—I was hoping you ould give me away."

He stares at me, his expression so full of emotions that for moment I can't define any of them. I see surprise, affection, quick flicker of loss and regret and finally, pleasure. "I'd e honored," he says, his voice deep with satisfaction. "I'd wim an ocean to be there."

"Let's hope you won't have to."

For an instant I think Dr. Kollman might hug me again, ut he keeps his hands in his pockets, though his eyes parkle as they sweep over my face. He studies me so ntently and with such obvious enjoyment that Peter clears

his throat again. "Should we—would you like to, I mean, g
for a cup of tea?"

"Oh, no." Dr. Kollman's gaze doesn't leave my face. '
have to run, but I can't forget the main reason I stopped b
today. I wanted to deliver this."

From his inner coat pocket he pulls a parcel wrapped i
brown paper and tied with string. The outer wrapping ha
been stamped CLASSIFIED and TOP SECRET.

"Sorry for the delay," he says, placing the package in m
hands. "These were discovered in Dr. Mewton's desk. I'
have given them to you straightaway if I'd known about then
Because I didn't know, they had to go through prope
channels before they could be released."

"Any news about Dr. M?"

"None I'm privy to. Still behind bars, I suspect."

My heart pounds as I weigh the package on my palm. "D
you know what this is?"

"Letters." He slides his hand back into his pocket. "To yo
from Renee. Apparently she wrote you for several month
before you met her. Unfortunately, they were never delivered

I pull off the string and run my thumbnail under the tape
seal, unwrapping the parcel. On top I see an envelope, addresse
to me in Aunt Renee's graceful handwriting. I flip the letter ope
and see that it's been opened, but that's okay. Whatever she saic
I know I'll want to read these letters again and again.

"Censors, you know," Dr. K says, his smile tinged wit
regret. "Fortunately, they didn't obliterate anything."

I hug the parcel to my chest as a feeling of glorious antic
pation fills my heart. I know what I'll find in these page
because I know my aunt. She would have written that she :
looking forward to seeing me, that she wants to tell me abou
my father, that she longs for the day when we can sit and talk. .

"It seems I'm always thanking you." I look up at Dr. k
not surprised to find myself tearing up again. "But I've neve
meant it more than now."

He places his gloved hand alongside my smooth cheek, then tenderly taps the beauty mark above my lip. "I'm glad you kept that. Call me with details about the wedding. And do give Judson a big hello for me." He draws me into another bear hug, but leans down to whisper in my good ear. "You *are* beautiful, you know. She would be so happy to see you."

I rise on tiptoe to reply. "If I am…it's only because of what she gave me."

"Perhaps not so much that—" his breath warms my neck "—as because of what she *inspired* in you. I don't think I've ever seen you looking more radiant."

I kiss his cheek and we pull apart. "Off to save the world, then," he says, tucking his scarf into his overcoat.

"Roger that." I send him off with a smile. "Be safe, Dr. K."

Peter slips his arm around me as I stand on the bridge and wistfully watch another connection to my past walk away. "What was that all about?" he asks. "It's almost as if you two were speaking in code."

I give him a smile that springs from a heart filled with contentment. "One day I'll explain it all," I promise, linking my arm through his. "One day you might need to know."

* * * * *

Dear Reader,

We hope you have enjoyed this thought-provoking book by
Angela Hunt.

Overleaf, we have provided some discussion questions on
The Face that will hopefully increase your enjoyment and understanding of this book.

The Editors
MIRA Books

QUESTIONS FOR DISCUSSION

1. As you will discover if you search the Internet for research on brain printing, Spanish poppy production, lie detection, CIA black sites, and propranolol (the trauma drug), most of the concepts featured in this novel are quite real. Did some of these concepts seem far-fetched as you read the story? Does knowing that these ideas come from actual situations change any aspect of your worldview? In what way?

2. When Sarah first learns that she has an aunt, she says "I have family…an aunt, a woman who *knows who I am*. If this is true, then this woman knows more about me than I know about myself. She knows where I have come from, who my mother was. She knows my father. Maybe she knows why I am here."

   How does Sarah's yearning to know her aunt reflect the yearning most people feel to understand and explore their roots?

3. How does the author use the setting to emphasize the theme of the story? Could the story have been set in another locale? How did the setting emphasize or detract from Sarah's plight?

4. When she's dreaming of the perfect face, Sarah thinks "I don't want to be breathtakingly gorgeous; I wouldn't know how to handle perfection."

   Would you want to have a perfect face? How would your life change if you had the world's definition of perfect beauty?

5. When Sarah confesses her feelings for Dr. Kollman and finds they are not reciprocated, she thinks "He doesn't love me because he can't love me. He has seen me at my ugliest and most misshapen. Even if I look like Miss America by this time next year, he will never be able to forget what I truly am."

   How is love influenced by beauty? Does the person who truly loves keep a record of faults?

6. What do you think about the idea of memory implantation? The information about the trauma drug is true. If you could remove unpleasant emotion from some of the past events in your life, would you? Should Sarah have opted to give herself new memories? Would you?

7. Think for a moment about the characters in this book. Which women truly had "no faces"—no emotional involvement with the people around them. Who came to have emotional involvement? What were the forces that brought these characters into a closer relationship with others?

8. What were some of the themes in the book? Are these themes relevant to your life? A year from now, will this story still resonate with you? Why or why not?

9. Would you say this is a plot-driven novel (the plot moves the characters forward) or a character-driven novel (the characters drive the plot)? What were the turning points for each of the major characters, and what might have happened if they had chosen the opposite path?

10. With which character—Sarah, Renee, or Glenda—do you most identify? Why? How did their histories make

them into the women they are? How will their lives influence each other?

1. If you were casting a movie of this novel, which actors would you choose for each of the main characters?

2. Have you read other novels by Angela Hunt? How does this novel echo themes in her other works? How does it differ?

ACKNOWLEDGEMENTS

While writing this book, I frequently felt like the circus performer who spins plates. Each plate—face transplants, brainprinting, computer technology, the CIA—required research and planning in order to remain airborne. Thankfully, I had help.

I owe special thanks to the father-and-son team of Ron and Andrew Benrey, who helped me with information about hanging computers. Athol Dickson was kind enough to share his wife, the Lovely Sue, who used her computer expertise to vet many of my computer scenarios. Thank you, Michael Garnier, for being an invaluable "test reader."

Thank you, Tom Morrisey, for being the go-to guy for details on pistols and weapons.

Also, many thanks to Don Maass, who helped me enlarge the story concept and suggested brain printing as a possible story development.

Thank you, Krista Stroever, Joan Marlow Golan and Terry Hicks, for wonderful editing and an eye for detail.

Finally, hugs and thanks to Dr. Mel Hodde and Dr. Harry Kraus, friends and medical experts who demonstrated (in public, no less!) how a woman should direct a bullet if she wants to donate her face to a loved one. I have such fascinating and knowledgeable Christian brothers!

I also received instruction and guidance from the following books and articles:

Adler, Jerry and Springen, Karen. "Can You Really Botox the Blues Away?" *Newsweek,* May 29, 2006, p. 8.

Ekman, Paul. *Emotions Revealed.* New York: Henry Holt and Company, 2003.

Ekman, Paul and Rosenberg, Erika L. *What the Face Reveals.* New York: Oxford University Press, 2005.

Kessler, Ronald. *Inside the CIA*. New York: Pocket Book
   1992.

Mason, Michael. "A New Face: A Bold Surgeon, an Untri
   Surgery," *The New York Times,* July 26, 2005.

Espinosa, Antonio J. *The Master of Disguise.* New Yor
   William Morrow and Company, 1999.

Moran, Lindsay. *Blowing My Cover: My Life as a CIA Sp
   New York: Berkley Books, 2005.

Polmar, Norman and Allen, Thomas B. *The Encyclopedia
   Espionage.* New York: Gramercy Books, 1997.

Shulsky, Abram N. and Schmitt, Gary J. *Silent Warfar
   Understanding the World of Intelligence.* Washington, D
   Potomac Books, 2002.

Siebert, Charles. "Making Faces," *The New York Tim
   Magazine,* March 9, 2003.

Talbot, Margaret. "Duped: Can Brain Scans Uncover Lies'
   The New Yorker, July 2, 2007.

NEW YORK TIMES BESTSELLING AUTHOR

KAREN HARPER

After spending nine months in a coma, Tara Kinsale awakes to devastating news. Her best friend has been murdered, leaving Tara as guardian to her daughter Claire.

Forced to start over, Tara focuses on reopening her P.I. firm and caring for Claire. But soon Nick MacMahon, Claire's uncle, returns from military service to take guardianship of his niece. The bad dream turns unbearable when Tara learns that something precious was taken from her while she was in a coma.

Working with Nick, Tara begins to investigate the missing months of her life. Together, they will find that secrets don't stay buried forever....

THE HIDING PLACE

"Harper spins an engaging, nervewracking yarn."
—Romantic Times BOOKreviews

MIRA®

NEW YORK TIMES BESTSELLING AUTHOR

SHARON SALA

Cat Dupree would love to settle down with fellow
bounty hunter Wilson McKay. But Soloman Tutuola—
the man who murdered her father and slashed
her throat when she was thirteen—haunts her
even from the grave.

An investigator is tracking down the person who
is responsible for Tutuola's death—and the trail leads
directly to Cat. To add to her bad luck, a junkie with
a vendetta is stalking Wilson and is willing to kill
anyone who gets in the way.

Desperate to start their future together, Cat and Wilson
vow to do whatever it takes to find freedom from the
past and the scars that have damaged them both.

"A well-written, fast-paced ride."
—*Publishers Weekly* on *Nine Lives*

BAD PENNY

*Available the first week of November 2008
wherever books are sold!*

A COMPELLING STORY BY

ROBYN CARR

Last Christmas, Marcie Sullivan said a final goodbye to her husband, Bobby. This Christmas she's come to Virgin River to find the man who saved his life.

Fellow marine Ian Buchanan dragged Bobby's shattered body onto a medical transport in Fallujah four years ago—and then disappeared. Marcie tracks Ian to the tiny mountain town of Virgin River and finds a man wounded emotionally. Yet Marcie manages to discover a sweet but damaged soul beneath his rough exterior.

Ian doesn't know what to make of the young widow. But it is, after all, a season of miracles and maybe, just maybe, it's time to banish the ghosts and open his heart.

A VIRGIN RIVER
CHRISTMAS

"The Virgin River books are so compelling—
I connected instantly with the characters."

—#1 *New York Times* Bestselling Author Debbie Macomber

*Available the first week of November 2008
wherever paperbacks are sold!*
www.MIRABooks.com

REQUEST YOUR FREE BOOKS!

2 FREE NOVELS
FROM THE ROMANCE/SUSPENSE
COLLECTION PLUS 2 FREE GIFTS!

YES! Please send me 2 FREE novels from the Romance/Suspense Collection and my 2 FREE gifts (gifts are worth about $10). After receiving them, if I don't wish to receive any more books, I can return the shipping statement marked "cancel." If I don't cancel, I will receive 4 brand-new novels every month and be billed just $5.49 per book in the U.S. or $5.99 per book in Canada, plus 25¢ shipping and handling per book plus applicable taxes, if any*. That's a savings of at least 20% off the cover price! I understand that accepting the 2 free books and gifts places me under no obligation to buy anything. I can always return a shipment and cancel at any time. Even if I never buy another book from the Reader Service, the two free books and gifts are mine to keep forever.

185 MDN EF5Y   385 MDN EF6C

Name	(PLEASE PRINT)	
Address		Apt. #
City	State/Prov.	Zip/Postal Code

Signature (if under 18, a parent or guardian must sign)

Mail to **The Reader Service:**
IN U.S.A.: P.O. Box 1867, Buffalo, NY 14240-1867
IN CANADA: P.O. Box 609, Fort Erie, Ontario L2A 5X3

Not valid to current subscribers to the Romance Collection,
the Suspense Collection or the Romance/Suspense Collection.

Want to try two free books from another line?
Call 1-800-873-8635 or visit www.morefreebooks.com.

* Terms and prices subject to change without notice. N.Y. residents add applicable sales tax. Canadian residents will be charged applicable provincial taxes and GST. Offer not valid in Quebec. This offer is limited to one order per household. All orders subject to approval. Credit or debit balances in a customer's account(s) may be offset by any other outstanding balance owed by or to the customer. Please allow 4 to 6 weeks for delivery. Offer available while quantities last.

Your Privacy: Harlequin is committed to protecting your privacy. Our Privacy Policy is available online at www.eHarlequin.com or upon request from the Reader Service. From time to time we make our lists of customers available to reputable third parties who may have a product or service of interest to you. If you would prefer we not share your name and address, please check here. ☐

BOB0